Novicess Hollydeva

Novicess Hollydeva

Volume 1
of the series
Hollydeva, Mystic Girl

by
Abella Blunk

Website for this book: www.hollydeva.com

© 2024 Abella Blunk

ISBN 978-3-7693-4117-1

Published by: Books on Demand GmbH,
In de Tarpen 42, D-22848 Norderstedt
Germany

Table of Contents

Fourth Part: The Festival Year on Linden Island

Fifth Part: The Battle for Linden Island

First Part:

At

Georgeburg Castle

Chapter 1:
Astrello. Guuz.
Seren

Astrello

Hollydeva saw Astrello, the star boy, for the first time when two strong bullies of the Dark Guards were dragging him into the dungeons.

»A boy, not much older than I am,« she wondered. »That is strange. A young boy, almost a child! How could he be dangerous enough to be brought to this place?«

She was equally surprised when her father, the Inquisitor, approached her the next day and told her to come along for the boy's interrogation. She had been to many interrogations before, that was not the surprising thing. But the father, Grand Inquisitor in the Order of the Secret Masters of the Nine Nacharya, determined that she would then conduct the further interrogations of this boy herself, without his guidance. A young person making contact with another young person would find it easier to achieve insight and repentance and the renunciation of harmful thoughts.

Hollydeva followed her father into the dungeons. He opened a door that looked like any door. But this door would lead to a maze of many underground floors that were full of cells and chambers and secret gangways.

Hollydeva loved these intermingled gangways. She loved the anguish that was burning within these walls, burnt by the fire of pain and terror of those who were incarcerated and oppressed in here.

The accompanying guard opened a dark cell at the third level down below. This cell was cold and barren. There was the shivering boy sitting inside.

»Come!« her father ordered. They led the boy into a special room for questioning.

»Do you want to drink or eat?« Her father tried to establish contact by appearing friendly, attempting to establish a kind of dependency, an entrance to the subconscious mind of this prisoner.

The boy was thirsty and hungry and nodded. Her father gave a sign to the guard, who went to fetch some drinking water and a soup or some bread.

»Boy, do you know why you are here?« Hollydeva's father asked. The boy remained silent, looking defiant. That was the usual stubborn behavior of the imprisoned.

The Grand Inquisitor took a piece of paper with some writings on it out of a case and showed it to the boy. »Look, you have written this! Do you admit?«

The boy took a look and kept on staying silent. As soon as you start talking, you are lost. That much did he seem to know. The talker would become a traitor, giving away his loved ones and himself.

»You are writing horoscopes in a new kind of astrology. You are making things even more complicated. We cannot prevent the planets to be called after some old gods from the polytheistic pantheons. Venus, Saturn, Mercury, and so on. But that is supposed to be all there is left of those. We cannot allow you to bring in more and new gods!«

Hollydeva realized that the boy was starting to say something to oppose the father's words. But he managed to keep his cool and stayed resistant to any cooperation.

»Well, right,« said her father. »You do not want to talk to me! That will have the consequence for you staying a bit further, down here in a cell! At the end, you will give in and realize that you are causing harm to people! You are confusing them! You will gladly stop to do so! We will support you with finding another profession! But it may also be, that you will not see your family and friends ever again! You could die sad and lonely down here in a dungeon! Take him back into his cell!«

Her father liked to frighten the inmates. He was threatening and intimidating. Hollydeva knew that it was helpful for the poor beings in the dungeon cells, as they would give in more easily. As soon as they had given in, they could be released in short. However, she had seen inmates in here who probably had been imprisoned for years.

She was interested in this boy. He seemed to be courageous and stubborn. She liked that. But she was sure that her father wanted the best for him, wanted to save him.

The guards took him to his cell. And her father told her that in the morning she should interrogate the boy on her own.

»He will talk to you more easily! We have to convince him to stop propagating his pseudo-science of the stars. Then we can release him quite soon! Befriend him! You may badger and bully him as well! You know how we do it! I am trusting you with this!«

Hollydeva was proud with this task, honored by this proof of trust by her stern and powerful father. His name within the order, as she knew, was "Seren the Stone".

And the stones down here were soaked with the despair and cries of desperate beings who had the bad luck of falling into the hands of Seren and his daughter.

The Powerful

»The rich or the powerful?« This was a kind of fun question between them. Father and daughter indulged in the feeling of having power over the great ones of the world.

Politicians and people with a lot of money, "capitalists" from the big banks and corporations, were welcome in the dungeon. But also priests, who either did not want to agree to the unification of their church with the general church of the One-God, or followers of the many gods, who did not want to bow to the supremacy of the OneGod, had been instructed and convinced here. And Hollydeva had already heard that the worst opponents of the lords of Georgeburg were the "Wizardeurs". The wizardeurs were magicians, sorcerers, "changers".

What would be more fun after questioning the star boy: the rich or the mighty one? Both were entitled, arrogant egomaniacs. They would leave in a much more humble attitude. They would not remember their time in the dungeons of the Nine Nacharya as the Inquisitor would trim down their controlling mind and put them into a waking kind of sleep. At the end, they would be put into a kind of hypnotic amnesia. There would be a story about their disappearance, which people would believe. But the "persuaded" rich or mighty would act different, and they would change their decisions.

»Let us start with the powerful, the politician! Let us see whether he is ready to stop supporting the creating of energy by destroying ur-kernels!«

They stepped into the cell of the politician. He looked exhausted. Hollydeva read his body posture, his depressed shoulders.

He was here for almost two weeks now. He did not get much to eat. At night, he was forced to stay awake. They had to let him sleep a little bit, however. A human being without any sleep for three days would get pretty crazy in the head. She had seen that, too.

Hollydeva did not like this politician. He had tried to talk or command using his power voice. As soon as he would try to use his power voice again, she would punch him into the area of his kidneys with her index finger. After six times of being punched like that, he started to talk more adapted to the circumstances.

Her father would probably give him the decisive suggestion into his subconscious today. In accordance with the teachings of the OneGod, the man should cease to demand and promote a dangerous and unnatural technology. And he should stop taking bribes.

»Ah, Mister Chairman, how are you? Will your party win the election?« Then her father changed his voice. »And now you may sleep and be quite relaxed.«

He took the man's head, pressed a certain nerve point behind the ear, and led him into a lying sleep.

»I'd like to tell you a pleasant story. You are floating in a sailboat on a sea. It is a pleasant day, the sun is mild, the air is warm.«

The man lay as if asleep, his deep soul open for the words of Seren the Stone. Nevertheless, he would respond to direct instructions. He was not in deep sleep, he was in the healing sleep of hypnosis.

»Do you want to listen to me and do what I say? Please nod with your head!«

The politician slowly nodded his head.

»Good, then listen to what I say. Soon you will be certain that generating power by destroying ur-kernels is an unholy and unnatural way. You do not want new power plants to be built! Do you understand that?« The man nodded.

»Speak aloud: I'm against ur-kernel power plants! I will prevent new power stations from being built!«

The tormented, hypnotized politician spoke the words in a muttering voice.

»Very beautiful. I am almost satisfied with you. I also tell you that you will not accept any more bribes from the energy corporations. You will not accept bribes from energy companies! Nod with your head!«

The man nodded, and gradually he could be awakened again. Her father told the story of the sail-boat on the sea a little further. Then he allowed the waking mind of the man to come back and take control of his body and senses again.

Hollydeva gave the man something to drink and patted his cheek. He should have been happy with himself, having survived so gladly.

For it had happened that one did not survive his stay down here. Three months ago, a particularly furious and rebellious fanatic had been throwing temper tantrums so hard that she had to give him a blow. The man had fallen down, pushing his head against the wall so that he became unconscious and injured.

She was only a girl without great muscle strength. But the hatred sent through her arms could shake every colossus.

Later, her father told her that the man had died and that this was the best solution anyway. There might arise an outcry in his country. The police would have to be blamed. Her father was fine with this event. Hollydeva, however, had felt badly that the man had died. Was she a murderess?

She had been worried about being a murderer for a while. "Murderess" did not sound like something she wanted to be called. Her father had obviously found it normal for people to die down here. He had even treated her a bit warmer. He was proud of her. She could kill and cause pains! And now he wanted her to be able to talk to the incarcerated, just as he himself was doing!

They were managing the mission of the Nacharya to save the world, to influence the world so that it would save itself. That was a big task. The assignment was not to be fulfilled without bloodshed. She wanted to be a good tool for the Knights of the Nine Nacharya. She wanted her father to be proud of her.

Guuz, A Flower Deva

That did happen on the same day in September when another surprise was waiting for Hollydeva, as she was watering a little plant, a daisy, on her window sill.

She had found a solitary daisy in the park, excavated, and potted it. Should it be a reminder of her mother and her brothers? No, she just liked flowers.

Suddenly, she heard a hiss, perceived a movement in the flower-head. Was there an animal?

Then, to her surprise, she saw a kind of very small man, a figure with a green suit and a hat that looked like a flower. Or maybe it was a lady of the good folk that live within plants. Hollydeva looked with great interest at this strange being.

Then she heard a voice. »Do not be frightened, Hollydeva! I am Guuz, the deva of this flower! May I talk to you?«

Hollydeva stayed silent. What was that, a "flower deva"?

As if the being could hear or read her thoughts, it replied, »Every plant, every tree, every flower, has a consciousness like you have one. Usually, we manifest ourselves as plants and are therefore very happy. We can also manifest ourselves as creatures of every kind, as birds or butterflies. But then we are not able to listen to the music as we can as trees or flowers. The smells are also not as wonderful! When you know how to contact us, you can contact each deva of each plant! And if you are a good person, every deva will speak to you and help you!«

»But I am not a good person!«

»If you were not a good person, I would not speak to you! You are a child and children are good. But you're exceptional! You are a girl with power and with the power to change this world. We accept and trust you! It is not a matter of whether you have caused pain to people and whether you have been present when killing happened! It's about whether you're ready to save this world!«

»This is what my father says. He will save the world! He does it on behalf of the Nacharya! But should not he do this with loving methods if he is to be a good man?«

»You are asking important questions! So you're not really a child anymore! We need your help! And it is the same to us whether you are good or evil! You just have to be our friend! I think you're that! Are you a friend of us, the flowers, Hollydeva?«

»Yes, I have longed for a flower here! I would like to be in a garden, in a park, on a meadow!«

»Something will happen, and you'll have to help the flowers and trees, Hollydeva! There is a change in the world going on that kills us! And when we die, everything dies in this world. First the bees and the butterflies and the birds die, and in the end everything is dead and gone! We must stop the change by any means! You must help us!«

»But how can I help? I am here in a dungeon assisting my father with torture and murder!«

»Listen carefully. Within a few days, the nine great nacharyas will come to this castle! It is a very significant meeting! Because the Nacharya know about the change! They will negotiate about it. You must listen to this meeting! For there are also those who bear responsibility for that fatal change! Those will explain what they are doing! We must know what they are planning! It is important that you hear what is spoken! Because, as you know, there is not a single plant in that hall! There is almost no plant within this castle, and we therefore have no way to hear what is being negotiated. You must help us! Please help us, help the flowers and trees and all the plants!«

»Alright, Guuz, I'll see what I can do! It will not be easy!«

»I'll send you another friend, the Lao cat. The Lao cat will show you how to best listen to the gathering! Beware of the nacharyas! They are very awake and aware and perceive every movement and emotion in their environment. Be sure you are calm and empty! I think you can do it!«

»Yes, I can do that!«

The Rich

Later that day, the day after she had seen Astrello for the first time, the first interrogation of the rich man took place. It began as usual. He asked for a "lawyer".

»Why am I here? What is this? I have done nothing wrong! I demand an attorney!«

Why did he think he was arrested by a regular police force?

Hollydeva's father had laughed. »You, Mr. Banker, are in a place where no one knows you and no one can find you. We have passed on a story to your relatives and employees that makes them believe that you need to relax, "Burnout Prevention". If you cause trouble, and we have to prolong your stay here, we would have to extend the story to the effect that you have gone into hiding with a considerable amount of money because the bank is about to go bankrupt!«

»Nobody would believe that! Stocks are at peak! Profits have risen steadily in recent years thanks to my work and foresight!«

»But people want to believe! You know what manipulation can do nowadays! Weren't you the head of marketing yourself? Didn't you say that you can sell anything as you understand the psychology of people?«

The rich man sighed. He was caught.

Hollydeva had listened with interest. Psychology. It seemed an interesting tool. She was eager to learn more about it.

Her father now made a friendly face. »Mr. Money Juggler, we just want to have a little influence on your investments and financing! We do it for the survival of the planet and the health of mankind!«

»Why do you have to kidnap me and lock me up for this? Why don't you buy shares and become a co-owner and have some influence?«

»You know how it works, and we know how it works. Shareholders are calm when they receive dividends or see price gains. Shareholders don't have any real influence

9

on company policy. The board of directors makes decisions. The directors fill their pockets and hope that if the share price falls, this can be blamed on bad government policies, some disaster, or even the cycles of the economy. And it is the board of directors that makes itself rich through salary and bonuses. And the supervising board consists of former directors and some powerful people who are in this way well-disposed towards each other, and you are a caste that does not make life difficult for each other. Meanwhile, similar conglomerates exist in other states and a certain pressure is exerted by them, provided they are cheaper and faster and more innovative!«

»Good, you know your way around, Mr. Inquisitor!«

»Yes, I do. That's why we're getting you, as the Chairman of the Board, to revise the policy of the bank a little! We want the group to give loans to companies that will not only make a profit, but do so in a way that does not harm the Yrth and humanity!«

The rich man laughed scornfully. »You are romantics?! Most profits are made with drugs, weapons, and prostitution! We are already holding back because of the image! What else do you want to put us off?«

»Drugs, guns and prostitution are just sideshows. The real money is made with compound interest!«

The banker went pale. Hollydeva felt that her father had hit a nerve. She also tried to understand what drugs, guns, and prostitution were. Witnessing this interrogation, she realized that she had spent the first years of her life in the tranquil world of a village and had been living in a castle, isolated from the world, ever since. There were things in the world — and these were supposedly being the most profitable things —, of which she had no idea.

»Yes, but you can't do without compound interest! There's nothing I can do about it!«

Seren shook his head. »Compound interest is frowned upon as usury in all religions of the OneGod. In the early Middle Ages, compound interest was completely forbidden. In Islamic finance, there was only participation in companies and in the profit of the participation, if it accrued.«

»Yes, but interest was allowed again! Because why should I lend money if I can't make any money from it?«

»Why lend money at all?«

»Because business needs financing!«

Hollydeva realized that money management was not her father's favorite subject. The banker seemed to be superior to him in terms of arguments. She had never thought about money before, as she didn't have any. Everything she needed, she got without payment. "But that's the way it is for children! Adults are to have the money to pay for things!"

Her father had meanwhile become angry with this unruly prisoner. He had given a sign to the guard who was watching the door so that he fetched the cloth and the water bucket. Hollydeva knew what would follow. The cloth would be put over the prisoner's nose and mouth. Water was poured over it so that he would have a feeling of drowning and panic. Her father wanted to soften up this banker.

When the guard came with the cloth and water, her father gave her a sign. She would use the rope she was holding in her hand to pull the prisoner's chair from under him. He would suddenly lie on the ground, the guard would hold him down and the Grand Inquisitor would cause him to drown.

Hollydeva was somewhat irritated. What did her father want to achieve? Was this measure sensible or justified? "Why am I beginning to question the procedure?" she asked herself. That had actually never happened before. She had always tried to please her father, to agree with him.

She was not even sympathetic to this rich man. But she had noticed that her father didn't know the right answers or guidelines to the banker's objections. He was simply against interest.

What was it? Hollydeva had never thought about interest. But she wanted to catch up on that. Then she pulled on the rope so that the chair buckled. The procedure took its course. The banker coughed and splashed the water out of his lungs. After five experiences of drowning, he was full of fear for his life.

»So now you can start thinking about interest and compound interest, Mr. Banker,« her father ended the interrogation.

When he noticed on leaving the cellar that Hollydeva had not completely agreed with the treatment, he justified himself: »If the person to be corrected feels it is irrational and unjust to be treated like this here, and if he even thinks he has the better arguments, then the treatment is all the more effective, as he then no longer knows what to stick to in this world. He will be punished for unjust acting and thinking, and he will be punished for right thinking and acting! So he becomes disoriented! When people in authority, then give him a direction, he follows, so as not to appear confused!«

But Hollydeva had still looked skeptical. Did her father know whereto the Nacharya wanted this banker to be directed to? Did they themselves know?

This had been the day when she realized for the first time that she had some doubts about what she was doing for her father and for the Order of the Nine. It had been the day after the day she had seen Astrello, the Star Boy, for the first time.

And it had been the day when Guuz, the daisy deva, had asked her for help.

Chapter 2:

The Order. The Nononn

Astrello, The Starboy

The boy sat on a chair, silently. The room was empty, illuminated by a dirty lamp on the ceiling. A guard stood in the corner. The boy's physical condition was tense and adjusted to defenses.

»What's your name?« Hollydeva asked. He gave no answer.

She knew that it was important that he would say something, any word. As soon as the channel was open, she would get even more out of him. In the end he would be glad to give in to the instructions to forswear his opinions.

»My name is Hollydeva!« she introduced herself, trying to use a friendly voice. »You'll surely want to get out of here as soon as possible, to the sun, and to your parents and friends. I can take care of this quickly. Just tell me your name.«

He still said nothing. She could not tell if he was afraid or defiant or angry. Was he arrogant and feeling superior to her?

She stepped up to him and held a finger in the direction of his face. »I can give you pain if you do not talk to me! Do you want that?«

When he did not move, she nodded to the guard who held the boy. She stabbed him in a place within the ear, causing pain with her index finger. »How is that?«

Astrello looked frightened and disturbed now. The pain was stronger than expected. He could not know that this twelve-year-old girl was trained to cause the greatest possible discomfort and unpleasant pain by the slightest means. And she was also trained to hypnotize people, and he probably did not realize that she was just seeking access to his subconscious mind.

She stepped back. »My name is Hollydeva, and what's your name? I am just a girl, and I would like to get to know you! Come on, tell me!«

»My name is Astrello,« the boy replied.

Hollydeva went out of the room, fetched a chair and placed herself in front of him. »Astrello, I greet you. Why are you here, Astrello?«

»I do not know. One morning, there were dark men holding a cloth to my mouth so that I became unconscious! Then I was here when I woke up again!«

»But you do not just come here! You must have done something, anything bad! What did you do?«

»I did not do anything wrong. I am only a little different from the others!«

»How different? What does that mean?«

»I came from the stars and I know the stars and I have to tell people on Yrth that they believe in something wrong, a false kind of astrology!«

»A false kind of astrology? I do not know any kind of astrology!«

»On the contrary, you know a kind of star science! You do know your so-called star sign!«

»Oh, that may be true, I am a Sagittarius!«

»But that's wrong, Hollydeva, or whatever your name is. These star signs are wrong! The sky has changed! You're probably actually a Scorpio! And that just indicates the sun in a region of the ecliptic! That is actually only a fragment of the overall picture! But you do not want me to explain your horoscope now, I assume.«

»Oh, why not? But I do not understand why that is important! Nobody is believing it anyway!«

»That's it! It's not true and therefore nobody believes in it! It, however, could be a great key to one's own understanding, to knowledge of one's own true nature, to the determination of one's own destiny!«

»So you're an astrologer, and yet you did not know you'd be sitting here in the dungeon today? How stupid!«

»But I suspected. Or better, I've seen that I'd meet someone important! And that's probably you, Hollydeva!«

Hollydeva liked to be someone important. The boy seemed to be nice. So he was an astrologer, a reader of the stars, seeing the future. He said that he had come from the stars.

»From what star did you come? Where is your spaceship?«

Astrello remained silent.

»Okay, enough for today. Can I bring you anything? Do you need something?«

»I need my ephemerides. And a window with a view of the sky would be beautiful.«

»Hmm, unfortunately, our "guests" here have only cellar apartments. "Ephemerides", I do not know what that might be, but I see what I can do.«

She told the guard to get him back to his cell, and went up the cellar steps to the dining room to eat supper with her father.

Father, Grand Inquisitor

Hollydeva had learned a lot from her father. For successful interrogation a mixture of inducing a kind of waking sleep and generating terrifying threats would deliver good results.

She had been in this castle for about three years. Before she had spent her childhood with her mother and her two older brothers in a small town about a hundred kilometers west of the castle.

Her mother was a loving woman to all human beings and creatures. She, however, apparently was determined to reject her daughter, complaining that Hollydeva was coming after her father, her gloomy father, who had left the family to work in some secret order.

Hollydeva's mother, Rosa, was a gardener who loved to see plants grow and bloom. Like Holly's father, she was a "monotheist", believed in an OneGod. But Holly had noticed that her mother was convinced that the OneGod was a woman, a primal mother. Wives, priestesses of the Great Mother, had come to visit them, and had eyed her as suspiciously as her mother did.

One day, the mother and the brothers, Einar and Baldar, both older than herself, suddenly had disappeared. Since they had probably packed suitcases and satchels, the disappearance had been carried out as planned. There was no crime, no abduction.

Hollydeva had suddenly been a seven-year-old girl who lived alone, left in a cozy house. She went to the neighbor, Mrs. Bromholle, who most likely had been informed by the mother. Mrs. Bromholle told her, that she could get food with her when she looked after the goats. Hollydeva went to school, cleaned the house, went to the neighbor, attended the goats, and wondered where her family had disappeared to.

She felt abandoned by her mother and brothers and swore retribution. One day, they would regret having left her. Leaving her had sown the seed of a plant that her mother should not have fostered.

For two years, she had lived alone. At Easter, three years ago, her father had suddenly been standing in the front door. She at first sight did not know, of course, that this man in a black suit and with a serious face was her father, as she had been a toddler when he had left the family. Hollydeva saw the black coat and suit as well as the intimidating attitude, saw a conspicuous seal ring on the finger of the right hand, identified the body as not menacing, and asked, »What do you want?«

»I'm your father, Hollydeva! I'll take you with me! You can not live here alone anymore!«

She had been reluctant to leave the house, but there was no choice. And she had somehow been interested in what that might be for a world, in which one was walking around in a heavy black coat, acting mysteriously. She had to say goodbye to her neighbor and had entered the big limousine. Her father had a driver and the car was big. He seemed to have money and means. She had liked it and still liked it.

With her father at her site, she could give the teachers and pupils at her school something to think about. They had treated her as an outsider, and she despised them.

»Can we pass the school? I have to take my things out of my locker!«

»Good, I'll come with you!«

Her father had accompanied her into the school building, and everyone had looked irritated. She was inwardly happy that everyone was envying her, wondering who the eminent and menacing gentleman was. How was such a man related to stupid Holly? The things in the locker had meant little to her. But this walk through the school building had been extra satisfying.

They had been driving through the countryside. Her father had been silent. Shortly before their arrival at the castle he had told her, »Hollydeva, we are staying in a dark, old castle, Georgeburg Castle. You will have your room there and continue to study and learn. There will be teachers there for you! The castle belongs to an ancient, secret order, for which I work. You will be my assistant! I hope you like it! You can always come to me with all your questions and wishes!«

At the gate, she had heard the man at the guard say, »Good morning, Lord Grand Inquisitor, sir.« Her father had handed her over to the care of an elderly woman who was the cook and housekeeper of the castle. She had shown her the room and told her the menu plan. Her voice had sounded friendly but worried. »Child, it's unusual that a young girl like you should live in this terrible place! Do not be afraid! Come to me when you need a woman's advice!«

Terrible place? It looked like an old, half-dilapidated castle. She had been anxious to explore this castle. And meanwhile she knew her ways in this place. And she also knew the dungeons and passages that crossed the mountain under the castle, as if she had lived in these since forever.

The Order of the Nine Nacharya

On her second day at Georgeburg Castle her father told her that this place contained the headquarters of the Secret Sentinel of the Nine Nacharya. He had led her to the castellan, who was supposed to be versed to explain her questions about the castle and the Order.

The castellan was an elderly gentleman sitting in a room with many books, a large globe and an aquarium. While it was generally dark and lightless in the castle, this room had a balcony. The door to the balcony was open. She saw the tall trees of a park that surrounded the castle.

»Good Morning, Hollydeva. I am Alleman, the castellan of Georgeburg Castle. My job is to ensure that this place is maintained, that everything works well, and that the outside world knows and perceives little of it. This castle is accommodating the head and heart of the Nine Nacharya. Would you like to know more about the Order, the "Secret Sentinel of the Nine Nacharya"?«

Hollydeva had nodded.

»Can you please use words?«

»I would like to know more about the Secret Sentinel of Nine Nacharya!«

»Thank you. I am reluctant to tell what the other does not want to hear. You do not need to be intimidated and can always ask me everything you want to know!

»The Secret Sentinel of the Unknown Masters of Nacharya, or briefly "The Nine Nacharya", was founded more than 2,000 years ago in the East. A mighty king selected nine people who were endowed with all that was possible to provide for the preservation and development of human society on Yrth. Since the King had become a Bodhisattvist, they were above all supposed to spread the compassionate doctrine of Bodhisattvism.«

»And are there still these nine?«

»Of course, they are not the same nine as 2,000 years ago. When a nacharya dies, a new one is found and inserted into the circle and trained to take over the functions.

Some pass their function on to their descendants. Some are born again and again. But for more than 2,000 years the Nine have provided for the world, remaining almost unrecognized. They intervene and steer when needed. No larger enterprise on Yrth is possible without the consent of these powerful knights!«

»Where are the Nine now? Are they here in the castle?«

»No, they live in different parts of the world. Every so often they meet here. You will probably meet them one day. But first we must know that we can rely on you to be silent and to keep secrets and to be faithful and loyal!«

Hollydeva had nodded again. She still wanted to be faithful and loyal and belong to this family.

»Shall I be a Bodhisattvist, then? What does that mean?«

»As you know, in the past hundred years the monotheistic religions have been united into a great movement, the Monodeus, the OneGod. The Nacharya put force into the effect that the monotheistic churches no longer fight each other. Bodhisattvism is more like a church without God, but it is also a world view of the OneGod. Whether one calls the unity of all being "God", "Allah", "Dharma", "Tao", or "OneGod" is basically not the issue. These are just names!

»It is important that people recognize that there is this Great Whole Totality and that they are part of this Great Whole Totality, and that they can make sure that they come to Heaven after death, that they are redeemed and resumed by God! So they do not have to wander around here forever with unfortunate karma. But excuse me, these were already a lot of religious or spiritual concepts! You will get lessons here and understand this by and by!

»You should know that we have enemies. These enemies have become more powerful in recent years. The one enemy is disbelieving the OneGod in connection with hedonism. This is a plague that rampages in the world and deprives the people of the higher. Drugs and the media and generally better lifestyle without hard work seduce people to a state of diminished consciousness, diminished conscience as well. Those are the plagues we have to fight against!

»But even more dangerous are the polytheists, the followers of the MultiGod, who keep the ancient variety of all kinds of gods alive. These are the magical and mystical cults that tap into the aura of the Yrth, which should be long forgotten! These lead to discord and war, and the illusion that one could go to Heaven without the OneGod, that heavenly happiness could be experienced here on Yrth, what do I know.

»So I hope you get in here, that your teachers can teach you to be a good assistant to your father, and that one day, like your father, you will be faithful to the Secret Sentinel of the Nine Nacharya as an effective servant!«

Navendra Raktah, The Nononn

The first nacharya to whom she was introduced was probably also the head of the Nine. Her father had told her one morning, after she had been at the castle for half a year, that she should wear her best dress. Someone special would come to see her.

The nacharya had first looked at her in silence. Then he had nodded to her father. »It could be her!«

She had been glad that she could be someone, and that her father was proud of her. The older gentleman with a small turban on his head and a long white beard was probably Yndian.

After this first meeting, her father had declared: »This was the Nononn. He is, so to speak, the nacharya with superior rank. They are all completely independent and have equal rights. But the Nononn has the deciding vote. And he is usually the mediator when two nacharyas disagree.«

The Nononn had come back every three months in the past years to spend a few days at Georgeburg Castle to see if everything was all right. Each time he spoke a few words with Hollydeva and asked her about her progress in school lessons.

During a meeting, he had explained his names to her in more detail: »My name in this life is Navendra Raktah, I am an Yndian again, just like in my first life as a nacharya. At that time, I was called Yogavaha and the Emperor Adiraja appointed me to the Council of Nine. I am also called the Nononn, the ninth and highest of the Nacharya. But we nine are basically equal. You could call me Sir Lancelot, for I was the father of Galahad, who found the Holy Grail and brought it back to the East. This sounds confusing now! You will learn that all people have several names, and that those with the most names are the most interesting. Because the names you have to work for, you have to make sacrifices for them. I would like best to be called "Nononn" by you.«

Once he had appeared when she was unhappy and the anger towards her mother was great. Her father had probably also rebuked her because she had not obeyed him as he would have liked. The Nononn had asked what was wrong with her. She had complained about her fate, abandoned by her mother and brothers, in an old castle with a rather closed father without other children, who most likely would have picked on her anyway.

»Hollydeva, you just have a special destiny, a fate that led you here. And it will lead to you having an exceptional task and position in the society of the people. Only those who have to learn to cope with strokes of fate at an early age and stand on their own two feet will make it to the heights. And the heights, there is your destiny! And you must follow this call!«

She had thought a long time about the words of the Nononn. The feeling of following a destiny had given her a kind of peace of mind. She would face adversity with the certainty that it would make her stronger.

At the recent meeting he had asked about her function as assistant to the Grand Inquisitor: »Hollydeva, so you are the assistant to your father, our Grand Inquisitor?«

»Yes, I am, Sir Nononn!«

»And do you like being that?«

»Yes, Sir Nononn, I like being my father's assistant!«

»That's fine, thank you, Hollydeva! We'll be hearing a lot more from you, I think!«

The Nononn, Mr. Raktah, Knight Lancelot, seemed like a kind, medieval gentleman to her.

An Assignment

Her father sounded as serious as ever. »Have you spoken to the boy?«

»Yes, I have. His name is Astrello. He says that he comes from other stars, that he would be an astrologer, and that our astrology is wrong! He needs his "ephemerides"!«

»His ephemerides. Those are tables with astronomical data. Well, he just wants to carry on with his astrology! But here it is safe. Maybe it is good, when you bring him something that is important to him! Then he is busy, and his deep soul is accessible!«

»What is the assignment? What shall I command him to do or be?«

»Hmm, that's hard to explain. There is a false kind of astrology in the mind of people, that is true. They are not the star sign that they all know. But this is intended!

So they fit in better and let themselves be guided! That is absolutely to their own best.

»The true astrology is an invention of the MultiGod. The twelve signs of the stars, the names of the planets: these are all MultiGod expressions. We definitely have to contain the beliefs of the Many Gods. Only the OneGod is correct. The OneGod is the source of all being. It is important that people know that. The Many Gods bring people to believe in different gods or idols, offer them sacrifices. And then they are starting wars in their names, and become possessed by them and rebellious. This threatens the planet, we must prevent it by all means.

»This boy is here because he has reached a dangerous degree of popularity. People believe in his story! They believe him to come from other stars! He has a few skills! He has made a few accurate predictions! We have to make sure that he falls into oblivion. He has to admit that there is no real science of the stars, that it is hocus-pocus and false belief. But work him up a little, talk to him, see if you can lead him and induce the waking sleep!«

»Besides, he was a teacher of astrology on Linden Island and I want to weaken the faculty of divination and its professor, a Master Betula, a little, especially since she's a polytheist!«

»Linden Island?«

»Yes, the Linden Island. I'm sure you'll hear about the monastery on this island. Mystics are trained there. The nine masters of the Nacharya also received part of their training there.«

He hesitated for a moment. She realized that he was about to tell her something important, but then decided to wait.

»You have handled the first interrogation with the boy well. I'll have the ephemerides brought to you from the library! You can hand that book over to him! Keep questioning him and get him to refrain from publishing his horoscopes and predictions. And it would also be good if he didn't return to Linden Island!«

Hollydeva liked her father for talking to her extensively. She felt herself taken seriously, almost like an adult, although she was only ten years old. She was grateful to her father for taking her with him to Georgeburg Castle.

Her father might have been in need of her as a helper with his interrogations. He was eerie, for he was the Grand Inquisitor, doing the dirty work for the Order of the Nacharya. But for her, he was her father, who treated her like an adult, telling her how to interrogate bad people, how to torture and possibly even kill them.

She had been outraged when her mother had disappeared. Mrs. Bromholle had told her that she did not need to worry about her mother and her brothers. They were simply cut off, submerged, without taking her with them. She had always been angry with her mother anyway, but after this separation it became special. This rage had been absorbed and channeled by her father and directed to the people in the dungeons and cellars below the castle.

Did Hollydeva feel sorry for these people? No, she hardly knew any feeling of compassion. She heard screams of pain, but that did not matter much to her. Her father and the Nine Nacharya, who instructed him, had reason enough to kidnap and punish these people.

But this innocent boy from the stars? Was he really that bad? She was not quite sure, because she liked him. She would have liked to have a friend, a person of the same age with whom she could speak. Astrology, astronomy, somehow that was sounding interesting to her. And it sounded even better to know more than all the other people and know the true and only science of the stars. Controlling the masses was one thing. But, of course, the members of the Nacharya Order wanted to have the true knowledge, know and cultivate it, withhold it from others. And Hollydeva felt as a member of this secret, dangerous, and powerful knighthood.

Chapter 3:
The Bhogi. Kalima

Astrello, Interpreter of the Stars

On the third day after his arrival at Georgeburg Castle, Hollydeva conducted the second interrogation with Astrello early in the morning. She had been looking forward to seeing him when she woke up.

»So you're called Astrello, and you're a reader of the stars?«

»Yes, that is true. Who are you?«

»I am the one asking the questions here!«

»And I like to give answers, as long as you talk to me as well.«

»Well, that's understandable. My name is Hollydeva, and I am the daughter of the Grand Inquisitor of the Nine Nacharya! And I'm his assistant! I can cause pain, kill, and, through consciousness control, get answers out of your subconscious!«

»That sounds dangerous!«

»Do not make fun of me, I'm not very humorous. I cannot understand whether something is true or ironic. So I take everything as true and literally meant and jokes then lead to misunderstandings and I add more pain than I actually should. But I have given free hand and ---?«

»Oh, you just want to scare me! But I understand you, there probably are Venus and Sun in the twelfth house!«

»And here we are already at the bottom of your being incarcerated here. You propagate the ancient gods, the MultiGod. We must stop that!«

»I do not propagate any gods! That's the name of the planets in this solar system, which provide important information for the astrologers! Or do you not call them Venus, Mars, Jupiter? Is Tuesday not the day of Tyu or Mars as in "Martedi" for you?«

»No, Tuesday is "Blood-Day" now!«

»Correct! Because of the color red!? The Red Planet, the Red God of War! It is all connotations, associations, symbol concatenations!«

Hollydeva looked at him furiously. He could not be right here! He was using words which she did not know! She felt that he had an argument! She would have to question her father! Were the followers of polytheism more powerful than she might have imagined?

»All right! Here, I will give you those ephemerides that you wanted.«

»Oh, thank you very much!«

»What does it help you? There is really no help for people like you!«

»I will tell you what will happen, and you will realize that I can help you! And you will support me with my mission!«

»Oh yes? Your mission, what is it?«

»I already said that I have to teach people the true astrology!«

»Why is your astrology more true than the kind people know?«

»My astrology takes the position of the stars in the sky, as they are to be seen! The planets against the background of certain constellations of the fixed stars indicate certain energetic patterns to Yrth, which are in correspondence with events on Yrth. I am able to produce precise predictions, but only when I take the actual position of the stars and not, as the superstitious do, the position within a fixed zodiac that does not exist in reality!«

»That's too hard to grab for me right now! But well, I realize that you mean it seriously and honestly! Maybe you can name the stars and the star signs so they propagate the only true God!«

»The only true God?«

»Yes, the OneGod, the foundation of all being, God Almighty, Bodhisattva, Tao-dharma!«

When Astrello looked a bit confused, she asked him if he did not believe in the one and true God.

»I come from the stars. And behind the stars there are stars. The scientists say that there is an edge to this universe. What there is behind the edge of the universe, one does not know. Other universes, I guess. And behind all the universes? There's probably nothing. I believe in myself, in the voice of my heart!«

»Yes, it is the OneGod speaking to you through your heart!«

»If you want to think so. My heart tells me to ask you about your date of birth!«

»December, 11th. In the 32nd year of the OneGod. Why do you want to know that?«

»I'll calculate your horoscope with the help of these ephemerides! What was the location of your birth?

24

»It was in a small village, 100 kilometers from here to the West!«

»Can you tell me your time of birth?«

»No, I do not know. I should ask my mother, but she has left me!«

»Your mother left you? When was it?«

»Five years ago!«

»Do you remember the exact date?«

»Yes. It was in the middle of autumn. I am quite sure, that it was a day after Halloween. November, first, year 38.«

»Perfect. So I can calculate the birth time! All I need now is a sheet of paper and a pen and light at night!«

»Oh yes? And what do you do for me if I bring you all this?«

Astrello looked at her directly. He took her right hand, solemnly saying, »I will always be your friend! I'll never hurt you, Hollydeva! I will always tell you the truth and look for the best answers to all your questions!«

Hollydeva was surprised. She did not want a prisoner to touch her. This should not happen! Her first interrogation without her father watching seemed to be going wrong! But she could not help it.

She became aware that she had allowed Astrello's touch as if paralyzed. Why hadn't she pulled her hand back? She wanted him to touch her and hold her hand! She wanted him to like her!

»I want to be liked! Really? Oh, no!« Her self-image as a hard-boiled jailer had just cracked.

»Yes, I'll bring you paper and pencil and give instructions that the lights stay on at night!«

»Thank you, Hollydeva!«

Good and Bad

Hollydeva's teachers were young priests. They were always introduced with blindfolded eyes, and probably did not know where they were. They were replaced after some months. She was not supposed to tell them that she was torturing or even killing people. No one from the outside knew that the world was influenced or even steered by the dungeons under Georgeburg Castle.

She learned to read and write and about natural sciences and history and was interested in everything. But she also needed answers to her most urgent questions. The question that mattered to her was: "Am I bad?"

It was clear to her that people who inflicted pain or even killed were not good, were not actually behaving according to the commandments of the OneGod, might reap a bad karma.

This year, the teacher priest was serious and intelligent. She had confidence in him. He was to be addressed as "Pater Septimus".

»Pater Septimus, could we learn anything besides the usual school material? Can we also talk about what is good and what is evil?«

»Yes, we can also add philosophy to the curriculum! Do you want that?«

»Yes, gladly. I want to know what is good and what is evil. I would like to be able to align my behavior!«

She hoped to be able to discuss her innermost questions with the priest without having to disclose what she had done. She did not want to talk about it with her father, as he was clearly of the opinion that his and her behavior were necessary and justified. Evil people must be led to rethinking. But how did he know that he had the right, how did he know that his cause was in accordance with a kind of Higher Law?

In her first philosophy lesson, Pater Septimus began by showing that ethics and morality, the occupation with good and evil, were a central theme of human reasoning.

»We have a conscience and that tells us whether we do good or evil,« the priest announced.

»A conscience? Do I have a conscience?« Hollydeva wondered. »Yes, obviously! Otherwise, I would not have asked to discuss this subject.«

»Conscience is our inner voice, which tells us whether we act good or evil, right or wrong!«

»Is good and evil the same as right and wrong?«

»No, right and wrong is based on a result. Good and evil is more of a foundation. The good man helps the other creatures. He or she acts out of compassion. The evil man has no compassion and harms other living things.«

»Compassion, how do I do that?«

»If another creature suffers pain, then you feel these pains as if they were your own pain! You feel the other, and then you feel the urge to help!«

She did not know that, and she did not want the Pater to become aware of that. She nodded and tried to act as if she had understood a deep truth. But she did not know what and how compassion was to be. That kind of conscience seemed to be somewhat too vague to distinguish good from evil.

Hollydeva was still in trouble. She needed answers with which she could evaluate her actions. So she asked the priest at the next philosophy lesson, »Pater, but if a man does not feel what another man feels, if he has no compassion, how does this man know what is good and what is evil?«

»Hmm, most people just require commandments and laws. They try to follow these. Otherwise, they will be punished. The laws are made by men and are to keep society in order. Man without compassion must first be obedient.«

Hollydeva did not like that. She did not just want to be obedient. She knew her father wanted more of her.

»But how can a man, who is not sure whether his conscience tells him right, decide whether what he is doing is good or bad?«

»It's the motive, motivation. If a person does something to do good, to protect others, to live pleasing to God, then good action will probably come out of a motivation like that!«

»Hmm, the motivation, the motive. So there are good and bad motivations?«

»Yes, all that is good for the fellowship of men and creatures or the Yrth is good. Everything that is selfish and greedy is bad.«

»Could it be possible to kill a man, and it is a good deed?«

»You mean, if you have compassion with a human being and kill him nevertheless, because the motive is the salvation of humanity?«

»Yes, like that!«

»Hmm, I'd say, yes, that can be justified. The act as such looks evil and may be carried out without compassion. But it can be meaningful and good on a larger scale.«

»But the performer must be very sure that the motive is actually justified?«

»Yes, of course. That is a profound question. There have been terrorists and fundamentalists who kill people because they think their God tells them that. And they want to save the world! They, however, are mistaken and do evil. Therefore, for a time, it has been said that every killing of a man is murder and must be punished severely! And that the murderer does not enter the Kingdom of Heaven!

»Today it is said that any deed is justified, when it is accomplished for the One-God, for the Great Whole Totality, for the happiness of mankind, for the survival of the Yrth. A killing will always burden the conscience! But this sacrifice may serve a higher purpose!«

Hollydeva had been thinking about the motivation to decide whether to do good or evil. And if you were just running instructions? One had to trust the higher-ranked issuer of the order. Would a person, intended to be good, have to check the motivation of the person who gave the instruction? She would have to continue asking Pater Septimus.

The Bhogi

And while she was writing down notes regarding the interrogation of Astrello and the question about the names of the days of the week and the planets in the dungeon masters' logbook, recalling the priest's philosophical lessons in her mind, she decided to visit the Bhogi. The Bhogi knew all the answers.

During her explorations in the large, winding castle, after a few weeks, she came across interesting objects that seemed to have been laid out for her there. She had followed the trail, and she had also been alert, as she could not know who was trying to lure her to where.

Finally, she had found a door behind which a library was hidden. And among the books and shelves she had found the next nacharya knight, an old man with a long beard who greeted her friendly.

He had been sitting in a wheelchair in front of a table that was full of books.

»Ah, there you are at last! Hello, Hollydeva!«

»Hello?«

»Allow me to introduce myself. I'm one of the Nine, the Nacharya. They call me "the Bhogi". I'm rather old now and love to be undisturbed. I had wild years in the world, and eventually, you get tired of parties, celebrations, and carousing. Now I dedicate myself to the history of our order!«

»How do you know my name?«

»Well, I don't only deal with the past, but also with the present. I have sources of information that tell me what is happening now. And your arrival at Georgeburg Castle was significant, perhaps even of great importance for our Order!«

»I am just some girl. I think you exaggerate and want to flatter me! What do you want from me?«

»Yes, you are right. I flatter you because I need your help! I'm not so good on my feet anymore, needing to be pushed around in a wheelchair. And I need to be taken to a place to prevent something happening! You're going to push me there! You're also going to make sure that the desired prevention is taking place!«

Hollydeva had looked skeptical.

»What place?«

»I'll tell you everything when the time comes!«

And she smiled as she remembered her first meeting with the Bhogi. The project in which he would require her help had not yet taken place. But just a few days ago he had said that she should be ready because it was imminent.

In the months before, he had provided her with some information about the Nine and their functions in the Order. But to what extent she could trust him, she would have to check on that imminent journey.

What had he said about the Nine? Which nine nacharya were there? And while she went up the stairs to have dinner with her father and to discuss the second inter-rogation of the Star Boy, she remembered and saw in her mind's eye once again the four with whom she had had experiences in the past years: the Nononn, the Bhogi, Tatu Njena and Peredur.

So she knew the numbers 9, 7, 3 and 5.

The Bhogi had warned her, at least subliminally, about the number 8, the "Boss". For several centuries, he had probably played a decisive role in determining the fate of the Nine. But in the current incarnation he had met with some rejection from the others. He did not want to be called Octonn or similar, as would have been consistent with his position as eighth. But the eight was a smaller number than the nine, and it sounded less important than the one or the two. So he named his position after the null number or zero, "Zronn". In his first life as nacharya his name had been Saphed, and he wanted to be addressed as such in the current incarnation.

The second, the Tworonn, was to be an influential doctor and healer. The Bhogi had indicated that she had a special relationship with him. He was called Daman in the days of Adiraja, and so he was called through all lives and incarnations and in the actual days.

The first one, the Onthronn, was probably a strong fighter. He was born an Arab and was called Achmar the "Red".

One of the Nacharya was Japanese, name Rokudan Aoi. He was the sixth of the Nacharya, the Sessionn.

The fourth, the Verionn, was called Quavert, which was a combination of the number four and green in the romanic languages. The Bhogi seemed to think not much of him. He was too "priggish". Whatever the Bhogi meant by this expression.

Kalima

The Bhogi had intervened when that person had landed in the dungeons that Hollydeva still had to think about: Kalima. About a year ago, this young woman had been taken to Georgeburg Castle. Two strong guards had to hold her. Her father, the Inquisitor, had led her into a cell. She was a beautiful woman, dressed all in black, with a black headscarf.

Hollydeva met them in the corridor and the arrested woman looked with dark, angry eyes at the girl who was at home in the dungeons of Georgeburg.

Then her father had even taken Hollydeva inside for the interrogation

This lady prisoner was by no means frightened or fearful. Rather, she immediately took charge of the conversation and asked in a sharp voice, »Who are you? Would you please release me?«

Seren, the Stone, had replied, »Gladly. We just need to talk to you a little first, dear Mrs. Kalima!«

»About what? I have nothing to tell you!«

»Please tell me if there's a God.«

»A God? There are many gods, at least in the minds of men. And in reality, there is no God! It's all an illusion.«

»So, are you a polytheist or an atheist?«

»Why do you want to know this?«

»Well, I want to convince you that it would be better to believe in the OneGod!«

»I believe in nothing. I am into experiencing.«

»In the crater?«

Hollydeva noticed a short clipping on the woman. She was surprised that this crater was mentioned.

»What crater?« She tried to dodge with a counter-question.

»You know what I'm talking about! You are the lover of a certain nihilist, a black mystic!«

Kalima had laughed and shook her head.

Later that day, Hollydeva had wanted to bring this woman, Kalima, some water and food. The door to the cell was open, and the two guards seemed to harass the woman as if they wanted to tear off her black clothes.

Hollydeva shouted at the guards to leave the woman alone, but she only got a blow to the head and fell to the ground.

She had picked herself up again and had rushed upstairs to look for her father. But in the corridor she met the Bhogi in his wheelchair.

»What's wrong? Why are you so excited, Hollydeva?«

»Down in the dungeon there is a beautiful woman, Kalima, and the guards want to hurt her!«

»Kalima, you say? Come on, take me downstairs!«

»You can't go down the stairs in a wheelchair!«

»Then you'll have to carry me!«

»You're too heavy!«

»Then sound the alarm!«

»How?«

The Bhogi had a pipe in a side pocket. He quickly took it out and blew into it, making a shrill sound.

»Shout: Alarm! Alarm!«

Hollydeva shouted, and immediately three of the gray wardens came running, as well as the castellan and then her father and another important man whom Hollydeva had learned to know as "The Informant".

The Bhogi ordered in a very firm voice, »Bring the woman, Kalima, up here to me immediately. Put the two guards who are harassing her in chains! Bring them up here too! Nothing must happen to this woman Kalima! Go, quickly!«

Only a few minutes later, all stood before the Bhogi as instructed.

»Why do you have this woman, Kalima, in the dungeons, Seren?«

»It was an order!«

»Order from whom?«

»Well, it is said that we should bring all those who fight the OneGod to their senses. And this woman is a nihilist who doesn't believe in anything!«

»So there was no specific instruction! You just happened to see her, and you took her!«

Seren was obviously feeling a bit guilty and shocked that the Bhogi was reprimanding him like that.

The Bhogi relented, »Perhaps it is our fault that our instructions on this matter were unclear! Maestra Kalima is a person above all laws and instructions. Remember that, Seren! Now release these two guards in your own way and leave me alone with Kalima for a moment! Organize a ride to take her where she wants to go!«

Seren, the Informant, the castellan, and the guards immediately rushed to carry out the instructions of the nacharya, who turned to Hollydeva. »Hollydeva, you stay here, please!«

Then he apologized to the young woman with the somewhat torn black clothes. Her headscarf was torn off and long dark brown hair flowed over her shoulders.

»Mrs. Kalima, the Nine Nacharya are sorry for any inconvenience you had to experience here today! What can we do to make up for this injustice?«

Kalima still looked a little angry, but maybe she always looked so intense and emotional.

»It's okay, Master Bhogi. It just went well again. I almost had to activate powers that wouldn't do your castle any good. Thank you for taking care!«

She turned to Hollydeva, »Thank you for standing by me, girl, and getting help. You seem to be very brave. I give you my blessing! What is your name?«

The Bhogi answered for her, »This is Hollydeva, daughter of the Grand Inquisitor!«

Then Kalima had touched Hollydeva's forehead lightly and a strange feeling of energy poured into her head.

»Believe nothing and believe no one! Walk the path of freedom and truth,« she had said.

Seren had appeared at the end of the hallway waving, and Kalima had to leave. After a few steps she had turned back to Hollydeva, »Strive to the heights, learn to love!«

This had angered Hollydeva a little, as she would rather not have anything to do with love after the experiences with her mother. Or did she merely want to blame her mother for an inability she felt?

»Could I love Astrello?« He was close to her, she felt connected to him. But he was sitting in a cell, and she was the inquisitor who was to guide him on the right path.

Chapter 4:
Tatu Njena. Peredur

Astrello, a Wizardeur?

»So you're an astrologer? And you come from another star?«

Astrello nodded.

»Are the stars and constellations as seen from where you come looking exactly like ours here, seen from the Yrth?«

Astrello looked a little puzzled. »I don't know that at all. I don't remember. I must have been there, on my star, and then I got into my spaceship, and I came here. Astrology I didn't start studying until I got here. Maybe I wanted to back up my claim of being the star boy with knowledge about the stars. Because when I say that I come from the stars, everyone laughs and thinks I'm crazy.«

»Yeah, that sounds crazy!«

»But I still have contact with my ship up at the edge of the atmosphere! And I can and know things that nobody else here knows about. My memory is just a little fuzzy. Ever since I got here, things have been getting more and more confusing.«

»Here at Georgeburg Castle?«

»No, here on Yrth. But that seems to be the general condition.«

»What do you mean?«

»Well, I began to study astrology, and found there is a lot of confusion about astrology on Yrth. The vast majority of people are using a kind of astrology which is wrong! And they do not know it! If you tell them, they do not want to hear this truth! And that seems to be the way it is with most truths. People would rather not hear it.«

Hollydeva nodded. She had been given another argument for the rightness of her assisting in her father's work. Truth had to be hypnotized into them. But she was aware that it sounded contradictory to let a person fall asleep in order to wake him or her up. But maybe one can only wake up if he or she has fallen completely asleep beforehand.

»But what could be wrong with astrology? It is superstition anyway!«

»No, it could be science! It works on the principle: "As in the big, so in the small!" and vice versa, of course. Everything is connected with everything and everything is reflected in all dimensions and orders of magnitude.«

»As in the small, so in the big?«

»Yes, you find the small and fine structure in the large structures. This is one of the principles of order in the world we live in. The number phi, 1 point 618, indicates a ratio that we perceive as harmonious, which is probably harmonious indeed, the so-called Golden Ratio, and you find this ratio realized in the shells and flowers, as well as in the galaxies and huge star clusters.«

Astrello painted a sign on the sheet of paper in front of him, while talking about the number phi: the number phi as a Greek letter: Φ.

Hollydeva wanted to keep his talkativeness going, »This is really interesting. So the stars we see reflect events and conditions on Yrth?«

»Exactly, right, they reflect. But even better: We can calculate the further course of events and thus see the reflection of future events. But the decisive phrase you just said was: "that we see". Because that is important. Stars and constellations of stars correspond as we see them. For this, we must look up into the sky, preferably at night.«

»Yes, of course.«

»As I'm saying! Yet, modern astrology calculates the position of the changing stars in a fictitious zodiac. And this zodiac shifts in the course of the years, but the astrologers still take a zodiac, which they have fixed, fixed even at a time, which now already lies over thousand years back.«

»Weird.«

»Yeah, weird. And I tried to tell people their true star signs, but they couldn't take that. So instead of the twelve signs of the zodiac, I prefer to take the 28 fixed stars, which are the background of the ecliptic, the plane on which the other planets circle the sun with the Yrth. In other words, these fixed stars, distant suns, give a special meaning to the planets as a background, while these planets seem to move across the night sky before them.«

»And astrology is wrong like that all over Yrth?«

»No, there are astrologers like the ones in Yndia, who take the planetary states as they are seen. But their interpretations are strangely pessimistic, and they have a system of 27 fixed star areas, which I found lacking the astronomical consistency.

However, it anyway is ultimately the main task and the mastery of the astrologer: the interpretation, the symbol linking. After all, they are all just symbols.«

»Symbols?«

»Yes, everything you perceive are signs! And how you link them together creates the meaning, the significance of the symbols.«

Astrello was now a little too enthusiastic about himself. But he was not to be put off, »The origins of astrology lie in the Orient, actually in Babylonia. The cultures that inherited the power of the Babylonians and Egyptians, like the Arabs, illuminated and expanded the observation of the stars. The clear desert sky is predestined for the observation of the night sky.

»I finally found the studies of a scientifically based astrologer, a great poet and magician as well, who lived a hundred years ago. Together with his wife he made use of a system of 28 fixed star houses, mostly in accordance with ancient Arabic astrologers. That was when I knew that I was on the right track, and so I went on!«

»He was a magus and did astrology as a science? And that's what you do?«

»Yes, exactly!«

»And these 28 fixed stars are the additional gods you are accused of?«

»Yes, that may be. But Regulus, Aldebaran, Altaïr, Spica...«

»Stop it! I don't want to hear those names!«

Hollydeva had ended the conversation carefully but also quickly. Outside the cell door, she thought. »He practices astrology as a science, as a form of alchymy! He is learning from a magician, a wizardeur! He may be nice, but he is deeply connected to the enemies, the alchymists and the wizardeurs! I have grown too close to him, too sympathetic. But I like him! I have to ask the Bhogi what I should think of it!«

For she would rather not give her father any sign that she was about to fail completely at the first assignment she was to take care of on her own, as she possibly was about to fall in love with the prisoner!

Who Are These Alchymists?

After meeting with Astrello, she remembered what the Bhogi had told her about the alchymists. And Tatu Njena had even shown her how the alchymists were harming planet Yrth.

Was astrology a form of alchymy, just as astronomy probably belonged to the physics department of alchymy? Perhaps it was right and important to dissuade Astrello from astrology or its proclamation for several reasons. For what she had heard and seen about the alchymists was not good at all.

»Who and what are these alchymists?« So she had asked the Bhogi.

»Hmm. The alchymists are a grouping that stands between wizardeurs and the mystics. They try to understand the world more deeply, so that their changes of the world do not require so much personal power, but are rather caused by mechanical interventions in the matter or even the spirit of the world. These alchymists call it "science".«

»A more profound understanding of matter, a knowledge, is not bad after all!«

»Yes, but. The world is not only what we can see, hear, feel and above all measure. Anyone who thinks he can understand the world by looking more closely at its surface is sitting on a fallacy.«

»But scientists do go beneath the surface! They study the primordial nuclei and the clockwork in the cells, the smallest structures!«

»Still surface. What we perceive is only an illusion, a reflection of the world soul, a universal consciousness.

The Bhogi explained: »The alchymists make a similar mistake as the magicians. We do not become happy and one with the whole by bending it as we please. Rather, it is we ourselves who have to adapt, who should come into resonance.«

»Then a science of the inner self might be helpful after all!«

»Precisely. This is what we mystics do: close observation of our inner life, our individual consciousness. This is what the alchymists originally did as well. They spoke of the philosopher's stone and the transformation of mercury into gold. But these were originally meant to be inner transformations.

»But then they were able to perform small miracles and could show these to the mighty rulers of the world. They could generate electricity and use it to make little lamps glow. Their engineers could run machines with steam. The alchymists could bridge great distances with balloons and airships. They could use gunpowder to shoot bullets at great distances, so that wars could be won.

»The alchymists formed subgroups: physicists, biologists, chemists, geologists. They wanted to find out what our world is like, down to the very smallest and up to the very largest. These people lived in the illusion that our world consists of the perceptible and measurable. They did not perceive that which cannot be perceived. That which cannot be measured did not exist for them. And they began to experiment and manipulate, and increasingly disrupted the order, the naturally grown order!«

Such the Bhogi had spoken about the alchymists. A few days later Tatu Njena had shown her the machinations of the alchymists, who could expect support from the powerful and the rich, since they could satisfy and encourage their greed at the same time.

Nacharya Tatu Njena

In the third year, after her father had taken her in, she had met a third of the nine Nacharya, after the Nononn and the Bhogi, the Dresonn, who preferred to be called by his birth name, "Tatu Njena".

One day, she had been asked to come to the castellan, who had introduced her to a strong, handsome man with dark skin.

»Hello Hollydeva, I am the Dresonn, the third of the Nine Nacharya. When the Adiraja founded the order, my name or the man who took the position at that time was Kriyendra. The Nononn would like to be addressed with his rank as the ninth of the order, and the Bhogi prefers the name that the Adiraja once gave. That is right. But please just call me "Tatu Njena"! This is the name my parents gave me when I was born in Eastern Afryka!

»I have heard that you have some weighty questions. And since we want you to play an important role for us sometime, we would like to answer all your questions. Perhaps we also think that the time has come that the Nine should not be made up of male knights only. Some of us probably do not want to be reborn. Who knows, maybe one day you will take over my position or that of the Bhogi, who is already very old. But no, the Bhogi is known for being too devoted to earthly pleasures, and you are rather abstinent! Am I right?«

Hollydeva hadn't been sure if she knew what he meant by that, but she nodded in agreement.

»Well, we shall see. It's important that you understand why we do what we do the way we do it!

»What do you know about archaeology?«

»Archaeology is a science that digs up ancient things!«

37

»Right. All over the world, you can find evidence of ancient cultures. They also find skeletons of dinosaurs that are said to have lived here a million years ago. But here, please read these books! I'll see you in a week and I want to know what you think of these books!«

Hollydeva had received the books from Nacharya Tatu Njena and read them in the days after. The authors, archaeologists, had studied strange finds on all continents of Yrth.

On a high plateau on the continent of South Ameryca, there were probably kilometers of ancient lines furrowed into the stones, which could only be seen from great heights and had therefore been developed by people who could do such things from great heights.

In the old writings of all cultures there were references to visitors from outside the Yrth, "extraterrestrials".

One book described the traditions of the reclusive tribe of Native Amerycans, the Hopy. The Hopy had passed down orally, generation after generation, the sightings of their tribe and the other tribes they knew. In their version of human history on the Yrth, there had been several advanced civilizations destroyed by high technology and wars.

The Hopy had lived through all the catastrophic eras, as they had learned to cope in rather adverse, barren environments. They had, as probably other similar groups on the Yrth, contact to an otherworldly world that gave them more than any earthly happiness, than any high technology.

Another book was by a strange sage born in the land of Armynia. His name was George Gurdjyeff, the book was called "Byelzebub's Tales for his Grandson". The book told a similar story of the people on Yrth as the Hopy. There had been numerous civilizations. The civilized people had developed high technology and destroyed themselves.

The destruction of a high culture on an island was mentioned in each of the books: Atlantys. Already while reading the word she had felt an inexplicable sadness. Something important seemed to have been lost.

»Well, what did you learn from these books?«

»There is an ancient history of the Yrth! It appears that the Yrth has been developed several times up to advanced civilizations and high technology, and that has always brought about the end of civilization!«

»Exactly. You got it right. There is a level of development that leads to a change, to an extermination. Certain weapons and technologies are so dangerous, their power is so destructive, that in the wrong hands they will bring about the end!«

Tatu Njena thought for a moment. »Perhaps the main causes for destruction are certain philosophies and world models. After all, technology is without evil will or any will at all. Even weapons themselves are without will. Man who wants to control others or the whole of Yrth is the cause of destruction.«

When Hollydeva nodded as if understanding, the nacharya asked what else she had read in the books.

»It seems that there are extraterrestrial beings!«

»Yes, this is another insight. There are probably extraterrestrials who influence the development of Yrth! Some bring knowledge, others bring destruction!«

At that time, in this conversation with Tatu Njena, Hollydeva did not know any extraterrestrials. But now she had met the star boy. He was sitting down in the dungeon. But Astrello would not destroy civilizations anyway. Would he bring a dangerous worldview with him?

Tatu Njena had praised her then. »Well, you did well. You have a quick mind and a quick grasp of the important things.«

»So it is the Nacharya's task to prevent the development of high technology?«

Tatu Njena nodded and thought for a while. »I can't say that at all. I'm sure there are one or two Nacharya who see things differently, who have nothing against high technology. Especially Saphed is more of an ally of the alchymists these days!

»The problem is not the technology, but the level of consciousness of the people using this technology. People who are conscious and supportive and loving of each other will probably be able to handle high technology in a meaningful way. The Nacharya were above all for spreading a kind of fear of God, or better: a reverence for Being!«

»What does Nacharya mean?«

»An Acharya is a teacher in the ancient sacred language of Sanskryt. We have an N before the Acharya, the classical letter of negation. Nacharyas are teachers, and we are not. We rather proclaim that the world is empty, that it is in some way a Nothingness, that people should not cling to anything, as everything is transitory.

»It may also be that it is more a matter of unlearning than of learning. We strive for an inner liberation, a transformation, a completion that is also a death.«

»That is why the Bhogi saved and dismissed the nihilist lady? The Nacharya are nihilists too?«

»Kalima? Kalima is not really a nihilist. And neither are we. We all believe in an afterlife, in a world to which we return after death. Maybe we even know that it is so. In any case, Kalima seems to know it. She is very convinced and very convincing!«

The Sacred Valley

»Come, let me show you something so you'll understand the world better!«

They had climbed a gondola that was hanging under a big balloon filled with gas. An experienced balloonist had been with them as helmsman.

»The first thing you see now from above is the surroundings of Georgeburg Castle. You see an old dark castle a little higher up, and a small village nearby. Around the castle there is a park and a forest. Then come many villages with fields and acres and woods. The County.«

»The County?«

»Yes, the castle is in the middle of the County. The Count is an old companion of the Nine. We let him do as he likes, support him financially, and he makes sure that the castle is provided for and protected and actually inaccessible to the world. And, yes, what happens in the cellars of the castle does not interest him either.

»In the southeast there is a large mountain range, where the northwest wind is blowing us now. And we must climb higher. Here, put on this anorak, it's getting colder now!«

After several hours of flying over landscapes and small towns, they had landed on a high plateau. Tatu Njena had helped her out of the gondola and said that they would have to walk for about half an hour. They had passed a narrow gorge that led through the rock and had reached a valley.

In the valley it was very quiet. A deep peace seemed to emanate from the trees and meadows. The valley looked untouched, no one around.

»This is the Sacred Valley, Hollydeva! This is what Yrth is like when it is left untouched by men and doers. We Nacharya keep it secret and protect it. Come, for once, we can take a walk through the valley!«

Hollydeva was overwhelmed. There was a scent, wild flowers were blooming everywhere. She saw birds and butterflies. Mighty trees stretched their crowns towards the mountains enclosing the valley.

»There are no predators here, no poisonous snakes?«

»Ah, there is nothing wrong with predators. They ensure a certain hygiene in the genome. Scavengers are also important. The crows and vultures probably do that here. It's a balance, a balance that is always restored in nature, if you let it!«

»So there are also predators and snakes and the like here? So there are also animals here that eat other animals?«

»Yes, of course. That is the essence of the world. Eat and be eaten. Only the threat to life makes the living beings fitter and healthier. It is an eternal changing, a flowing.

»Come on!«

They had hiked for several hours, and Hollydeva had enjoyed the idyll of the Sacred Valley. It was fragrant and radiant. The air was filled with the songs of birds and the humming of millions of insects. Against the bites of the mosquitoes, Tatu Njena had given her an ointment that scared off the mosquitoes, which they applied.

At the end of the valley Tatu Njena led her up a path that led into a small side valley. It widened after a while and opened into a plain with a village in the middle.

»Come, I want to show you how people live who live in harmony with nature, with God's creation!«

When they were at the entrance of the village, a man came towards them. Tatu Njena quickly went up to him and hugged him. He turned around and pulled Hollydeva towards him.

»Hollydeva, allow me to introduce you to Peredur. He is the fifth in the succession of the Nacharya and the protector of the valley and this village and its inhabitants!«

Tatu Njena turned to Peredur, »Peredur, this is Hollydeva, the daughter of Seren and Rosa de Valmere! I want to show her how wonderful this world can be and how much the alchymists threaten the world in their hubris!«

Peredur bowed lightly with his palms of his hands put together: »I greet you, Hollydeva! I have heard about you! Come along, it's the celebration of Thanksgiving!«

On the way to the village square, where all the inhabitants were gathered to attend a kind of procession and blessing, Peredur explained to her that all the inhabitants were at the same time farmers in the fields, meadows, and gardens of the valley. They also had houses in the village where they practiced a trade: blacksmith, potter, tailor, baker, builder, carpenter, weaver.

She had seen merrily celebrating people who had put on their best festive costumes. There was dancing and food and drink. As Peredur's companion, she was respected and left alone. So she had observed and absorbed everything.

But she had also felt strange and unsuitable. When Peredur had asked how she liked the village, she had said that she would fit better at dark Georgeburg Castle. Tatu Njena and Peredur had laughed mockingly.

But she had got a nice guest room, slept exceptionally well, and the breakfast the next morning was as delicious as she had ever eaten before.

Then Tatu Njena had said that she should arm herself, as now he would show her the other side, the world that had been corrupted by the alchymists.

They had been given a horse-drawn carriage and had driven out of the valley and over some more ridges. Then they had reached a landscape with fields and other plantations.

»Remember the fruit trees in Peredur's village?«

Hollydeva had eaten an apple that Peredur had picked from a sturdy tree at the edge of the village. »Yes, of course, there was this strong apple tree!«

»Exactly. And here you see these crippled, high-bred apples lined up in a row.«

Hollydeva was surprised when she saw this orchard where trees were only about six feet high and looked like crippled.

»Wait until I show you the stables for the animals, and the slaughterhouse where they are turned into meat.«

At the edge of the fields, there had been warning signs: "Beware of pesticide!"

»What's pesticide?«

»The farmers spray chemicals, which they got from the alchymists, on the fields, so that no insects and no worms can live there, as they could eat away some of their grain!«

»And the farmers in Peredur's village don't have that problem?«

»No, it's not a real problem. It is right and proper to sacrifice a part of the harvest to the small animals. These are food for other animals, and they pollinate the flowers!«

Hollydeva had seen masts with strings stretched between them. There had been such masts in her home village, but not so many.

»There's a power station back there. Electric energy flows through the cables! But the energy also creates harmful force fields!«

»And what are these towers?«

»They are transmission towers. The people here can send messages over the ether, invisible waves.«

»And that's surely not healthy?«

»No, it's not healthy. You will have slept better yesterday than anywhere else. Because in the valley and in the village there are none of these waves in the air. We can't see them or smell them, but they affect our sensitive brain waves and our immune system and everything.«

Then they had come to a disgusting place where it stank and smoked.

»This is the garbage dump! People throw a lot of things away here. In the village of Peredur everything is used and reused and can be composted into fertilizer. Here, materials are used that cannot be reused. The alchymists have invented plastic. It's pretty colorful, but it's unnatural!«

They stopped at an inn. The people looked tired and pale. Or they had puffy faces.

»The people are usually discontented here. They eat and drink too much. But the food does not have so much positive energy and does not really nourish them! They also drink alcohol, which numbs them and makes them forget the effort they put in to be able to afford more plastic and pesticides and electricity!«

Then a man came into the inn, who was treated with respect.

»This is the government tax collector here. They have elected this government for themselves. But the taxes are high because the government likes to waste money and give it to the alchymists to produce more of their questionable achievements!«

The tax collector was accompanied by a uniformed man who had heard Tatu Njena's last words and was probably also irritated by his skin color, which was unusual in this region.

When he approached them with a stern look, Hollydeva had to laugh. He reminded her of her father when he wanted to question prisoners.

But then a man behind them had stepped out of the shadows and showed this policeman something so that he went back to the tax collector grumbling.

»Here we can only travel around with a companion who protects us. Above all, you can't speak the truth out loud here!«

Tatu Njena had thanked the guard who protected them, and they had been driven back to Georgeburg Castle.

Chapter 5:
Lyndonia. Miona

Lyndonia

On the fifth day after Astrello's arrival at Georgeburg Castle, the Bhogi had summoned Hollydeva early in the morning so that she could not visit Astrello.

»I have a journey to make, and I want you to accompany me!«

»Where are we going?«

»We have to go to Tangent Alley!«

»Where is this alley? I've never heard of it!«

»It's a little alley in the big city of Lyndonia!«

»How do we get there?«

»We are driven to the coast, board a ferry, get to a big island, take a train and get to Lyndonia, the capital of this island, where we are sometimes driven by carriages. But in the end, you have to push me so that we can get into that alley and prevent an occurrence.«

»What do we prevent? Who wants to prevent us from preventing it?«

»Yes, these are excellent questions, and I can only answer them there when I see how people react to our presence. Our adversaries are the wizardeurs, people who wave magic wands and upset the balance of the world so that they have an advantage. But, as you can imagine, an upset balance is no good!«

»When do we leave?«

»Let's leave right away now!«

Then the old nacharya added, »And, please, you call me Bhogi, without sir, master, lord or any such polite form of address. If you respect me, we will not get far!«

Then he suddenly looked at her firmly, »But if you don't respect me, we neither will!«

Hollydeva thought about this contradiction further during the drive and came to the conclusion that he probably meant two different kinds of respect. The general respect of the person was good and necessary. Respectful politeness in a critical situation, in a battle, would be obstructive, unnecessarily time-consuming.

So she pushed the Bhogi, who sat comfortably in his wheelchair, from Saint Pancras train station through the streets of Lyndonia, which seemed to be a really big city. She could not judge this, however, since she had never been in a city before. Everywhere were houses, streets, a swarm of people, carriages that drove by themselves.

»The station is called Pancreas, that is a digestive gland!« Hollydeva amused herself. They had just been studying human anatomy in Father Septimus' class. She found the internal organs fascinating, especially since Father Septimus believed that every organ had a physiological and an energetic function.

The Bhogi looked over his shoulder at her, »The station is not called the pancreas station! It is named after Saint Pancras, one of the Ice Saints! Saint Pancras Station is the anti-pole to Valhalla, where the Nordic gods dwell!«

»Ice Saint? Nordic gods? Are you a follower of the MultiGod, Bhogi?« Hollydeva was irritated, but she had already suspected the Bhogi of being an old heretic ever since the Kalima incident.

»I am not a follower and not a believer at all, Hollydeva! I have always believed only in good food and beautiful women! See that one?«

Hollydeva saw a gracefully dancing, dark-skinned woman, probably about 20 years old. She sighed. With what kind of lecher was she traveling here? She surely wanted the rulers of the world to behave better than that!

»But I am not a beautiful woman!«

»Just wait a few more years, you'll be fine! Beauty comes from within! If you think you are beautiful, you will be! But I think you'd rather be inconspicuous like a nacharya! Instead of being stared at, you rather want to be the observer!«

Hollydeva had to nod slightly. The Bhogi understood her all too well.

»But we are out of the station. So we're not going to Valhalla today?!«

»No, Valhalla doesn't exist anymore, Holly. But that's an entirely different story. Push me down that street, Romilly Street, that's where we have to go!«

It was a dark street. She had read somewhere along the way that they were in the Soho district. The Bhogi asked her to stop in front of a dark pub, which was inconspicuously located between a bookstore and a store, where music on round discs was probably available. "The Haughty Herring" was the name of the dive.

»Come on, we have to get in there! Inside is the entrance to the alley we want to go to!«

It was dark and a little eerie in the pub's guest room. There were about seven guests, who stood up, immediately looking suspiciously at the Bhogi and Hollydeva.

The landlord approached them. »We're closed! Private meeting!«

The Bhogi replied, »Yes. I am invited. I just have to see what I engraved back there on the tiled wall in my youth, when I had been here with one of the most beautiful women of her time, Boadica, you will remember. Yes, thank you, I will find the way myself!«

The Bhogi had given Hollydeva a sign, and she had pushed him past the baffled innkeeper to the tiled wall. Quickly, he had hit some tiles with the walking stick he had with him. But nothing happened.

One of the guests approached. »The Bhogi, once again! We have changed the sequence, Mr. Nacharya! There will not be another visit of His Eminence to the Alley of the Tangents! Last time you robbed us and the loss was painful!«

The Bhogi had turned the wheelchair around to confront the man, who had a wooden stick in his hand.

»I must go to the alley and I must prevent an apprentice of yours from acquiring a certain wand! He'll only do mischief with it!«

»We'll take care of that ourselves! And I think we know who you're talking about here! The young Cevaine will not do any mischief, but will help the wizardeurs back to their old greatness! You mystics will hear and see more!«

The Bhogi examined the man and the other wizardeurs who gathered behind him. They all seemed to be bizarre figures, boldly dressed. On the street in front of the Herring, they would most likely generate rejection or laughter.

»Master Deekelly, don't be foolish! You know that you cannot or must not do anything against me!«

The person addressed laughed: »Times have changed, Nacharya Bhogi! The mages –who you call wizardeurs- are just regaining their power. We have a new hope, a new prince!«

The Bhogi continued to provoke the wizardeurs in the tavern, »A prince of the wizardeurs? Where is he supposed to come from? You have become barren!«

»Yes, but the curse laid upon us does not work in distant lands! And from those lands the prince came to us! And we heard of other neophytes who are on their way to Vowharts!«

»Oh, and they still stock up on the necessary equipment here?«

Deekelly realized that he had already revealed too much and raised the wand for a curse.

»You must do something now, Hollydeva!« the Bhogi whispered to Hollydeva.

»Me? What do you mean?« Hollydeva was surprised. What should she do against the magic of an experienced wizardeur in his own territory?

»Yes, that's why I brought you with me! You have powers! You can get us out of here safely! I was just bluffing! I am old and weak and have no more power!«

Hollydeva mouth stayed open in amazement.

The wizardeur hurled his staff in their direction and shouted something that sounded like »Scabbers!« And it began to itch.

Hollydeva felt panic. What should she do against these superior forces? Where were allies here? Nowhere.

Why had the Bhogi brought her into this situation? Was he really so weak? Was it a test and she just failed dramatically?

Deekelly and the other wizardeurs laughed loudly and gloating. She grabbed the wheelchair and pushed the Bhogi out of the Haughty Herring with vehemence.

Outside on Romilly Street, they paused.

»You did that wonderfully, Hollydeva! Splendid! You have shown them,« the Bhogi shouted back to her.

Splendid? Did he mean it ironically? Was running away really the option?

»I just pushed you out! I have not been able to do anything! I can't do any magic!«

»Running away is great magic!« laughed the Bhogi.

And what about the scabies?

»It itches!« she complained.

»Oh yes!« admitted the Bhogi. He pulled a magic wand from a hiding place on the side of the wheelchair, waved it over his head, made a big circle and shouted, »Get away!«

In fact, the unpleasant skin feeling was gone instantly.

Miona

A dark-skinned girl, probably two or three years older than Hollydeva, crept up the otherwise deserted alley. She looked closely at the houses as if she were searching for a particular house.

»Here, dear!« shouted the Bhogi at her. »Surely you want to get into the Haughty Herring to get into the Tangential Alley?! Shopping, isn't it?!«

The girl came to them and nodded, saw the pub and wanted to go right in.

»Wait, wait!« shouted the Bhogi. »The Haughty Herring is closed today! You cannot go in now! We stand here as welcoming committee and advisers. We are already waiting for you. But you are…«

»Yes, I am Miona Yaboah. I'm supposed to go in here, and inside is the entrance to the alley where I get the things on this list!«

»Go on, hypnotize her,« whispered the Bhogi to Hollydeva.

Yes, she knew the basics of hypnosis, which she had learned from her father. But now here, at such short notice?

»I also wanted to come in here and to the alley, but I can't now. Do you want to rest?« She had left her post behind the wheelchair and walked towards the Afrycan girl.

»Don't you want to rest a little?«

The girl, Miona Yaboah, looked at her without understanding. She had been prepared for something completely different, for a new, exciting world, for her apprenticeship as a wizardeur. She did not want to rest.

»You do not want to rest now! But a little sleep would be wonderful as you come from so far away! It was a great journey, and you have mastered this journey. And now you are here, and you don't know whether you should sleep or just rest. Sleep a little…«

Hollydeva had spoken in an increasingly soft and mumbling voice. And the Bhogi had started with a deep and evocative voice: »Yes, you can sleep now, you just follow our voices, and now you become very heavy and just let go, Miona! Miona, you can trust us!«

And Miona stood there like she was asleep.

»Wonderful! Great again, Hollydeva! I knew you had it in you!«

Hollydeva was still not sure if the Bhogi was teasing her a little. But anyway, the other girl, the aspirant of the wizardeurs, was in a hypnotic trance.

»So, Miona, you will just go with us now! We will take you wherever you want to go!«

And like a sleepwalker, this aspiring wizardeuress followed them to St. Pancras train station.

But on the way, the Bhogi beckoned a street boy. He wrote something on a piece of paper, folded it, wrote an address on the back.

»Boy, can you take this to that address, please? Here's your reward!«

The Bhogi gave the boy a coin that was probably bigger than the boy had expected because he made big eyes.

»If you carry out the order well, and I know you will, I will give you more orders that will be just as well paid! What is your name, boy?«

»Oliver!« answered the boy.

»Oliver, that's good. Run along, my boy, and bring the message to the man at that address! Do you know where it is?«

Oliver nodded

»Then, go!«

Oliver ran.

»What was that message?«

»Oh, the wizardeurs have a newspaper. It will interest them that a young aspirant came from far away; from Afryka! But she was intercepted and kidnapped by the Nacharya!«

Hollydeva looked a little surprised.

»Don't look at me like that! We did not get into the realm of the wizardeurs today. So we must provoke them so that they come to us!«

»This Miona here is a decoy?«

»Yes, cheese for the mage-rats, so to speak! As soon as she is nicely stored in our dungeon in the castle, they will have to come to free her. Then we will know how powerful their new prince is!«

Hollydeva thought that the plan might have some risks and felt some compassion for this girl who had been distracted from her path through them.

But Miona stayed in the relaxed trance, followed them on the train to Dover, boarded the ferry with them and was driven between Hollydeva and the Bhogi, sitting in the car, to Georgeburg Castle, where she was laid down on a cot in a room in the castle cellar to wake up from the hypnosis that the Bhogi had refreshed from time to time during the journey.

No doubt, the place of her awakening would be surprisingly frightening for Miona.

»This will not be a nice awakening for this Miona! It is not her fault that she wanted to go to the wizardeurs!«

»Oh, no? Well, it honors you to speak for her! Why don't you put her with the starry boy! She'll see a nice face for a start!«

But Hollydeva had chosen the Starboy for herself. She did not want to breed a competitor! And this Miona really looked attractive, strong with even features and a little more feminine than she herself.

»Maybe I will introduce them to each other! But I will keep control,« she said to herself.

The Highest, the Most Important?

On the train ride, the ferry crossing and the car ride back to the castle, she had given further thought to morals and ethics. And she rather would not discuss these with the Bhogi, as she was not sure whether she could or would approve of his actions, in which she had become an accomplice.

Hollydeva had been thinking about the Septimus' statements for some time. The motivation should be good. Good was what was oriented towards the preservation of life. Those who were not aware of the motivation and felt no conscience had to subordinate themselves to the instructions of the higher-ups. Their motivation either had to be trusted or it had to be checked.

»So what is the highest, the most important thing?« she had asked the Pater.

»What do you mean by that?«

»You said that it can be justified to kill another human being if only in this way the survival of humanity or nature can be assured.«

»Yes, you can see it that way!«

»Could it happen that all of humanity would have to be sacrificed to preserve the Yrth?«

»Hmm, you mean, if people destroy the Yrth and there is possibly other intelligent life of equal value, or if there is a chance that there could be a new beginning for humanity?«

»Yes, but does that sound like man is the highest of the Yrth?«

»We are human, so I guess we have to look at it that way. First, we are concerned with our own survival!«

»Ah. So we are ourselves the highest, the one at whom we orientate our behavior?«

»Yes, you could say so. And the question will probably not arise. For no one has the power to extinguish humanity as a whole!«

Hollydeva had to agree and had some time again to think up questions about it.

What is right action? How should I know if my actions help humanity or life in general or the Yrth?

How do I know if I am acting out of greed or out of magnanimity?

How can I speak to the OneGod so that he or she tells me what to do, whom to follow?

She had learned on the journey to the Sacred Valley of Tatu Njena and Peredur that there was something beautiful and natural to protect on the Yrth, that there was something like the OneGod's creation, which was increasingly defaced, filthy and endangered by the alchymists.

And the rich and powerful whom her father sought to influence had become lackeys of these alchymists!

She had looked at the sleeping Miona, to whom she felt a connection, who in her own way probably was forced bay motives as recognizable as her own, and said to herself, »I must toughen up! As soon as I am sure that my motives and those of my father and the Nacharya are such that they are undoubtedly on the side of the good ones, then I must be able to carry out deeds that seem to be evil, I must be able to imprison people like Astrello or Miona in order to snatch them from the clutches of the pests!«

Values, Criteria

Hollydeva was almost certain that she really had to dissuade Astrello from his astrology. At least, he had to stop telling people something that was misleading them.

She remembered a conversation with her father, whom she had asked about the motives for his actions. Because it was important to her that she could justify the evil-looking actions with the rescue of the Yrth, with a higher motivation.

She wanted there to be no discrepancy between the commandments of the One-God, and especially those of Bodhisattvism, and her actions for this worldview, as these discrepancies would cause her to doubt and hesitate in her actions.

Hollydeva had reflected for a long time on the various questions concerning good and evil. She had to know that what she was doing and aiding and abetting was not reprehensible. She had to question her father's motives, even if she wanted to trust him.

»Father, we imprison people and torture them: Why are we doing this?«

»We work for the Nacharya. The Order of the Nine Masters keeps order and preserves Yrth.«

»Are we sure about this? Are they really doing this?«

»Do you want to check this?«

»Yes, I think we have to know that and be sure that we're working for the right people!«

»Hmm, you've been racking your brains over weighty questions!«

Hollydeva had sensed that her questions made her father uncomfortable or that he didn't take her seriously. But she did not want to be fobbed off with the idea that she was too young for these questions. After all, she hadn't been too young to poke forefingers into sensitive areas.

Her father had tried to point out the impossibility of the idea: »You would have to study all the decisions of the Nacharya and see how they changed or preserved the Yrth. These are probably over 2500 years of records. Allman will have them! But it will take you several years to read them!«

Hollydeva had looked at him firmly and tried to hide that she felt a bit of annoyance.

»What are the Nacharya's ventures, and by what criteria do they intervene in the events?«

»This is a good question. Although I would say that I have been working for them for almost twenty years and I have never had the feeling that I was doing something wrong. I have traveled around the world, seen what is going on, and have entered into the service of Nacharya with conviction. As my daughter, you should trust me and believe me that we are doing the right thing!«

He had looked firmly at Hollydeva and noticed her displeasure.

»Well, you are probably like myself, and you are not easily impressed and above all you are not willing to blindly trust, not even your father!«

Hollydeva had nodded slightly.

»I think that the Nacharya have above all ensured that good and just rulers govern the states of the Yrth. We want the people to be as well-off as possible, that they do not go hungry, that there are no wars and diseases. The greatest deed of the last hundred years was probably the unification of the monotheistic religions into one, the OneGod. This has greatly reduced wars and especially civil wars on Yrth. Faith sometimes turns people into murderers.

»On the other hand, the Nacharya are most likely working for the fairest possible markets. No one should have a monopoly, no one should take advantage of others with prices that are too low or too high or with bad goods.«

Seren had thought further, »There are threats to the Yrth. Asteroids or large meteorites can cause damage. There are natural disasters, epidemics. We must work to ensure that humanity is prepared and can cope with all threats.«

He had looked at Hollydeva, »Do these explanations make sense to you?«

Hollydeva had nodded. Her father seemed to have given it some thought and respected her suspicions. She would continue to assist him. She would eventually take over his position.

Chapter 6:
Zronn Saphed

Astrello Meets Miona

So, on the sixth day after Astrello's arrival, the day after the eventful trip to Lyndonia, Hollydeva had time to "visit" the star boy in his cell again in the morning.

»Where were you yesterday? I missed you! No one spoke to me!«

»Yes, that boils you soft, eh? Now you're going to swear off soon!« Hollydeva grimaced, but didn't really succeed.

»What's the matter, Holly? You're different!«

»Yeah, you must have calculated that! Is my Jupiter at its zenith?«

Astrello laughed, »Jupiter at its zenith? There's no such thing. No, I didn't calculate it. I can tell by looking at you! Or, it's such a feeling! You experienced something yesterday that is still bothering you!«

»Yes, that's right. I was in a big city on an island out west, Lyndonia, with Nacharya Bhogi. Do you know Lyndonia?«

»Yes, I've been there! A really big city! What were you guys doing there? Who is Bhogi?«

»The Bhogi is one of the nine Nacharya, an old gentleman. We like each other, I think. He explains some things to me. We were going to a street where the wizardeurs buy their tools and implements. But we didn't get in. Maybe he didn't want to and just wanted to test me in a difficult situation. But then something happened that just bothered me.«

»What is it?«

»We kidnapped a girl, a wizardeur, and took her with us!«

»A girl? She's in a cell next door?«

»Yes, something like that. She's a few cells away. We hypnotized her and took her with us. The Bhogi wants to attract and fight the wizardeurs that way. But I feel sorry for her. She's an Afrycan and I guess she wanted to go to this street because she goes to the wizardeur school. I don't really know anything about her. Her name is Miona.«

»Hmm, but you didn't mind me being stuck here either. You like to detain people and torture them, don't you?«

»Well, you haven't been tortured that much! All the people I've seen here so far for treatment by my father were somehow harming people or damaging Yrth! I am confident to do the right thing when we pester them a little and motivate them to change their behavior!

»But how can people like you and Miona, who are only slightly older than me, be so evil that they deserve to be locked up here? I don't feel like I'm doing the right thing in these cases!«

»Oh, a conscience!«

»Yes, strange. I thought I didn't have that!«

»Everyone has a conscience!«

»Really? But then why are there people who harm the Yrth or humanity?«

»Good question. Greed is just stronger than conscience then. Or their own survival is preferred to that of humanity or the Yrth, which is understandable. Making sacrifices is just what heroes do!«

»Heroes! I'm not a hero!«

»That's not what the stars say! People like you, with the moon in a strong area — it's even the throne itself —, can only be brave and thus be heroes!«

»Can you calculate what will happen to Miona? When will she get out of here? When the wizardeurs will try to get her out of here?«

»I can try. But I need birth time and birthplace, and I might need to have an impression of her, too, see her.«

»See her? You want me to take you to her cell?«

»Yes, that would be a feat! It would give her courage to see who else is in here like that!«

»You mean she'll see that there are heroes in the neighboring cells, and then she'll get a whole lot of confidence!«

»Go ahead and make fun of me! Rather, show me that you're brave, that you can make a difference here. You, the daughter of the Grand Inquisitor!«

»I'll see what I can do!«

She exited the cell and immediately saw that Miona's cell was guarded by two men of the Grey Wardens.

»I need to talk to the prisoner I brought here yesterday!«

She had tried to speak in a slightly lower voice of authority so that the two guards would let her into the cell right away. But, of course, it wasn't that easy.

»We have orders to let only the Grand Inquisitor or the Septonn see her!«

So she had to ask the Bhogi for permission. He quite liked the idea, though, especially since Hollydeva promised to tell him what time Astrello would have calculated the wizardeur's attack to free Miona. He summoned a guard to accompany her and gave appropriate instructions to the guards outside the door.

»Come along, Miona, I have someone to introduce you to!«

The wizardeur girl was a bit irritated.

»Where am I? Why am I in a cell?«

»You are in a castle of the Nacharya! The Nine Nacharya are the guardians of the Yrth! We kidnapped you!«

Hollydeva had decided that only the absolute truth would allow real contact.

»Why? What have I done?«

»Oh, actually, you're probably innocent! We want to attract the wizardeurs! They will come for your liberation!«

»Wizardeurs? What is that?«

»Wizardeurs, — it should sound French — that is our word for those presumptuous magicians and sorcerers!«

»Are you sure? The wizardeurs don't even know me yet!«

»We've already given them a message! And if they don't come, you'll just stay here!«

Then she introduced Astrello and Miona to each other. But the two were suspicious. Hollydeva was somewhat reassured: this was not love at first sight, and she herself would remain at the top of Astrello's sympathy list.

»When and where were you born, Miona?« asked the astrologer, then.

After Astrello explained that he could then tell her when she would finally arrive at the wizardeurs, she told him.

Astrello explained that he needed a time for calculations. After about two hours, he told Miona that she had an interesting birth chart. She would probably have important siblings, too. And yes, she would have magic abilities.

Miona confirmed that she had two younger sisters.

»So what now? When do I get out of here?«

Astrello glanced at Hollydeva. He wasn't sure if he should really tell her that. Hollydeva nodded encouragingly.

»You'll be freed by the wizardeurs the day after tomorrow!« informed Astrello.

»Well, that's good then! Thank you, Astrello! If you ever want to learn about astro-magic, come join us at Vowharts! That's the school and the central castle of the wizardeurs! I'll speak for you!«

Hollydeva took her back to her cell. And still wondered about this invitation to the wizardeur's castle.

Astrello then confirmed to her that Miona had probably been with the wizardeurs for some time. »By my calculations, she must have been with the wizardeurs for two years already. She must have just seemed like a newcomer to you! Maybe she was pretending! She possibly is something like a Trojan horse here with you!«

Hollydeva thanked him and told the Bhogi these findings.

»The day after tomorrow! Yes, that's exciting. Then there are the other nacharya here, too! We are capable of as much magic and sorcery as these wizardeurs have got! They are in for a treat! But I already figured that the girl was deceiving us. She's in a cell where she can't use her magic!«

The Names of the Nine

In the afternoon, Hollydeva was summoned to the castellan's office, where the Nononn was waiting for her.

»Hollydeva, tomorrow all nine nacharya will be here at Georgeburg and I want to introduce you to them. You will eventually take a post in our order, perhaps even a significant post. I want you to be able to answer questions about the order well and make a good impression!«

The Nononn paused for a while, thinking about something.

»Who of the Nine of us have you met so far?«

»The Bhogi and you, Master Nononn. Then I was with Master Tatu Njena on a trip to a valley and there we met Master Peredur!«

»Good, so that's four. Let me tell you again about the Order! Then I'll introduce you to the other five you haven't met yet!

»The story of the Nine begins with the Adiraja, a king in Yndia about 2,500 years ago. His grandfather and father, as kings of a smaller empire, had already expanded it considerably and subjugated the neighboring kingdoms. The Adiraja continued these subjugations. In itself, he and his ancestors did this to establish a unified great empire so that the many wars between the small kingdoms would cease, and they could prepare together against threats from greater powers outside the Yndian subcontinent.

»At that time, there were several religions on the subcontinent. Most Yndians were followers of one form of the MultiGod religion, Hynduism. But several generations earlier, some wise founders of religions such as the Bodhisattva and the Mahavira had appeared. They had taught either a OneGod religion or a religion without God but with a unified divinity of Being. These had gathered many followers around them in their time, had appointed successors and founded mass religious movements.

»When the Adiraja had overrun and subjugated another neighboring kingdom with war, he traveled through this conquered land and saw the devastation, the dead and the suffering, and decided that it could not go on like this.

»He had contact with the Bodhisattva's teaching, which had taught compassion in the face of the impermanence of all being, and the suffering associated with impermanence.

»Can you follow me?«

Hollydeva nodded.

»The Adiraja converted to the Bodhisattva's teaching and decided to bring compassion and forgiveness to his subjects. The cause of suffering is attachment to impermanent items, to things! In short: greed!

»He also decided to infect the great empires that might want to conquer or threaten his kingdom with the world view of Bodhisattvism. So he sent out preachers, ambassadors, and missionaries. He hoped that the principle of compassion would spread throughout the world.

»But above all, a certain order had to be maintained. He understood that in a way, by giving up violence, he was weakening his position of power. People obey kings and emperors and presidents whom they fear. They fear being punished, robbed, murdered. A gracious, forgiving, compassionate ruler is usually considered weak, and citizens seek to take advantage of this.

»The Adiraja decided to find or train nine masters who could secretly and by all means exercise power in his kingdom and possibly in the neighboring kingdoms and the other great kingdoms.

»The eighth of the Nacharya is a special case. He is the leader, the boss. He actually always determined what we stand for. But something happened in the last few years. It's like he lost his moral compass. Well, actually, he didn't even have that when he was King Arthur himself. In the time of Adiraja, he was the majordomo of the palace, used to giving orders. Saphed was his name, and that is how he wants to be addressed now. He is the Zronn, the Zeroth Nacharya.

»I myself am the ninth, the Nononn. I am the mediator, the president. Back in the days of Adiraja, I was called Yogavaha. I was a Bodhisattvist who had already taught him some things and whom he trusted.

»The Yogavaha should be the highest number, the number nine, the mediator.

»The first of the Nacharya, the Onthronn, should be a warrior, a perfectly self-disciplining, worthy man. This he found in his tailor, Swami Sampanna. At present, the Onthronn is a man born in Palestine, an Arab, that is, el-Achmar.

»The second Nacharya, the Tworonn, was the physician of Adiraja, a healer. He is at this time a Western European, a Frank, like yourself. He is always called, in all incarnations so far, Daman.

»The third, the Dresonn, was Kriyendra, a high officer. In this life, his name is Tatu Njena. This means 'Three Yellows' in the language of his East Afrycan homeland.

»The fourth Nacharya, the Verionn, was the father of Tristan, Riwalin, in the time of the Arthurian knights. Indeed, we Nacharya had inspired the Knights' Round Table at that time. It was one of our most intense times, and some of us still like to be called by the names of the knights they were then! But his name is actually Nacharya Quavert now.

»Prathari, in the time of Adiraja, was a singer and actor who could give an inspiring performance of the ancient exploits of the Bodhisattva and his disciples. He is the Fionn. And is now called Peredur, a name of probably his most powerful role, back in the days of King Arthur.

»The sixth Nacharya was an advocate, a prosecutor. He is the Sessionn. The function of the Session is not inherited or continued through rebirth. Rather, personalities of merit are invited to fill this honor. At present, the Session is a Japanese. He has chosen the name Rokudan Aoi. He is also a martial arts master and versed in dark arts, I think!

»The seventh, the Bhogi. You know the Bhogi. The Bhogi is ancient, perhaps the oldest soul in this world. He loves women too much to disappear into nirvana.«

»And you were always the same, only freshly reborn? Do you remember all those lives?«

»No, that would be too much remembering in my head! I know what I need to know! But now, can you tell me the names of the Nine? It would be good if you at least knew the names of the ones you're going to step in front of tomorrow!«

»Alright, I don't know if I remember them all. But I'll try!

»So the ninth one is you, the Nononn. Mr. Navendra Raktah.

»The eighth is the boss, Saphed, once King Arthur himself.

»The seventh is my friend, the Bhogi!

»The sixth, the sixth. Tell me again, please.«

»The sixth, the Sessionn. His name now is Rokudan Aoi. You should address him as Master Rokudan. He's not a good person to deal with otherwise.«

»Thank you, Master Nononn. The fifth was the Fionn. His name is Peredur now.

»The fourth is a beau. The fourth green one, Quavert.

»The third is Tatu Njena, the one who took me on the balloon flight.

»The second Nacharya is the Tworonn, the Daman.

»And number one is the Onthronn, an Arab, Mr. Achmar!«

Saphed, The Zronn

Then she had told the Nononn about her work in the dungeons. Realizing that he would like to hear some compassion for prisoners, some heart, she told of Astrello and Miona.

»Ah, Hollydeva, you don't just bully! You also enjoy playing matchmaker?«

»Matchmaker?!«

»I'm probably turning pale or red with embarrassment right now!« she thought to herself at the same time.

»Aren't you going to set them up?«

»No, not really! But the astrologer might know when the wizardeurs will try to free the girl! But he'll have to do some calculating!«

»And you're sure the astrologer is a friend?«

»Yes, he is my friend!«

»I rather think he is an alchymist or a wizardeur! Yet we'll see! What do you think of the girl?«

»Miona? She's nice. But of course, she doesn't approve of Bhogi and me kidnapping her!«

»Yeah, that wasn't a too smart move either! You have to be a little careful with the Bhogi's ideas! Sometimes it's better to pretend you're in on it, and then let it all go to waste!«

»Yeah, I guess I've thought of something like that!«

»Come on, I have to introduce you to one of my brothers! Well, he's another na-charya, not my biological brother. I told you about him: Saphed, the boss of the Na-charya, also called Zronn. He wants to check you out a little. Don't worry. Just answer honestly and openly!«

The Nononn led Hollydeva to the better floors of the castle and to a cozy room, furnished with sofas and carpets.

Saphed, Nacharya number eight, the boss, was waiting there.

Saphed nodded to Nononn, who left the two alone.

»Hello Hollydeva! Nononn will have told you that I am Nacharya Saphed. I have been so for very many lifetimes and consequently have experienced much and helped guide the fortunes of the Yrth. Sometimes better, sometimes worse! May I ask you a few questions?«

»Yes, please ask, Master Saphed!«

Saphed had a slight Russian accent. He was of stout, medium build and probably forty years old. A certain coldness and hardness in his features made him rather un-appealing to Hollydeva.

»All right. Hollydeva, you are assisting your father, our Grand Inquisitor, after all! Do you enjoy this activity?«

»I haven't thought about that yet. It's interesting, anyway. It feels good to bring bad people back to the right path!«

»Yes, it's good, too. I was told that you asked your teacher questions about what was good and what was bad!«

»Yes, I did! Wasn't I allowed to do that?«

»Oh yes, of course you were. Those are perfectly valid questions! And you came to the conclusion that what you were doing in the dungeons was justified?«

»I don't know. It might take me to hell!!!«

»To hell?«

»Yes, murderers go to hell!«

»Hmm. Hell is a term from the world model of some cults that flowed into the OneGod, that's right. After all, we Nacharya tend to follow the Bodhisattva. There is the model of rebirth, incarnations. And the law of karma. If you do bad things, you will experience bad things. Everything is balanced. Do you believe in such things? Are you going to end up in a dungeon?«

»I don't know.«

»If you believe that you should be punished for your actions by a higher justice, then I guess it will happen that way. We create our reality, mostly unconsciously.«

»I don't think I would have to be punished, since I am working for the preservation of the Yrth, for naturalness, against the alchymists!«

She perceived that Saphed flinched a little.

»The alchymists? Oh yes, you were with Tatu Njena and Peredur in their Sacred Valley! Well, let me tell you that I have a slightly different attitude towards the alchymists!«

Hollydeva became aware that she was beginning to put on her mocking face of defiance. There was nothing she could do about it. She also didn't really care whether the Nacharya boss liked her or not. Her connection to the Bhogi and to her father was enough for her.

»It looks very nice in the valley and in the village in the neighboring valley. And then in the small town, not so much. But I must tell you that the valley is an artificial world, protected with great effort and kept alive by my friend Peredur.

»The world of people has always been characterized by a hard struggle of survival. There are diseases, natural disasters, enemies. Everyone experiences loved ones dying and being lost. Everything is ephemeral, and every loss can challenge one's survival.

»People in worlds before civilizations did not ask themselves whether they were acting ethically or morally good or right. They simply wanted to survive.

»So people invented tools to build shelter, to domesticate animals, to improve the odds of survival. And now we're at a time when we can invent and build considerably more effective tools. Science has moved into a new dimension. We can shape the environment and ourselves to live a life of peace and freedom. Then we won't have to worry about ethics and morality, as there will be no more motivation for evil deeds!«

Hollydeva was at the same time confused and somewhat defensive about this long lecture of Zronn Saphed. She somehow felt that she did not want to agree with him. She wanted the idyll of the Sacred Valley to be stronger than a life simplified by science. But she didn't feel strong enough to argue with Saphed.

»I just want you to remain neutral. As an assistant to the Grand Inquisitor, you are an executive body of the Nacharya. You carry out orders and do not question them. There are some among the Nine who rather indulge in idyllic concepts! There are some like me, who welcome the successes of the sciences and want to promote progress! You can be sure that all actions and attitudes will be openly discussed and dealt with in our Council of Nine. Then we will find the best solution!

»The solution is always a synthesis of possibly extremely different looking points of view or attitudes or even world views. The Bodhisattva has taught the way of the middle, and this is also followed by the Nine Nacharya. Do you agree with this explanation and your role, which after all may expand and change as the years go by?«

Hollydeva nodded, »Yes, thank you, Nacharya Saphed! I thank you for taking this time and effort to explain to me exactly the procedure and my role! It gives me the confidence to accomplish my task!«

»Good, just don't be too influenced by the romantics among us!«

With that, he dismissed her, and she thought about a few things as she made her way back to Astrello, whom she had to talk out of his connections to alchymists and wizardeurs, and especially to this Miona. "Talk him out of it?" She laughed a little wickedly as she imagined this dissuading, reinforced by some emphasis.

»Talking to Nacharya Saphed made me a little more evil!« she said to herself. That wasn't so wrong after all, actually.

Chapter 7:
The Alchymists

The Arrival of the Alchymists

During the seventh day since Astrello's arrival at Georgeburg Castle, an unusual number of cars had advanced and obviously important guests had appeared at the castle. Hollydeva knew that the nine nacharyas themselves had come. During her life here in the castle, all nine had never gathered like that before.

The Nine were in the castle. They were dressed in dark clothes, and had probably become accustomed to behave, act, and be inconspicuously.

Then came a big carriage and three persons, two men and a woman, got out. These were rather conspicuous and expensively dressed. Those were the ambassadors of the alchymists. They were led into the hall.

Hollydeva quickly looked up the secret spot which the cat had shown, and went to the place from which she could observe the room.

The Nine sat in their seats in a half-circle. In front of them, three chairs were placed for the guests. So these three alchymists sat down in front of the Nine.

Her father, the Grand Inquisitor, stood a little apart, as did two other strong men, the Executive, and the Informant.

Hollydeva looked to see who she recognized and knew among the nine and who was previously unknown to her.

In the middle sat the Nononn. To his left she saw Tatu Njena, dark-skinned in dark clothing, looking almost menacingly black. To the right of the Nononn sat Saphed, the alleged boss.

Next to Tatu Njena on the left, the Bhogi had driven his wheelchair. Next to the Bhogi was a nacharya she had not yet met, but who seemed strangely familiar. Daman, the healer.

On the far left sat Peredur, who watched the proceedings with alert eyes and was probably ready to put the alchymists in their place.

On the far right, she spotted Achmar, the burly Arab nacharya. Between him and Saphed sat Rokudan Aoi and Quavert, whom she had not yet met in person.

The Nononn, acting as a kind of primus inter pares, addressed the three guests. »Valued alchymists, dear Madame Negara, Doctor Albedo, Professor Rubedo, thank you for coming here today to discuss the subject with us! As you know, concerns have arisen about what you do with your clockwork studies! It could be that we have to prohibit you from continuing this! Please describe what you do and why you do it!«

One of the alchymists, the white-dressed, stood up. »Gentlemen, Nine, we have been working for some time to decipher the deepest secrets of the mechanics of living cells, as they occur in plants and animals. We see the creatures like clockwork, with small wheels and programs interlocking. If we know how these programs and cogs work, we can possibly optimize and eliminate diseases or disorders. We can improve harvests and defeat hunger on Yrth! Yes, we are able to cure diseases!«

The alchymist, Doctor Albedo, made a significant pause and announced, »We think we have succeeded in deciphering this innermost mechanics and have already achieved success! We have planted fields with our improved grain and achieved excellent crop!«

The other alchymist, Professor Rubedo, also rose and declared, »We ask the Nine to support us! We are not looking for a quarrel with the Nine! But you know how powerful the League of Alchymists is! And the decoding of the clockwork strengthens us further! We ask for your approval. But we also say that here we have a key that we can not easily give out of our hands! We have come into your sphere of power here, as we trust your decency and hope that this debate will be beneficial to the world!«

Nacharya Achmar, who was sitting on the far right as seen from Hollydeva's perspective, answered with some sharpness in his voice, »You should be aware, Mr. Alchymist, that we should forbid you to continue these experiments and researches, and that you will then omit these!«

Tatu Njena tried to calm him, »Well, brother, let us proceed with calm. We thank the alchymists for coming here! We have come to know the dangers of your clockwork experiment! It could be that your altered grain causes problems with digestion. Changed or optimized cogs, as you call it, can move to other plants and animals also changing them uncontrollable! There is a possibility that your plants kill the insects, and thus remove the food other animals depend upon!«

Doctor Albedo replied, »Yes, these are legitimate objections! But of course, we have already considered this! We assure you that these consequences are not existing! With this technology, we are making use of a natural process of mutation and breeding and improvement, as it occurs in nature. We only speed up evolution and natural selection a little!«

»I am afraid you are downplaying the problems!«

»But you have to realize the advantages!« The woman, dressed in black and gold, stood up. »And we offer the Nine a considerable share of the profits!«

Nacharya Saphed reprimanded her, »As you know, we do not need money!«

Tatu Njena exclaimed with a harsh voice, »We need you to put aside the Multi-God, fight polytheism like we do!«

The black dressed Madame played innocent. »But we alchymists are no followers of any gods! We are scientists, believing only in what we can measure! Therefore, we believe in the One, that is a measurable world. We are physicists, chemists, biologists, physicians, mathematicians, believing in the true unity of nature that we can decipher!«

»What do you do with the key? What door do you open? What's behind the door?« Achmar asked, obviously still agitated.

»Behind the door is freedom, happiness, health. We think that the mind is the highest, the intelligence, the science that can fathom everything! So we turn dirt into gold! We have said farewell to the hundreds of gods long ago! Some of us see the unity of the whole symbolized by a single true God! Perhaps there is this demiurge, a creator of this world! But otherwise we have discarded the faith and found out what and how reality is! We want to know!«

The Nononn wanted to conclude the interview with a positive tone, »All right! We see you as a division of those scholars who have overcome polytheism! We welcome you as allies!«

The three alchymists nodded and bowed. Then they sat down again.

Saphed scribbled on a little blackboard and showed it to the Nononn who then asked, trying to sound innocuous, »You said that you would only accelerate natural evolution. As you know, we propagate the OneGod, who once has created a perfect world, and accept a blind process of evolution somewhat reluctantly.«

Professor Rubedo probably sensed that a trap had been laid and had a ready-made answer: »Ah yes, you want to test whether we really believe in the OneGod, in the creation of this world? Or are we more convinced of a world created without a creator, subject to the process of evolution, not perfectly created by a supreme being? Our answer is that both are true! The evolutionists analyzed and described a natural process of the continuous adaptation of the living beings which the OneGod has started, or better: has given as a natural law!«

Nacharya Nononn pondered, »The OneGod is the original creator of evolution?«

»That's how we see it!« Professor Rubedo evidently felt that he had given an answer which was well received.

»All right,« proclaimed the Nononn checking with the other eight of the Nacharya. Nobody was protesting, nobody was even making a critical face. The answer was good. Evolution, and the natural selection and continuous adaptation of living beings was evident and thus could be combined with believing in a Creator OneGod.

»Well, well!«, the Nononn declared. »The alchymists may continue the research on the internal mechanics of the plants and creatures, and let these discoveries flow into products that benefit mankind!«

Hollydeva perceived astonishment and indignation with some of the other eight nacharya.

The Nononn told the alchymists that they could retreat and go home.

When the three alchymists had said their goodbye, Hollydeva wanted to retreat. But she still heard a dispute unfolding between the nine men.

Onthronn Achmar exclaimed excitedly, »You can not really want that! We must vote! I do not want to cooperate with the alchymists!«

»Brother Onthronn, let us sleep over that matter for one night,« the Nononn tried to calm him down.

Tatu Njena agreed, »Let us discuss and vote on the matter tomorrow. Brother Nononn gave the alchymist a free hand and I agree with the approach!«

Achmar became more aggressive. »Oh yes, Tatu Njena!? Because you and Nononn want it so, it has to be done like that? This is quite new! We could have sent them home and let them return after a week to listen to our decision!«

»But then we would have to be hanging around for a week as well, and there's just something more to be done for us! Do not you want to go back quickly to the Middle East, Achmar?« Daman had spoken plaintively.

»Yes, I will, dear Daman! But I insist that we vote tomorrow and think about how we control the alchymists!«

»I, too, think that their actions are dangerous and support Achmar,« stated the far-left sitting Peredur.

The Nononn concluded somehow tired, »Yes, we thought that you were thinking like that too, Peredur! We meet here tomorrow morning, after breakfast!«

Hollydeva had watched her friend, old Master Bhogi, who had stayed silent during the meeting. She could not detect from his expression or body language what his opinion on the proposal of the alchymists was.

Predictions

»Bring me back to Guuz, cat!« Hollydeva whispered to the Lao cat. The cat ran off, and Hollydeva followed her through the entangled secret ways in the walls of the castle.

Finally, she was in her room and hurried to the window sill, where the daisy in the pot looked thirsty and almost withered.

»Guuz, where are you?«

The daisy-deva appeared. He looked sick and exhausted.

»Guuz, what about you? How are you?«

»The flower is dying, and I'm dying with it. You gave us water, and there are also some beams of sunlight here. But it is missing what all life needs in this world. Around here there is not enough vitality. Where there is no green, where the fellowship of the plants is not, there life can not live, and everything becomes desert!«

»I'm sorry, what am I supposed to do?«

»It's not your fault, Hollydeva! I wanted it that way, I had to come here to be able to report to the other beings what the Nacharya are discussing with the alchymists! It is the sacred task of the Nacharya to preserve and protect life on Yrth! Will they uphold and fulfill their task? Tell me!«

»They want to finish this tomorrow! I think some will reject the request that the alchymists proposed. But some are also in favor of it. And the chief nacharya and his right hand are not yet decided.«

»Yes, I thought so. Daman and Fionn Peredur are friends of the plants! You have to keep watching tomorrow as they decide! We must then communicate it to other beings! And maybe we have to stop them all!«

»But you are dying!«

»Yes, but I can last two more days! Understand, Hollydeva, I'm only one deva and not as important as all life! I like to be the one who makes a salvation possible, which puts an end to the actions of the alchymists.«

Guuz looked a little concerned.

»I do not want to poison your mind, Hollydeva! The alchymists are not intentionally bad! They think that they are doing something good, that they can improve crops and destroy vermin! They just do not understand that they see a limited image and not the whole complexity. Without vermin, there will soon be no crops! Bees and birds will die! Grain, which does not need to protect and defend itself, will be weak and all the more susceptible! And besides, it is unhealthy for those who eat it! I can hardly understand this stupidity!«

»I wish we had the alchymists down here in the dungeons!«

Guuz laughed. »This might come, just wait!«

»I must go back to Astrello! My father will expect a report and some kind of progress!«

»Go to Astrello, Hollydeva! I have to sleep for a little while!«

When she came into the cell where Astrello now "resided", he was bent over his ephemerides, scribbling into a book.

»Do you figure out what will happen?«

Astrello looked up and smiled, »Yes, something like that!«

»How does it look?«

»There's a crisis coming, we know that! Saturn is declining in the sign Shaula, "The Sting". This is where the sun was at your birth. And your sun is in the eighth house, the house of death, when your ascendant, your first house, is in the region of the Pleiades. You are an assassin, a deadly weapon in the hands of those who give the orders!«

Hollydeva shrugged, feeling exposed. She had already killed a man! She actually was deadly, a weapon! She was bad! She should not be on Yrth!

»Do not look like that, Hollydeva! I would rather not judge it! The assassin is as important as all the others! Sometimes you have to kill! It would only be good when killing was used for survival, for the good, for the preservation of life on Yrth!«

»Do you really mean that? It is said, "Thou shalt not kill!"«

»Yes, but have those who believe in these commandments ever held to it? In the name of the prophets they killed believers of concurring faiths, sometimes even exterminated whole populations! The commandment really read like, "Do not kill those who are like you! You shall preserve life on Yrth and populate it with your own off-spring and keep the others from doing so!"«

»But I do not know if I am! Maybe I am one that kills all lives! My mother has seen me like this, and possibly she was right! She had hoped that I would starve, left alone.«

»I do not know about that. But I think you need to know your entire horoscope to really know who you are. Your moon is more important than the sun. The moon represents the female side and sun the male. You're a woman. The moon and the position of the moon in the horoscope is more important to you!«

»And? Where is the moon?«

»Your moon is in the ninth house, the house of the father, in the house of values. The moon and top of the ninth house are in the sign Aquila, "The Eagle". Could it be that your father is an eagle?«

Hollydeva thought of her father, the Grand Inquisitor. »He is an eagle of the Nacharya. He does what they ask of him!«

»So he's the eagle! Your female side is deeply connected with him, and together you want to realize high and honorable values!«

Hollydeva looked up at Astrello. »I thank you! You intend to save me and comfort me. You want to make it easier for me!«

»Yes, I will!«

»Listen to me, Astrello! I have overheard a meeting of the Nine who are just all in this castle right now. Alchymists have come to receive permission to experiment! They intend to adjust the inner mechanics of the plants! In my room there is a plant deva, which considers this adjustment as very dangerous. Tomorrow I will observe the Nacharya again, whether they decide to give the alchymists permission. It may be that I must stop them!«

»You alone?«

»Support might only be found outside these walls!«

»Maybe you should talk to your father!«

»He must not know I overheard the meeting!«

»Talk to him anyway!«

»Can I tell him that you will abjure?«

»Tell him I'm ready to do the astrology just for my private pleasure. I will publish nothing more!«

»And what can you live on then?«

»I will support your struggle against the alchymists!«

Hollydeva laughed. Astrello as a warrior and fighter!

»They will no longer be able to do their research because of laughter!«

»Just wait! I can be dangerous!«

He made an eerie grimace, and Hollydeva laughed even more. She understood that he wanted to make her heart easier. She felt warm in her heart for it. It was good to know that someone recognized her, was able to see through her, and yet was still well-disposed towards her!

Assessment

Later that afternoon, Hollydeva was called into the Great Hall, where the Nine Nacharya had resumed their seating.

The Nononn addressed her, »Hollydeva, you stand here before the Great Council of the Nine Nacharya because we want to know if and to what extent you will stand with us. Do you realize the importance of this questioning here now?«

»Yes, Master Nononn, I am aware of the significance!«

»I simply ask in advance: are you ready and willing to be present at the side of the Nine Nacharya for justice and social cooperation according to the commandments of the OneGod and especially the Bodhisattva?«

»Yes, I am, Master Nononn!«

»Good! Does anyone have any questions for Hollydeva?«

Tatu Njena spoke next, »Hollydeva, after all, we were together in the Sacred Valley. Are you of the opinion that it is justified to care and advocate for the preservation of nature and, in a sense, the idyll in the world?«

»Yes, I am, Master Tatu Njena.«

»Would you be willing to kill for that, to kill people?«

»Wait, brother!« interrupted Peredur, »Hollydeva, despite everything, is still only a child. She doesn't need to have a firm attitude about such hard decisions of conscience yet! In fact, she can't have a firm opinion about it yet!«

»Let her speak!«

Hollydeva had heard Peredur's objection and decided to be appropriately mild in her response. »I think killing can only be a very last resort, and there really must be a need! After all, I have never been faced with such a decision. But I don't want to rule out that I would be willing and able to kill a person who endangers the nature of the Yrth and the survival of animals or plants.«

Hollydeva hoped that her answer was well received.

Now Saphed took the floor, »Hollydeva, but now if we Nacharya are wrong and decide something that you think would be bad or dangerous for the Yrth, would you also kill one or all of us?«

»I didn't say I was sure I could or would kill myself. But I think that yes, this Order has been around for quite a long time and has quite a bit to show for it and has steered the Yrth well. Anyway, I'm proud to work for the Order alongside my father!«

Saphed had asked her a sort of trick question, and she didn't like it.

Nononn put a hand reassuringly on Saphed's forearm, »I think, Saphed, that Hollydeva has been very loyal so far and plans to continue to be so!«

»Hollydeva, until now, you were a child, the daughter of the Inquisitor, our revered Seren. However, you are now getting older and should be allowed to work for us by your own right. You will also soon be able to choose whether you want to continue schooling here in the castle, or whether you would prefer to go to a boarding school. In any case, we want you to get a good education!«

Hollydeva just nodded. She didn't understand what she was supposed to do at a boarding school.

Daman now asked, »I understand you lived alone in your family's house for some time. Your mother and brothers had left home. How do you feel about them today?«

Now, why did he want to know that?

»My mother will have had her reasons. I had no problem living alone in the house. But I was happy when my father picked me up and brought me here. I feel meaningful here!«

She had probably noticed that Nacharya Daman had been watching her closely, trying to interpret her body language and facial expressions. Why did he care how she felt about her mother?

»Hollydeva,« the Nononn continued. »You were in the special care of our eldest brother here, Nacharya Bhogi. Did he treat you well and appropriately?«

Was there any doubt? An old gentleman, the kind Bhogi.

The Bhogi protested, »Navendra, why are you asking her in this deceitful way? Since I lived out my libido in my younger years, I don't need eroticism with a 12-year-old now in my old age! I hope you can say the same for yourself!«

The Bhogi turned to Hollydeva, »You'll have to excuse the Nononn and the others here, Hollydeva. I used to have a bad reputation. But you will confirm, I hope, that I have never touched you indecently or spoken to you ambiguously?!«

Indecent? Ambiguous? What was that supposed to be?

»Master Bhogi was always kind and reserved. He showed me Lyndonia and I felt safe with him!«

»Lyndonia? What did you want in Lyndonia?«

»I wanted to prevent the new prince of the wizardeurs from getting a certain wand. But I didn't get into the alley where the wizardeurs go shopping. Instead, we took a schoolgirl, a becoming wizardeuress!«

»A schoolgirl? Now that sounds a bit inappropriate again, friend Bhogi!«

»No, it was not inappropriate. This wizardeur adept is, as far as I know, of importance for the wizardeurs. I want to see what the wizardeurs will do to get her out of here. Which, as you know, is practically unfeasible! But we'll have to see if the wizardeurs are still amateurs, or if they've become opponents again who challenge us a bit. We need sparring partners, after all!«

»I hope he doesn't underestimate the wizardeurs!« grumbled Onthronn Achmar.

The Bhogi looked a bit surprised at Achmar, nodded, and slid back in his wheelchair.

»Good, Hollydeva! Thank you for answering our questions so well! We'll reconvene here this time next year, and maybe by then you'll know if you want to go to boarding school! You can go now, thank you!«

Chapter 8:
At Night in the Dungeons

Inattentiveness

Hollydeva was not sure, if she really wanted to tell her father about Astrello's giving up and renouncing. But in front of his room a guarding man prevented her from entering, saying that because of the presence of the Nine, her father could not speak to her. He would be very stressed on these days. He would call for her.

Hollydeva was kind of relieved. She went back to her room, lay down early, dreamed of the weird alchymist Magnificentia Negara.

She was eating breakfast in the dining-room, when she saw the cat, who was trying to get her attention. Hollydeva understood and followed her. The discussion of the Nacharya was about to continue!

They reached the place again, from which she could observe the hall through a peeping hole. The nacharyas sat in the same sequence as at the day before.

The highest ranking nacharya, Nononn, was just opening the debate, »I somewhat hastily gave the alchymists a free hand in their research yesterday! Some of you would like us to vote on whether we actually allow the alchymists to tinker with the inner clockworks of plants and probably animals.«

Nacharya Nononn looked around, »I want to hear a statement from each of you! Onthronn Achmar, you were pushing forward yesterday. Please start!«

Sitting on the far right of the semicircle, the stout, somewhat weathered nacharya stood up. His black coat was subtly trimmed with red stitching and edges. Upon closer inspection, Hollydeva got the impression that the otherwise black cloaks of the other eight nacharya were also marked with certain colors.

»As you know, I'm against the alchymists. We have always had trouble with them. All our predecessors have had trouble with them! They lie and cheat! Their dirty labs have now become places of "science", academies! But have plastics, ur-kernel power, and machines brought humanity any further, made anyone happier? We should impose strict rules on the alchymists!«

»Thank you, Onthronn Achmar! Who speaks and supports the alchymists' request?«

The man next to the Arab nacharya stood up. Hollydeva was able to identify him from the pictures the Bhogi had shown her. He was the Japanese, Rokudan Aoi, number six of the Nacharya.

»I speak for the alchymists! Let them do it! They operate with sober research and patent new plants! It is nothing more than breeding and refining! We should not be so upset.«

»I agree with Sessionn Rokudan!« The one next to him was also standing up. He was younger than the others and appeared "fashionable".

»Ah,« recalled Hollydeva. »Quavert, the green one, fourth in the sequence of nacharya knights.«

Nacharya Quavert spoke with arrogant vehemence. »We're partakers with the alchymists, after all! Their results will bring money! We deserve that! It's good! Anything that makes money is good! We have always promoted capitalism! And I certainly think that plastic and machines have improved the lives of mankind!«

»Thank you, Verionn Quavert!« The Nononn nodded. »So now two of us have strongly spoken in favor of my decision from yesterday to allow the alchymists their research! Thank you!«

»Oh what, are you depending on the approval of these money-grabbers and snobs!« Master Peredur, sitting on the far left, had jumped up. Hollydeva was surprised. She had got to know him as restrained and friendly. But he obviously took the preservation of nature and naturalness very seriously.

»Nononn, do you really need that?! Your decision yesterday was premature! I agree explicitly with Achmar! The alchymists are neither our friends, nor are they our cash cows! Their research is dangerous! We should forbid them to proceed!«

Tatu Njena, the nacharya who had shown and explained parts of the world to Hollydeva, stood up, »Yes, I have to agree with Peredur! You could have waited, Nononn!«

»You agreed with me yesterday, Tatu Njena!«

»I did not want a quarrel as long as the alchymists were still in the castle!«

»And do you know if they do not have spies in our ranks anyway?« Peredur looked scornful.

And the scorn electrified Nacharya Saphed, who had been sitting silently to the right of Nononn, »What do you mean? Are you insinuating that I am spying?«

Hollydeva remembered her talk with Saphed the day before. He seemed to not be friends with Tatu Njena and Peredur, her own friends. Had he been trying to win her as an ally? Had he been attempting to neutralize her as an ally of his enemies within the council?

»I am probably overestimating my role!« Hollydeva tried to stay realistic.

Peredur continued insulting. »I am insinuating, Saphed, that for money you do everything!«

»I'm not reporting anything to the alchymists. But I am having sympathy for their enterprise!«

»Tworonn Daman, what do you say regarding this matter?« The Nononn was taking control of the conversation again.

Nacharya Daman, who was sitting next to Peredur, rose, »I am undecided. I would like, of course, that the healing power of the plants is preserved. They therefore should be left untouched! We have not yet revealed all the secrets of nature! We should not intervene before we know the basics! But I do not want to exclude the fact that the alchymists also think like that and are already carrying out their research and developments accordingly!«

Then Nononn asked the Bhogi, who had sat there silently and as if absently, »Master Septonn, Bhogi, what do you say to the matter?«

Nacharya Bhogi, sitting between Daman and Tatu Njena, remained sitting. That was his privilege due to old age and frailty. Seeing him reminded Hollydeva of the young wizardeur, they had kidnapped at Lyndonia. Miona was still staying downstairs in the dungeons. Hollydeva hoped that the Bhogi knew what he was setting in motion.

»The alchymists yesterday were not to my liking. But in my long term as one of the Nine Nacharya I usually cooperated well with the alchymists. Like here, a new generation is at their helm!«

The Nononn then closed the discussion, »Good, everyone has spoken! Let's vote! Who is for narrowing our consent of yesterday and sending a delegation to the alchymists to review their research more closely and, if necessary, to withdraw our consent?«

Hollydeva had to prevent herself from leaning forward too much, as she wanted to see how the voting was going. In a corner of the room, she perceived her father with the Executive and the Informant. She saw that, as expected, Peredur, Achmar, and Tatu Njena were raising their hands. Surprisingly, Nononn himself also raised his hand. He was no longer sure of his decision from the day before. Tatu Njena nudged old Bhogi and he also raised his hand.

Then there were three votes in favor of working with the alchymists: Saphed, Rokudan Aoi, and Quavert. Nacharya Daman did not move, stayed undecided.

»Good,« stated the Nononn. »I think that it is the best like that. We have shown our good will to the alchymists. But they also know that we need to control. Their labs are on Mount Lead. I'll go there. The Executive will accompany me. Is there any brother to come with us?«

»Yes, I will accompany you,« came Onthronn Achmar's strong voice.

»That is good! Thank you, Achmar!«

»I'll come too, so that someone who is positive about the alchymists is there as well,« declared Saphed.

»Good, so be it!«

Nononn turned to the corner, »Perhaps the Inquisitor may come along as well?«

Hollydeva leaned forward even further to have a better look at her father. By accident, she pushed at the wall, wherein the peephole was cut.

The Informant was immediately alerted, »What was that sound?«

With unexpected velocity her father, the Executive, and the Informant rushed to the place in the wall, behind where Hollydeva had been watching.

»Quick, guards!« her father shouted.

»Behind the wall, there is a corridor!« one of the nacharyas knew.

Hollydeva looked around for the cat, who was already running down the corridor. She followed behind and around two corners. But the cat was not there anymore. She had lost her guide. She went on quietly. But then a secret door in the wall was opened, and the Executive stood in her way.

»There we have the spy! What are you doing here?«

»I was walking in these corridors a little!«

»Come along!«

The Executive grabbed her by the upper arm and dragged her to the Nine.

»This is your daughter, Seren!« Nononn thundered.

Her father nodded.

He looked at her and asked, »Were you eavesdropping?«

She nodded and explained, »In my room is a plant deva, who wants me to tell him what you have decided, so that the plant devas can prevent the plans of these alchymists!«

»This is treason!« exclaimed Nacharya Rokudan Aoi.

»Seren, bring your daughter into an interrogation cell. She shall not talk to that plant deva!«

»Perhaps someone else should take my daughter into a cell!«

»Yes, right! Soort, please take Seren's daughter to a cell! Seren, go to her room and explore and kill that plant deva!« The Nononn had given these orders to the Executive and her father with a harsh voice.

Hollydeva was terrified. But she did not dare to say anything as not to cause any more trouble for her father. So she landed in one of the cells in the dungeons.

Braked

After some time, the door of the cell was opened and her father came in, closed the door, and sat in front of her.

»Why did you eavesdrop on the meeting of the Nine, Holly?«

»In my room I had a daisy! A plant deva came from the flowerpot, Guuz, who was talking to me! He asked me to help the plants! They fear that the alchymists will do evil to plants and bees, to birds, and to all creatures!«

»Plant deva, there is no such thing!«

»Then you could not find and kill him?«

»I've found the flower head with a wilted daisy! I should have known that you did not get rid of your mother so quickly! She has hypnotized you to see plant devas and to even talk to them.«

»No, she did not hypnotize me! And Guuz was real! And after what I've seen and heard at the meeting, yesterday and today, he's probably right! I would not trust these alchymists! I'd like them down here in the cells!«

»Ah, I understand! It even could be that I see this similar! But you must by no means violate the rules and laws here! My position with the Nine has suffered great damage through you!«

»I'm sorry! I did not want that.«

»I know, I understand! You are still a child!«

He looked at her mildly, and she felt understood in this predicament.

»I'll get you some food! You'll probably have to sit here for another day! By the time the Nononn and Saphed are on their journey to the alchymists, I can release you, and it will be forgotten again!«

»But I have to inform Guuz! It is good that five of the Nacharya have voted against the alchymists!«

»Yes, maybe! But let the Nine accomplish their tasks themselves! They do not need you for that!«

Her father made an encouraging gesture and left.

So she sat there trying to imagine that she was a prisoner of the Grand Inquisitor of the Nine and his daughter, the dangerous Hollydeva. »Am I a rich one or a mighty person? Not at all, I am a nihilista!«

Then she heard a voice, »Holly, Holly!«

Was it Guuz? How had he found this cell? But she saw no one and no being.

But she heard this voice again! And then she saw a cockroach! And after a short while, she was sure that this cockroach was talking to her!

»How did you get in here, friend cockroach?«

»We're coming in everywhere! We're living in the walls of old buildings!«

»My respect! What can I do for you?«

»Guuz sends me to you! You have to free the star boy! He is important! And you must prevent him from spending any extended time with the Afrycan wizardeur!«

»Yes, I think so, too! But why is the star boy so important? And how should I free him? I am sitting in a cell now myself!«

»Yes, I do not know either! Guuz does not live much longer. I am to tell you that you have to release the star boy!«

»Well, maybe I'll get out of here soon! Can you inform Guuz that the Nine have voted against the agreement with the alchymists with five to three!? But they have already given it a certain kind of consent yesterday! The highest of the Nine, Nononn, with another, who is in bed with the alchymists, Saphed, and Achmar and the Executive will go to the alchymists!«

»I'll let Guuz know that!«

»I thank you. It's great that we can talk to each other!«

»Yes, that is strange, that the other people can not talk to us!«

Dungeon Party

Hollydeva had the feeling that evening had come and night was approaching. It was strange to be sitting in a cell herself. After all, she had only been down here as her father's assistant for a limited time in the years before. But now that her father had not reappeared, it probably meant that she would have to stay here for some time. A guard had put some more water and bread inside for her, but refused to speak to her or to even make eye contact.

There was still the bulb glowing in a corner of the wall, so there was some light in the cell. She lay down on the cot and took the old smelly blanket to cover herself.

How did air even get into these cells to breathe? But yes, there were small openings at the top of the cell wall. There must have been a sophisticated ventilation system. At any rate, she had not heard of any prisoners suffocating.

Then she heard banging noises. It was as if inmates were signaling each other. She had once heard of Morse code. Three short, three long, three short, that was S.O.S., "Save our Souls", the call for help. But these knocking sounds were more complex.

Then, very slowly and carefully, the door to the cell opened. Startled, Hollydeva sat upright on her cot.

Looking into the cell was a man with little hair, very pale skin and staring eyes.

»Hello, who do we have here? A child! What have you done wrong?«

»I haven't done anything wrong! Who are you? How did you get in here?«

»Oh sorry, for not introducing myself. I'm Mollum, I've lived down here for a long time. And now the wizardeur lady girl has unlocked all the cell doors and I can finally see what's going on in the cells and who's in here right now!«

»The wizardeur lady girl?! Which wizardeur?«

»Well, she's sitting two cells over, not much older than you, dark skin.«

»Yes, that's Miona Yaboah! But she's only an aspirant. She wants to become a wizardeur first!«

»No, she can do things! How do you know her?«

»Oh, we were brought in here together and had a little chat!«

»Well, the doors are open, the guards aren't down here at night. They prefer to sit up at the front door. No one can escape here, after all. But we can communicate. I've been teaching the prisoners the knock code for years. And now even the doors are open, and we can have real parties here and all meet and get to know each other. Come on out!«

Hollydeva couldn't believe it. What was going on in "her" dungeon? She had obviously only seen a facade so far. And her father, too, it seemed.

She had known that there were some sorts of dregs of prisoners in the dungeon who had been here for some time. Had they made themselves somewhat at home down here?

»I need to talk to this Miona! What's she up to? I may have to warn my father!«

So she accepted Mollum's invitation and went out into the corridor, which was also dimly lit. Here prisoners were already walking around, introducing each other, shaking hands, laughing or whispering to each other.

In front of her cell, Miona stood looking happily at the hustle and bustle that was beginning.

»So you opened the cell doors! How did you do that?«

»Oh, there's a simple spell for that! But wait, what are you doing here? There was no guard or inquisitor here at night the last two nights! Are you all alone down here? That's brave! Inquisitor's daughters could be a popular supper in these dungeons!«

»I'm not an inquisitor's daughter now. I'm actually a prisoner like you! I have violated the laws of Nacharya and am suspected of being a spy!«

»Spy? Who are you spying for?«

»I overheard a meeting of the Nacharya with the alchymists! I was spying for the plant devas, as their very existence is threatened by the research!«

»Plant devas, so so. Well, they're not down here, and they can't very well help you!«

Miona came closer to her.

»You tricked me, hypnotized me, and made sure I'm down here and not with my lover, the Prince of Sorcerers, Cevaine Mire!«

»Beloved? Prince of Sorcerers? I thought you were fresh out of Afryka and going to Tangential Alley, or whatever it was called, for the first time!«

»Yes, you thought! No, as you can see, I'm a little further along. I already know the spell that unlocks door locks! I can do a few more, too! Would you like me to put some pimples and warts on your nose?«

»No, thanks, don't do that! I was just doing what the Bhogi told me to do! I didn't know who you were or what he was up to.«

»All right, that's how I met the star boy! We certainly could use him on Vowharts!«

»Vowharts?«

»Yes, that's where our castle is, and the school of the young sorcerers. I started together with Cevaine Mire, and we've been through quite a bit together. He's even more powerful than I am. But he also has a powerful enemy, a magician who was once banished. The more powerful the enemy, the more power you have to develop!«

»Hmm, the Bhogi will surely release you tomorrow or the day after. He wanted to lure the wizardeurs here. But they'll be smarter than to walk into a trap here! And if no one comes, you can surely get out again!«

»Make no mistake! They will come! And as your astrologer said, I'll be out of here tomorrow. But tonight I want to create some atmosphere here! I'll leave you alone, but don't get in my way. Somehow you seem to me a little inexperienced and untrained. Well, I have to admit, I was hypnotized. I guess it happened because I kind of liked you, as I actually thought you were one of us, a wizardeur. You're going to have some kind of power.«

»Yeah, I guess I can talk to plant devas and cockroaches!«

»You can talk to the cockroaches here? Oh yeah, that's something! I should really leave you alone on that one!«

Miona pranced away, greeting some inmates groping their way out of their cells, demanding music.

Astrello? She had to see how the star boy was doing! And keep him away from that Miona.

On the way to his cell, however, she encountered the rich man, who, after all, had only had one opportunity for interrogation.

»There's the inquisitor's daughter! She tried to drown me!« he roared.

Others of the dungeon folk were drawn to his shouts and desire for revenge. And came closer.

She had to get to the exit and alert the guards! But a small gathering had now formed around her, and she would not be let through.

But that's when Miona intervened, who had taken Astrello from his cell and came prancing down the sparsely lit basement hallway, hooked arm in arm.

»Leave her! She's locked up too, isn't she! Maybe she knows where to get a drink and some music!«

Hollydeva was glad to have the attention diverted from her. Drinks and music?

»Yes, there's a room down here for the Guardians, for the Grey Guardians people! I'll show you!«

The guardians were hardly allowed to drink alcohol down here. But they weren't allowed to rip the clothes of attractive prisoners like this Kalima either!

So the pack followed her to the guards' room, which was empty because the guards preferred to keep vigil in the room at the entrance to the dungeons.

Miona quickly found the hiding place behind a loose stone and there was a sip of burning whiskey for everyone. Then she spoke aloud a sorcerer's spell, directed probably to the table and chairs in the room, which began to bob and tilt and stomp an impressive rhythm.

»Let the party begin!« shouted Miona, waving poor Astrello around. Anyway, he gave Hollydeva a somewhat irritated look.

What was she supposed to do? The party wasn't bad after all! Maybe she could use the confusion to get to Guuz.

Dancing and feigning her enthusiasm for the party, she crept toward the stairs and the exit from the dungeons. The door upstairs was locked from the outside, so she knocked on the door. Sure enough, one of the stunned night guards opened.

»How did you escape from your cell?«

»The wizardeur girl knows a spell to open the doors! All the doors!«

Immediately, the guard produced shrill sounds with a whistle. More guards and the Executive and her father also approached.

»Thank you for alerting us, Hollydeva! We need to keep things quiet down there and this wizardeur girl needs to be put in a special cell, it seems. Unfortunately, you can't get out yet! Please, go back to your cell too!«

She hadn't planned that so well! Somehow, the party had been more exciting than the restored order.

Chapter 9:
Wizardeurs

Cevaine Mire

Hollydeva took the blanket her father had brought her and tried to sleep in the windowless, barren cell. It was dark and cold.

Then the cell door was yanked open. Nacharya Peredur, in whose Sacred Valley she had spent such pleasant hours a few months ago, stood in the doorway.

»Wake up, girl! You have to come! You are in danger!«

She threw open the blanket and hurried to the cell door. »Why am I in danger?«

»Because you kidnapped the wizardeur girl! There are wizardeurs in the castle, attacking us! Probably some traitor among the Nine let them in!«

»What are the wizardeurs up to?«

»The wizardeurs are allied with the alchymists! They want to limit or end the power of the Nine on Yrth since the beginning! We had always limited their spheres of influence, and they hated it!«

»Where are the wizardeurs now?«

»I do not know that now! I do not know how many they are! You need to get out of the dungeon and probably away from Georgeburg Castle! We have to get to your father! He can protect you!«

»I have to set the star boy free!«

»What star boy? Why do you have to set him free?«

»The cockroach told me! The plants want it! He is Astrello, the star boy! He comes from a star. He is interpreting the stars! He must come with me!«

»Well, do you know what cell he is in?«

»Yes, of course, sir! Come, Master Peredur!«

»Just Peredur, please Hollydeva! We don't need any formalities!«

She looked up at the nacharya in the half-dark of the cell. She trusted him.

»So come, Master Peredur!«

She knew where she was and how she could get to the star boy's cell.

But in front of the door of that cell stood a boy she did not know. He had a stick in his hand and waved it around.

»He wants to seal the door,« realized Peredur.

The boy was surprised and interrupted his spells to seal the door. He turned to the approaching Peredur and Hollydeva.

»Ah, I've been waiting for you,« he exclaimed.

He was a boy, a youth, perhaps three years older than herself. He had a scar on his forehead.

Peredur had pulled a long knife. But the young wizardeur had already built up a wall of air, that they could not penetrate.

»I am to render you harmless,« he cried. »And I'll do that now! This boy should stay in this cell! And this girl has to come with me! She has abilities that we can use!«

Then, from the farther end of the hallway, Miona, the dark-skinned wizardeur girl student, approached hurrying.

»Cevaine, let Astrello out of the cell! I want him to come with us!«

»No, I want him to stay here! I want this girl here with us!«

Hollydeva shouted, »But I don't want to come with you! And I want the star boy to be free, too!«

Cevaine shook his head and waved his wand.

»He's staying here! I can't have any competitors!« he grumbled.

»Competitors?« Miona asked incredulously. »Cevaine, you're not jealous, are you? You know I only want to be with you!«

Peredur intervened, »But he'd rather have Hollydeva with him, girl!«

Divide and rule. It was worth a try.

»That's not true!« exclaimed Miona.

»What do you want with her?« she asked Cevaine, whom she had now grabbed by the shoulder.

Cevaine looked almost desperate, »This is my mission! I'm freeing you, Miona, arresting this girl and making sure that star boy doesn't get in our way! This is about saving the world! The clockworks in the plants are set wrong! The alchymists must not be prevented from correcting this!«

Then Hollydeva saw black shadows streaming toward the boy, affecting him seemingly! He began to flail wildly. The cockroaches came to their support!

The young wizardeur couldn't help himself, he started to retreat. As he tried to grab Miona's hand and pull her with him, she broke free and ran away, past Hollydeva and Peredur, down the hallway. Cevaine shook his head in disbelief and ran away from them. Hollydeva tried to open the door of the cell where Astrello would be sitting, but she couldn't. There was no key in the lock.

Peredur called out, »Come on, we have to follow him. He will meet with the other wizardeurs and attack the nacharyas in the main hall! You can free the boy afterward!«

They ran through the castle, following the boy's clattering footsteps. They saw him again in the great assembly hall.

Where Miona had run to, they could not make out. But she did not seem to be such a burning threat anyway.

The Power of Burping

There were four nacharyas standing in front of Nononn, drawing crosses, calling prayers and invocations. Hollydeva recognized Tatu Njena, Rokudan Aoi, Daman, and Quavert.

Obviously, prayers and invocations temporarily protected them from the attacks of two wizardeurs, an old white-haired woman and a man with very long hair, standing before them, waving their wands and screaming curses in an incomprehensible language.

The boy, Cevaine, now stood by the other two.

»Good to see you, Cevaine!« Hollydeva heard the man call the boy.

»Where is Miona, is she alright?« the white haired lady asked.

»Yes, Owleya, she's fine! She went to settle a score somewhere else in the castle, I think! Let's show those vampires!«

Vampires? Hollydeva hadn't sucked blood yet, and no one in the castle would do such a thing! She was outraged.

Peredur told her that they had to stop and scare away the wizardeurs. The Nononn had to be protected!

She would have liked the knights of the Nacharya to be so powerful that three wizardeurs could not harm them!

Hollydeva did not know magic. She could talk to little animals and plant devas.

She wanted to run to the wizardeurs and stab them in the ears. But the air around the three wizardeurs seemed to be condensed, impenetrable. She found herself as if paralyzed in a cloud of magically compressed air.

She looked around. Peredur was close to her. »Can you hear me?« she cried. The nacharya nodded.

»Can I speak to the air? Would the air help us?«

»Try!«

She did not get any inner relation to the air.

»Try it with the nitrogen in the air!«

Nitrogen was not answering.

She had struggled to generate energy to interact with the elements. The tension in her stomach discharged with a strong belching.

»Take the belch!« Peredur had observed her well.

»Burps, stab them into their ears! Prick those three wizardeurs in their ears!«

She could see the air that had escaped from her stomach. The air of the belch was dirtier than the condensed air. She felt that this air still belonged to her, still smelling of her. She intensified the command.

Her belch could quickly move through the condensed air, it connected with the air, had been absorbed in it, and yet found itself together again and again. Then the belched air splashed into three beams and attacked the wizardeurs!

The three wizardeurs were longing for their ears, trying to scare away imaginary insects, not knowing what was happening.

The older woman told the boy and the long-haired that they should put everything into one last, lethal attack! Then they would have to disappear!

The three stood up in full size, lifted their arms, and hurled energy at loud shouts of magical curses toward the nacharyas.

Seren the Stone had entered at the same moment, had jumped into the way of the curses, had spread his arms to protect the nacharyas entrusted to him. The wizardeur's attack threw him down immediately. But it seemed that he had protected those five nacharyas standing behind him.

The three wizardeurs ran to a door. As they opened the door, fire struck them. Georgeburg Castle was on fire!

They ran back, took off and jumped through one of the windows on the west side of the hall. Hollydeva wondered whether they had spread wings after leaving the window frame.

She hurried to her father.

Nononn had also rushed to him. »Quick, you must disappear! The castle is on fire! The wizardeurs will come back with reinforcements!«

Seren groaned and was unresponsive.

Peredur called to her, »Bring your father to the gate! I'll get the star boy! We meet there!«

Hollydeva nodded. But when Peredur hurried away, she remembered Guuz. »I have to rescue the deva in my room,« she told the Nononn. »Can you bring my father to the castle gate?«

Nononn called two of the other nacharya, they were Tatu Njena and Daman, to help him carry the massive Seren out.

There was heavy smoke in the hall. The fire came close quickly.

Hollydeva ran down the corridors to her room. Fortunately, the fire was on the other side of the castle. She called for Guuz, who was lying on the flower-head, exhausted. She took him and whispered, »All will be well, Guuz! We repelled the wizardeurs! We will stop the alchymists!«

She carried the plant deva out with her hands and met Soort, the Executive, in the hallway.

The Rescue of the Bhogi

»Where is the Bhogi? Have you seen the Bhogi?«

»Most of the time he's in his library!« recalled Hollydeva.

»The library! That must be where the fire started!«

They ran as fast as they could to the library.

Inside it was very smoky and some shelves with books were still burning. The Bhogi was sitting in his wheelchair, had his wand out and was trying to keep Miona at bay, who was waving her wand and intoning strange spells just as he was.

Miona had started the fire! She was indeed not a beginner! She had started the fire and still wanted to show the Bhogi who had kidnapped her that she was not a decoy but a dangerous eagle-woman!

The Executive struggled to beat out the flames and open the windows, so the smoke could drift out.

»Miona, leave the Bhogi alone! Let's talk!«

Quickly, the Afrycan had turned and struck in her direction as if with a whip. Sure enough, a blow of compressed air burned across her hand, which she had extended to protect and warn.

Almost Guuz was hit, and that made Hollydeva angrier now.

»Hypnotize her again!« the Bhogi shouted.

But when Hollydeva started purring phrases to suggest to Miona that it would be better to rest and relax and sleep now, the latter had put on headphones as if she would rather listen to music now. She made another big movement with both hands, ran to the window, pushed aside the Executive who tried to stop her, and jumped out.

Hollydeva rushed to the window and saw that the long-haired wizardeur was waiting in front of the window as if he could stand in the air. He caught Miona, and it appeared as if they were flying or floating away!

But the library was still burning and smoking, as was the entire wing of the castle where the library was located.

»Quick, Bhogi, we have to get out of here! The air is sooty!«

»I can't! I have to save the documents! So much has already been burned! They are the most important writings from our Nacharya history!«

»Yes, but if you have smoke inhalation, you can't save them either! The Executive will extinguish and take care of them.«

And already she was pushing the wheelchair and thus the Bhogi out and into the courtyard of the castle. As she continued to push toward the gate to the front court-yard of the castle, the Bhogi raised his hand and asked her to stop.

»Wait, Hollydeva I have something to tell you before we meet the others!«

Hollydeva stopped the wheelchair and came to the Bhogi's side.

Aspirantess

»Hollydeva, I don't have long to live in this body anyway. And I don't want to be born again then either! And this fire and this defeat I have to answer for! I have underes-timated this girl quite considerably, and the wizardeurs as well! I'll see what I can salvage in the way of important documents, and then I probably won't have long!«

Hollydeva wanted to say something reassuring, confident, but the Bhogi raised his hand and looked at her firmly.

»Now listen to me carefully! In over a thousand years, some of us have always been reborn after death. We had ways and methods of finding and identifying our-selves again! Occasionally, however, one of the nacharya would tire of performing this function and would give instructions on how to train a suitable candidate as a successor. Each of the nine of us has a secret medallion that is passed on to the successor or family in which the rebirth is to take place. The medallion is one of the proofs for the other nacharya that the particular person is the rebirth or successor!

»As I said before, I believe that we are failing and that it was a mistake to have an all-male group of nine. The only woman in the castle was always the cook! And now you have come as the daughter of the Inquisitor, and I see great potential in you. I want you to succeed me as Bhogi!«

Hollydeva's eyes widened in amazement. How was she going to do that?

»Wait, don't worry, Hollydeva! You must go to Linden Island! There is a monastery of mystics there, where the nacharya always go through the training like other mystics. It is even a monastery of a certain superior mysticism, a kind of meta-mysticism. You will find it exciting. That's where you have to go. The training takes a few years, and when you have completed it, you seek the Nononn and show him the medallion and explain that you are the Bhogi. You may be called Bhogini or Bhogeva! Do you understand?«

»And if I find that I can't or won't?«

»Then you give the medallion to Nononn or Saphed and explain it to them, and they will have to find someone else. But that would be very messy. I want you to pull yourself together and do this! Please promise me that you will do everything you can to develop and practice to the point where you can do my part! I will write you a kind of manual and send it to Linden Island! You won't get it until you complete the training on the island, though!«

Hollydeva nodded.

»Swear it!«

Hollydeva raised her hand. »I swear it by the OneGod!«

»Well, I'm not even the nacharya who stands up for the OneGod! Swear it by the daisy in your hand!«

Hollydeva had almost forgotten about Guuz and was now not sure if the Bhogi had seen the Deva.

But she did the Bhogi the favor and swore by the daisy, even though it seemed a bit weak to her. But the Bhogi seemed satisfied.

»You, so now, I guess, we, do not represent the OneGod?«

»Yes, that will surprise you. The OneGod thing was only because the monotheists were fighting each other so much in the world and the Yrth was damaged by it, especially since such fighting is completely unnecessary. The nine of us stand for different principles, the special observance of which we practice and spread.«

»So what is my faith now?«

»I don't want to give you too many guidelines. You should develop and find your own way. But the Bhogi is the representative of ecstasy.«

»Ecstasy? What is that? I don't know anything about that!«

»Wait and see, it will come! But the important thing is: do what is difficult for you. You will find that you are rather not an ecstatic person. Ecstasy, after all, is something crazy where you lose your head and go into chaos, lose control. And a part of this way of practice is also to find the equanimity, the inner center! Although this is only of value when you are in the chaos! The equanimity in the midst of ecstasy, the completely still observation of the outer loss of control, that is great strength!«

With that, the Bhogi took out a medallion from the side pocket of the wheelchair. It was a heptagon with a heart in the center the size of a large hand, forged from a gold alloy. Hollydeva accepted the medallion.

»Thank you for accepting it, Hollydeva! Take ten years and have many experiences. And when you encounter the chance to ecstasy, gather your courage and dance and shout with the other ecstatic dancers without losing your center! Go now!«

»My father has been badly injured, cursed by the wizardeurs in the main hall!«

»The Nononn will probably want to take him to your grandmother. It's on the way to Linden Island. You can do that! Your grandmother is also a special woman. She'll pave the way to Linden Island for you! This is the last time we see each other, and I'm glad we met. It may be that you don't have the best impression of me. The action in Lyndonia looked like me, crazy and amateurishly executed. You will do better and so will the Nacharya! Maybe along the way you will have fellow female nacharyas who could replace some of my Nacharya brothers, that wouldn't be wrong. So go ahead. We will never meet again, and if you want to feel me, then turn around yourself for one hour. Then I will appear to you and give you the advice you are asking for!«

Tears stood in Hollydeva's eyes at this parting. She felt that the Bhogi was a special encounter for her, an old wise man who had become her friend. She hugged him and then came the Executive who offered to push the wheelchair to where the Bhogi wanted to go.

Going Away

Hollydeva ran to the gate of the castle where the other nacharyas were already debating wand arguing with each other.

»Why could you, the mighty nacharyas, not finish these wizardeurs?« she asked, somewhat sobered.

Nononn admitted, »Oh, they're just very strong. They have found new strength with that boy. The Nacharya have lost much power over the centuries, much knowledge has fallen into oblivion. Ultimately, we are just politicians. We have power because we are involved everywhere, as we know how to put politicians and business leaders under pressure. But against such magic we have little defense. You are our hope! You can connect with the animals and the elements and use them for us!«

»But you have defended yourself well!«

»Yes, we can activate the OneGod's help! But that too has become thin! We do not know if the OneGod really exists! Probably he is only a thought construct that has no real power! I'm sorry to disappoint you!«

»No, I'm not disappointed! We must fight the alchymists and wizardeurs by every means!«

Peredur came with Astrello! Behind them was the burning castle. The servants, the personnel, and the dark guards had run out and gathered in front of the castle wall. Meanwhile, eight nacharyas were assembled there.

»Who of us has let the wizardeurs in?« Onthronn Achmar asked, angrily.

»They've just came in! They are powerful,« replied Saphed.

»I'm still going with Achmar, the Executive, and Saphed to Lead Mountain,« Nononn declared. »The others go back to their areas and castles and organize themselves! The attack must not be left unanswered! We should start campaigning against magic! We declare it to be cheap tricks, deceiving spells, fairy-tale entertainment!«

Peredur suggested, »The girl should go with Seren and the boy to her grandmother! Her grandmother can heal the Grand Inquisitor! He is suffering from a fierce magical attack!«

The strong nacharya turned to Hollydeva, »Could you find the way to your grandmother? You must always go west! The star boy has to go to Linden Island! He can reach there from your grandmother's place, the Refuge!«

Hollydeva's father was conscious again. He straightened himself, stood up. »I know the way,« he moaned. »I can do it!«

»Seren, are you sure?«

»Yes, Peredur! You have to find out what and who is behind this attack of the wizardeurs!«

»We must save the castle! We must clear the fire! The library!« the Informant shouted, missing the old Septonn Bhogi already.

Citizens had come from the village when they had seen the fire. There probably was already a fire extinguisher on the road.

»Good!« Hollydeva was now determined. »Let us go! Astrello, Father!«

They left, heading west.

Nononn followed for some way, telling her with force, »Hollydeva, you have to go to Linden Island and continue your education! You must practice and strengthen your mystical power, your power to connect and communicate with everything! It may be our best or even only protection against magic!«

Second Part:
The Road Towards the
Noviciate on Linden
Island

Chapter 10:
Ostreaux. Druyds. Odiën

Road Signs

Georgeburg Castle was burning. Hollydeva looked over her shoulder and saw smokes and flames. Astrello grasped her forearm and shouted, »Quick, we must go! Far away!«

She dragged her injured father, who was moaning, through the bushes and undergrowth. In her arms she held Guuz, who was weak and tired, unconscious.

After about an hour they reached a small hill, from which they had an overview. The fire of Georgeburg Castle was shining in the distance. The night was quiet around this place of rest.

»Where are we going?« Hollydeva asked. Astrello did not answer. The father had dropped to the ground. In a weak voice, he moaned, »I must go back! I have to protect the Nacharya!«

»But you're hurt! And those wizardeurs have curbed you with a curse! The nacharyas should be able to assert themselves against the wizardeurs! You need a doctor!«

»And a wizardeur who takes the curse away from you,« added Astrello, who was probably not sure whether he really wanted to see the Grand Inquisitor at full force again.

»You're right,« sighed Seren the Stone. »We must go west! We must go to your grandmother, Holly!«

»West is the opposite direction of where the sun is rising,« Astrello knew.

Hollydeva looked around. »There's a light on the horizon! There is west where the sun has set! So we must take that direction!«

Seren rose again, groaning. He spat some blood and held his side, where ribs had been broken, pressing on the internal organs.

When Hollydeva looked worried, Seren whispered, »You can not help me, Holly! We just have to see that we are reaching to Granna's property! If I can not stand and have to lie, you must go further and look for me after you have found her garden, the Refuge!«

Hollydeva remembered her grandmother, who was the mother of her mother. She had always been friendly to her, had not rejected her. Granna was living at the edge of a wood, some three hours walk from the house in which she herself has lived, next to the house of Mrs. Bromholle. Would she find the house in which she has spent her childhood? She should be able to find the village where the school was. They had been passengers in the car that brought her to Georgeburg Castle.

But she then had not paid any attention to the names of the towns and villages they had passed.

»But you know the way!?« she asked the father. Seren, however, was already almost unconscious. »I do not remember the way,« he murmured.

They simply had to trust that their feet would carry them on the right path or that benevolent forces would support them.

When morning dawned, Guuz woke up in her arms. Hollydeva stopped. »I need water for Guuz,« she called to Astrello, who immediately opened the water bottle. Hollydeva was somewhat surprised that he had this water bottle with him. When had he filled it? Did the stars tell him to take care of water? Would he always have such a good foresight?

Guuz whispered to her that he had to sit in front of a tree to speak to the tree's deva. The deva of the tree would tell them the way.

She told Astrello and Seren to take a break, and sat down in front of a large oak. Guuz crawled from her arm and sat in front of the tree. He laid a hand on the tree trunk. After about ten minutes, the deva of the tree actually appeared.

»Greetings, cousin!« Guuz whispered. »How are you?«

»Better than you seem to be,« the deva of the oak grumbled. »What can I do for you?«

»I do not know how long I still have. Please tell these three people the way.«

»Where do they want to go?«

»They do not know exactly!«

»Then I can not help! A way is for getting somewhere!«

Hollydeva entered the conversation, »Do you know one Mrs. Bromholle?«

»I have to ask the mushrooms!«

Guuz told Hollydeva that mushrooms had a network of roots in the earth and that they would be in contact with each other around the world. Mushrooms would always be well-informed.

The deva of the oak spoke to them again, »Yes, there are mushrooms who know a woman Bromholle! She lives in a village by a pond in the west!«

»Which way do we have to go?«

»From here you can see an oak standing on a hill. That is my brother. He is standing in the direction and he has a better overview. He will help you!«

It was now already deep night. »Maybe we'll try to spend the night here. His brother is hardly recognizable in the dark!« Astrello sounded reasonable.

»But it will get cold!«

»Then we'd better keep moving!«

The Wizardeur with Wolves

They had been passed on by the oaks. To stay in touch with the trees, they had had to take detours through forests. It anyway was probably a good tactical plan to avoid the open fields and meadows.

Then a great wolf stood before them in the forest road. Astrello threw a stone at him. But the wolf did not budge. He was glowing at them with fiery eyes.

»We must turn back and look for another way,« Astrello suggested, a little disgruntled.

But as they turned, a man stood behind them on the forest road. He had lifted his arms and began to speak magic formulas.

»Wait!« Hollydeva shouted. »Who are you? What do you want from us?«

»I have the order to stop you! My name is Charles Ostreaux!«

He had spoken with an accent, and in her mind Hollydeva had his name written as in the language of the neighboring country, which her father once had called "land of the frog-eaters".

»You confuse us with somebody else!« Astrello shouted. »We have to take our sick father to the next city! He's sick and has to go to a doctor!«

»He's not your father, boy!« the wizardeur replied. »This is Seren the Stone, one of our enemies, now mortally wounded by a magical curse, which the three most powerful of our guild have cast! Nobody can help him with that! You can leave him here! And I am sorry that I have to freeze you!«

He again started to raise his arms and his wand, muttering magical formulas.

»Monsieur Ostreaux, what's there behind you?« Hollydeva tried to distract him, while Astrello rushed forward to beat him with a branch he had picked up.

But Ostreaux was alert and had erected an invisible wall of energy that Astrello could not penetrate.

For a moment, however, the paralysis spell was weakened. Hollydeva looked around for possible allies, beings like those cockroaches in the dungeons of Castle Georgeburg.

She only saw that there were more wolves behind Ostreaux. Hollydeva sent an inner question to the wolves, but she felt that they were under the wizardeur's power. They appeared to her as torn inside. It pleased them that the wizardeur offered them prey, through which they could quench their blood thirst. But they had abandoned their freedom very reluctantly. They hated to bow to the ban of this wizardeur. Obeying a human was not to their liking.

Astrello had crawled back. He took up Guuz again, whom he had put to the ground before his attack. The deva, however, had come to his senses and asked Astrello to place him back into the grass. He stroked the grasses and muttered something. Then he showed Astrello a dandelion and asked him to blow.

Suddenly, Guuz sat up with his last strength and spread his arms. »Bind!« he shouted.

Hollydeva saw that the wolves suddenly fought with something that came out of the ground. Grasses and flowers had twisted around their fetters.

Mageur Ostreaux also stepped out and tried to free the shoes from the grasses and flowers that came to him.

There was a butterfly in front of Hollydeva's nose. »A peacock's eye,« she thought, remembering that her brother Einar had once taught her the names of the butterflies.

»Butterfly, get help!« she sent with her mind. And she felt that the butterfly, like the cockroaches a few hours ago, understood her wish. The peacock's eye flew away quickly.

»This wizardeur is "Saturn at Acubens". We must send a message!« Astrello shouted.

»I've sent a message already,« Hollydeva said.

»Then we need a moon and a sacrifice! We must call the moon, offer a sacrifice to the Moon Goddess!«

Hollydeva could not grasp much out of Astrello's astrological statements and suggestions. But he had begun to look up and summon the moon, which was still invisible this late afternoon.

She quickly searched the inner pockets of her father's jacket. In fact, she found a small pocketknife and opened it. She cut herself into the hand, so that blood started to flow.

»Moon, I'll give you this blood!« she cried, looking hopefully at Astrello. The star boy nodded, calling the Moon Goddess with an even louder voice.

The wizardeur, however, had kindled a magical fire that burnt the grasses at his feet. The fire blazed around him, but it did not attack him. He saw what Astrello and Hollydeva were doing and prepared his counter-attacks.

Hollydeva felt that he had sent out his paralytic spell again, that her movements and thoughts slowed.

Astrello was still panting, »Moon!« He now sounded as if he was talking very slowly.

Then the bees arrived. Had the butterfly alerted these bees? They were clearly on their side. Some swarmed around the wizardeur, who struck out wildly. Others flew around Hollydeva. Hollydeva tried to open her sleepy mind. »Follow!« she heard.

She grabbed Astrello by the arm, pulling to move. Astrello picked up Guuz. She shook her father, who struggled to his feet, stumbling with them.

The Druyds

»Come, come!« the bees demanded.

Hollydeva realized that Astrello and her father could not hear the bees, and shouted, »We must follow the bees!«

But the father was unable to walk fast or hurry. He was very exhausted, chalky-pale.

It had become evening and increasingly darker. They heard the wolves howling behind them. Ostreaux and the wolves seemed to be still struggling with grasses and bees. But the wizardeur was quiet for now. The moon probably had effected something at last.

The bees led them to a fire burning in a forest light. Around the fire were some half-naked men and women lying around or dancing. Hollydeva counted about fifteen men and seven women.

Hanging from a tree halfway up was another man, tied to the tree with ropes.

When Hollydeva, Astrello, and Seren came to the fire, those who were seated at the fire looked up. The dancers approached with unwelcoming faces.

»Who are you?«

»I'm Hollydeva, that's Astrello, and that's my father who's hurt!«

»What is his hurt?«

»He has broken ribs and was cursed by a wizardeur! They were three wizardeurs, actually!«

»Oh, that's not good! A white-haired woman, a boy, and a long-haired man?«

»Yes, those were the ones!«

»They had passed by! Powerful wizardeurs! What do they have against you?«

»My father is the guardian of the Nine Nacharya at Georgeburg Castle. These wizardeurs are fighting the Nine Nacharya!«

»Ah yes. Well, we're keeping out of those wars!«

»Who are you?»

One of the men with a long beard came from the fire into which he had thrown new logs and answered, »We are the druyds! We are reviving the old traditions of our ancestors!«

He pointed to the women who were now moving around the fire, »Those are fire maidens!«

When Hollydeva looked a little confused, he added, »Druyds were the shamans, the medical men, and the priests of the ancient nations, here in this region. Before the Romans and the priests came, people trusted the druyds, the wise men! It is time for the druyds to rise again and heal the Yrth from those who have polluted her!«

Another druyd shouted, »Tonight is a good night for soma, the potion of the fly amanita, the holy mushroom!«

One of the dancing fire maiden came up and cheered, »Today we want to fly! Soma lets us fly! Will you fly with us?«

»No, thanks. I think we have to move on!«

They heard the wolves.

»Wolves?« asked one of the shamans at the fire, who had hitherto been silent.

»Yes, a wizardeur had wanted to stop us, and he had wolves!«

»You better stay here tonight. The wolves will not approach the fire, nor us!«

»Sit down there! Put your father near the fire!«

Another, lightly clad woman came up and brought some water, which she held to Hollydeva's father's mouth.

»I'm going to give him life,« she decided, snuggling up to Seren.

»He probably does not need that now,« Hollydeva stated, fearing that the woman would misuse the weakness of her father.

But Astrello suggested, »Let her! Your father could use some life force!«

There now was a bowl of brew from fly amanita mushrooms, the ominous soma, and all the shamans drank from it. Hollydeva and Astrello let the drug bowl pass. Guuz lay asleep in Astrello's left arm.

»Here, girl, bring that to the man hanging in the tree!« one of the druyds, the one with a pointed hat on the wild hair, told her. He seemed to be a sort of ceremonial master. He handed her the bowl with the soma remains.

Odiën

Hollydeva took the bowl and went to the tree. The hanging man seemed quite thirsty. But how was she to bring the bowl to his mouth? His feet were just above her head. She would hardly be able to climb up to him with the bowl in her hand.

The bees were buzzing around her. »Shall we help you?«

»How could you help me?«

»Release the bowl! We will carry it to him! We can do that!«

Hollydeva trusted these bees. »Good, thank you, lovely bees!«

In fact, the bees were able to transport the bowl as a swarm. The man drank thirstily as they held the bowl to his mouth.

»Ah, good soma!« he muttered.

The man looked down at Hollydeva and whispered conspiratorially, yet decisively, »Come back in half an hour, when the effect sets in! Then I will answer one of your questions!«

»He will answer a question for me,« she reported to Astrello. »What shall I ask him?«

Astrello shrugged, »Ask him how to escape the wolves!«

After half an hour Hollydeva returned to the man hanging from the tree. The question with the wolves seemed a little too boring.

»Do you have a serious question?« asked the druyd, hanging at the tree.

»My name is Hollydeva!« Hollydeva called to him.

»I am Odiën! I am hanging at the tree to get knowledge! I get insights! What do you really want to know, Hollydeva? I will answer your most important question!«

»Hmm. I need to know whether I'm good or bad! Am I a good or an evil human being?«

»This is a good and important question! I have to travel a little for it! Wait here!«

Hollydeva wondered how the druyd tied to the tree wanted to travel, whether he was going to tear out the tree and use it as an aircraft. But she quickly saw that he meant an inner journey, that he had left, had gone into a trance.

Then he came back, opened his eyes.

»Hollydeva, you are a wicked human being! You are bad!«

»That is what I feared!«

»Rejoice, the wicked are the good ones!«

»I do not understand that! How can the wicked be the good?«

»The evil people are called evil because they cause pain. Pain is good!«

»Pain is good? But people avoid pain!«

»Yes, they have learned it that way. They are superficial. They have learned a superficial life of pain relief. But in their deepest depth, in their innermost core, there is pain. The pain contains truth. It contains the door to their true self, to the divinity of the whole from which we were once separated!

»The evil human being forces them into their pain, and thus they are forced from the surface into their depths! Thus, evil works good, for in the depths lies liberation!«

Hollydeva was confused. But she felt that Odiën had said something important to her. She did not have to be ashamed of herself. She did not have to feel guilty, as she would bring depth, even if depth hurts.

»Thank you, Odiën!« she shouted.

»You have a dangerous way ahead of you, girl! Be watchful at every step! Choose well who you trust! Now let me go on!«

The man hanging on the tree fell into a trance again and was no longer accessible.

Hollydeva went back to the fire. Astrello looked, and was probably reassured, when he saw that she looked relieved.

»Was the answer satisfactory?«

»Yes, the answer has made me stronger!«

The druyds and fire maidens lay or sat or danced in their soma trance. The wolves and wizardeur Ostreaux stayed away.

»Get some sleep. I'll keep watch!« Astrello suggested. Hollydeva put her head on his right thigh, rolled in, felt the fire on her back.

But she could not fall asleep at once. She watched the shamans, now fierce by their soma ecstasy.

The druyds staggered around and hooted. One danced around the fire and shouted something in a strange language. One of the fire maidens shrieked wildly.

Another fire maiden tore off her clothes and raced toward one of the druyds, whom she dragged into the bushes.

The scenery was a bit menacing. The disciples of soma had lost control and now lived in a chaotic, wild world.

But they left Astrello, Hollydeva, and Seren in peace. Guuz lay quietly in Astrello's arm.

A Taste of Ecstasy

Hollydeva didn't feel threatened and remembered that the Bhogi had said something about ecstasy.

»Astrello, are you awake?«

»Yes, Hollydeva, I'm still awake!«

»What are they doing?«

»They brewed a potion from fly amanita and drank it, and now mushroom poisoning is helping them to a wild frenzy!«

»Yeah, that was obvious. Is that ecstasy they're experiencing?«

»You can call it that!«

»Do you know what that's like?«

»No, I don't think so! I didn't take soma or anything like that! In my world there is no such thing!«

»Is there ecstasy without drugs?«

»Yes, I think I've read that mystics get into ecstatic states! Or by certain drum rhythms and chanting and spinning in circles.«

»I guess the Bhogi wants me to experience all that!«

»Who is the Bhogi?«

»The Bhogi is an old man, one of the Nacharya! He lives in Georgeburg Castle! But he soon will die! He showed me some things and explained them. He is the nacharya who should know about ecstasy, he said. I would find out about that too!«

»Do you know his date of birth?«

»No, I don't. I actually don't know much about him! Four days ago, I was with him in Lyndonia, and then we kidnapped Miona Yaboah!«

»Oh yeah. That's who that was. Miona mentioned an old man. But that's too few clues to make a horoscope.«

»I need to taste a little ecstasy!«

Astrello tried to hold her back, but she was already up. She had no intention of drinking from the soma. It was drunk up anyway.

She just wanted to get some sense of what drove the druyds and fire maiden. She wanted to have an idea of what ecstasy was.

Then Guuz spoke to her. He must have overheard the conversation. »Hollydeva, do you see that little mushroom there in front of your left foot? That's a psilo. Eat a little of the hat, but not all of it. That will give you a little idea of the gang's experience here!«

Hollydeva saw the small, brown mushroom and ate a piece. After a few minutes, she had a strange sensation, an energy rising up from her guts. It buzzed in her ears. She stood rooted to the spot and a joy filled her. She didn't care what yesterday had been or what tomorrow would be. It did not matter what the world would become. Nacharyas, alchymists, wizardeurs: all were very far away.

She saw the stars above her and they were wonderful. She wanted to dance, to sway her hips, to stretch her arms into the night air. Hollydeva couldn't help but laugh.

»That's what ecstasy is like?«

»Yes, Hollydeva!« replied Guuz. »I guess it's like that for humans. We plants are always in that ecstasy. It is easy for you, too. You just have to stop thinking! And you have to stop thinking that you know how the world looks and feels. Because the world is entirely different. You perceive only a section that corresponds to your learned and handed down concepts. The ecstasy comes closer to the truth! And do you feel gifted that the world is in truth wonderful!«

»Yes, it is wonderful!«

She stood for a while longer, enjoying the feeling and the perception. Then the ecstasy caused by the little mushroom ebbed away, and she finally lay down to sleep, inspired.

Chapter 11:
Medea, the Seeress.
Rokudan Aoi. Quavert

Medea, the Seeress

In the morning, Hollydeva woke up. The druyds and fire maiden slept lying around wildly, recovering from their soma intoxication. Whereto Odiën had disappeared from the tree, she could not make out. Astrello had also fallen asleep. He lay halfway over her, and it felt pleasant to her.

She looked at her father. The fire maiden, who had wanted to give him vitality, was still lying in his arm. He looked relaxed.

Guuz lay in Astrello's arm and seemed to be sleeping, too. She listened and heard that he was still breathing.

Everything seemed to be all right, in peace.

She stood up and walked around. A tea and a bread would be really nice now!

As she crouched down in some bushes, she saw a woman cooking something on a different fire. Hollydeva went to her.

»Good morning, my name is Hollydeva! Do you have any tea for me?«

The woman looked up. She was probably forty years old, wearing leather and looking not very friendly. »You are the daughter of the strong man with whom my sister made it tonight?«

Made what? Hollydeva did not know what the lady meant, but she nodded.

»Where are you up to go to?«

»We want to see my grandmother!«

»Oh, how cute. Are you the good girl, bringing goodies to the grandmother, and the evil wolf has threatened you?«

»I'm not Little Red Riding Hood!«

»Oh, is that so?! But I am to believe the fairy tale with your grandmother?«

»It is not a fairy tale! My grandmother can heal my father!«

»Is he ill?«

»Yes, the wizardeurs have thrown a deadly curse on a few of the Nine Nacharya, and he has caught it!«

The woman looked up. »Do you always tell such stories?«

»It's the truth!«

»All right. Actually, nothing in this world surprises me anymore. I am Medea, seeress of the druyds. I am pleased to make your acquaintance, Hollydeva!«

Hollydeva was relieved that the woman had introduced herself and not chased her away.

»What do you mean? You are a seeress of the druyds?«

»We are an ancient coven of women who live with nature and harness the power of nature. We call upon the forces of nature, the devas and gnomes, so that they come to our aid. But times have changed due to the supremacy of the OneGod and in many areas we are no longer welcome.«

»You don't believe in the OneGod?«

»No, do you?«

»I don't know. I used to live in the Nacharya's castle, Georgeburg Castle. And as I understand it, the Nacharya want the people to believe in only one god, a OneGod. However, the Bhogi also said something different there. But that confused me and I tried to forget it again.«

»The Bhogi? You know the Bhogi?«

»Yes, the Bhogi taught me a little.«

She better not mention the medallion.

»How is he? He is an old friend of mine. You must know that the Bhogi is a friend and confidant to the druyds and fire maiden. If he hadn't protected us, the fanatics of the OneGod would probably have wiped us out completely by now!«

»The Bhogi doesn't have long to live. Georgeburg Castle has burned. That was yesterday. And he must have been trying to protect his library. But he inhaled a lot of smoke. Then he told me goodbye that he didn't have long anyway, and he didn't want to be reborn either.«

»Oh, poor man. Yes, the Bhogi is very, very old. Then he is still at Georgeburg? I will go and see after him! I must also know who is to be his successor.«

Hollydeva took pains to give no sign that she knew who was to be the Bhogi's successor. That Medea would laugh at her anyway.

»That will please him, I think!«

The seeress looked at Hollydeva with a slight smile. »So there, that will please him. You're a bit precocious, aren't you? You don't know anything!«

»Oh, I can talk to a flower deva! And with the cockroaches!«

»Flower deva? What flower deva?«

»Guuz, the deva of the daisies. He approached me a few days ago to tell him what the Nacharya and the alchymists are up to. I think the devas are worried that the clockworks in the plants will be changed and then everything will die.«

»Oh dear. Show me this Guuz! Bring him here, please!«

Hollydeva ran, taking the pot of daisies from Astrello's arms, who was still asleep and looking all childlike and pure in his sleep.

In fact, Guuz stretched his head out of the daisy and seemed to be pleased to see this Medea.

»Guuz, how are you?«

»Oh, we are rather short-lived, we daisies. Please protect this girl, Medea. She is the Hollydeva. She can influence the course of events!«

»What makes you think that?«

»She can fight the alchymists!«

»The alchymists? What about them? They do a little tinkering with their vapors and distillates, trying to create gold. But that's rather ridiculous!«

»No, they've evolved a lot in the last few decades. Since they no longer believe, but only think they know, their alchymy has changed! They bring about some dangerous developments! They want to optimize everything now! And their research into the innermost mechanics of the cells that make up animals and plants must be stopped!«

»All right, all right, calm down. I've actually always gotten along with the alchymists. Do you want me to protect this girl? Is she being threatened?«

»I don't know. It's not like I'm keeping track!«

»Tell me, girl! Where's the threat?«

»We're on our way to my grandmother's house, like I said. Yesterday, the wizardeur Ostreaux threatened us with his wolves. But I think the real danger comes from three of the nacharyas, who want to make common cause with the alchymists and the wizardeurs!«

A voice came from the edge of the forest: »Come on, we are friends! We're no threat to you after all!«

Pursued

Two figures came out of the shadows of the trees. The druyd lady had jumped up.

»Who are you? Do you know these gentlemen?«

»Excuse me, lady! We do not want to frighten you! We need to talk to this girl! We'll be off soon!«

Hollydeva told the seeress, »These are Nacharya Rokudan Aoi, the Session, and Nacharya Quavert, the Verionn! Quavert is the younger one who looks slightly perfumed. Rokudan Aoi is the rather bad-tempered Yapanese!«

»What do they want from you?«

»They probably want to prevent me from going to my grandmother. They are siding with the alchymists!«

The seeress wondered, »There is a quarrel among the Nine?«

»Yes, there is. And these two gentlemen here are those knights of the Nacharya, who are hostile to me!«

»Who are hostile to you? Are you the top nacharya?«

»No, I am only Hollydeva, the daughter of the Grand Inquisitor of the Nine Nacharya!«

The nacharyas Rokudan Aoi and Quavert had followed the conversation bored, yet politely. Now Rokudan, who had noticed that some other druyds and fire maiden had woken up and started to gather at their little talk, declared, »There is no quarrel between the Nine! A delegation from us, headed by our primus inter pares, Nononn, is undertaking an expedition to the alchymists to check their research! They will find that everything is in the interest of the Great Whole of Existence and will continue to allow it! The alchymists are our allies, as are you here, of course!«

Quavert added, »You are the druyds? Our pleasure to meet you. We, the Nacharya, have supported your resurrection since quite some time now!«

The seeress grumbled, »Hogwash! You are some blatherers!«

Then she announced with a determined voice, »This girl is under our protection! So say what you have to say to the girl or her father! And then she decides, whether she will go with you, stay here, or go her way!«

Rokudan Aoi admitted, »Good, then. We, the Nine, must do everything to settle the war against the wizardeurs! The castle is badly damaged. Our power has got a damper. Our disagreement weakens us! We need the Inquisitor now more than ever before! After Nononn, Achmar, and Saphed will have met with the alchymists on Mount Lead, the Nine will be re-gathering in a still secret place!«

He turned directly to Hollydeva, »We want you to come there with your father!«

»My father was badly hurt by the wizardeurs! I do not know if he will be of any use to you ever again! We'll go to my grandmother, who may be able to heal him!«

»But you have learned the techniques of your father! You can replace him! We want you to come with us! The druyds can take your father to your grandmother!«

»No! I do not trust you both! You are allies of the alchymists! I have to stop the alchymists! They shall not be allowed to continue their research!«

»You are not to decide on that matter!«

»Oh, now she's only a young girl again!« the seeress spat.

»You do not want it any other way,« Quavert said, rushing forward. He spoke a magical mantra that sounded as if he were using a distant eastern language.

The Nacharya Quavert was throwing a kind of net over Hollydeva. Meanwhile, Rokudan Aoi was producing a kind of bad smelling mist to keep the druyds and fire maiden from protecting her.

Hollydeva could feel a kind of paralysis creeping up on her. She was really getting tired of these paralyses. The net lay over her and she felt caught.

Defended

But then another energy came from behind her. Suddenly Odiën stood there, the man who had hung on the tree! He swung a large branch and shouted, »You are littering this sacred place of the druyds with your attitude! This is not going to go unpunished!«

The paralysis went away, and Hollydeva saw how the two nacharyas, who had been siding with the alchymists, were retreating. Medea helped her to get free from the net.

But, of course, the two mighty nacharyas did not travel alone and without escort through these forests. From behind the trees, archers and armed men of the Gray Guard stepped forth.

»Surrender and nothing will happen to you! These archers here are very accurate!« called Rokudan Aoi.

Several of the druyds had stepped forward and bravely shielded Hollydeva with their bodies. All the druyds suddenly had strong wooden sticks, that were as long as they were, in their hands, swinging them back and forth. Would they be able to fend off sharply shot arrows?

Hollydeva felt Astrello had joined her with Guuz in his arms.

The fire maiden, which had been with Seren, had pushed the Grand Inquisitor into an upright position and supported him so that he now stood with the druyds.

»Let your archers shoot, and you'll hurt your own important man!« she yelled over to the two nacharyas,

Suddenly, a big magpie was sitting on Rokudan's shoulder, who flew over very quickly and snatched an amulet from the fire maiden that she had been wearing around her neck.

»No!« she cried, »Give me back my amulet! It's loaded!«

Quavert had both arms raised. Around his arms, two snakes writhed out of nowhere, as if they had been hiding within his wide cloak. The nacharya hurled his arms forward so that the two big snakes swiftly lurched onto Hollydeva, twisting around her legs, bringing her down. At the same time, the two nacharya and their troops had moved closer.

Odiën and the druyd with the pointed hat, however, had swirled their sticks around the free ends of the snakes with a swift and whirling motion. They detached these snakes from the stunned Hollydeva, throwing them back to Quavert.

Some other druyds had begun a roaring song. Or were they calling stags that way?

The seeress lady in the leather dress, whose tea Hollydeva had just drunk, made a loud hissing sound through the air. Several cats materialized around her.

And another fire maiden had stepped beside her, evidently able to summon bees and wasps, so that swarms first attacked the magpie, who immediately dropped the amulet. Then those swarms rushed at the two nacharyas and their troops.

The attack seemed to be warded off when they all heard the howling of great wolves that had appeared at the edge of the clearing. Mageur Ostreaux stood there, seeming to summon a thunderstorm from the sky.

»Wizardeur, leave that! We're allies!« Rokudan Aoi shouted.

But Ostreaux shook his head and shouted back, »Do not talk nonsense! You are Nacharya! On behalf of the wizardeurs, I will prevent the Grand Inquisitor or his daughter from being of any more use to you!«

The two nacharyas, Quavert and Rokudan Aoi, found themselves between two fronts and realized that they had behaved strategically awkwardly, especially as they were being struggling with bees and wasps.

Rokudan Aoi shouted, »All right, bring Seren to Grandmother Algard for him to heal! We will tell you where the Nine meet again! Where you have to appear!«

They called their troops to retreat and quickly disappeared from the scene.

But Mageur Ostreaux and his wolves had to retire as well when the druyds rammed their wands into the ground and sent shock waves that spread like earthquake waves against the wizardeur and his wolves.

Hollydeva was impressed by the power of her protectors, who they had met coincidentally the night before. But no, these bees had brought them here. Hollydeva saw the fire maiden calling the bees and wasps back.

Initiation

Hollydeva looked around. All the druyds and fire maiden were standing behind her now.

»Thank you, you saved us!« Hollydeva exclaimed. »You could save the whole world! You could put a stop to wizards and alchymists! You could also make those nacharyas see reason!«

»Why should we do that?« Odiën was not taken with her suggestions.

»Don't you want the world to be saved, to be all right?«

»No, that's a misconception! But aside from that, we who you see here, at least in Eyropa, are all that is left of the once mighty druyds and fire maidens. We live underground, in hiding. And we will come out only when we can be sure that the henchmen of the OneGod faith and the powerful and the rich will not be able to exterminate us again.«

Hollydeva nodded. »I understand. Sorry, I didn't realize you had been decimated so much.«

»These are tests, girl! Only those who are tested can grow, can finish the path. And exams where there is no failure, no not-being-good-enough, and no flunking are just not very interesting!«

»But possibly, we have dared too much in the past centuries and are have been tested too much!« added Medea.

»Yes, I'm afraid that's the case!« sighed Odiën.

Astrello came with Guuz in his arms. Seren also had managed to stand up, supported by the fire maid who had spent the night with him.

The seeress in the leather put a hand on Hollydeva's shoulder, »Girl, we'll protect you! My name is Medea. Call my name to the bees and I will hurry to you! Now bring your father to your grandmother! The bees will lead you! Where does your grandmother live?«

»Her garden is about three hours from where I have lived, next to Mrs. Bromholle's house. My grandmother is known as Mrs. Algard!«

»Mrs. Algard? Yes, we know her! We also know Mrs. Bromholle! The bees know the way!«

It seemed to Hollydeva, as if Medea would make a few signs with the hand and communicate with the bees directly.

»Thanks for the tea,« Hollydeva said.

Then Odiën, stood before her, »Let these manners with the courtesy go, maid! Do not thank and ask nicely! Rather, pay attention to how you can cause pain, pain that leads into the depths hidden deep inside! These are the treasures that most people are not even self-aware of! This is your gift!«

He looked hard into Hollydeva's eyes. She had to make an effort to stand by his gaze.

Through her lips she pressed defiantly, »I thank you, Medea, for your tea!«

Medea laughed and answered her, »Thank you for drinking my tea, Hollydeva! Use courtesy to conceal that the pain within you burns like the fire deep within the Yrth!«

Hollydeva had continued to resist the eyes of Odiën. »No politeness!« he barked.

Medea was now standing close behind her. »Be always polite,« she whispered.

Odiën had moved close to her and whispered, »Be direct and without polite phrases!«

In the other ear she heard Medea, »Be polite and so keep your distance!«

Hollydeva noted that the confusion about the two opposing instructions prevented her from thinking or moving.

»If you need us, tell a bee!« Odiën and Medea whispered together.

And together and impressively they intoned, »One day you return to us as if you were our daughter, who, after a long journey full of dangers and pain, finds strength and forgiveness with father and mother!«

Then Hollydeva's mind was free again. She looked confused to the druyd and the seeress and nodded, being aware that she would not be able to recall what the two had just told her.

Her traveling companions had received tea and bread. Soon they wandered west, guided by the bees. Undisturbed by wolves, wizardeurs, and nacharyas, they passed through a fertile landscape of fields, acres, and woods. They passed small villages and felt guarded by the little river that mostly accompanied the way.

The druyds had given Seren a small donkey that pulled a little cart on which he could travel half sitting, half lying down, so he didn't have to exert himself.

Astrello seemed to be in good spirits. This hike was clearly preferable to the half-dark dungeon of Georgeburg. Hollydeva was still not sure if she could forget her home of the last years so easily.

In the evening they reached the cottage in the garden of her grandmother.

Chapter 12:
Grandmother Algard.
Creature

Mystics and Magicians

»You have a little paradise here, Granna!«

»Yes, this is the Refuge, a sheltering retreat for plants and animals!«

Hollydeva had now been for two days with Granna, her grandmother, who lived in a cottage surrounded by a large garden.

The garden was designed in the form of a large octagon. Each side of the octagon was probably more than 500 meters long.

Her grandmother planted mainly herbs, as she was a well-known healer. But there were also fruit trees and shrubs and many, many flowers, which were especially enjoyed by the bees and butterflies.

The day before, the grandmother had also shown her the patches in which she was cultivating vegetables. Beanstalks. Red tomatoes ripened on the house walls.

Attached to her croft, the grandmother had a bakehouse. There was a small windmill to grind the grain that grew on the eastern side of the garden.

Hollydeva had admired the apple, pear, plum, and cherry trees.

It was late summer and a plenty of fruits were to be reaped. Gardeners and helpers were all over the patches.

At the cottage, chickens and other poultry, geese, and turkeys were running around. Hollydeva had seen a goat and a few sheep. The collie dog Rhea was always near Granna, keeping watch.

Everywhere in this wonderful garden songbirds flew singing and chirping.

And at a daisy flower, they had laid Guuz to his last rest. When Hollydeva wept over the plant deva, hundreds of devas who had watched the funeral had consoled and thanked her.

Granna's retreat, this shelter for all plant devas and all the helpful and good spirits, was a special place, the Refuge.

»Granna, how did you manage that no threat could enter here without your permission?«

»Yes, that was not easy! It's not the time to explain it to you, Holly! But one day I will introduce you to the secrets of the Refuge.«

Hollydeva and her grandmother strolled through the beds and hedges and groves.

»I fled from an argument between the Nine and the wizardeurs! Then there were these alchymists! Are these all sides of this war? On which side do you stand, Granna?«

»Oh, that's a lot of questions! There are basically two ways in the world, Holly: the way of magic and the path of mysticism. In a way, both want the same thing! They want to restore the unity of the inner world with the outer world! This is not easy to attain, and the masters on both sides take great trials in order to restore unity within themselves and possibly also in others and within the world!«

She was silent for a while.

»It's a very long story! The wizardeurs want to restore unity by changing the outer world, by gaining power over the world. To be able to do this, they must develop their powers, they must acquire power.

»The mystics, on the other hand, take the world as it is, declare it as perfect as it is! Mystics undertake many efforts and a lot of purification to adapt themselves to this perfection to become as perfect as the outside world!«

»The nacharyas are the mystics?«

»Well, they are not the only mystics! But they have once arisen from a mystical tradition that followed an Awakened One, a Bodhisattva, who lived almost 3,000 years ago in the East. They were masters of Eastern mysticism, practiced in physical exercises of the so-called "Yoga", sitting silently for hours in meditation. They were close to the Center of Being, connected to it, thereby had power. And they followed the principle of "Karuna", compassion, the attitude of the Bodhisattvas, to protect the Yrth, to reduce suffering.«

»Are they no longer so connected to the Yrth? Are they no longer close to the Center of Being?«

»I am afraid that they have been very slack in recent generations. They became attached to having political and economic power, and they are very much in demand. The training of successors was neglected. The mystical schools in all the religions became kind of flat, partly because the religions, who wished to impose their laws and commandments on all men, had persecuted and suppressed their own mystics. It was certainly a great achievement of the Nacharya to unite the religions that believe in the OneGod. But it has not revived the mystical sentiments in the world-views of the OneGod as they had hoped for!«

»The wizardeurs are stronger?«

»No, not necessarily. Classical magic has also experienced a great decline. But the alchymists were a branch of magic, quite close once to the mystics as well. The alchymists are responsible for helpful inventions, for technology. People have invented a form of magic that allows them to experience miracles without much development of their personality! However, that is a dangerous error!«

»Personal development is more important than mastering the world?«

»Yes, I would say so. Mastery of the world is a big mistake! The world is wonderful, perfect, divine, as it is!«

»So you're more of a mystic?«

»Yes, I am a mystic. I nonetheless respect the wizardeurs, use some magic skills to protect my garden. I once was a master on Linden Island. Linden Island is the refuge of the mystics of all directions, of all the spiritual ways!«

»All directions? There are directions different from those of the OneGod? Oh yes, I have met the druyds!«

»Correct. Yes, there are other directions, different worldviews than that of the OneGod.«

»And on Linden Island all are preserved and taught?«

»Yes, and the masters of Linden Island create a super-ordinate view of the world in which the similarities of all mystical world views are perceived and accepted. They are convinced that every facet of the world is entitled to a certain extent. That mystic is a true mystic who can choose his world-view depending on the situation! That mysticess is a true mysticess, who can choose her world-view according to the situation, the environment, and the requirements!«

The Relative and The Absolute

During the evening, Hollydeva had to ponder over the explanations which her grandmother has given her. And she could hardly find her sleep. In the early morning, she had to continue questioning.

»There is nothing so true that it is superior to other faiths?«

»No, it all was developed at a certain time and in a certain environment and has authority in this environment only! We can accept and utilize truths, but not always. There, however, is one super-ordinate truth that sets a certain evaluator to all concepts!«

»A superior truth?»

»Yes, there is an end point to the development of the soul at this level. We call it "enlightenment". There are many names in the different traditions for this final state, for this final achievement! The mystic state of unity with everything. Everything that serves to achieve this condition is good and justified.«

»And there were heathens and followers of the OneGod, who have achieved that state, alike?«

»Yes, and there were also followers of the MultiGod and atheists, who do not believe in any god, who have achieved it! Personification is only an aid, a thought-construct that can be helpful, but which should not be confused with the absolute truth!«

»There is a relative truth arising in the environment and time, but there is also an absolute truth, that is eternally true?«

»Yes, I know that the assumption of an absolute truth is dangerous terrain and may lead to fundamentalism, the fundamentalism we have just overcome on Linden Island. But yes, there are absolute truths! And we are now in agreement, that we are souls, who go through a lot of lives to achieve development, which, with experience and purification, enables the soul to return to the Great Whole Totality, overcoming any separation from the Center of Being.«

Hollydeva nodded. She would have to digest and think about it.

»And the wizardeurs and the alchymists?«

»Wizardeurs and alchymists want to change the planet so that they like it. Now they are attempting to change the planet to eliminate the disturbances they themselves have caused! They have fallen prey to the arrogance of the human mind! But there is also the knowledge of the soul in magic and alchymy. They are not so dissimilar to mysticism. But, frankly, this is not the place to understand the wizardeurs and alchymists. They attacked, and we have to take up the fight against them! Let, however, the nacharyas do it themselves! They will learn from it, and especially in Daman and Peredur I have great hope! And in you too, my wonderful granddaughter!«

Hollydeva snuggled up to her grandmother. She had not yet been valued and honored like that before.

»I promise I'll never disappoint you, Granna! You shall be my absolute truth!«

»You'll disappoint me like everyone, Hollydeva! Yet, you should know that I'll forgive you almost any failure! I or the masters of Linden Island or even the nacharyas will be hard and serious with you and tell you truths that you will not want to hear. But you ought to know that we just want you to grow and learn and improve yourself! You will always have our forgiveness, our trust, as long as all that you undertake comes from caring for life and love for all and everything!«

On the way back to the cottage, they were silent. Hollydeva tried to explore in her heart whether the care for life and the love for all and everything could justify her actions. She, however, was well aware that she felt no love for all and everything.

It was a mild evening. At a table, sheltered by the overhanging straw roof of the cottage, her father and Astrello were sitting. Astrello was probably happy that he could make calculations about the stars, that he could write them down in his little book, that with the ephemerides he could fathom how the world would continue.

The grandmother gave Hollydeva a hand sign that she should sit down. Granna went into the house and after a short time she came back with hot tea and warm carrot soup. Then she went back and fetched a large loaf of bread, from which she cut a few slices.

»Good appetite!« she wished her guests.

The three others replied, and they silently spooned the soup and let themselves be heated by the tea.

»Seren, how are you?« Grandmother Algard asked.

»I still feel dazed! Physically it's better, but -«

»But that dizziness? It comes from the curse of three wizardeurs that you have caught! We will need some things to mitigate the curse, to take the consequences of the injury from you! But be assured that it is feasible and that I will manage to heal it! I've already ordered that the things I need are to be brought from the Island!«

»That is good! I thank you!«

Hollydeva then slept well and deep for the third night. She felt safe in her Granna's cottage like nowhere before.

Pain?

Hollydeva again stood up at sunrise and stepped out of the house. She saw her grandmother hacking in the beds, plucking the weeds, spreading water with a hose. Had she nursed her garden all night?

She went to her Granna. »And why did not you take me in when my mother left me?«

Her grandmother looked up and Hollydeva saw pain in her face expression.

»I could not do it! I could not take you!«

Hollydeva recalled what Odiën had said about her gift to lead people into deeper pain. Not the grandmother, or should she dare!? Would pain really be received like a gift?!

»I have to learn to understand that being bad is good,« she had to convince herself.

»What prevented you from taking me in, Granna?«

»I had to promise your mother! Your mother had a request good with me. I did not always do everything right with my daughter. I fear that the parents will not do it right with any child! But your mother also felt pushed back by her mother, me! I made her a gardener, as I was myself. She had been studying gardening here for years. Then she went to Linden Island, just as I myself once did.«

Granna stopped and remembered. »One day she came from Linden Island on vacation. She was very angry. Rosa cried that she'd followed me for a lifetime. She would have healed and raked, sown and harvested in gardens. Meanwhile, however, my daughter had now learned that this was not her Dharma, that she was a different one. And now she would also have to be in the garden on the monastery island. Everyone would see her as a gardener! But she did not really desired to be a gardener! She wanted to be a wild beast! And she was furious like a wild beast!«

»Rosa went on journeys, got to know your father, or met him somewhere. Or he'd gone after her. When Einar and Baldar and you were born, we were able to get together again, and I could help her in the first years, especially since your father was mostly on his way fulfilling orders of the Nacharya.

»Then she got the call to return to Linden Island school. Rosa was glad to be able to return! Your mother asked me to give you an opportunity that she herself had missed. She wanted you to go the difficult way, the path, which is not always just

121

good and noble! She wanted your father to get you and that you have the choice to discover the shadow, the evil side, within you, so that you could grow beyond the evil within you! I do not know if you really have such a thing in you! I perceive you as a good girl!«

»Because you are good in yourself and at ease with yourself! But it is true, there is evil in me! I do not feel the pain of people. I like to give pain!«

»You like to give pain?«

»Yes, I like to see people suffer!«

»You're scaring me!«

»A man died through my hand at Castle Georgeburg. I regret that. I wondered whether I was a murderer! But I was reassured. Father was even proud of me. It is a good thing to erase evil people from the power games of the world! Odiën and Medea, whom we met in the forest, have encouraged me to be a deliverer of pain!«

»Oh, child, Holly, what are you talking about? That truly worries me!«

Hollydeva's grandmother was showing an unhappy face. Hollydeva became a bit afraid that her grandmother would throw her out of the Refuge, that she did not want anything to have to do with what she was.

»But the bees showed you the way?«

»Yes, they have protected us from the wolves!«

Granna made a strange hand movement and hummed something. A swarm of bees came to her. The bees had risen from the flowers and had come flying, following her signals.

It was as if the grandmother were talking to the bees then. Hollydeva felt the bees answering. The bees were moving between them, flying around them, some were sitting on their bodies.

Finally, the grandmother stated, »The bees are not afraid of you, they have no dislike of you whatsoever. The word of the bees counts with me! The bees say that you have a higher destiny, that you will go beyond good and evil! You would need some guidance. But you would be needed to save the world! Especially you. Because all good people would not be consistent enough to fight those who endanger the world and thus will ultimately unintentionally be defeated!«

Hollydeva felt recognized and again honored and valued.

Her Granna hugged her. »Hollydeva, I'm always there for you! Your path is not as clear as the way of your brothers! But you will be fulfilling your Dharma! And if you require a place to retreat, you can always return here! That is my promise to you!«

A Creature

Several gardeners and shepherds used to work at the grandmother's estate. They came from the surrounding villages and were probably paid for with the fruits of agriculture. Hollydeva had the impression that all these people loved and admired Grandmother Algard and liked to work for her.

Then she saw her grandmother opening her clinic room for consultation hours. Sick people from the surrounding villages and small towns were brought. Hollydeva understood that the workmen and helpers were probably coming and working to reward the good and the healing which the grandmother had given to loved relatives, children, and the elderly. The grandmother did not accept any payment for her healing work.

After Hollydeva had stayed with her grandmother for a week, however, not a single patient came to the morning consultation, and only two of the gardeners had appeared.

Granna had called Hollydeva, and together they went to the gardener who had come. »Robert, why, besides you, almost nobody appeared today?«

Robert looked up. He was a middle-aged, somewhat grumpy man. »It is said that wolves and wizards block the access to your estate, Mrs. Algard. I know all the hidden paths here in the area and I therefore went round making detours. But it is true. I heard howling wolves and angry voices!«

»We've been waiting for that,« Granna said to Hollydeva. »This will be the wizardeur you described, the one with the wolves! We need to know if Quavert and Rokudan Aoi are still there! And whether other allies of the wizardeurs and alchymists are present!«

»Would they be able to enter here?«

»If they have enough power, they can do it! But first they will besiege us! The unfortunate thing is that I am expecting medicine for your father brought from Linden Island!«

Grandmother Algard thought for a while. »The gardener Robert has to show you his creeps! You have to remember them well! Maybe you can spy a little! I will call the bees! The druyds will help us!«

Hollydeva left the Refuge with Robert through the hedges and bushes that delimited and protected the estate. They remained unnoticed, and Robert said goodbye. The grandmother had told him to stay with his family for some days.

At their farewell, he had shown Hollydeva a way that would lead her toward the Linden Island ferry. From there the messenger would come. Granna had asked her to look for this messenger.

Hollydeva went down the path for a few miles and climbed a half-high tree. She heard voices and movement and wolves in the direction of the Refuge.

Then one of the wolves was under the tree. He was sniffing at the tree and the surrounding area vigorously, probably sensing her.

Only a few minutes later, she saw a young man coming along on the way. That had to be the messenger from Linden Island!

She had to warn this messenger! She had to distract the wolf!

But then something very strange happened! It seemed to her as if a door had opened out of the nowhere. It was as if the world had become a painted background on a stage and a door had opened, through which a stage worker could enter. But it was not a stage-man who went into the world, but a creature of a kind she had never seen before. It somehow looked like a human being. There seemed to be no eyes, no mouth, no ears. Hollydeva saw only two small ridges, like horns, on its forehead. It moved smoothly but without direction, back and forth.

The wolf howled when he smelled this being. He barked at it. His howl was answered by a dozen wolves in the neighborhood, who were probably hurrying to support him.

Then the creature reached out. Its arms could not touch the wolf. Yet, its fingers suddenly grew longer, shooting at the wolf. The wolf was hit by a blow and fell dead.

The creature was making random movements, as if it were looking and orientating. Then it ran in the direction of the Refuge.

Since the wolf did not move and the other wolves were not visible, Hollydeva climbed down from the tree and ran towards the messenger. »Stop! Stay right there! It's dangerous here!«

Chapter 13:
Baldar. Daman.
Mechanical Flies

Baldar, Brother

The messenger was a young man who asked, »What's the matter? Who are you?«

»I'm Hollydeva! Grandmother Algard sent me to lead the messenger coming from Linden Island. There are attackers and wolves all over this place! The Refuge is under siege!«

»Holly? It is me, Baldar!«

»Baldar?«

Then she recognized her brother, whom she had not seen for several years. She looked and took a step back.

But Baldar rushed toward her and hugged her. »Holly, I'm so glad to see you!«

His joy seemed genuine. He had missed her! She allowed her brother to draw her to him.

»Holly, Einar and I, we felt so bad that we had left you! We have often asked ourselves how you are! Where have you been all this time?«

»The first two years I was all alone at our house! Then I was with our father at Castle Georgeburg. But he is seriously injured and lies at Grandmother's cottage! She is going to heal him! You are expected to bring medicine from Linden Island!«

»Yes I do! Let us go to the Refuge as fast as we can!«

»I've just learned some hidden paths! Follow me!«

They actually got back to the property without any disturbance. Granna was also happy to see Baldar. Hollydeva started to introduce him to Astrello. But the two young men already knew each other!

»I've learned something about astrology from Astrello. I was a novice in the third year when he arrived at Linden! But there were too many gods in it for me!«

Astrello laughed, »Yes, the admirers of the OneGod are always kind of afraid of astrology! Although you'd rather had one of the novicesses from the first year in mind anyway!«

Baldar laughed, sounding a little bit embarrassed.

»And have you been able to land with her in the meantime?«

»Giustizia? No, not really. She is very disciplined and strict! We are in the same house, Agnus, right-hand path monotheists. I will have to ask her if she wants to marry me as soon as she is finished with her third year and has become an adept.«

Astrello remembered, »Hmm, I have not seen any married couples in the monastery!«

»Oh, but there are some! It is rather private! And yes, it does not really fit into the place. I probably have to forget about lovely Sister Giustizia!«

Hollydeva shook her head. This Linden Island seemed to be a strange place!

She told her grandmother about the otherworldly creature that had come through a door into this world.

»That's not good,« Granna explained. »There's most likely a gap in the boundaries to another world! Beings from other worlds can be dangerous! I hope it has something against wolves and wizardeurs! Or that Ostreaux has something against alien beings! But if he himself had called it, we have a problem!«

Then she took the remedies that Baldar had brought and went to her kitchen. She started cooking teas and ointments for her son-in-law.

»Come,« Hollydeva invited Baldar. »Father will be glad to see you!«

Baldar was hesitating. But he followed her into the room where Seren the Stone was resting and recovering. The stone now seemed more as if he had become an old piece of wood.

The injured Grand Inquisitor barely opened his eyes. »Holly! Are you okay?«

»Yes, Father! I'm fine! I love the Refuge of our Grandmother! Look, who I bring!«

Baldar came to his father's bed. »Father, it is me, Baldar!«

»Baldar!?«

Seren took the hand of his son. »It's good to see you again, Baldar! I am afraid the wizardeurs have struck me so hard that I do not have a lot of time left!«

»But Father, I have brought medicine from Linden Island. Grandmother will heal you!«

»Yes, she will. How is your brother? How is your mother?«

»Einar finished the novitiate one year before me. He's doing very well. We are both in the same Yana with our mother!«

»It's good! Good thing, you're together!«

Baldar nodded. Seren still held his son's hand and pulled him closer.

»Baldar, promise me something. When I'm gone, you and your brother must protect Hollydeva! She is an exceptional person! Your mother is afraid of her! But she should not have to! Holly is just a little different! Baldar, I beg of you, do not leave your sister alone!«

»If I can, Father, I'll do it! I'll protect Holly! And I know Einar would do it anyway!«

Hollydeva had pursued the conversation and felt repulsed. She did not need the protection of brothers who had left her before! And she was frightened at how much her father had assumed that he did not have much longer.

Then Granna came into the room, offering tea. She smeared an ointment on Seren's forehead.

»He has to rest! Come!«

Hollydeva, Astrello, Baldar, and Granna sat in the kitchen, eating a strong stew. Hollydeva had told her grandmother how it looked outside the Refuge.

»How long can we endure?«

»Oh, enough food is growing in the garden! I do not think the wizardeur or the wolves can break through my barriers! It is only a pity for the beds which are not cultivated and for the fruits which are not harvested!«

»We'll help you, Grandmother!«

»That is fine! But I fear that we will still need a healing wizardeur for the father, who can lift the curse of the three wizardeurs!«

»Where to get one from?»

»Maybe we can get the wizardeur outside our borders to do that,« Granna suggested, somewhat audaciously.

»We should get him under a pretext!«

»We need to make sure he does not use his magic in here against us!«

Nacharya Daman, Uncle

A bell alarmed them. »There's someone at the gate! Come! Perhaps the wizardeur will come on his own accord.«

At the gate, Nacharya Daman was standing.

127

»Oh, Daman, my dear! Come in, my son! Your niece is here!« Grandmother Algard exclaimed. Hollydeva remembered that this nacharya had something to do with healing. He was her uncle?

At some distance she saw Quavert, Rokudan Aoi and the wizardeur Ostreaux. They were watching how and whether Daman would be allowed to enter the Refuge.

The grandmother spoke to the oak, which stood beside the gate. The oak guarded the access to the Refuge.

Finally, Granna stepped forward and pulled at the gate so that it could go inward and Daman could enter.

They went back to the cottage. Before they went inside, Daman stopped, turned and shouted, »Ah, what a beautiful place! I am always impressed, mother!«

Granna looked at him, »And as you know, Daman, the medicine from these plants could help a lot of people!«

»Yes, I know!« the nacharya agreed.

They drank tea and the grandmother asked, »What brings you to us, Daman?! As you can see, my workers and gardeners are not here because we are besieged from the outside! I hope you can help to end this kind of situation!«

»Yes, I should like that. On the one hand, I would like to see and know how our Grand Inquisitor is doing! We urgently need his services! The situation of the Nacharya is not very good at the moment, and that may be threatening for the Yrth as well!«

»The Grand Inquisitor is greatly affected by a strong magical curse! I do not know if he can survive this! I have just received medicines from Linden Island today, which could alleviate the effects of the curse! But we must wait!«

Daman turned to Hollydeva, »My name is Daman, as you know by now! I am one of the Nine Nacharya! And I am the brother of your mother, so I am your uncle! I am on your side! We need your help! You must take over the function of your father!«

»What shall I do?«

»Stop,« shouted her grandmother. »Daman, I forbid it! Holly is a child, she can not be your Grand Inquisitor!«

»But she knows more about her father's methods than any of us!«

»Then you must find new methods! You require a new Grand Inquisitor! I will send Hollydeva to Linden Island in order for her to receive further training and education!«

»I understand that! But we are in a difficult situation! The Nine are at odds. We have been attacked by the wizardeurs! The prisoners in the dungeons have died or fled. Our power in the world has never been endangered like that during the two thousand years of our existence!«

»Stop, step by step, Daman!«

Grandmother Algard interrupted her son, who had become one of the most powerful individuals on Yrth. Daman seemed to be under a enormous amount of pressure.

She saw that he calmed down, and asked, »Tell us the position of the Nacharya, Daman! How have you been quarreling?«

»There may have been some antipathy between some of us. It probably also depends on the fact that our training has flattened. We have paid too much attention to political and economic power! And of course, the world is different and more complex nowadays! Dangerous and endangered!

»Now the alchymists came with an offer. Their research makes it possible to cultivate plants which yield and are resistant to insects and disease. In addition, these plants do not form seeds, and the farmers have to buy new seeds every year. With this invention, the alchymists would be able to control the food production of mankind and thus become very powerful. They offered to let us participate in this power and the profits.

»But some of us do not trust the alchymists. Some are also of the opinion that this research is unhealthy and unnatural!«

Hollydeva could hardly keep her still, »This change in the plants will kill the insects and thus the birds and ultimately all life! Guuz explained it to me! He died for it!«

Her grandmother put her hand on Hollydeva's arm, soothingly.

»Daman, continue! Tell us! Which knight of the Nine is on which side?«

»It is clear: Achmar and Peredur have always been enemies to the alchymists and would like to avoid them altogether. Rokudan Aoi and Quavert, lurking outside the gate with the wizardeur Ostreaux, are eager for power and money and would like to be allies with the alchymists and wizardeurs. Nononn and Tatu Njena are rather undecided. They are above all concerned with the survival of the Nine, whose leaders they are. Saphed is a special case. He certainly wants to make a pact with the alchymists, to trick them out later. He is notoriously thwarting. The Bhogi is very old and not a factor. Or better said, he follows the Nononn.

»Nononn, Achmar, and Saphed went to the alchymists to look closely at their research. Tatu Njena remains at Castle Georgeburg and brings some important books and equipment to a new place far to the north. Peredur will be somewhere nearby.

Rokudan Aoi and Quavert are in front of the gate and want to bring Seren and Hollydeva under their control.«

»And you, Daman? You did not talk about yourself!«

When her grandmother spoke to the nacharya, Hollydeva remembered that he had been undecided in the discussion of the Nacharya and had not reported in the vote.

»I am concerned above all with the healing power of the plants. Alchymy is a science which explores this healing power and develops remedies. In a sense, I am an alchymist and my ancestors and teachers were alchymists. But these new researches give me discomfort. Too much seems to me to be undertaken from greed! I trust the Nononn that he draws the right conclusions from what he sees on Mount Lead.

»I am particularly concerned about this attack of the wizardeurs on Castle Georgeburg. This is very unusual! They risked a lot! They must be of the opinion that the Nine are very dangerous for them or what is important to them! Actually, we have not taken them very seriously in the last decades. That was a mistake!«

»What about Ostreaux? Could we make him lift the curse that has bewitched Seren?«

»Ostreaux seems to be a sort of independent wizardeur, who had accepted an order from the guild of the wizardeurs, to hinder Hollydeva's ways! And he kind of managed to fulfill his task! The death of one of his wolves has, however, troubled him.

»But I do not know if he can lift the curse! It would surprise me!«

»We must try!«

»What about you? You're a good healer, too!«

»Yes, I would like to look at Seren! I can not influence injuries afflicted by magic, however!«

»Let's get Ostreaux in!«

Daman nodded and accompanied Granna to the gate.

Baldar said his goodbye to Hollydeva, »Holly, I must go back to Linden Island! I hope you to arrive there soon as well!«

»Yes, I hope so, too,« joined in Astrello. »I will accompany your brother. I am a teacher at the monastery and would like to prepare for the new school year!«

Hollydeva became sad, as she would have to miss these two now. But she nodded and wished them a good return home to Linden Island, where they seemed to have found their place, »Yes, go! Baldar, do you remember the way we went in here? I will accompany you to the hedge!«

Council of War

When she came back to the cottage, Granna and Daman were just coming back with the two other nacharyas and the wizardeur from the country of the frog-eaters.

Since the two nacharyas who had attacked her in the days before had obviously been obliged by the grandmother to exercise restraint, Hollydeva did not protest their presence at the Refuge.

Ostreaux bowed. »Mademoiselle Hollydeva, my respect!«

»Respect?«

»Yes, you are a worthy opponent!«

»I have not done much! I have only called the bees!«

»Yes, and these bees were equal to my wolves! And then you won the protection of the druyds! And I must respect them, too!«

Granna interposed, »Enough of the courtesies! Ostreaux, I want you to look at my son-in-law!«

»Very well, Madame Algard! But I have one condition! I have been commissioned to prevent the Grand Inquisitor or his daughter from continuing their office!«

»I promise you that neither my son-in-law nor my granddaughter will ever again, or for the first time, perform this office! I promise and will make sure that this agreement is being kept!«

Ostreaux nodded.

She turned to Hollydeva. »Hollydeva, listen to me carefully! You will never take office as the Grand Inquisitor of the Nine Nacharya! Do you understand me?«

»Yes, Grandmother, I understand!«

Ostreaux explained, »Madame Algard, your word is good with me! I know that you have the power to attend to this promise!«

Grandmother led the wizardeur, the three nacharya, and Hollydeva into the bedroom, where Seren was lying.

He lay with half-opened eyes. Daman sat down on a chair beside the bed. »This wizardeur is ready to see if he can lift the curse!«

Ostreaux looked, strutted around the bed, sucked in the air, murmured.

»So it was a threefold curse, spoken by Cevaine, Owleya, and Andalf?«

Hollydeva nodded. »When the old lady and the long-haired are called by those names, then it was as you said.«

»Good. I need a special ingredient from your garden, Madame Algard! I need one of the very rare blue strawberries!«

»Oh, well. Yes, there are still some. Most are probably picked and eaten! Come on, Holly, we pick them up and bring them to our Monsieur Magus!«

Hollydeva followed her grandmother into the garden. Just as they were standing in front of the beds of the berries, where a few blue strawberries were still shining beside the many red ones a roaring and humming filled the air.

Flies

»Help! To help!« cried Granna immediately, and the three nacharyas and Ostreaux rushed out of the cottage.

There were thousands of flies that had come rushing around to sit on the blue strawberries.

»Call the bees!« Granna called at Hollydeva, who immediately began calling the bees with her inner voice.

The three nacharyas tried to scare away the flies, which moved up as a cloud, but then attacked all the green and everything that was alive.

The bees came and began to fight with the flies. But these flies were very resistant and vicious.

»I'm afraid they're modified flies, small flying machines, produced and sent by the alchymists,« Daman was concerned.

»We need the blue strawberries,« stated Ostreaux. He waved with his arms and shouted magical incantations, but the flies were not affected.

The blue strawberries were quickly destroyed. Peculiarly, the flies had left one of the strawberries intact. They had taken this one up now, and several flies came together to take it away through the air. The rest of the bed was completely destroyed.

»How did these flies know that we needed the blue strawberries just for the healing of Seren?«

The suspicions were directed to Rokudan Aoi and Quavert. But they were as dismayed as the others.

132

»The alchymists could have listened to our conversations!«

»We were talking in the room! The listening device must be there!«

They searched and looked at everything in the room. Ostreaux remained conspic-uous. Hollydeva had watched him and had the feeling that he knew what the device was.

But then Rokudan Aoi said that if signals were transmitted to the alchymists, it would have to be something that Grandmother Algard would have received or bought from the alchymists.

»I have painkillers here, which I bought in a pharmacy in the village! I thought these pills would help my son-in-law better than my teas!«

Rokudan Aoi looked at the pillbox and the pills more closely. »They are clearly from the alchymists,« he recognized.

Quavert and Daman examined the pills and the pillbox. »That's impressive with what means these alchymists can work now,« said Quavert.

»So you really believe that the pillbox transmitted our talk to the alchymists?« Grandmother Algard asked disbelievingly.

Hollydeva had watched Ostreaux and saw his discomfort. »I think it's like that,« she confirmed. »Monsieur Ostreaux, please confirm it! The blue strawberry is now stolen and inaccessible!«

»Yes, I think it's like how you found out!«

And already Daman started crushing the pillbox. Granna swept the remnants to-gether, went out and threw everything on the trash, non-compostable trash, which was a tiny bunch.

»Someone has to go to the alchymists to get the blue strawberry back again!«

»We could send a message to Nononn and Achmar!«

»How can the message reach them fast enough?«

»Nononn can talk to the bees as well!«

Hollydeva's grandmother called the bees and gave them the news they were to bring to Nononn. They had understood and buzzed.

A little hope remained.

Ostreaux suggested, »I want the given promise to be preserved so that my assign-ment stays fulfilled. I'll prefer to stay here and keep Monsieur Seren alive and keep the curse at least at a low level. I can not completely dissolve it! This is the curse of three wizardeurs and therefore too strong! But I think I can keep Mr. Seren alive until the blue strawberry is brought back!«

»What about your wolves?« Hollydeva was not convinced that she wanted to leave the wizardeur with her father and grandmother.

»There was something strange about the wolves. One of my wolves was found dead. He looked as if he had died very suddenly!«

»I saw him die,« Hollydeva replied.

»Say, did you kill him?«

»No, I could not! I sat on a tree and the wolf had taken in my scent. Then a strange creature came through a sort of door in the air, killed him with a sudden blow, and ran away.«

Rokudan Aoi stepped in, »A strange being?«

»Yes, it did not seem to have a face and moved a little chaotic. I've never seen anything like it!«

»Did you call it, Ostreaux?« Daman asked sharply.

»No, of course I did not! I would not call the murderers of my wolves!«

»Unfortunately, this is no good news! It is a being from another dimension or from a parallel world! Hopefully, not more of them will come! We need to find it and eliminate it!« Rokudan Aoi seemed really worried.

»What about the wolves?«

»I command the wolves to return to our hiding-place!« Ostreaux was actually doing his best to win their approval.

Granna nodded, »Do that, Ostreaux! I'll let you through the gate. Gentlemen, why don't you go and look for that creature from another world?«

»Yes, we have to do that! We're coming! We call some of our men from the Gray Guard!«

Hollydeva's grandmother went with the four men to the gate, Ostreaux called his wolves and sent them home, the three nacharyas went to look for the creature.

Granna came back with Ostreaux. »I have to take my granddaughter to Linden Island. There she is safe and also a little out of notoriety. That should be right for you! Can I trust you with my son-in-law, Ostreaux? My son, Daman, will represent me here for the time!«

»Yes, you can, Madame!«

»Tomorrow the gardeners and workers will return. Then we go!«

So she went with her Grandmother Algard the way Baldar and Astrello had already taken. She wondered what it would be like on the now often mentioned Linden Island.

Chapter 14:
Abbess Tilia. Maestra Fraxina.
Exam

Ferry Crossing

Slowly the little boat glided through the mist. The ferryman stood at the stern and moved the boat forward by swinging movements of the stern rudder. Granna sat calmly and composed in front of the ferryman. Hollydeva was sitting at the bottom of the boat at her grandmother's feet. Pierre, the foster son of the ferryman, sometimes poured water over the edge of the ferry boat, while he was observing the surrounding sea.

Suddenly, the ferryman stopped and gave a sound, telling his passengers to be quiet. The fog cracked, and a jetty was visible at about thirty yards away.

»This will be the jetty on Linden Island!«

But the boatman had stopped for something else. A large figure suddenly rose out of the waves just before them. Whitish, gazing eyes were staring at them.

»Skipper!« An eerie dull voice from came the watery mouth of a water demon, simultaneously sounding desperate and threatening.

The ferryman answered, »What can I do for you, friend from the water?«

»Whom are you bringing to the island, skipper?«

»Who wants to know that?«

»My mistress, the Princess of the Nereïdes, would like to know! And if you give me no answer, I shall tear your boat down so that my mistress can see for herself whom you are bringing to the island!«

»I am a ferryman, and I am bringing the healer, Mrs. Algard, to Linden Island, so that she can heal a sick nun there! I have often driven Dame Algard to the island! Your mistress knows her well!«

»Yes, that may well be! Who else is on the boat?«

»There is only my son, useless Pierre!«

»Throw him overboard! With us, he may become useful!«

»No, good spirit of the waters, I can not do that! His mother would be very sad, and I would have to suffer badly!«

»Well, there is somebody else on the boat!«

»There's no one else! We are three on this trip!«

Hollydeva made herself smaller and crouched on the floor of the boat. The sea demon grew bigger.

»There's someone else! I feel it! The Princess told me that a person, who is going to be a danger to us, is heading to the island! I'm supposed to prevent this person from reaching the island!«

»But what kind of person is that? Who can be a danger to the Nereïdes and to the mighty demons of the sea?«

»Do not mock me, skipper! The Princess has told me.«

Granna interposed. »Here, demon, bring this ring to your Princess! There is a stone of amber attached to it, which she once sent me to the beach, where I found it. She will recognize this stone! Tell her that I know whom she is talking about, whose path you should prevent! Tell her that with this ring I give her my word, that this person is in my care, and will not be the enemy of the beings of the sea ever!«

»But she'll have to obey the Abbess. And the Abbess is our enemy!«

»Yes, I know!« Hollydeva's grandmother sighed. »I assure you that I will tell the Abbess that the obedience of this person shall and can not be forcing her to act as an enemy against the creatures of the sea!«

»I will return your words to the Princess!«

Granna threw the ring to the water demon, and the scary fellow dived back into the water.

The skipper nodded his thanks, and drove the boat safely to the jetty.

When they got out, a big man, dressed like a monk, was expecting them with a lance. »Stop, where are you going? Who are you?«

Granna responded, »I am the healer Algard, formerly known as Maestra Malus! I am going to meet my friend, the Abbess Tilia! I am accompanied by my granddaughter Hollydeva! The boy of the ferryman is coming with as he is carrying some things, which I bring to the Abbess!«

The guard seemed to be satisfied with the answer and invited them to follow him. Hollydeva saw a wall in the morning mist. They came to a gate, which the guard opened. Behind the wall, Hollydeva perceived a monastery of several two-storied stone houses grouped around a square. On one side of the square a majestic house, the entrance of which was reached by a broad staircase, dominated the other eight houses. In front of this house stood a tower with a bell. That was where Hollydevas's grandmother led her and Pierre.

Abbess Tilia

»Wait here,« advised Hollydevas's grandmother and followed the guard into the main house. After a time, she returned accompanied by two women, who were dressed in a kind of floor-length robe of solid fabric, the edges of which were marked by different colors.

»High Maestra, this is my granddaughter, Hollydeva, for whom I ask your protection! This boy is the ferry boatman's boy. His name is Pierre and I would like him to be able to stay here, so my granddaughter has a friend at the monastery!«

»As I heard, she already has a friend here, the star boy, who came back here a few days ago,« the stern looking lady frowned.

She continued, »The star boy came with one of our adepts, a brother of your granddaughter. And her oldest brother and her mother are here in the monastery as well! So she would not be very alone!«

»Good, Tilia, I understand. You play to be "the difficult" again! I want the boy here to be a novice!«

»The ferryman's boy, like your granddaughter, and a few other young people who are here these days, may apply for the novitiate!«

She turned to Pierre, »But know, boy, the trial is not easy, and it is that only those who really intend to stay here will enter the novitiate!«

Pierre nodded and muttered something. Granna pushed him. »Say it aloud, boy!«

»Yes, I want to be a novice here,« Pierre stated firmly.

»Good,« the Abbess approved. »And you, girl, do you want that too?«

Girl? Hollydeva was feeling inwardly indignant at this turkey, who was so very self-confident. But she felt her grandmother's sharp eyes on her.

»Yes, I, too, want to be a novice, as my two brothers were.«

Grand Maestra Tilia pointed to the nun next to her. »All right, Maestra Fraxina will take care of you! She is the prioress of the novice's house and will lead the examinations! But for the time being you will be silent for a week! We do not want you to

137

speak with the other aspirants and find allies or the like! Whoever speaks a word must leave the island! The examination is already starting now!«

Hollydevas's grandmother spoke up again, before Hollydeva and Pierre would go with Fraxina. »On the ferry crossing, a sea demon wanted to prevent Hollydeva from coming here! I promised him that Hollydeva would stay neutral in your war with the Nereïdes!«

»My war with the Nereïdes? Maestra Malus, you know the sea demons have attacked us! I do not even know why they did it!«

»Well, then it is no problem!«

»But the sea demons will probably come back! And the Nereïdes themselves with them! We must defend ourselves!«

»Hollydeva can defend herself! She can defend those who are attacked, as long as they are close to her! The Nereïdes will not object to that, I think!«

»Do you have any more conditions?«

»My daughter, Maestra Castanea, always saw something evil, coming from Hollydevas's father, in her daughter. I want you to make clear to her that she is projecting her own evil on the child!«

»But Castanea is our Garden Maestra! She cares for flowers! She is like goodness itself!«

»Yes, those are the worst, as you know. She does not even know her shadow self! But I blame it on myself and I can not blame it on her! I only ask you, dearest Tilia, to order mutual cooperation between my daughter and my granddaughter! They are both very strong people, and we absolutely need them both!«

»Well, I'll try to mediate!«

Granna turned to Hollydeva, »I am going back to my garden. You're safe here, Holly! Follow the instructions of the masters and adepts! Choose well, when choosing the Yana comes up!«

They hugged each other and the guard led her grandmother, who, as Hollydeva now knew, was also called "Mrs. Algard" or "Maestra Malus", back to the ferry boat.

The Red Prayer

Maestra Fraxina led Hollydeva and Pierre to a meadow. There was a bonfire, the sparks of which sprang into the evening sky.

Around the fire about twenty girls and boys were silently sitting, looking frozen, even though they were close to the fire.

»These are your competitors for the twelve novice places! You will be here for four more days with them on this meadow! Remember that you should not talk to them! Do not make any signs or anything! You may sit side by side at the fire. But do not touch!«

She led Pierre and Hollydeva to stables at the edge of the meadow. From a box, she took two sleeping bags and gave them to the two tired aspirants.

»There are straw balls in these stables. Take your sleeping bag and spread it out! This is your sleeping place for the next nights! Behind the stable is a water pipe, where you can wash! Food is brought by two adepts and offered where we have entered the meadow. The exam will begin in four days.«

Maestra Fraxina left. Hollydeva and Pierre took their sleeping bags, went to the stables, then to the fire.

Nothing happened for four days. They were twenty-two young people waiting for a test.

Hollydeva sought communication with plants and insects, but they all seemed to obey the orders of the nuns. She would have liked to know whether her grandmother had returned safely. But she felt that Granna knew very well how she could move unharmed in this world of dangers. »Oh, I want to be like Grandmother Algard,« she said to herself.

She wondered if the other aspirants were a competition for her. Most of them were looking rather frightened. But there were also some who seemed to be very well-equipped with power and charisma.

A girl, who was probably a year older than herself, made an impression through her tattooed bald head and a sinewy, athletic figure. Hollydeva felt that she had respect for her. This girl observed the environment and the other actors closely, just like she herself was doing.

A boy walked around, confidently and vigorously. He looked like a prince from a royal house.

Another boy juggled with stones and sticks, keeping himself busy.

Some of the aspirants were dark-skinned. A girl who kept herself in the corners mostly was probably from the far East.

Hollydeva enjoyed these four days, resting, wondering if her mother knew that they would meet soon.

On the day of the exam, the Abbess, Maestra Fraxina, and several other masters of the convent approached.

The Grand Mistress told them that before the exam they would say a prayer together. It would be the Red Prayer. And they would learn this and the other six prayers during their training in the monastery. The aspirants who would not manage to be accepted as novices today would still receive a booklet with these prayers, since the daily recitation of at least one of these prayers— it would be one for each day of the week — would be very helpful in mastering life. So she read line after line of the Red Prayer aloud, and all the aspirants chanted it after her.

»I breathe red light into my Mars center, my "root chakra"!
I let the red from the earth flow into me!
It flows in my veins, my heart.
I am ready for fight and work!
I give myself the right to live!
I have the right to be who I am!
I breathe out compassion and send it into the world!
May all living beings be fulfilled and victorious!«

Maestra Tilia called out that in the spirit of this prayer, they should go into this test with full commitment, and above all, fair to the other aspirants.

Maestra Fraxina had her stand up and shouted, »Aspirants, aspirants! Only twelve of you will be accepted as novices of the monastery on Linden Island this year! You will run through a labyrinth and there will be three tests in this garden. If you solve these correctly, you will find the way and will get to the exit of the garden, which leads to the reception as a novice. The others will be brought back to the shore today, and we wish them all the luck in their life!«

Fraxina showed in three directions. »We have three mazes. There you will see three entrances! There will be three of you, one at each entrance, to go into the maze. Fifteen minutes later, the next three are to follow. If you meet in the maze, you should ignore the other! But there is no one of us in the garden who observes or evaluates your behavior in the maze! It's only important where you get out! There are three exits from each maze, and only one leads to the monastery! I wish you luck!«

She took a list and shouted, »The first aspirants are: Pretem from Brabant, Ellianne, and Pierre, the ferry boat boy!«

Hollydeva had to wait for an hour. Then she was to go with the fifth group. She ran to the labyrinth to the right and entered. The paths were lined with privet hedges.

She followed her feeling and decided to take turns for the right or the left way. Then she came to a small round clearing with a fountain in the middle. There were benches to sit at the fountain. She sat down and looked at the fountain.

The Fountain

A mysterious voice addressed her, »Hello, aspirant!«

Hollydeva became a little startled. Then she saw a face in the water fountain, and said, »Hi, Mister Fountain!«

»I have a small task for you,« said the well. »You can see a trough in the rear at a water line leading into the deeper maze. It is very important that you fill exactly one liter of my water into the line! Under the bench are two pots. One pot holds five liters. The other pot holds three liters. You can measure exactly one liter with the two pots in two trials. More attempts can not been made! Pour that liter into the trough!«

The face smiled. »Hmm, a mathematical problem!« Hollydeva thought. She had not been good at arithmetic. But she was still convinced that she could solve the task.

Should she fill the five liter pot and then pour it into the pot, which contains three liters? Then there were two liters left. That was not a solution. »Five and three are eight. Five minus three is two. That's not how it works!«

She tried to get the inner contact with the hedge. She immediately felt that the hedge already knew this trick and would not give any clues to any aspirant.

»I need a liter. Ah, three and three is six and that is one more than five! So I take three liters into one pot and fill it into the larger one. Then I do that again and keep a liter left. It's easy!«

She did it and poured the one liter into the trough.

The fountain spoke to her again, »Excellent, aspirant! Calculating is not too complicated for you, I guess! Tell me where is the water that flows through me? Will I get this liter of water back? Can you please pour the five liters in the big pot back into my basin?«

Hollydeva did as the fountain had asked for. »The water is coming from the groundwater,« she answered.

»Groundwater?«

»Yes, everywhere there is underground water, groundwater. In the depths, there is probably a thread or a line which brings this water upwards!«

»That could be! And where does the groundwater come from?«

»The groundwater is coming from the rain!«

»Oh yeah. And where does the rain come from?«

»The rain comes from evaporated water that has risen over the seas and the lakes!«

»Where are the waters of the seas and lakes coming from?«

»Those are coming from the rivers that flow into the seas and lakes!«

»Right. Where do the rivers come from?«

»The rivers come from the springs!«

»Where did the springs draw their water from?«

»The springs are probably collecting the groundwater in the mountains! They come from overflowing groundwater!«

»And where is the original source?«

»The original source?«

»Yes, the groundwater has come from rain that has risen over the seas, fed by rivers whose springs are pouring groundwater. You explain the causes of the phenomena with the phenomena themselves. This is a circular argument! That does not explain anything!«

Hollydeva thought about the fountain's statement. She had learned the explanation of the Church of the OneGod: The original source is the omnipotent OneGod. But she had the feeling that such a preconceived or parroted reasoning would be badly received.

So she said, »I am afraid that everything is circulating in such circles. There are no first causes! It has always been there and has always begun to circle forever!«

The fountain smiled. »You said it nicely! I like that! Do not follow the direction of the water line, take a different path!«

Hollydeva looked around. The line from the trough went in one direction. Opposite this direction were two exits from this fountain plaza. On one side was the entrance through which she had come. On the other side was another exit.

Should she trust the well? Had she answered the questions so that the fountain would point her the right way?

She decided to trust the fountain and took the right exit from the two who were facing the water line.

Again it was about a few corners, and again she had to choose right or left. Then she met one of the other aspirants, a long, thin boy, slightly confused at a fork.

»Well, do you not know where to go to?« she asked. The boy was frightened and stammered. He had not spoken to another person for several days.

»I've been here a couple of times. I'm going in circles.«

»Have you been at the fountain?«

»Fountain?«

»Yes, I'm coming from there. The fountain has shown me the way!«

»No, I was at an aviary. The birds asked me a question and I answered them. Then they told me the way and I ended up here. But I'm going in circles somehow!«

»Hmm. So, where I come from, there is a fountain! Maybe you should go there and I go to the aviary! Do you remember where it was?«

The boy looked around and indicated the direction.

The Aviary

Hollydeva thanked and went in the direction. She wondered that they had both been at different stations.

And there was already the aviary, in which some colorful birds fluttered around.

»Oh, girl! Let us out!« they shouted.

»I thought you'd give me a test question,« Hollydeva said. »I'm here for an exam. Give me the examination task!«

The birds shrieked and seemed to laugh. »Oh, you mean, because of the lanky chap who just left? We just teased him! Here, every year, these aspirants come by and want us to do examinations! But we do not belong to that game! Let us out! We want to fly and have a little freedom! We're coming back! There's always food here!«

Hollydeva saw a door that she could open.

»I think you are trying to spoof me,« she said. »Probably my loyalty to the monastery is examined here. I let the birds out, the monastery is in danger, things can get lost, get into the wilderness and in danger! And then I have the blame! That would be very much like me! And, unfortunately, I have to be accepted as a novice in this monastery! Because only here I am secure!«

»Here you are secure?!« the colorful birds, parrots, finches, and vultures shrieked. They seemed to be laughing again. »This monastery is the most dangerous place on Yrth!« they exclaimed. »Flee as long as you can! The nuns and monks are all scammers!«

»No, I do not think so! I met the Abbess and the Novice Maestra, and they made a very serious impression on me!«

Again the birds shrieked. »Serious impression! Crazy!«

Then a bird came close to the grating. »We're pied vultures! Vultures live on carrion. Here we get only old living worms from the alleged nuns and monks! Please let us out! Then we can fill our stomachs with the warm bodies of lost aspirants who died in this labyrinth!«

»Nobody's going to die from starvation in here!«

»You will not be the first to starve in here! Do you not have a peculiar feeling in your stomach already?«

Hollydeva realized she had not eaten anything for a long time. She should at least have been drinking from the water of the well! But she wanted to get this test done as soon as possible and leave the labyrinth!

»If you tell me where to find the next exam, I'll let you out!«

»For real? Let us out first! Otherwise, we tell you, and you cheat, and leave us, and we will not get out of this disgusting cage!«

Hollydeva looked at the aviary and found that it was actually a little tight for the poor birds. The pied vultures were smaller than ordinary vultures. They were about the size of geese. But they were very airy and agile.

»Someone will have thought of something here,« she told herself. »But I really do not care whether I pass this test or not! When I have to go, I go back to Granna and the Refuge! It was good there! I am for the birds and bees to live in the air! No animal should be imprisoned!«

She opened the door of the aviary and stepped aside.

The six pied vultures stepped out with an attitude and flew to nearby branches in trees, which were between the privet hedges.

»Ha, you are making big eyes now! There are trees here as well! You just have to look up!«

And when she saw that an apple was hanging on a branch, she understood that the vultures had shown her this apple, as if it was part of the next test!

»Thank you, good vultures!« she shouted.

»Thank you, aspirant! And we remind you of what we've said about the feeling in your stomach!«

They flew farther up and over the hedge. Hollydeva wondered how the aspirants who were coming after her would be able to carry out their examination. But the parrots and finches had remained in the aviary and whispered to each other. They would probably help the other aspirants.

The Apple

So Hollydeva climbed the tree, plucked the apple, and climbed down again. When she was about to bite the apple, the tree started speaking to her.

»Hello, Hollydeva. So you are the granddaughter of Maestra Malus!«

»Oh, Mr. Apple Tree! Yes, I am the granddaughter of Maestra Malus, my grandmother!«

»Malus is the Latin word for apple tree, you must know. She was not just named after the apple trees. She was very fond of us. Maestra Malus is the priestess of apple trees! Wherever she is in the world, she will find an apple tree and be heard by us! And that could also be transferred to her granddaughter! Are you liking us like your grandmother does?«

»Yes, why not? Can I eat this apple?«

»Please listen to this story!

»At their wedding, Adam and Eve, the first couple, were presented with an apple, an apple from the forbidden Tree of Knowledge, which is in the middle of the Garden of Eden.

»They stood there looking at this apple, which they had laid on a marble base.

»Earth came and said, "How stupid you are! Aren't you ashamed? An apple is for eating! He can only fulfill his destiny if one of you eats him."

»They did not want to turn against the destiny and not deny this apple its fulfillment, so Adam began to eat this apple.

»Then Water came and cursed and said, "Why does the man eat this apple? How can he starve his wife, who is to give birth to a child, who needs strength?"

»Adam gave Eve the apple and she took a nice bite. But then Fire came and shook her head and snatched the apple from Eve and said, "Do you have no honor? You must always take your food together! No one is allowed to come short! No one is allowed to eat before the other! Only so can your marriage succeed! And it would be critical that you succeed and become the primeval parents of humanity!"

»So they took the apple and bit it from both sides at the same time! But Air hurried toward them. Air shouted, "Stop! What are you doing? You are eating away the greatest gift the Gods ever made! The poor apple! The beautiful apple! Do not you know anything?"

»They were very intimidated and put the apple back on the pedestal. The Akasha, the Fifth Element, came and was indignant, "The apple is quite nibbled! What does it look like? You must give it from yourself so that it can be whole again! Now it is embarrassed!"

»What should they do? They each cut some meat from their lower back! And they added it to the apple! Thanks to miraculous powers and the magical power of the marble pedestal, it became a whole beautiful apple from the Tree of Knowledge again!

»What is the right choice now? Should the man eat the apple or the woman? Or both? Or none? Or shall the apple eat of the two?«

Hollydeva had to laugh. »You are telling quite some stories, friend apple tree! There is probably no right answer!«

»Is there not? But you will have to give an answer because your way is determined by your answer!«

The apple tree pointed in five ways, which branched off from a small clearing behind them.

»Oh, alright! What is the answer that leads to the novitiate? So, I do not think it's right if only the man eats the apple. In the myth of Genesis, the woman eats the apple and that also leads to punishment. If both of them eat it, at least it leads to an equality of the sexes. If none of them eats of the apple, which is of the Tree of Knowledge, no one comes to know. I think the island is a place of discovery. There should be nothing added to apples, I am sure!«

»What is your answer, then? Both should eat from the apple at the same time?«

»Yes, I imagine it is a pity that there is no one here to bite into this apple with me!«

And she took a big bite because she was really hungry now. The apple tasted really good, and she ate it with pleasure.

»You have chosen the way of Fire! This is a good way. You did not understand some of the deeper meaning of the story, but it does not matter. You want to learn something here, too! Do you see the light there in the middle way? This is the way of Fire! Go through the fire and you will reach your destination!«

Hollydeva did as the apple tree had told her. The path led to a burning ring of fire. The ring was bigger than she was. She would be able to jump through without bumping.

146

So she took off and jumped through. And when she landed, she realized that she had left the maze.

A female maestra stood there with some of the other aspirants. She also saw Pierre and was happy to see him.

»You did it, girl!« the maestra congratulated her. »Welcome to the novitiate of the monastery on Linden Island!«

Pierre took her by the hand, and two other girls, one dark-skinned and a radiant redhead, came to her and embraced her.

They had to wait another hour, got tea, and were then led through a gate, so they entered the central courtyard of the monastery.

Hollydeva saw that they were a total of twelve youths, who now were to become novices.

She was about to ask Pierre how he had answered the apple question, when the maestra, who was leading them, explained, »Each one of you had a different, personal experience in the labyrinth. It brings you nothing to share these experiences now. So be silent about it! And now be ready for what the Grand Maestra and Abbess has to say to you! Leave your old life behind you! Your novitiate begins, and nothing will be for you like it was in your childhood.«

Chapter 15:
Eight Priors. Novicess Scorpio

Different Lines of Mysticism

»You are now here as novices in the monastery school of Linden Island! We are a monastery of trans-religious mysticism. Mysticism is the school of experience within the religions of the world, in which the male or female seeker seeks a direct contact to God or to states of religious consciousness, ecstasies!

»All religions on Yrth have a mystical aspect or a mystical subgroup. And on closer study, we find that these forms of mystic spirituality are very similar, despite all differences of these religions on the surface.

»Mystics have always dealt with healing and other arts. Mystics were talking with animals and plants, getting information about their healing power and other things.

»So I want you to understand that you are not supposed to be followers of the MultiGod, or of the OneGod, or of the gods within nature, or be without any gods as an atheist. You should be able to stand above and know the connection and also the differences of different worldviews! You can then choose what you want to believe, or whether you want to believe anything at all. You should be able to choose the faith that offers you the greatest advantage, the most promising attitude within any situation.

»For that is what worldviews and belief systems are: thought patterns and models through which certain abilities can be achieved!

»Foremost, religions have always had a social character. The religious men and women are more willing to sacrifice for the community, as he or she hopes that the good deeds will be rewarded by God or the Gods or by a Law of Karma. The belief in a common God or in a pantheon of Gods creates an identification. Believers stick to believers who confirm the belief or worldview.

»Unfortunately, identification with one God, several gods, or even no god has caused much suffering in human history. We therefore want to be able to stand above it and not take any faith too seriously!

»But we would like to get to know the different teachings of mysticism. So for certain times you will accept and believe each of these schools, or at least pretend to believe it. You will argue and discuss with the other novices. You will learn the benefits of acting in a particular belief system! What kind of forces do you gain access to?

»What is common to these mystical worldviews? How do they differ from those of the mages, alchymists, or all the other philosophies? This is especially important as we may have partnerships and clashes with the wizardeurs and alchymists, as well as with mystical secret organizations.

»Above all: we want to know ourselves, our true self, our deepest self. And we intend to know each other so that we can go beyond ourselves! We as mystics expand the limits of our self so far that we can become one with animals and plants and stones and everything that is! Becoming one with the Great Whole Universe!«

Maestra Tilia paused for a moment, gathered herself. »For the sake of completeness, and none of my Masters here shall accuse me of inconceivability or misleading of novices, there is also the mystical tendency which sacrifices the union with the Great Whole Totality of the Universe for a union with a Great Nothingness!«

She raised her voice, »If a man whom I call the Black Mystic, a man who raves to you about the great, black, empty, silent Nothingness, wants to take you with him to this very Nothingness or Emptiness, then run and come to me! And let me know! For nothing is as dangerous in this world as this man, the Black Mystic!«

Hollydeva noticed that the Abbess's warning had tended to arouse her interest in the man.

Novicess Sister Scorpio

The Abbess continued, »You will receive names! These names are your novitiate names that you will wear during the three years of your basic novitiate! When you have completed these three years, you can become an initiate!

»After three years the Yana, to which you belong, may accept you as an adept. Then you will receive a new name again! It is probably obvious to you that some trials are waiting for you on this way! And I wish each one of you that one day you stand next to the person who then is abbot or abbess of this monastery, and you have become a master yourself.

»The new names are supposed to indicate that you have left your previous life, that you want to be someone else here, someone newborn!

»We choose these names according to the names in various esoteric traditions, such as the Tarot cards, the astrological sign, the names of the angels or saints. This year again the astrological signs have their turn. You are twelve young people. There are twelve zodiac signs! That fits perfectly!

»The star signs, as we know them as signs of birth, are orientated at the position of the sun at a time of birth.«

Abbess Tilia gave a sign and an adept brought a large bowl, which contained twelve lots.

»Each of you is going to draw a lot! Your novitiate name is written on the lot! And these names correspond to the Latin names of astral constellations, and perhaps that name is significant to you!«

So they went to the bowl one by one, taking a lot, went back, opening the lot, reading their future name, which they would at least carry on Linden Island, with which they could be called.

Then, Grand Maestra Tilia announced that she was going to baptize the twelve newly born novices.

»Come to me as I call your name!«

So Tilia called, »Ariëa!«

A strong girl with dark skin color went forward, bent her head, the Abbess placed a hand on her forehead, proclaiming, »Sister Ariëa!«

And so, all the twelve girls and boys came forward one by one and heard their new names, "Tauro", "Gemina", "Cancra", "Leo", "Virgo", "Libra", "Scorpio", "Sagittario", "Capricorno", "Aquaria", "Piscio".

So Hollydeva had become "Sister Scorpio" and Pierre was now "Piscio". Hollydeva was born in Sagittarius. But she remembered, that Astrello had said, that these zodiac sign calculations were based on an error, and that her sun had to be around 25 degrees earlier. And thus her sun should be in Scorpio.

»That's all right,« she thought. She liked being a scorpion, even if she had never seen such an animal.

Then the Abbess told them to go to the novice's house. In the cellar there was a clothing store, and the Cellar Master of the monastery gave them new clothes, their novice's cowl.

Yana of Ravens

So they were twelve novices, newly clothed in simple plain gray dresses, named after the star signs. Expectantly, they sat in the courtyard. It was cool, a little raining.

Hollydeva looked at the other novices. "Sister Scorpio" was her name now. To her right sat a boy, probably two years older than herself, who wore glasses on his nose and seemed to be thinking all the time, muttering softly as if he were making calculations. So this was "Brother Sagittario". To her left sat a girl who seemed to be the oldest of them. She appeared to be a young woman with long brown hair loose and flowing over her shoulders. She was strikingly feminine in shape. Hollydeva noticed the impulse to tease "Sister Libra" in a darker corner of her brain.

On the right edge, the ferry boy, now probably called "Piscio", winked at her. They were both the youngest and smallest of the twelve novices.

Then the Abbess returned to the novices. At the back of the court, eight nuns and monks were approaching, each carrying a banner hanging from a flagpole. The end of the flagpole was put into a foot left in the ground. Hollydeva saw that symbols or shapes were embroidered on the banners.

The nuns and monks were probably masters, as they had better cut dresses. On the edges, these robes were deposited in different colors. The cowls themselves were black, brown, gray, or white.

»The monastery on Linden Island consists of the Abbey and eight Houses, which we call "Yanas". Yana is a word from the holy language of Sanskryt, and it means "vehicle". The House or Yana shall be your vehicle on the spiritual path, that you have chosen. The prior or prioress, the masters, adepts, and novices of that Yana are special to you! They are the main part of the vehicle that will support you on your way to the final state!

»One of these Yanas will be your home! You'll spend most of your time here in your home house, your Yana! Furthermore, you will spend two or three weeks in each of the other seven Yanas during the first 12 months! And you will insert yourself in the Yana that you are living in, into the ways of thinking and living of that Yana, whatever Yana it is at that time!

»For the first month you will be allowed to make your choice, and this choosing has a special meaning! The Yana you select now is your home, to which you will return from the visits of other Yana at the end of each visit!

»Behind me are standing the eight Masters of the eight Yanas of Linden Island! These will now present their Yanas to you! You can then pick! According to experience, all novices want to move to different Yanas, so that all Yanas at the end of the choosing have one, two, or three novices.

»It could be that you all want to go to the same Yana! That would not be in the best sense of the monastery. We need a good distribution. So do not be afraid to pick the Yana of which you think that it might be unpopular. We usually learn the most where it is difficult and uncomfortable! But since the choosing will be secret, and you do not know what the others will choose, we will trust in the harmony which is flowing through you and all that is responsible for an appropriate distribution!

»Dear masters, please introduce to us the eight Yanas, the eight families of the island!«

The twelve novices sat in a semicircle with their faces to the main building of the monastery. The eight masters stood with their backs to the main building.

The person on the far left began the short performance. He was an elderly man with a long beard and a knobby stick on which he was leaning. His robe was brown with yellow edges.

»Novices! My name is Master Alyapis! I introduce the Yana of Bees to you! We, the masters and adepts in the Yana of Bees, believe in nature. In nature, we see, hear and feel living beings. We are friends with tree spirits and flower devas, with the waters and the clouds, the stones and the animals. Members of the Yana of the Bees are also called shamans of the right-hand path, medicine men, medicine women. We strive to be good and gentle and eager like the bees!«

»Thank you, Master Alyapis!« Abbess Tilia exclaimed.

A woman, positioned on the extreme right side, stepped forward. Her black robe had a silvery hem. She was wearing a skull in her hand. »Greetings, novices! I introduce to you the Yana of the Ravens! We, too, are shamans! We, however, pay homage to the dark forces of nature, decay, fall, autumn, and winter! We can do great deeds with the powers of nature! I am Maestra Corvanya!«

Hollydeva was aware that the Beemaster's speech had been more sympathetic, and she already had reference to the bees. But she herself was not very good and industrious, and she thought she might be better off in the Raven's Yana. That Maestra looked dark and had poisonous eyes, but perhaps she would be able to understand her.

A man, a master, who had stood to the left of Maestra Corvanya, now advanced. »I am showing you the Serpent's banner! We, in the Yana of Serpents, know many

152

Gods! All the forces in this world are represented by Gods whom we can call, whose powers we can ascertain! And like my neighbor, the mistress of Ravens, we, the Snakes, like the dark forces, the dark Gods. We teach the curses, bring sacrifices of all kinds. And laugh at how our Gods are outshining each other and trying to get rid of each other with intrigues. Choose me if you want to have fun! We are the Snakes, and I am Master Anguinaga!«

Master Anguinaga wore a black robe like Maestra Corvanya, but it was decorated with a green border. He appeared like a snake to Hollydeva, poisonous and sneaky.

»Thank you, Anguinaga!« said Tilia and pointed to the second Maestra from the left side.

»I greet you. I am Maestra Sura, from the Yana of the Angels. We also pray to the many gods! And we consult the messengers of the gods, the angels. We pray, offer sacrifices, perform secret rituals. The gods give to us, they test us, they enable us!«

Hollydeva looked at the eight Yana Masters and found that Maestra Sura was clearly the prior or prioress who looked most sympathetic. »But I am the one who does not pick the sympathetic,« said Hollydeva to herself. The Serpent, however, appeared too creepy for her. Maestra Sura was wearing a light gray robe with gold ornaments.

To the right of Maestra Sura stood a white-dressed Maestra, who now stepped forward and held up her banner, which showed a lamb. Her robe was marked by a black border.

»Bless the Lord, the OneGod. We at the Yana of Agnus, the Yana of the Lamb, pay tribute to God, the God Almighty, the Taodharma. Everything is one, and one God rules over everything, Godfather or Godmother, as you will. Come to us, we are masters of the most impressive worship services! My name is Urana!«

»We, too, believe in a single God, the symbol of all creation,« roared the Master, who was the third from the right. »We are the Tigers! But this one God is not merciful or good! He is cruel and challenging! My name is Master Baghora!«

Baghora wore black with yellow stripes, almost imitating a tiger's fur. He made a strong impression on Hollydeva.

Beside him stood a very young Mistress, who jumped slightly prancing. »Hello. Allow me to bring to you the Dragon Yana. We want to discover ourselves, as we do not believe in any gods outside of us! So we are about to realize our true self, to grow above ourselves! We, the Dragons, fly high, higher than the gods. I'm Maestra Shyena!«

Shyena was dressed in a gray cowl with a purple edge.

Left of her stand a gentleman, dressed in gray with turquoise, who proclaimed, »We do not believe in Gods; we are the scientists, the alchymists. We explore the laws of Existence inside and around us all! This is the Yana of the Dolphins! The name indicates that we encourage pleasure! My name is Professor Griseo!«

Hollydeva was startled. The professor's name reminded her of the professor who had spoken at the meeting with the Nacharya. He could also be one of the alchymists! She had to watch out! Alchymists and wizardeurs were also represented here!

Will You Follow Me?

Abbess Tilia, then, asked them to take a good look at the masters and the banners, and then decide which Yana they wanted to start with and live in.

Hollydeva thought, »Bees are close and dear to me.« But Maestra Corvanya of the Ravens was probably more similar to her own attitude. The Snakes paid homage to the polytheists and appeared to have to be approached with caution. There she would be as little at home as with the Angels, even if Maestra Sura appeared to be so bright and friendly. She had grown up with the OneGod, she had believed unto now. Lamb or Tigers? She wanted to be as good as a Lamb, but she knew that she could not be that easy, and that the Lambs would be rather frightened of her. Tiger, that was interesting! Master Baghora seemed powerful and strong. She certainly would not want to go to the Dolphins, which were represented by an alchymist, as her home. And the Dragons, Maestra Shyena? She could also feel some attraction with her.

She thought for a while. Then Hollydeva wrote "Raven" on the piece of paper that the Maestra had given her.

All the papers were gathered, and the nun who seemed to be the Abbess's assistant pushed the novices to their newly elected Yana Masters.

When all stood by the banner they had chosen, the Abbess exclaimed, »You have chosen well and divided yourself well. Each Yana now has one or two novices. May you all have your home here! May you grow and learn in the Yana you have chosen, and finally become Lord Master or Lady Maestra!«

Like her, the dark-skinned novice, "Sister Ariëa", had picked the Ravens and eyed her disparagingly.

Hollydeva looked up at Maestra Corvanya, beside whom they now stood. The Maestra turned to them and then went down on one knee to be at eye level with them!

She turned to Hollydeva first.

»I have heard of you! You are the daughter of the Grand Inquisitor of the Nine and the local Garden Maestra! Welcome to the Ravens! What is your name?«

»I'm to be called Scorpio now!«

»Scorpio, that's good!«

Then Maestra Corvanya turned to Ariëa.

»I welcome you to the Ravens. What is your name?«

»I am Ariëa here!«

»Ariëa, ram. You are a Raven now! Why did you choose this yana?«

»Ravens are as black as I am, at least on the outside!« replied Ariëa.

Corvanya laughed and rose, giving them further direction, »You will join me in the Yana of Ravens tomorrow morning! Then I will show you our world! You will like it! I sometimes do darkly. Do not let it frighten you!«

»I was my father's helper at Georgeburg!« whispered Scorpio.

»Good, then I can't scare you! Do as I tell you, Ariëa and Scorpio, and we'll get along just fine! And if you get mad at me, let that be a sign that I've hit a sore spot that we can use or heal! Agreed?«

Scorpio and Ariëa nodded.

Maestra Corvanya turned back to Hollydeva, Scorpio.

»Do you agree?«

»Yes, I agree?«

»Will you follow me?«

»Yes, I will follow you!«

»Even if you don't know where the flight is going?«

»I will follow, Maestra!«

»Very well. The Ravens and I, we will protect you with our lives! I swear it!«

Scorpio seemed impressed.

»Will you follow too, Ariëa?«

Ariëa had probably just been trying to categorize her impressions seemingly special position of her fellow novicess, feeling somewhat sidelined.

She looked the Maestra in the eye and put her strength into her answer, »Yes, Maestra, I will follow!«

»And will you assist Scorpio here, now that you are in a swarm together?«

155

Maestra Corvanya had probably noticed that Ariëa was eyeing this sister Scorpio beside her suspiciously.

»As she will stand by me!«

Maestra Corvanya looked mockingly, shook her head with a sigh, and indicated to Ariëa that she was asking something of her without expecting anything in return from the other raven novicess.

»Now go to dinner with the other novices, Ariëa and Scorpio! I will see you to-morrow! Keep a distance from the other novices! Be friendly and cooperative! But bind yourselves to none and nothing!«

Chapter 16:
Eleven Fellow Companions.
Older Novices. Einar

Eleven Fellow Companions

The twelve novices gathered in the refectory, the dining room, of the novice's house.

They ate a stew in silence. The Novice Prioress, Maestra Fraxina, told them after the meal that they should introduce themselves to each other and choose a speaker or spokeswoman. They should do this on their own. She would return in an hour with the novices of the second and third year, from which they would each receive a tutor.

Hollydeva looked around. She was sure that she would not be chosen and that she should not start talking.

A strong boy began, »We are the lion. "Brother Leo" we shall be called. Otherwise, our name is Bjarkerik. We are the son of a king in the north. Where we are from, it is usually pretty cold. We shall be king one day. Therefore, we should learn a lot here and, above all, no longer feel so entitled due to our origin.«

He laughed, a little unsure. Most of the others laughed with him, asking themselves whether he was aware that he was talking about himself in the plural form, which was a bit embarrassing.

The strong girl with the red-blond curls taunted, »We will cast out the entitledness! But just as you look, you will not have to put up with a lot of spanking. This makes it more difficult. But it would be worth it!«

Leo laughed and nodded. »And who are you?«

The redhead turned to the circle of the twelve novices and introduced herself, »Here I shall be, "Sister Aquaria", the "water-bearer woman". I have chosen the Yana of the Dolphins. I would like to know truth. Truth without belief and superstition. Professor Griseo seemed to be a good teacher for me. I come from the Brytish island, that is the kind of mainland, which you see when you look over the seas on the western side of Linden Island!«

Hollydeva wanted to warn her of Professor Griseo and the alchymists. But the others should not know yet where she was coming from and what she had learned already. And maybe Griseo was not allied to Rubedo. She liked Aquaria, impressed by her strong appearance.

»Let us all here and today speak our earlier names. And then we'll just address each other by the novice names!«

They all looked surprised at Hollydeva. She herself was surprised at how calmly and convincingly she had spoken.

»You are right,« agreed Aquaria. »My name before and probably one time again is Ellianne!«

They all looked at Hollydeva now, and so she said, »I was called Hollydeva, and now I am "Sister Scorpio", the Scorpion. I previously lived with my father at a castle on the mainland, east from here. But we had to flee! I came here because my mother is the garden maestra at this monastery! But my mother and I do not like each other! I hope you learn good from her. I have gone to the Ravens, and I will learn how to talk to the birds!«

The others laughed. They did not know that she could talk to the bees and plants already.

»I already knew Hollydeva, oh, sorry, Sister Scorpio. My father and I have rowed her with a boaty. My name is Pierre, and now I am Piscio, the little fishling, the tiny Bee!«

Hollydeva looked kindly at little Piscio. He had introduced himself well. Did he use these diminutives to ask for protection? She would protect him. But others probably would feel provoked.

The young woman, with her flowing brown hair, introduced herself, »I am Sister Libra here. Previously I was Vimala. My mother is a midwife in a small town on the continent. I went to Yana Agnus! I will serve, I will be close to the OneGod! Like a rose in his garden!«

Aquaria asked that they should leave their religious preferences from before out. They would probably have enough to discuss. All agreed. Libra felt reprimanded and would try to get back at Aquaria one day.

A lean girl with a very dark, almost black skin took the floor. »He, listen to me! I was going to say that I seem to be a seeker of the dark side of nature, and that's why I went to the Yana of Ravens. We go together!«

She gave a nod to Scorpio, but it didn't seem like she was excited about this companion or competitor. Hollydeva found her attitude kind of condescending or even aggressive.

»I am Sister Ariëa now. Before, I was Cita Yaboah. I come from a country far in the south where nature mostly is sand and stones. My father is a scholar who has heard of this monastery! He wants me, when my time is over, to tell him everything so that he knows all that is being discussed in the world.«

»We are far from the world! How are you going to learn what's going on in the world?« Hollydeva was indignant or astonished. For she had just fled to this small island to be protected from the events of the world.

»Are you dissing me? What the hell do you know, Scorpio!« Ariëa responded with some disdain.

»Believe me, my dad knew what he was doing when he sent me here! A lot of information strings are running together at this place! All the powers of this world, all true powers, have their representatives here and exchange their information!«

Hollydeva knew immediately that Ariëa was right, and that she herself possibly had been sent to this island for other reasons than she had thought!

»Zss. The little scorpion ran to her mommy in the garden and finds it as dangerous in the garden as it is in the world!« The ironic voice of the slender, pale woman without hair, her skin covered with tattoos, guided the attention of the other eleven to herself. Hollydeva smelt an enemy whose first address to her confirmed this assumption.

The tattooed pale hissed, »Zss. I am called Sister Gemina, "Twins". I went to the Yana of Snakes. Outside these walls I am called "Dirt". You need nothing more to know about me!«

»Mio dio, we do not want to know more,« growled a boy, who was sitting next to her. She looked at him poisonously and Hollydeva's sympathies for him grew, even though he was more of a fat boy.

»I am now Brother Tauro. That fits. I'm like a bull. Or mostly like an osso, an ox.«

His self-irony arrived well. The other novices laughed.

»I come from a rich merchant's house. We are acting over many seas and have caravans in all countries. But I'm more of a sognatore, a dreamer. I was interested in the stories of holy men and women more than the prices of goods. But my father is a very wise man. He said I should learn more about stories and saints. This would be the best way to find trading partners and friends in distant countries. At home in Ytaly my name was Fibonardo, after a famous traveler and mathematician of ancient times.«

»The one who invented the number zero,« Brother Leo interjected, probably to interrupt the flow of words from chubby Tauro.

Tauro, however, did not let himself be puzzled. »Si, the one with zero, amico Leo. I go to the Angels, to the Yana of the many gods!«

»Me too,« interjected a black-skinned boy who noticeably spoke the "a" vowel prolonged. »I am now "Caapricorno"! I am supposed to be like a mountain climbing animal, I guess. You can say "Caapri" to me. I come from Afrycaa. We have many gods there, and I will get to know some new ones. At home, I am called Ndenju.«

Chubby Tauro and more athletic Capri looked at each other. They seemed to have come to some instantaneous sympathy and understanding.

The boy, who was sitting to the right of Hollydeva, the bespectacled calculator, introduced himself, »I am Sagittario, "The Shooter". Otherwise, I'm Jack. I am a programmer and researcher. I will develop the science of faith here. I am also with the Dolphins like Aquaria.«

A skinny boy, who had watched everything with waking eyes, spoke up, »Excuse me, I would like to introduce myself.«

»Shoot,« Leo sitting next to him boomed and punched him lightly on the upper arm.

The skinny boy looked a bit unsettled, but then took courage. »Vertigo! Oh no, Virgo! I am now Brother Virgo, the Virgin.«

When he revealed his comedic talent by imitating a virgin gaze, all clapped applauding, shouting for more.

»I was part of a traveling show group. We heard about this island and were allowed to play here last month at the invitation of the abbess. She asked my parents to leave me here. I would become a gifted mystic. Agra!«

He pronounced the word "mystic" in a creepy and exaggerated manner, and everyone laughed again.

»I was in the Gaudio squad, and here I am a Bee like the other dwarf over there!« He pointed to the slightly sourish Piscio.

»Well, I hope I do not have to protect Piscio from that joker!« Hollydeva thought.

»Who has not spoken yet?« Aquaria looked around, then nodded to a somewhat timid Asyan-looking girl who was sitting to the left of Leo. He wanted to box her on the upper arm as well, but Aquaria's eyes held him.

The shy girl said in a low voice, »I from Chyna. I cook. Master Ulmus brought me here for being cook. Masters like Chynese cooking. But first shall learn mysticism and be novice! Name Lin Tao, now Cancra, Sister of Cancer. Me Tiger.«

»Hmm, Cancra sounds kind of sick!« pondered Aquaria. »We'll call you "Shrimp"!«

Everyone shouted "Shrimp!", until the little Chynese girl also laughed. »Good, I Shrimp,« she agreed.

»We are to vote for a speaker,« Libra shouted.

»I'm suggesting Leo. He is a king, he can stand up!« responded Aquaria.

But Leo shook his head. »No, we should rather learn to fit ourselves in. We think you're the best choice, Aquaria!«

»More candidates?« Libra asked.

No one proposed anyone else, Libra asked, »Who is in agreement?« All the other eleven raised their hands.

Libra announced. »Then Aquaria is our spokeswoman from now on! Bravo Aquaria!«

And "Bravo Aquaria!" was repeated by all of them!

The Older Novices

Maestra Fraxina came back, followed by a total of thirteen novices.

»Well, did you choose a spokesman?« she asked the round of twelve novices.

Leo answered, »Yes, we have unanimously elected Sister Aquaria to be our spokeswoman!«

»Good. Then I would like to introduce you to the other inhabitants of the novice's house! Some of them will take you to the residence of your chosen Yana tomorrow. Others will tell you what you have to do here in the novice's house! You have to follow the instructions of the older brothers and sisters!«

Then she asked three novices to step forward. »I'll introduce to you the three novices of the third year. The novices of the third year are named after the first twelve cards of the Greater Arcana of Tarot cards!«

Maestra Fraxina touched one, as Hollydeva found, very beautiful young lady at her upper arm. »I'll introduce to you Sister Bagatto! We took the Ytalian names of the Tarot cards! Bagatto, that is the card "The Magician". She is resident at Yana Tiger.

161

Bagatto is currently the top novice here in the house, and I'm glad about it. When Bagatto goes on like this, she shall be abbess of Linden Island Monastery in a few years' time!«

Hollydeva saw Sister Bagatto blushing slightly. The top novicess indicated a slight curtsy and took a step back.

Maestra Fraxina gave the boy a sign. He, too, stepped forward and bowed. »Here we have another hope of the local academy! Or is he the greatest misfortune here? Brother Amantes, "The Beloved", from the Yana of Angels!«

»And the third is our Sister Giustizia, "Righteousness", from the Yana of Agnus!«

Sister Righteousness made a bow, but she looked sharply at the novices, and Hollydeva felt particularly patterned. She felt uncomfortable with her. She wondered how Baldar could have fallen in love with that novicess.

»Now I'll introduce to you the novices of the second year,« announced Maestra Fraxina.

Hollydeva was surprised. Where were the other novices of the third year? Had so many given up? Was the training so challenging or even dangerous?

The ten novices of the second year were standing in a row.

»Tell your names and Yanas,« demanded Fraxina. »They are named after the cards of the Major Arcana, second series, also in Ytalian.«

On the left stood a slender boy who began. »I am Brother Matto, Yana of Bees.« Then he made, »Humm, humm,« and fluttered with the forearms. "The Fool", obviously.

The next one was like him, slim and cheeky. »Brother Appeso, "The Hanged Man", Yana of Ravens.« And he imitated a man hanging from the gibbet, with his head tilted to the side.

Hollydeva looked at Appeso more closely, as he was in a Yana with her. She would probably have more to do with him. He had eyes that watched everything closely, she noticed. Her eyes met, and she held his gaze. Appeso nodded, as if seeing her again after a long time.

Third came a girl with a round face and blond hair. »Sister Sole, "The Sun". Yana of Angels.« She blew open her cheeks, pressing air through her lips as if she were farting.

Then came a dark-haired, rather stern-looking one, »Sister Giudicia, "The Last Court". Yana of Serpents!« She made an appropriate hissing sound.

The boy next to her shouted, »I am also in the Yana of Snakes. My name is Brother Mondo!«

Hollydeva liked Mondo for not making any grimaces.

The next brother from the series of novices of the second year was as serious. »I am Brother Temperan from the Yana of Agnus! I am the current speaker of the novices of the second year! May it be better for you than us!«

»Hey, hey, Temperan, do not scare the little ones,« the athletic boy next to him snapped. »Torre, "The Tower", Yana of the Tigers!«

A lascivious redhead, who had her arm into his, added. »I am Sister Luna, the moon woman in the Yana of the Tigers!«

»I am Brother Bastoni, also "Ass di Bastoni", the "Ace of Wands". Yana of the Dolphins.« He made a somewhat unfortunate impression, seemed to be not particularly happy with his neighbors from the Yana of the Tigers.

The last one in the row, far right, he or she, looked a bit mockingly and did not seem to want to say anything. Fraxina cut short and introduced, »Diavolo, Yana Dragon, speaks only with Dragons! And we still have no word to replace the words brother or sister in the case when one of us is both or none. Diavolo, of course.

»The novices of the second year will look after you and guide you, especially those who are from your Yana. The novice's house here is run by Sister Bagatto together with Sister Giustizia and Brother Amantes!«

Dormitories

At ten o'clock, they were to go to sleep. The novices of the first year had two bedrooms. "Dormitorium Puerorum" and "Dormitorium Puellarum" stood at the doors. Boys and girls would live in separate dormitories.

Hollydeva joined the other five novicesses into their dormitory. There were six beds in the room. So here they would live together for a year or even longer! Each of them six took a bed. Libra chose the one on the left window, Aquaria the right one near the door. Gemina went to the left at the door. Hollydeva took the bed between Aquaria and the dark-skinned Ariëa, who probably wanted to be at the window. The little Shrimp took the bed between Aquaria and Gemina.

Everyone had a small shelf and a cupboard at the bed where they could place their things. She did not have much. Moreover, each had a wardrobe.

The boy's room was opposite. In addition to the dormitories, they each had a washroom with showers. The water was basically cold. But Sister Bagatto, the "big sister" in the novice's house, had come and said that she had made sure that the kettles were heated so that they could have hot water and clean themselves thoroughly after the days outside at the test ground.

At ten, a bell would ring, and the night rest would begin.

The Cellerar had given them clothes. Their things brought with came into a bag. They would be washed and kept. All of the novices had received what they needed for writing and washing themselves.

They had been allowed to keep three things that were important to them personally.

Hollydeva had not been able to save any such things from Georgeburg Castle, and she watched the other five for a time.

Shrimp had the bed facing her. She was concentrating on clearing little bottles into the drawer of her cupboard. Surely, these were Chynese cooking elixirs.

Aquaria chose her place between Hollydeva and the door. She was quickly ready to leave and wrote something into the writing-book which she had received. »She probably takes notes about her voters,« Hollydeva said to herself. Aquaria seemed to be a politician.

Ariëa looked out the window. On the shelf she had put a wooden figure.

Libra watched her opponents out of the corner of her eye, while she had placed her mirror on the shelf to brush her long hair thoroughly.

Hollydeva wondered whether she was more likely to be on Aquaria's or Libra's side. »I'll stir up some animosity between them,« she thought amused. »I'll have to take care that Libra is not becoming Aquaria's best friend!«

Then there was Gemina. The bald enemy had laid two poles on her shelf. They were probably made of hardwood. Hollydeva had heard when the Cellerar wanted to take them away. He had ordered, »No weapons in the novice's house!« And Gemina had insisted that they were musical instruments from her home country. Their eyes met. They both looked steady, without blinking or wavering. Gemina was dangerous, and she would be the one Hollydeva wanted to have at her side, if she came to any fight with wizardeurs or alchymists or demons or the novices of the second year.

Then there was a knock on the door and Amantes stuck his head in. »There's a young man who wants to be bitten by Scorpio,« he said.

»Astrello!« Hollydeva thought, happy. She jumped out of the room.

»They're waiting downstairs,« Amantes shouted.

»They? Several?«

164

»Yes two! They say, they know you!«

Einar, Brother

When Hollydeva came to the door of the novice's house, there were two strong young men standing there, her two brothers.

Baldar had said goodbye only a few days ago. But she had not seen Einar for a long time. He was tall, strong and radiated a calm, which she had already admired as a little girl.

»Einar! Baldar!«

»Little sister! Let me hug you!«

But Hollydeva backed away. »Why do you want to hug me? You abandoned me at that time! You left me alone!«

Einar lowered his head. »Yes, you are right. Mother had suddenly told us that we had to pack our things! We went! After about a kilometer I asked her what was with you, why you did not come along! She answered that you belong to your father, who would pick you up soon! I protested and said that I did not want to go without you. Baldar will confirm that! But she insisted that it had to be like that!«

Baldar nodded, affirming his brother's version of that day.

»Holly, I'm sorry. I am really sorry! I hope you have made the best of it! I want to be your big brother again!«

Hollydeva saw the honest depression in his eyes. She stepped forward and snuggled into his arms. She felt Baldar leaning against her from the side.

Her tears came. She had missed her brothers, and it felt good to know that the two had not forgotten her.

»My name is Scorpio now.«

Einar and Baldar parted from her. Einar laughed, »Yes, I once was "Aprilus"! We were named after the monthly names! And Baldar became novice a year later, and was called "Iwain", after the knight of legendary Arthur.«

»And what are your names now?«

»Well, you can continue to call us Einar and Baldar! We are, so to speak, the secret bond of the three siblings! Otherwise, we are both adepts at Yana Agnus, the Yana of the Lamb!«

Baldar said, »From Einar and Aprilus, he became "Brother Avela", the "Oat Brother". I am the "Brother of Love-grass", "Eragrostis"!«

»We can not really get rid of our mother, it seems!«

»Mother is a maestra in the Yana of the Lamb?«

»Yes, she is the garden maestra of the entire monastery. All masters are also in a Yana or from a Yana. Mother like us is in the Yana Agnus. But she is a little dissatisfied with Prioress Urana, as for her the OneGod is the OneGoddess. Which Yana felt most attractive to you, little sister?«

»I am in the Yana of Ravens!«

»Uh, how creepy!«

Baldar added, »On Sundays there are always competitive games between the Yanas happening. I think the Ravens are afraid only of the Tigers! It is a strong Yana with a strong Master!«

»Thank you, Baldar!«

»What attracted you to the Ravens?«

»Some druyds and fire maiden helped us to escape from Georgeburg Castle! A swarm of bees had led us to them. They were probably a kind of shamans. They impressed me! And since I already knew the bees and Maestra Corvanya seemed to be stronger than Master Alyapis to me, I landed with the Ravens!«

»Yes, you'll have an intense time! Sometime in this first year, you are also with us! This may get you bored!«

»Your Maestra has praised the services!«

»Yes, we have beautiful worship services!«

Einar exclaimed, »And you were with the Nine, the Nacharya! They also pay homage to the OneGod!«

Hollydeva nodded, »Yes, that's true! But ultimately, my impression of some of the Nine Nacharya was not the best! It turned out that they behaved more like politicians, and without our father they would be even less! I hope he's all right.«

»The father? Oh, Baldar has said that he is ill and at Granna Algard's Refuge!«

»Yes, the wizardeurs have hurt him very much! But he is strong!«

»And our grandmother is the best healer!«

»So you were close to our father?«

»Yes, very close! He has taught me many things!«

»That's nice! I wish I could see him again!«

»If Baldar could reach to the Refuge, you must be able to do it as well!«

»Yes, that's right! I'll ask Maestra Urana for permission to leave.«

»It was great to see you! Come back here soon!«

»Sleep well, sister!«

»Sleep well, Scorpio! Tell us if you need help!«

Hollydeva hugged Einar and Baldar. She felt calmness passing from them to her.

»Faith in the OneGod gives a certain kind of unconditional trust,« she thought.

She went back into the novice's house. Did the others also have allies or relatives here? She would have to watch them.

Gemina and Ariëa looked out of the window as she entered the girl's dormitory.

»Zss. You have sweet brothers! Will you introduce us?« Then the two warriors laughed like stupid young girls. Hollydeva shook her head incredulously.

»She does not want us in her family,« Ariëa snapped.

»Be quiet! I want to sleep now!« Libra growled.

Aquaria, who already acted like the boss of the novices of the first year, supported this request with a strict kind of face expression.

So Hollydeva had to let go of further talking to these two future "sisters-in-law" and also lay down.

There was a bell in the courtyard which stroke ten times announcing the beginning of the night.

The day had been long and eventful, and they slept soundly and quietly.

Third Part:
The First Week on
Linden Island as Novice

Chapter 17:

Appeso.
Maestra Corvanya. King Krama

Bloodday (Tuesday)

At six o'clock, Sister Bagatto called into the dormitory of the novicesses of the first year, »Get up, novicesses!« In the washroom there was now only cold water for the morning freshening.

Then they were supposed to make their beds, fold the blankets accurately, and arrange their things. The dormitory was quickly swept out.

In the refectory, the dining room, there were tea and small sandwiches. In the back of the refectory was a kitchen and Hollydeva saw the woman, who were the cook of the novice's house, and an assistant hurrying around, busy to ensure that the novices were nurtured.

At seven o'clock, Ariëa and Hollydeva were to meet Brother Appeso at the front door of the novice's house. Appeso was already waiting.

»Come, you should make the best impression on your first day with Maestra Corvanya! If she has the impression that you do not have discipline, she will be happy to teach you! She is the strictest of all the masters on the island! And according to what happened to the novicess in the year before, she takes things even more serious at the beginning of the training!«

On their way to the Yana of Ravens, Hollydeva asked the "Hanged Man", »What happened to the novicess from the year before?«

Appeso answered, »She was called "Papessa", "Sister Papessa", the "High Priestess".«

»And, what has happened?«

»You will have noticed that the ranks of the novices of the third year are very much thinned! Of twelve novices, only three are left! The others died last year when we repulsed an attack! The novices of the third year have heroically defended the monastery and sacrificed themselves! From my year two novices ran away, as staying here appeared too dangerous for them! But there has been no attack since then.«

»Attack! By whom?«

»I do not know exactly. There were demons and creatures from the sea. We, the novices of the first year, had just been here for two weeks, and the masters ordered us to seek shelter in the cellar of the novice's house. We only saw and heard that it cracked and flashed. It is said that the nacharyas wanted to destroy the monastery, since it does not propagate the OneGod properly!«

»But the OneGod is propagated here, too!«

»Yes, but just as one worldview among several. The Nacharya do not like this indifference. I have just heard so.«

»The Nacharya want to destroy the Linden Island?! I can not believe that!«

»What do you know?! Do you even know who the Nacharya are?«

Hollydeva would almost have answered in a streak of anger. But she'd better not reveal where she came from. She noticed that she still had the impulse to defend the Nacharya.

And yes, the Nacharya were nine and divided. With Tatu Njena she had flown in the balloon over the Yrth. She had had a protector with Nacharya Peredur in the fight against the wizardeurs. And with Daman, her uncle, she now had a connection. The Bhogi wanted her to be his successor. The Nononn had told her quite a bit about the Nacharya, and when she left, had told her to get an education here on Linden Island. Only Rokudan Aoi and Quavert had attacked her. And Saphed seemed to be a particular problem for all of them. Who was missing from the list? Oh yes, Achmar. He was still a stranger to her.

They reached the building that hold the Yana of the Ravens. Like the novice's house and all the other Yana houses, it was a two-story building with a large door and about ten windows on each side of the door, and probably on the back. There was no front yard or trees in front of the building.

Appeso opened the door and they entered an entrance hall. »Wait here,« he instructed them. »Someone will fetch you!«

They stood in the entrance hall for some minutes. Then a young man in a black robe came. He was wearing a black feather in his hair.

»Hello, you must be Sister Ariëa and Sister Scorpio! I am "Brother Jackdaw", adept in the Yana of Ravens! Follow me!«

Prioress Corvanya

They followed Jackdaw up the stairs to the first floor. At the end of the passage to the right Jackdaw knocked at a door and opened it. He encouraged them to enter and shut the door behind them from the outside.

Maestra Corvanya was sitting at a powerful, dark desk. The skull was on the right side of the table. She looked direct and strict at Hollydeva, "Scorpio", and Cita Yaboah, "Ariëa".

»Ariëa and Scorpio, you are our new novicesses! You are eager to learn the way of Ravens!«

Ariëa and Hollydeva nodded, but said nothing.

»Scorpio, I've collected some information about you!«

Now Hollydeva could not hold on to herself, »But not from my mother!? My mother does not like me and just left me five years ago!«

»Psst!« Maestra Corvanya hissed. »You answer when I ask you something! Otherwise, you keep the beak shut! Do you understand that?!«

Hollydeva nodded.

»You answer to a question verbally! Did you understand what I said before?«

»Yes, Maestra Corvanya! I've understood!« Hollydeva had answered more correctly than necessary to express a certain displeasure in this unassailable way. She looked at the Maestra, who had probably registered it. But Corvanya most likely knew she was dealing with a not very simple novice.

»Good. Just follow my rules and we will understand each other! Your mother? Oh, you are the daughter of the gardener. No, the gardener and the ravens do not like each other. I really do not speak to her. Ever so often I have to defend my ravens against her accusations. No, do not worry, I'm an ally if you want to fight your mother! The High Maestra told me that you lived with the Nacharya on Castle Georgeburg and had to flee from there. You freed Astrello and he accompanied you!«

Astrello? Hollydeva remembered that the star boy had to be nearby in the monastery. Why had she not visited him already? She wondered.

»And I've heard that you've probably gathered some knowledge about dark practices. So there are things I do not have to teach you! And you are able and ready to kill!«

Hollydeva became slightly concerned. »I've probably killed a man, but I did not want it!«

»Shh! I did not ask you! We'll talk to each other about it when it's time!«

Corvanya looked at Ariëa. »Do you also have experience in the dark arts and killed men, Ariëa?«

Ariëa shook her head and probably was asking herself whether she had landed in the right yana.

From outside the room there were sounds, drums, to be heard.

»You're going to go there tomorrow like the others! The Raven dance at the beginning of the day! There is a meeting, a meditation, with drums and dancing! We are the wildest group here in the monastery, and we like to remember that at the beginning of the day. Do you like drumming?«

Ariëa laughed confirming, »I am from Afryka!«

Hollydeva was not sure. »I do not know, I've never drummed!«

»Good, then you're dancing! You will have the experience of it! Appeso will take you to the morning ritual of Ravens tomorrow! When that is over, you come here! You do not need to knock at the door, but go in here, sit down on the chair you are sitting on now, be quiet, do not say anything, regardless of what I am doing! Wait until I speak to you and ask you or give you instructions! Did you understand that?«

»Yes, we have, Maestra Corvanya!«

»Do not be too polite! I know this is a form of insubordination!«

Their eyes met and Corvanya nodded. Hollydeva felt she was looked through, but still accepted.

»Do you have a question?«

Hollydeva replied, »Yes. How did Sister Papessa die?«

Prioress Corvanya's eyes narrowed. The question pleased her little.

»Did Appeso, the little talker, make himself interesting?«

Hollydeva was about to protect Appeso, when Maestra Corvanya continued, »A year ago the island was attacked! The masters of the island, their adepts, and initiates, as well as the novices of the second and third years, have defended the monastery against demons coming from the sea! Three masters, eight adepts, six novices of the then third year, and nine novices, who would now be in their third year, have perished! But we have thrown back the attackers, and they have not come back. Not yet!«

»Who were the attackers? Who sent them?«

»Why do you want to know that?«

»Appeso said the Nacharya had ordered the attack to destroy the monastery!«

»Yes, that was a theory we had. But you will surely want to tell me now that there are different points of view among the Nine! And, that there is no reason for the Nacharya to extinguish the monastery!?«

Hollydeva nodded.

»Well, we have good relations with the wizardeurs and with the alchymists, and we know very well that they were not behind the attack!«

She paused, then said, »The monastery has a great adversary! He used to be a master and a teacher here. We call him the "Black Mystic", or "Master Finster"! He has developed a kind of dark mysticism with the experience of nothingness and blackness and the dissolution of all being! The Abbess and the Council of Masters had to dismiss him and send him off! He was not happy about that! It might be that he has the power to call such demons!«

The Black Mystic? Hollydeva shuddered as she imagined this powerful and evil mystic.

»But I do not think the Black Mystic would kill novices! It seems to me that these demons came from a different dimension, another sphere, and we hardly knew anything like this so far. In any case, we have researched and investigated and found nothing within the year. The bodies of the demons killed by us suddenly dissolved, leaving the ruins of some houses and stables, and the corpses of our dead brothers and sisters, as the only proof of this attack.«

Maestra Corvanya rose from her chair. »Come, Ariëa and Scorpio. I'll introduce you to the ravens!«

They followed Maestra Corvanya outside. Behind the house of the Yana of Ravens there started a path leading to the coast.

Raven King Krama

»All schools have secret areas and buildings on the island that you can enter as novices, only accompanied by a master or adept from the respective Yana. This grove of our ravens, no novice of the other Yanas will ever enter. You must know that the eight Yanas compete with each other! We even did have wars. The ravens are one of our most dangerous weapons!«

They came to a small forest consisting of high leaf trees. And there were many nests in the branches. Maestra Corvanya led Ariëa and Hollydeva to the inside of the grove.

Above them, a hundred ravens were flying and croaking with excitement. They flew circles, sat down on branches, came down, flew up again.

»Stand still! They will want to examine you! Be friendly to them! Do not be frightened!«

Ariëa and Hollydeva were standing in the middle of the grove. The first ravens were tugging at their hair, sat down on their shoulders, fluttered around their heads. The two novicesses remained quite still and confided in the Maestra.

Then Maestra Corvanya stood before Hollydeva and grasped her hands. On the shoulder of Maestra Corvanya sat a powerful old raven, who seemed to look at Hollydeva.

»Scorpio, look! I introduce you to the king of our ravens, King Krama. Raven King, here is our new novicess, Sister Scorpio!«

Hollydeva heard his croak and understood, »Good day, Scorpio! We have heard of you and know that you are Hollydeva of Castle Georgeburg. Hello and welcome!«

Hollydeva bowed, and replied, »I salute thee, King of Ravens.«

Corvanya looked surprised. »You can already talk to the ravens?«

»I did not know that I could. But I can speak with the flowers and the bees, so now as well with ravens?«

»That is rare. It is good. What more can I teach you?«

»Bring her to believe in herself,« Krama suggested.

»She seems quite self-conscious,« replied Corvanya.

»She is impatient! She wants to wage war against the alchymists, and now she sits here on an island with quirky nuns and monks!«

»Is that so, Scorpio?«

»Yes, I must admit that I left Castle Georgeburg because I have to fight the alchymists who are tinkering with the inner mechanics of the plants, thus endangering the existence of insects and all life on Yrth. I have to hide here for some time and think about how the fight is going to be led! But yes, it is my mission to fight the alchymists!«

King Krama approved, »Thank you for being so honest with us! But you certainly know that you can not lie to the raven anyway!«

»Yes, I could imagine!«

Maestra Corvanya turned to Ariëa, who had listened intently but also enviously to the conversation with Hollydeva.

»Here, King Krama, I introduce you to another new novicess, Ariëa!«

Krama looked at Ariëa and seemed to shake his head.

»I don't know if she will fit in!« he doubted, probably thinking that only Corvanya and Hollydeva could hear him.

But Ariëa answered loudly, »I don't know if I fit in with you guys either! I was not so attracted to the other yanas! Please accept me! I never understood animal language before! But just now I heard what you said, King of Ravens!«

»Oh, you already know the language of ravens too!? That's unusual. Yet nice. We are eager to get to know you better, Sister Ariëa!«

Krama cawed loudly, »Good novicesses this year!« All the ravens were now cawing loudly and wildly, flying aloft, cheering with sounds that probably sounded unpleasant and shrill to the ears of other creatures.

Maestra Corvanya intervened again, »Good, I'm glad you understand each other! We will think about how to stop the alchymists! Come, Scorpio, Ariëa, we must return! See you soon, King of Ravens, my old friend!«

The ravens were croaking loudly and wildly, flying high, screaming at the sky.

On the way back, Hollydeva said, »Thank you, Maestra. I know now that I have chosen the right yana!«

»Why did you choose us?«

»At the end I was choosing between you, who seemed to me to be the most truthful of the masters, and Maestra Sura, probably the friendliest. I'd then rather have chosen the tougher path.«

»This is the proper choice! Only in overcoming resistances you will develop your full potential!«

Back in the Yana of the Ravens, there was a soup. The Maestra told them that every day after the soup at noon they would go to a different training, together with the other novices of their year. On Bloodday, this would be a lesson at the School of Martial Arts. They were to go past the abbey building. Then they would see a hall on the right, Mars Hall. There, the shifts for the night watch would be assigned as well.

Martial Arts

On her way to the main building, Hollydeva saw a few of the other novices approaching the Hall of Martial Arts. The house of the Ravens was the first on the left, then came the building of the Snakes. The shaggy, tattooed, lanky Gemina just stepped out of the Snake's house and joined her. Ariëa had already gone to the hall.

»Zss, shall we start fighting already?«

»Do you want to feel the scorpion's thorn?«

»Zss, snakes get done with scorpions quickly!«

»Oh yes? But I am guarded by ravens!«

She pointed upwards where a raven hovering above them floated in front of the dark rain-clouds blowing from the sea. There was no protecting snake around. Gemina understood and remained calm.

But after a short while, she could not let the tease go. »Zss, and has your mommy greeted you and took you in her loving arms?«

»No, she has not! And she will not! She, however, will not like you either! She likes flowers and people who are like flowers!«

Gemina laughed. »Zss, be glad that we are both brush! Thistles! Weeds like us are not plucked so easily!«

Hollydeva felt that Gemina's aggression was that of a kindred soul.

They entered the martial arts hall, and after a short time all twelve were present.

Three teachers entered. The oldest of them stood before the novices and shouted, »Welcome to your first hour in Mars Hall! You will learn something here every Bloodday, that you should practice during the following days and months! My name is Brother Abiës! With me, you learn some movements and attitudes! Brother Cedrus here will teach you a more mental form of fighting or defending yourself! And Adept Vigilio here is the head of the night watch and will instruct you afterwards! Forgive Brother, Vigilio is your function, your name is -?«

The slim adept, the night watch man, said his name earnestly, »I am Brother Laburnum.«

»All right, let's start with taking a position and standing!«

Master Abiës showed them how to get the best stand. He let them stand with their knees bent, with their knees pressed. Then he let them feel the flow of energy in their legs. He asked them to lay a hand on the lower abdomen, where the center of gravity of the body would be. He made them connect with the heavens so that they could feel drawn up into standing in a strong, upright position.

Then they stood for a quarter of an hour, with their knees slightly bent. In between, Hollydeva's legs trembled a little, but she felt that with a little practice, she would be able to stand for a long time, as she would be rooted in the earth.

Master Abiës then let them go some more and make prancing movements. In the end, he gave them sticks, with which they were to strike down on logs, which lay on one side of the hall.

»We must strengthen your arms and shoulders,« he explained.

Master Cedrus then gathered them around and explained that beside the physical, the mental component of fighting would be important. »We have to be desiring to win! We need to insist against the attacker! And maybe we have to have quotes or curses with which we can impress the opponents or even paralyze them!«

Hollydeva found that this combat training was extremely inspiring. Cedrus showed them some exercises and made them practice. The best part to Hollydeva was, as they were to face each other in pairs to fight the opposite with the eyes only.

After two hours of training, the Vigilio explained to them that the novices of the first two years had to participate in the night watch. As the attacks of demons could return, it would be very important to observe the sea at any time. The night watch would, of course, also guard the sky and everything. There would usually be a master, two adepts, and two novices at any night watch. There were two shifts, one from ten to half past one o'clock and one from half past one to five.

They were twelve and would be arranged in groups of two on the days of Treeday, Seaday, and Flowerday. So every one would have to don night watch service once a week.

The Vigilio wrote down their names, arranged them for days, and gave Sister Aquaria the list to hang it up in their rooms. The first guard would have to be at ten o'clock at the main building. The second shift would be woken up by the first, and then would have to go to the main building to receive the instructions from the master on duty.

Hollydeva had the second guard in the night from Treeday to Seaday along with Libra.

They then were told to go to the novice's house, where there would be a schoolroom on their floor. Maestra Fraxina would give them instruction in arithmetic, reading, writing, natural science, social science, and languages, mostly Latyn.

There were fish and potatoes for dinner in the refectory. Then they should wash the dishes of all novices and clean the room. Sister Giustizia, the third of the three surviving novices of the third year, supervised them and gave instructions.

Before falling asleep, Hollydeva let the day run before here inner eye and in her dreams she flew with the flock of ravens high above the island.

Chapter 18:
An Oath of Allegiance by the Twelve Novices

Skyday (Wednesday)

On the second morning, Bagatto woke them, the novices of the first year. She explained that from the third morning on would have to get up on their own. Like yesterday: cold washing, dressing, porridge and tea in the dining room, pack writing materials.

Then they saw that some novices of the second year were coming in from outside, sweaty and energetic.

»Hey, scrubs, have you slept well?« asked the unsympathetic Brother Torre.

»Was the tea warm enough for you?« His mate Luna, of course, was not far off, and equally nasty.

»Leave them alone!« shouted Bagatto, the chief novicess. She stepped up to the novices' table and explained, »We get up an hour early every morning and go outside for a run. There is a place where we sit for a quarter of an hour in silence! Then we do some gymnastics and come running back! You may join us!«

»You are doing that voluntarily?«

»Not entirely voluntarily. You will soon find that a little more physical and mental fitness is needed here. That extra exercise will be approved by the masters! It may be good for some extra points!«

»And why do we need those?«

»Well, at the beginning, all are nice and friendly to you. But you will soon notice what happens to those, of whom the masters are of the opinion that they show less talent and less commitment than the others! They are brought to giftedness and dedication! You should spare yourself from that!«

After clearing the tables and washing up and arranging the sleeping place, Hollydeva and Ariëa went with Appeso to Raven Yana House, like at the first day and probably numerous days to come.

»You shall take us to drumming and dancing!«

»Yes, of course. You'll like that! We are wild heathens for an hour every morning!«

»Do the other Yanas act the same?«

»Yes, every Yana has its morning ritual. But the others are much quieter! We Ravens are the wildest. The Bees are the right-hand path shamans, that is, our opposite. They are probably also drumming, but with discipline and violins and trumpets!«

»What does that mean: right-hand path and left-hand path?«

»Well, there are four kinds of divine faith, and of every kind there is a right-hand and a left-hand path. The rights are the orthodox, who set up and obey rules. The lefts are the unorthodox, breaking the rules and understanding mysticism as a kind of combat mysticism!«

»Combat mysticism?«

»Yes, lone fighter mysticism. The right-handed path wanderers are also fighting. But they are more into blessings. We rather use curses. They are the notoriously good and we are the notoriously naughty! You'll know when you're in the other Yanas for two weeks. Next month you will be with the Angels, that is a different world!«

They entered the Raven's house, and Appeso showed them the dressing room. A sister adept gave them a black linen dress like they all were wearing. There were probably all the Ravens gathered, except Maestra Corvanya. Jackdaw and another adept had great drums before them. The dance room was empty of any furniture and had sides about twelve meters long. There were two masters present whose linen dresses had a golden hem. Then there were ten adepts, with a red border at the hem of the linen dress. One of them was the Vigilio, whom they had already met yesterday.

Brother Jackdaw came to Hollydeva and Ariëa. »You're here for the first time. Do not be frightened! We're pretty wild for an hour. In the first quarter of an hour, we make grimaces and just play crazy. Then we jump high and steady to the drum music! This goes for ten minutes! After that, we dance wild and crazy. In the last quarter of an hour, we stand in a circle, hip by hip, and dance and jump together!«

Maestra Corvanya also came in and took a tambourine. She gave a sign and the wild drumming began.

Hollydeva was astonished at the wild, crazy energy in the room, which arose after a short while, when the seventeen dancers were making wild and loud animal sounds or screams and shouts, flinching, jumping, trampling.

In the end, she stood in the circle. She did not know whether there was a master or an adept or another novice beside her. It did not matter, they were all the same. They were all Ravens. She was happy to be one of the Ravens.

Sometimes the circle moved to the left, sometimes to the right, sometimes they jumped up and down, sometimes they swung like trees. Then they bowed back and forth and shouted, »Raven, Raven!« Or they croaked like the black birds.

Hollydeva was bathed in sweat when the hour was over. The linen dresses were thrown into a basket, which a female adept carried away.

When Hollydeva was dry and dressed, she felt the Maestra's hand on her shoulder. »Come,« Corvanya prompted. »Come, Scorpio, Ariëa, let us go back to King Krama!«

Raven Cemetery

They would go into the grove of the Ravens first at every day of the month, and the King of Ravens would inspect and question them.

They would tell the Raven King and their Maestra everything they knew. Hollydeva would state that she had to stop the alchymists. She would warn of the wizardeurs. She would tell how she judged every individual nacharya.

The King of Ravens and Maestra Corvanya would sometimes look concerned.

Hollydeva would no longer feel alone with her task.

On that second day of the novitiate, a Skyday, the light blue Day of Heaven in the middle of the week, Maestra Corvanya went with them over the island.

»We in the Yana of Ravens represent and live the worldview of shamanism in its left-side version, the unorthodox form, as you know!

»Shamanism, that is the original natural religion of all peoples. "Animistic", "Pagan". We are not interested in whether there are many gods or one only god or no god. This Yrth is our god. Nature lives, is animated!

»The ancient people, the primal hordes, hunters and collectors, dealt with whatsoever was there. They needed hunting and gathering luck. So they talked to the souls of the animals and plants and asked for this happiness and asked forgiveness for killing animals and taking fruits, leaves, and roots from plants. Survival in this world is inevitably connected with killing and destroying other living creatures!

»But the people of the tribes wondered where the souls of their dead relatives and friends went! The grief is profound, and you require a consolation like the idea that the souls of these deceased still live in a good place.

»They presented sacrifices to their ancestors, gave them presents, and placed precious things in the grave. We would not be who we are, if not a long chain of ancestors had been before us. They have developed and passed on achievements so that we can pass them on to our children!«

They came to a small grove. Hollydeva saw that it was probably a cemetery.

»Like all these early people, we also practice an ancestral cult. We worship our ancestors and ask for advice, ask for their protection, their intercession with the spirits of animals and plants!

»Since we usually arrive here without parents and remain without family, it is seldom that we bury parents or grandparents here! Scorpio, you may eventually bury your mother here! But I think she will not want to lie in the cemetery of Ravens as she is a Tigress!«

»I thought she was Lamb!«

Corvanya looked surprised and rebuked her sternly, »Speak, when I ask you, and do not talk silly! Your mother is a Tiger! Do not underestimate her! She, too, is on the left side!«

Corvanya pointed to the stones. »Here are the dead Ravens of the last three hundred years! My predecessor as Prioress of Ravens is lying here, Maestra Kaua! She was an impressive woman who showed me the way that I am to show you now!«

Corvanya showed them a rather fresh grave, »Here is our sister, novicess Papessa. She died when the demons attacked a year ago as she faced the demons in front of the Raven Grove. She had just finished the second year of the novitiate. Papessa was a strong, brave woman of Ravens, so promising! I thought she would follow me one day in the position of the Prioress of the Ravens!«

Then Maestra Corvanya spoke to the grave itself, which consisted of a landfill and a wooden carved shield on which "Papessa" and the date of death were to be read. At the bottom, her name from the time before the arrival on Linden Island was written. "Paola Parmain, from Savoy".

»Please sit here for an hour and meditate and see if you find an inner contact with Sister Papessa, novicesses! Then you may wander a little around on your own!

Eat your soup then again in the refectory of the Yana of Ravens and then go to Myrcury Hall! Today there will be lessons on architecture, the sacred geometry.«

Hollydeva and Ariëa nodded and did as the Raven Maestra had told them.

After a few minutes, Hollydeva tried to establish an intimate contact with an unknown entity that was connected with the grave. But there seemed to be nothing. At some point, she sensed to hear something like a warning. It sounded like, »Beware of the demons coming from the sea!« But Hollydeva was almost certain that her imagination produced these words because it would sound interesting.

»Did you hear anything?« she asked Ariëa.

»I'm not sure. I think I imagined something!«

»Yeah, that's how I feel. What did you imagine?«

»A warning. About the demons coming from the sea!«

»Yes, I got that too, or imagined it. Maybe Papessa actually said something to us!«

»After all, those sea demons must have brought her to this tomb!«

Hollydeva and Ariëa looked at each other. The shared shudder created something like a tenuous bond between them.

Art of Geomancy

After lunch, the novices of the first year met in the Hall of the Builders, "Myrcury Hall". Behind the hall, they had seen wooden and stone-made structures.

A master and two adepts entered. One of the adepts was probably a Raven. Hollydeva had seen him at the morning dancing.

»I greet you. I am Master Fagus. I am the master in the faculty of architecture and sacred geometry. Here we have Sister Coryla, who teaches about yantras and mandalas. And Brother Crataegus here is our best stonemason. I myself am a carpenter, a master of wood.

»In this faculty, we deal with the structures. We can generate and control certain energies with structures.

»You will have heard of the free-masons who built cathedrals in the so-called Middle Ages. Actually, however, they have founded mystic secret societies, in which they cultivated and passed on esoteric and occult knowledge.

»One particular branch of this faculty is the science of geomancy. We intend to know how and where certain energy lines run on the surface of the Yrth. We aim to use and influence them. So we would know where our buildings are best placed.«

Master Fagus then ran with them around the island. They were asked to tell him where there were special energies, points, or lines on the Yrth. He wanted to know if the energy coming from the ground was stronger at certain places.

Most of the time during this exploration, the novices did not agree with each other. But almost everyone noticed that the way from the lighthouse, which was on the east side of the island, seemed to be easier to walk to the main house than any other way.

Master Fagus confirmed that the road was on a so-called "Ley Line". He was, however, less satisfied with the places they had identified as energy points.

»But that's why you're here! You will learn about it during your time at Linden Island monastery school!«

They then worked a little with the materials of wood and stone, learned to know the tools, could carve and chisel for a while.

The Oath

After the evening dinner, Aquaria summoned all novices of the first year to the girls' bedroom.

»We've had our first experiences here,« she opened the meeting. »I want us to meet in the evenings and share our experiences as far as we can. I want us to promise to keep together. I want us to understand the confrontations about concepts and worldviews as exercises. But we are not what we believe and think and mean.

»I feel that a special arrangement has brought us together. I want us to swear that we support each other. If there is a dispute, we will clarify it here together and dissolve it! That would be of high value for me! Do you agree with that?«

First, everyone was silent and a little surprised. Aquaria had taken the lead, to which she had been elected, with great strength. Hollydeva found that they were actually all sympathetic, that she herself, and maybe Gemina, were possibly the most disagreeable of these twelve.

Of course, Leo agreed with Aquaria as the first of them, »Yes, we like that! We will do so, Aquaria!«

Libra, who was probably not quite happy with Aquaria being their leader, weighed her head a little.

Hollydeva felt the impulse to speak. »Aquaria, you spoke well, and it would be a good thing if we agree. But you do not know me and I do not know you! You do not know my story! I can not promise that we are not mortal enemies!«

»Oh, that sounds dangerous,« Leo laughed ironically.

»Zss. You do not look like the most dangerous of us, little Scorpio!« Gemina muttered.

»Yes, maybe you're more dangerous than me, Gemina! But I do not know how long I am here. I'm on a mission! And I'm hiding here! My enemies are the alchymists and the wizardeurs! And this hostility has already claimed sacrifices! And perhaps two or three of the nacharyas, at whose castle I have lived, are my enemies and are looking for me.«

»You have lived in the castello of the Nacharya?« well-fed Tauro asked incredulously.

»You said you lived with your father in a castle,« Aquaria added.

»Yes, I said that. My father is or was the Grand Inquisitor of the Nacharya! I was his assistant! We have lived on Castle Georgeburg! We have been attacked when the Nacharya wanted to ban the alchymists from certain experiments and changes on the plants! Outside, on the mainland, a great war begins, and we may be on different sides!«

Now everyone was silent. They had heard of clashes and threats of warfare. They felt that Sister Scorpio was talking the truth.

Piscio wanted to jump to support Hollydeva, »I'm small, but on your side, Scorpio!«

»Thank you, Piscio. But maybe I am lying to you! Be careful with your support! You owe me nothing! You have helped me to come here safely, and I owe you something, at least something of my truth! All of you deserve the truth! But you will not even be able to tell me what I would find in the secret groves or temples of your Yanas!«

Aquaria agreed, »That's right, we all have secrets after one day only! But that should not prevent us from being there for each other, to keep together! That would be significant, I am sure!«

Ariëa gave a sign, »I want to say something! If war is, and we are on different sides, we can still be friends! War is not real! It's a mistake! As we sit here, we are youths who are at a school and learn! We belong together! Let us decide that before we harm, injure, or even kill another of us, we ask ourselves whether the reason why we are doing this, is so holy and important that our deed is justified!«

Aquaria nodded. »That sounds right! I thank you, Scorpio, for making us aware that we live in a world where everything is not good and easy! We will have to make decisions! We will have to keep secrets from each other! But I swear to you and everyone that I will always see and always remember that I am sitting here with you, and that you have a heart like me and you are a novicess like me and I will support you in your way as far as I can!«

Hollydeva felt a barely known grasp. How did Aquaria do that? She felt a bond between them that she had not known before! Aquaria tried hard and worked hard, and she had to honor it.

»I swear, I'll always remember how we're sitting here! I will always help each of you along the way, as far I can!«

And one by one spoke in the same manner, which was solemn and holy.

Sagittario had written down their words. »Let us find a symbol which reminds us of this evening, that no one else will decipher and possibly destroy! I suggest that we change the hands of the watch and keep it interchanged!«

»How? What do you mean?«

Sagittario gave Virgo a sign, and together they opened the big wall clock, which stood in the girl's bedroom, and exchanged the hands. From now on, the big hand would display the hour and the small hand the minutes.

»We're doing the same thing with the clock in our room!«

»The twelve digits on a dial of a watch are like petals! They may remind us that we belong together, that our fate is a common destiny, that we want to bring peace to this world together!« Libra wanted to have the final word and had spoken it.

All nodded and agreed. They sat in a circle, clasped their hands, and sang the song of Linden Island,

»On the island of the lime,

there we will find,

what was never lost,

as it was never acquired,

once died,

now reborn,

now reborn!«

And they repeated three times, »Reborn!« Then they embraced each other and felt that they were not alone in this menacing world.

Chapter 19:
Maestra Castanea, Mother

Fruitday (Thursday)

Early in the morning, Hollydeva was jolted awake. Gemina was bent over her and whispered, »Zss, come, Scorpina, let's run with the smugs!«

Hollydeva, Scorpio, jumped up and followed Gemina. The others, however, were still asleep. Should she envy them for an hour of sleep? She was not sure. But she wondered why Gemina had woken her, of all people.

In front of the novice's house, the thirteen older novices were gathering. It was cold and dawn was breaking on the horizon, but it was still quite dark. And Piscio, Virgo, and Sagittario were there too.

»Where is Tauro, he might need it!« Gemina asked. And indeed, the fat boy stumbled out of the house as well.

Bagatto shouted, »Follow me!« The pack ran to the little ferry jetty, where a path around the island began.

»We're running around the whole island! That's ten kilometers!« Amantes exclaimed enthusiastically to the newcomers.

»In three quarters of an hour?«

»No, we're just running today. One hour. If you have to stop, just walk back!«

»But we can not go back across the island!?«

»No, there are forbidden areas of the Yanas in between! But there is the allowed way back from the lighthouse. I'll show you when you need it!«

The older novices set a fairly fast pace. They obviously had practice and were good runners.

After a little more than half an hour, they arrived at the lighthouse. Hollydeva looked at Tauro, who probably had the most trouble running the entire route. The boy was actually very red-faced now and out of breath.

»Come, Tauro!« Hollydeva encouraged the novice from the Yana of Angels. »I'll walk you on the path back to the novice's house!«

Tauro held back gratefully and rested his arms on his knees. Piscio looked, but Hollydeva gave him a sign to keep running.

She went to the lighthouse and peered over the sea. The sun was rising. So the sea lay in the east. There was a gentle breeze. Seagulls were screeching over them.

Tauro was already on the way, and they walked back together.

»I better become physically adapted pronto!« Tauro gasped.

»Yes, but step by step! The second years wanted to show us how good they are and intimidate us! Let us get better day by day!«

»You could have made the whole percorso!«

»Yes, I could have. But I wanted to orient myself a bit!«

She had seen some statues along the way, and hidden gardens. At least three of the forbidden gardens or buildings were located along this path from the lighthouse to the novice's house.

At the novice's house, they had to hurry to get breakfast.

Ariëa and Appeso were already gone. She had to go alone and probably arrive late at the Yana of Ravens. Capri had been waiting for Tauro, both of whom had to go to the house of the Yana of Angels. They took Hollydeva in their midst. So she had two great and powerful "angels" as protectors.

»What a pity you cannot come with me to appease Maestra Corvanya, as I'm late.«

»We'd rather not quarrel with Maestraa Corvaanya.«

»How is it with the Angels? Next month I will have a visit two weeks at the Angels!«

»Oh, it's rather holy and very nice. Now a kind of worship takes place. The Dio die Giorno is honored and all his angels and saints. It will not be noticed when we come late!«

Capri added, »Maestraa Suraa is as nice as she looks!«

»Hopefully everything is the way it looks!«

Hollydeva had learned that everything is usually different than expected.

The other Ravens had been waiting for her. She quickly dressed and joined the wild dance of the Ravens.

Ariëa and Hollydeva then went to the study of Maestra Corvanya and sat down on the chairs. Maestra Corvanya was not present. They looked around.

Corvanya had many books in her room. Maps were hanging on the wall. Bones were lying around.

When Corvanya did not come after an hour, they went into the porch. An adept asked if he could help them.

»Maestra Corvanya is not in her study! We waited for an hour at her room.«

»The Maestra had to attend a meeting with the other masters! If she is not there and does not come after a quarter of an hour, you should report to the kitchen and help there! I'll show you the way! I am Brother Rosecrow, you will meet me again in the garden with your mother!«

At the door to the kitchen, he left them. Hollydeva was taken aback a little. She had almost forgotten about her mother! She was so close and so far away!

The cook of the Yana of Ravens came towards them. »Ah, two novicesses who want to do something meaningful! Start with the onions!«

So Ariëa and Hollydeva spent the time with cutting onions and other vegetables. They felt quite right with that.

»Does each Yana have its own kitchen?«

»Yes of course! The tastes are very different! But we sometimes exchange recipes or even whole dishes! We are ten cooks here at the monastery, and we work together well. Every so often, there are festivals for everyone, and then we prepare a great feast! I am "Marjorie". I come from Eastern Yngland.«

The cook's friendly manner increased their appetite, and the lunch soup tasted particularly well.

Healing Arts

It was Fruitday and the program for the afternoon was the first lesson in the Art of Healing.

They went to an edifice behind the main building, which had already been indicated to them as a temple of healing. "Jupiter House". They were told to report there, whenever they would feel pain or illness.

Behind the building was a garden with a fountain and a small temple.

An elderly master dressed in a white robe with a belt came up to them.

»Sit down, children!« They sat down on the grass in front of the temple.

»I greet you in the faculty of medicine. My name is Master Salix! I am the doctor in this monastery!«

Master Salix took a chair and sat down before the twelve novices.

»Healing art covers several areas! In the building in your back, some of my students and adepts practice a few approaches! But the most important thing is the prevention! We want to cultivate a healthy lifestyle here to keep diseases and afflictions from us!«

Master Salix paused and pondered. »Our territories are, therefore, medical science with herbs and salts, pharmacology. Of course, we have to rearrange bones and possibly even operate inside, surgery. We should know about poisoning. Oh, that's probably part of pharmacology! We know about infectious diseases and how we protect ourselves against them. What else?«

The master had lost his thread.

Virgo, the juggler and entertainer, spoke up, »Odonto! I have a little toothache! Can you cure that, Master?«

»Yes of course. Accompany me afterwards to the adept, who functions as our healer of the teeth.«

He scratched his head and tried to clear his thoughts, »There are certainly more areas. But above all, we plant herbs and pick their leaves, flowers, roots, and berries and make teas and ointments and the like. So you should know many plants! We do this like that: You will meet a plant every day! Then you know 365 plants at the end of the year! That's a lot! For you shall know of every plant what it looks like and what it is capable of healing.«

Master Salix looked at his feet. Then he bent down and tore a weed from the grass. He held up a dandelion seed head.

»What kind of plant is that? And do not say "blowball" now!«

»This is a dandelion, and it has faded,« knew Libra.

»Good, girl. This is dandelion. What does the flower look like?«

»Yellow!« Cancra, "Shrimp", exclaimed. She seemed to suddenly be more present.

»Correct. We all know the dandelion and its yellow flowers and the blowball. This is one of the most versatile medicinal plants available. Above all, the root can also be cooked for a tea. The leaves are rich in vitamins and nutrients. What can we do with the juice of the stalk?«

He held up the stalk of the blowball from which the white juice swelled. Nobody knew it.

Master Salix admitted, »I just do not know either! There is a book for it somewhere! You do not have to have everything in your head, you know. You just need to know where to look it up! So come every Thursday, and we learn together about healing.«

»Thursday?«

»Yes. Oh, forgive me, the day is called something else now! What was the new name again?«

»Fruit Day, Master!«

»Ah, yes. Thank you! Fruit Day! The thunder god became fruit.«

»Which plants shall we collect tomorrow?«

»Oh yes. Tomorrow. Run around a little and find a plant and bring it with you in a week. We then find out together what it is and what it can do! So, best of all, you'll pick this plant up shortly before we meet here. But you should have gone around to know where you find a plant!«

They then went to the novices' house to learn about arithmetic, literature, reading and writing Latin.

Maestra Castanea

Hollydeva was called out of the class by an adept. She was to go into the main house to speak to the Abbess.

When she was let into the room, where Abbess Tilia used to run the monastery, she saw that another maestra, her mother, was in the room.

Abbess Tilia welcomed her, »Scorpio, good you are here! You will soon have lessons at the plant nursery! In that faculty Maestra Castanea, your mother, is the teacher! I have learned that you have tensions with your mother, that you have not seen each other for a long time! I do not want these tensions to affect the lessons! You have to say here and now what is on your mind!«

"Castanea". Her mother's name was Rosa, as she remembered! Well, good, that she had become somebody else during these years on the island!

»What would you like to say to your mother, Scorpio?«

»She left me alone! She is my mother no longer! I do not need her!«

»Why did you leave your daughter behind, Maestra Castanea?«

»I once learned here at the monastery school. All the seven years! I was a novicess, an initiate, an adept. I am deeply attached to the Yana of the Lamb! Then I was told to spend the next three years in the world, on a journey. On my travels, I met my

193

husband, Seren, and married him. I did not know who he was. But he told me on the wedding night. We were both adherents of the worldview of the OneGod. That was good. But for me, the OneGod is a woman. And his OneGod seemed more like a dark demon to me!«

Hollydeva's mother seemed to remember difficult times. »Seren traveled a lot. I lived mostly on the property of my mother, Lady Algard, who herself was living mostly here on the island as she was gardening Maestra Malus then. Later we lived in that house where Hollydeva was born in. For a while, Seren and I had a time of happiness.

»I could not help but love Seren! But it seemed to me that I was going a wrong way! Then my children were born: Einar, Baldar and you, Hollydeva. Einar and Baldar were bright and light. But you came after your father, rather dark, more closed. You were scaring me!

»Stories about the Great Mother did not interest you! You loved to be in the forest.

»Then came the call from Linden Island! I would be needed! I should lead the nursery! Gardening is my favorite occupation! Einar and Baldar would be accepted as novices! It seemed to be my salvation, especially since Seren had visited us less and less! What was I supposed to do with you? I did not want you to be a novicess here! So I sent a message to Seren at the Castle, urging that he should come and get you. I'm sorry if he took longer to get to you than I expected!«

Abbess Tilia nodded, »Thank you, Maestra Castanea, for your frank words! Now your daughter has been accepted here as a novicess! What do you think about that?«

»I do not understand why you did it! I do not think she'll stay here for the whole period of seven years!«

»We took your daughter in here because she was in need, as your mother asked us to do so! You know that your mother still has some status here! We can not refuse her, and she has spoken a lot on behalf of your daughter! There are significant things happening in the world! There is great danger ahead!«

Tilia walked over to Hollydeva and laid an arm around her shoulder. »Your daughter has already experienced a lot at Castle Georgeburg and on the way towards the Island. She has learned about these dangers. Her father, your husband, is sick and perhaps dying. Scorpio has received an order from the plant devas! It is an important assignment! And she has become a factor in the power games between the feuding Nine! That's all pretty much for a young lady!«

Maestra Tilia looked hard at Hollydeva's mother. »I see she's different, Castanea! But as you know, we have eight yanas here, and we have very different novices here!

With Corvanya she is in the best hands! How dull it would be if all were Lambs like you and your good sons! I want you to respect your daughter!«

»I'm supposed to respect my daughter? Since when is it not the child that should respect the parents?«

»It should be mutual respect! But you know, Castanea, that the age of a person has nothing to do with the age of the body in the particular life. Your daughter is far older than you, than most of us. She has gone through great trials in past lives and has seen terrible things. Show her respect, and ask her forgiveness that you were an inadequate mother to her!«

Tilia had spoken with sharpness and emphasis. Castanea lowered her head, turned to Hollydeva, and stated somewhat reluctantly, »Please forgive me that I was a bad mother! I respect that you are a novicess here!«

Tilia turned to Hollydeva, »Novicess Scorpio, are you content with this ask for forgiveness and this amount of respect?«

Hollydeva realized that the High Maestra seriously meant it and was paying her respect. The Abbess seemed to be on her side. That surprised her. Hollydeva suspected that her mother was not high in favor on the Island these days.

She thought to herself, »Am I really older than my mother? An interesting thought!«

Loudly, she exclaimed, »I've been here for three days at the Linden Island school. I've learned so many interesting things and found eleven friends! I would like to continue my education here and carry it through to the master's degree.«

»Stop, stop!« the Abbess interrupted her. »You do not have to promise! You do not know yet how things will develop!«

»I really want it! It may be that I have to go away and have to help the plants, but I will always ask your permission, and I will tell you what I am up to. I understand that my mother has left me and that she could not help herself!«

Hollydeva noticed that she still showed a kind of slight contempt.

»But that is how I was set on my feet and I arrived at Castle Georgeburg, and I finally ended up here! Everything has its meaning, and you too, mother, have had to complete your role for me! I forgive you and will not disturb your lessons! Please forgive me, however, that I will often pretend that we are alien to each other!«

She saw that tears shot into her mother's eyes. Maestra Castanea nodded and muttered, »Yes, I understand. Thank you!«

Maestra Tilia pressed Hollydeva's shoulder, »Yes, thank you, Sister Scorpio! I know that one day you will recognize that your mother loves you just as much as your brothers! But the love found again is greater than the love that is never questioned, is it not?«

It seemed to Hollydeva that the Grand Maestra was wondering about that statement herself, unsure about the answer.

»Run, go back to class,« Maestra Tilia advised her, reclaiming her status.

After vespers, they all ran a little around the novice's house to look for plants, to look, to recognize.

Hollydeva joined Shrimp, who seemed to be well acquainted with plants. The Chynese girl told her that her aunt at home in Shandong was a herbal healer. She would have often accompanied her on her walks and learned a look for medicinal plants.

»But the best plant is the ginseng,« she explained. »The best ginseng is from Shandong!«

Hollydeva was happy with herself as she could establish communication with the little Chynese girl.

Aquaria

Later, Hollydeva sat down on a bench behind the novice's house. She wanted to think about the day in peace.

But soon Aquaria stood before her. »Can I sit down with you, please? It would be important to me!« she asked. Hollydeva nodded.

Aquaria explained, »As you know, I went to the Yana of the Dolphins. My prior is the master who calls himself Professor Griseo! You will have already thought that he is an alchymist! My first two days with him have confirmed that! He gets along well with Sagittario, who is just taking notes. So I can stay low back somehow and make my observations!«

Aquaria grasped Hollydeva on the forearm, »Please, it is important to me! I do not want us to be enemies! You're right: Something with the alchymists is wrong! And Master Griseo, I'm sorry, I'm not at all happy with him! I have probably chosen the wrong yana! But I felt attracted to science and a world of faith built on reason!«

Hollydeva put her other hand on the hand of Aquaria lying on her forearm. »It's good, Aquaria! I understand you! And maybe it's good when one of us observes Professor Griseo! Learn as much as you can! We will need the knowledge of the alchymists to be able to reverse any harmful effects of their experiments and inventions!«

Aquaria nodded. »Good, that makes sense!«

Hollydeva found, »There will be good and evil alchymists! Just as there seem to be good and evil nacharya as well! And I've heard of a Black Mystic! So there are evil mystics as well!«

»Oh yeah! I was told about the Black Mystic! He must be bad! He probably sent the sea-demons to attack Linden Island!«

»I hope, he'll leave us alone!«

They went back to the novice's house together. Before sleep, Hollydeva thought about how odd it was that she suddenly had girlfriends. The girls at school, where she had been as a child, had excluded her. And there were no other children at Castle Georgeburg. Here she had met at least five other girls, who wanted to be close with her, who were respecting her.

Chapter 20:
Maestra Betula. Nightwatch

Treeday (Friday)

On the morning of the fourth day, a Treeday, the novices of the first year were all up early to run around the island with the other novices, or whatever they were going to do. Hollydeva had already prepared Aquaria regarding the problems that Tauro might have. Aquaria was willing to go back with him from the lighthouse. Perhaps she herself was not a runner with the breath for an hour yet.

But Amantes told them that they would run for half an hour to a special place, where they would watch the sunrise and meditate for a quarter of an hour, then return. A whole round of the island they would run on Clouddays and Fruitdays only.

The place on the east coast of the island was actually very nice and well suited to look over the sea, where a reddish glow was just pushing above the horizon.

After breakfast, Hollydeva returned to Raven House with Ariëa and Appeso. Appeso was a little taciturn.

»What is the matter? Are you in love?« Ariëa asked a random shot.

Appeso looked puzzled. »How do you know? I have not told anyone!«

»I've only guessed, Appeso! I just wanted to tease you! Who is it?«

»Why would I tell you this?«

Ariëa laughed. »Then I ask the ravens! They will know!«

»Oh, no, have you ever been the mocking of those ravens? You would rather not experience that!«

»Then say!«

»I am in love with our chief novicess!«

Hollydeva affirmed, »Bagatto. I can understand that. She is wonderful! Have you shown her?«

»No. She had a lover and friend, a novice from her class, who was like her at the Tigers, a Brother Carro. I almost did not get to know him. He has perished at the demons' attack, and Bagatto has since then become rather unapproachable for potential lovers.«

»Hmm, understandable. But she should get over it now!«

»Yes, I hope so. But of course, I am not the only admirer! She will surely choose an adept, who will pave the way for her into the ranks within the monastery.«

»No, she does not need it! Yet I doubt that she will become interested in a Raven!«

»Yes, it is said that one should look for his lovers in his or her own yana!«

»Oh, that would be a bit desolate!«

»Scorpio, I heard you arrived here with Astrello, the legendary star boy!«

»Yes, I have. And?«

»You'll see him this afternoon. He is in the team of the prediction artists! He, of course, is the astrologer!«

»Oh yeah. I have not seen him since our arrival!«

»Have you not missed him?«

»Oh, come on. I've never been in love and will never be! I like Astrello and we have helped each other! But I would not want to be kissing him now! I'd rather punch a Raven!«

Hollydeva gave Appeso a push, and Ariëa puffed him from the other side. Appeso had to laugh, and they were glad that they had someone to talk about their attractions to other people.

After the dance of the Ravens, they entered Corvanya's office. The Maestra was already waiting.

»And, are you still willing to be Raven?«

»Why should we not be, Maestra?«

»Well, you, Scorpio, grew up with the OneGod!

»And you, Ariëa, probably rather believes in the many gods of Voodoo!«

Hollydeva replied, »Yes, but the OneGod has never come to my aid! I love nature! Nature shall be my God! The animals and the plants are talking to me! I understand and feel them! I do not feel people!«

»You do not feel human beings?! I almost thought so!«

»Am I different from other people?«

»Yes, probably! You have little or no empathy with the other people. For this, you have all the more feeling with the beings of nature! You will always have to ask them to tell you what people, who you are dealing with, really feel! You may have trouble figuring out if people are lying to you or talking the truth! Difficulty with understanding irony, probably!

»But it does not matter! The shamans in the old days have been just like that! The young people were observed by the old ones. The strong became warrior. The empathetic became healers. The strange ones became shamans. And the shamans were of high status! They could foresee the future! They could talk to the devas of plants and animals!

»And you will be able to kill and hurt people! Therefore, you were a good assistant to the Grand Inquisitor, and perhaps you will be his successor! And maybe we, the Ravens, will need you as an assassin!

»That is why you came to us and have not gone to the Bees! The Bees are the good shamans, who are concerned exclusively with the preservation of nature and nature spirits. They heal and nurture and protect. But they do not kill or injure those who endanger or harm nature and living beings. I have respect for the attitude of the Bees, the right-hand path shamans!

»But we, the left-hand path shamans, are ready to get our hands dirty! Therefore, you are here at the right place! And I'm glad you're here, Scorpio! Saviors must be merciless! And I assure you that you have a very strong global army at your side!

»But, as I said, I am the maestra and you are the novicess! Whatever you plan to do outside our curriculum, I need to grant permission. Be assured that I will give you this if your plan is right! I will allow you to ask the ravens at any time how the clashes between the nacharyas and the wizardeurs and the alchymists are going on!«

»Thank you, Maestra Corvanya! I feel well received!«

Ariëa agreed.

»And do not try to influence me with courtesies and sweet words! I am immune to that! I like it when you end your sentences with the title "Maestra", but otherwise it does not need any thanksgiving!

»You'll see the star boy today! What binds you to him?«

»I like him! He came to Castle Georgeburg, and I was to question him! Then I wanted to help him! I felt I had to free him, that he was part of my destiny. He is not of this world!«

»That's right! He is part of your destiny. Trust him! But do not trust him too much. Do not reveal to him all of your secrets!

»Good, visit the ravens and the dead Raven shamans in the cemetery! Then you can go to lunch! I'll see you tomorrow, Ariëa, Scorpio!«

»Thank you, Maestra!«

Art of Prediction

After lunch, they went to the building, the temple, of the divination artists. There was a building shaped as an octagon, located on a small hill.

They were led into a small room, that was octagonal as well. Then the Maestra of Prediction came in, accompanied by Astrello and two other adepts.

»I am greeting you, novices, I am Maestra Betula, the teacher of predicting arts. I will tell the future through dreams, visions, divination! I am a seeress, and I will teach you to see!

»But we have a variety of ways to find out what's in the future and how we can influence the outcome of occurrences!

»My three assistant teachers here are not direct adepts or masters of Linden Island. I have rather "imported" them because they are masters of their specific arts! And I would like to benefit from their knowledge and skills. In these times, Linden Island needs multi-level perception of the future like never before, and so it was right for the Linden Island Masters to have these three invited to our place!

»Astrello is a scholar of astrology! He can calculate the future from the movements of the stars! Astrello himself is not of this Yrth!

»Achillea, here is our card reader. She is skilled with the tarot and sees the future from all kinds of card sets!«

A young woman had stepped forward and curtsied. She looked like a woman from the travelers, with a long colored skirt and a headscarf and big golden rings in the earlobes, with black hair.

»And Master Ai Min is, of course, familiar with the Yi Jing, the Book of Changes, a wonderful Taoist book with which we can also explore the future.«

The little Chynese with goat-beard, Master Ai Min, nodded, murmuring, »Confucian, not taoistic!«

Hollydeva tried to make eye contact with Astrello. She had almost forgotten him in the last few days because of the many new experiences. But he did not look at her and did not want the other novices to know about their special connection or to assume a different treatment.

Maestra Betula explained that people have always wanted to know what the future would bring. They would have selected special people, people who could have access to unusual levels. The future is only an aspect of the present, as is the past. It

201

actually is a great continuum of time-space and the initiate can travel it and pass through all the times.

»But it is by no means the case that the future is fixed. It is a vast ocean, and every stone that would be thrown into the ocean would change the pattern of the waves.

»Never forget that you can only decipher the pattern of the waves! Not more! The ocean remains the ocean!«

Maestra Betula made a strange leap into the air. When she landed again, she exclaimed somewhat exaggeratedly, »It may be that we are jugglers, and that we learn these arts because one can make the most easy money with them. We'll determine what people want to hear!«

She laughed, »Do not take it too seriously.«

Hollydeva saw that Betula's three assistant professors were looking a bit sour. They probably did not agree with that statement of Betula.

Maestra Betula explained, »In ancient and not so ancient times the future has been predicted from all sorts of things: from the flight of birds, from the innards of slaughtered sacrificed animals, from coffee grounds.

»The principle is: everything is connected with everything in this world! As things are on the small level, so they are on a large scale as well!«

The novices looked at each other somewhat confused. Should they take predicting seriously or not? Maestra Betula seemed to be a confusion artist.

»So if you want to be a prophet, or a clairvoyant, or a fortune-teller: it's good to have your audience confused, at least a bit.

»You'll learn something about the prediction of the future here at every Treeday! It will be interesting and fun! And maybe we will actually find out what might happen in the future!«

Hollydeva could not hold back any longer, »I met a shaman in the woods just a few days ago, he had drank a mushroom brew. He could travel to the future and to the past and to every place with his spirit and answer questions!«

Maestra Betula walked towards her very quickly and stood before her. »Quiet! What yana are you in?«

Hollydeva did not know whether she was supposed to be quiet now or whether she should answer.

»You're probably a Raven?«

Hollydeva nodded.

»If your shamans can travel so well into the future, and so they should know what will happen, why then were the shamans almost exterminated? Do not feel too important, child!«

Hollydeva swallowed the rebuke and understood that Maestra Betula could be funny and appearing non-serious. But in reality she was not to be trifled with! Hollydeva liked that. But she also thought of revenge. She lowered her head.

Maestra Betula went back to her seat. »Do not get me wrong, novices! What we are doing here makes sense, and it even is science! We can answer questions, give directions, and help others, give them good advice! We develop an understanding for tendencies of development in the world! We can warn! There hardly can be too few warnings nowadays!

»Let me flip a coin! Who has a coin?«

The novices looked at each other questioningly. They had handed over all their belongings at the inauguration.

»Do not tell me. At least one novice always has a coin!«

Then a sound came from Pierre, who was now called Piscio. »I have a silver dollar here! This coin is my lucky charmlet! It once was given to me as a gift by a traveler whom we ferried over with our boaty.«

»Stop, boy, do not tell me your whole story! I just want to flip your coin now!«

Piscio gave her the coin. Maestra Betula showed the two sides of the coin. »We have a head, and we have numbers!«

She exclaimed, »In the near future, there will be a small lecture of our revered Astrello on the foundations of astrology.»

She turned around herself one time, »And when the number is showing, the revered Confucian Taoist will show how Yi Jing is capable of explaining the future!«

She threw the coin, let it drop to the ground, looked, and cried, »It's head! Astrello, your performance! I have predicted the future 100 percent correct! The oracle of the coin has told me the truth!«

All novices had to laugh. They understood that Maestra Betula wanted to teach them something and make them laugh at the same time. And you probably never knew exactly what she was driving. So the listener had to be very careful and attentive with her.

Hollydeva noticed that Piscio took care of getting his coin back.

Astrello stepped forward and explained, »This planet is in a space. The planet circles around a sun, like some other planets as well. Circling this planet is a moon. The sun is part of a galaxy of several thousand suns. And countless galaxies exist in the vast universe. Stars, wonderful stars in abundance!

»The stars, which we see in the night sky, show a picture to us, show us a relationship in the sky. We can calculate how the starry sky will look tomorrow, how the energetic relationship will have changed. That gives us clues!«

Astrello told a little more about astrology. Then Achillea showed them how she used to lay the cards. She had very vivid tarot cards. And Ai Min gave a brief introduction to the 64 signs of the Book of Changes.

When the twelve novices left Venus Temple, they were very impressed and excited about the lessons of the coming year.

Maestra Fraxina then taught them about the history of humanity.

Hollydeva went to bed early as she would have to get up in the middle of the night to attend her first night watch together with Libra.

Nightwatch

When she was awakened by Leo in the middle of the night, she had jumped up quickly, had thrown over her cloak, and, with Libra in tow, had stormed to the meeting point at the bell tower.

A Master, whom she had seen with the abbess before, was waiting with two adepts, which she did not know.

The master introduced himself, »I am Master Ulmus, the deputy of the abbess. Is this your first night watch?«

Libra and Hollydeva nodded.

»Well, most of the time nothing happens. We must, however, observe whether something is gathering beneath the surface of the perceptible. The two new ones go clockwise around the island! The two adepts go counterclockwise! You meet at the lighthouse and then finish the round! Every few minutes, you stop and listen and feel if there is something unusual going on. Be back here after three hours! If this bell rings or storms, there's an attack somewhere! Then you should rush and defend the monastery from the attack! Oh, here are weapons and flashlights!«

They each got a kind of short sword. It all seemed a little absurd to Hollydeva.

»Oh, and the whistles!« Master Ulmus gave them whistles hanging from a cord that they could hang around their necks.

Then they left. After some minutes, they stopped and listened to the night. It was quiet.

After an hour of silent walking, Hollydeva and Libra sat down at the lighthouse. There was nothing to be seen from the adepts.

»They probably know better and are sleeping somewhere,« Hollydeva said.

Libra looked surprised. »Do you think so?«

»Yes, the whole thing is obviously absurd. Older students know the tricks!«

»But if last year's attack really happened, it would be better to be careful!«

»You're right. Let us have a look at the sea!«

The sea was quiet. But Hollydeva had the impression that there was something lurking there, listening to their noises just as they listened to the noises of the sea.

After some time, they went on and sat down on a bench about a hundred yards from the shore. Behind the bench, a grove seemed to dream.

»Here is the Lamb's grove,« revealed Libra. »I'm sitting at this bench quite often! It is probably my favorite place!«

»Oh, yes, it's a beautiful place! Thank you for showing it to me!«

»You and the others think I have something against you guys and that I feel like a rose in the midst of scrubs!»

Hollydeva wanted to contradict, but remembered that she should not be polite. She felt a pain in Libra's words and waited for her to speak on.

»I've met your brothers! They are also planted into the Yana of Agnus, like myself! If you are like your brothers, I can trust you!«

»Unfortunately, I'm not like my brothers! And so I am a Raven! Do not trust me!«

»Oh, Scorpio! I thought we could be friends!«

»I think we're six girls in the first novice's year who are holding together, plus six boys to whom we stand! These are quite a few friends, though perhaps not close friends! I'm not such a girlfriend anyway!«

»Hey, you're right. But somehow you're all more like fighters! I'm just not combative.«

»You said your mother was a midwife. Did you even help with births?«

»Oh, yes, a few times! When it gets tough, my mother always needs some extra hands!«

»This is more bloody than a battle, as far as I have heard! You're braver than you think!«

Libra looked at her with surprise and relief. »Yes, you are right. Thank you for reminding me!«

»With pleasure. Make sure you do not compete with Aquaria!«

»Competing with Aquaria? Oh, I sometimes interrupt her when she talks!«

»For example. Aquaria remembers that. She is the born leader, I believe.«

»Yes, that may be. And Prince Leo supports her! I think I feel closest to you, Scorpio! Libra and Scorpio are signs lying next to each other!«

Hollydeva felt Astrello would agree with her. She thought to herself that she was closer to Gemina or Ariëa, as they were as tough and hard as herself. But Libra might be complementing them well. »But she's going to get more interest from the boys,« Hollydeva thought. »And that will probably make me and the others angry or jealous!«

»Libra, may I tell you something else? From friend to friend?«

»Yes, of course. Tell me!«

»You will be receiving more interest from the boys than we lean fighters! Never play it off against us or boast with the advances which are made to you. Enjoy, but stay silent about it!«

»That was a little wiser than I would have expected from you, Scorpio!«

Hollydeva sighed. She hated herself when she was so precocious.

Libra added. »But it was good advice! I know what you mean!«

Back at the bell tower, the Master sat like a meditator. Hollydeva had the suspicion that he could sleep like that. But when they were close to him, he jumped up, took his short sword, and cried, »Parole!«

They had not received a parole. Hollydeva answered, »Parole!«

The Master shouted, »I asked for the parole first. Answer!«

Libra protested, »You have not given us that word, Master!«

»Any intruder can say that! What a cheap trick!«

Hollydeva had an idea, »The parole is "coffee"!«

»This is a good parole! How do you know that the second night watchers get coffee in the abbey's kitchen?«

»I smelled something!«

Master Ulmus laughed and invited them, »Come with me!« They went to the already active kitchen in the main house, where the two adepts had already made the rare enjoyment of a hot coffee to be their morning prayer.

Chapter 21:
Master Sycamor. Seven Prayers

Seaday (Saturday)

Bedtime had been short because of the vigil. Libra and Hollydeva had skipped the morning run and rested a bit, but deep sleep had not been forthcoming. Master Corvanya had not let Hollydeva sleep either, but had told something about mushrooms that Ariëa and Scorpio would soon take to find their power animal. The Raven prioress had shown them the mushrooms in the meadow near the Cemetery of Ravens, and had headbutted Hollydeva when she felt that the novicess was not paying attention.

Now Hollydeva had ended up in class with Master Sycamor after the soup at noon and could hardly keep her eyes open, especially since the master began, somewhat very theoretically, lecturing about the prayers and rituals in the traditional monasteries of earlier times.

He wanted to teach them seven prayers that would empower and strengthen them.

»Very well,« Hollydeva thought to herself. »There will be nothing wrong with that. I should pay attention!«

But her eyes were already falling to shut again, and Aquaria, sitting next to her, nudged her.

Aquaria seemed quite taken with this Master Sycamor anyway. Yet, he was rather unimpressive, slight. But he led the Saturn Academy, the Institute for Self-Empowerment, for Soul Power. That sounded good, and Aquaria expected a lot from it. The other novices, including Libra, who had been on vigil with her, seemed genuinely interested as well.

Master Sycamor explained that the prayers they would learn would be independent of worldview. Whether a person would believe in the OneGod or the MultiGod or in nature or in no god at all would be selectable depending on the environment. The prayers and what he would teach would be superior to the concept of faith.

»Our prayers are ultimately directed to ourselves! The powers invoked are our own powers!«

Hollydeva shook her head inwardly. This was all too high. After all, when she had lived alone in the house, she had prayed to the OneGod almost daily because she had felt alone and lonely. And the OneGod had been with her then!

And in the dungeons of Georgeburg Castle, she had prayed for the imprisoned so that they could quickly confess and repent and be released. There, too, the OneGod had mostly helped. Or had she imagined that?

She still had to digest that the belief in the OneGod, for whom she had worked in the Georgeburg dungeons, was not the only and not the true belief. The Bhogi had already sown doubts in her mind. But he had probably taken nothing really seriously anyway.

Master Sycamor was a master from the Yana of the Tigers. It was obvious that he wanted to convey some kind of magical empowerment. They themselves were finally the gods to whom the prayers were addressed. The prayers were to remind them of their own power. Hollydeva had to admit that she actually liked the concept. But she wondered whether the Dark God of the Tigers would thus be planted into them as well.

Saturn Academy. They sat on rather hard chairs in a semicircle. The room was quite large and round, with a roof of thick glass through which light fell into the room. On the walls of the seminar room in the Saturn Academy seven large posters were hanging. These seven prayers, so important to the Master of Soul Power, were listed on these posters and to be read. The posters were in seven colors and Hollydeva saw that the days of the week, which could be named after the seven colors, were written in large letters on the upper right corner of each poster.

Then they were to stand up, as Master Sycamor was going to explain and demonstrate the chakras to them. Hollydeva was glad, as sitting down made her eyes fall shut faster. So she could stretch a little and take a breath.

»The first chakra, the root chakra, is below where the two legs meet!«

They were to feel there with both hands. Some of the others giggled and grinned. The first chakra was at the genitals, and they must have found that suggestive or somehow exciting. Hollydeva yawned. She found the others embarrassing.

The second chakra was in the lower abdomen. She put her hands on her belly and listened to Master Sycamor explain something about the center of gravity of the body. They were to move their hands up and down and energize the chakra. It felt good, awakening some energies that she could desperately use.

Master Sycamor also had them feel and vibrate the other five chakras, in the solar plexus, heart, larynx, third eye and above the head. Hollydeva was grateful to the Master for this exercise. It was considerably more lively than sitting on chairs listening to his lecture.

Master Sycamor explained that these seven chakras were connected with seven bodies, six of which were subtle and therefore not visible. Furthermore, these seven bodies were connected with other seven entities, corresponding to the days of the week, the needs, the Higher Emotions.

»Please go around and look carefully at the seven posters on the walls. On them are written the seven prayers. They address all of these seven entities respectively. With the correspondences, we can exercise power by addressing them as if we were magicians, wizards, so to speak. As you know, I am from the Yana of Tigers like your sister Cancra here and the Tigers are in communication with the Wizardeurs.«

Hollydeva was alarmed. Hadn't he also praised the alchymists before? Was Master Sycamor possibly an enemy? He seemed to have a great deal of knowledge and exuded a certain self-control. She decided to observe him further and closely.

So they were to go around and write down the correspondences they found in their notebooks. After a tea break, they reconvened.

»So, who will read us the correspondences for today's sea day, the dark blue day?«

Of course, Aquaria dashed forward and exclaimed, »I'll do it, please!«

And off she began, »Dark Blue Day, Sea Day, Sixth Chakra, which is also called Third Eye, Need for Support, Higher Emotion: Devotion.«

»Very good, Aquaria!«

He pronounced Aquaria somewhat haltingly, as if he were actually calling her something else.

Then they were to stand in front of the Sixth Chakra poster and read and say the prayer aloud together:

»I breathe dark blue light into my Saturn center, my "Third Eye Chakra"!
I allow the dark blue from the seas to flow into me!
It flows into my sense organs and nerves!
I am ready to learn, to know and to realize!
I myself give me support and challenge!
I am helped, having support given by the whole existence!
I breathe out devotion and dedication and send it into the world!
May all living beings dance in eternity and infinity!«

209

Master Sycamor asked, »So what are the topics that are addressed in this prayer? We should not just rush down these prayers as if memorized but feel deeply what is being addressed and stimulated, what we are connecting with! What is the first?«

»Dark blue light in the Saturn center, the Third Eye!«

»Yes, right! But before that, we had to be aware of what day of the week we are saying this prayer! So what is the heading?«

»Sea day prayer! Dark blue prayer!«

»Exactly! We have a correspondence to a day of the week and a color! Some of you may know a different name for the days of the week, naming them by numbers, like first day, second day, third day! Some perhaps still use the old names of the week-days, as they were called for centuries before the unification of the monotheistic churches to the OneGod, at least in Eyrope! Tell me again, please, the names of the days of the week in the order and with the colors by which they can also be named!«

They shouted all at once. Sycamor interrupted them and let some answer the question one after the other:

»Today is Dark Blue Day, Sea Day, before Saturday!«

»Tomorrow will be Flower Day, Yellow Day, once called Sunday!«

»Horrido! Then comes Cloud Day, the Silver Gray Day, Monday!«

»Zss. Red Blood Day, had been Tuesday!«

Sycamor interrupted, »This day, Blood Day we see today as the first day of the week and Cloud Day as the final day of the week associated with the seventh chakra and the moon! Novice Leo, please tell us the next day!«

»Wednesday is now the Sky Day, the Blue Day, Day of Mercury, Fifth Chakra!«

Ariëa shouted, »Listen! Fruit Day is the Day of Jupiter, before Thursday, Orange!« And Libra was awake now too, »I plant the tree day! Green like the tree! Friday.«

Master Sycamor then had them read the other six prayers and say them aloud. These read similarly. It was just the colors, the Social Needs to be met, and the High Emotions that were different.

He gave them two versions of the posters so they could hang them in their dormitories.

Then he gave each of the novices small copper plaques on which a heptagon was drawn in such a way that the connections of Day, Color, Chakra, Need and Higher State were engraved in the respective sevenths.

Needs

The inquisitive Aquaria inquired, »Can you please explain the Social Needs, Master Sycamor?«

Hollydeva saw that it pleased the master very much to be asked like that. Apparently, he was not used to the novices in the first week really trying to understand what he was trying to give them.

The master was from the Yana of the Tiger. He had said that right away. The only one of them who had chosen this yana was Shrimp. The small Chynese had however enough to handle with following the language. Aquaria would have been more at home with the Tigers than in the Yana of the Dolphins.

The master explained, »As living beings who have a body, we have needs. Physical needs must be met in order for us to survive! What are they?«

»Breathing air!« »Food and drink!« »Protection from storms and demons!«

Sycamor nodded, »Exactly! What else? I like to organize everything into sevens, and we actually have seven basic physical needs. We have breath, food, and shelter so far! What else could kill us if we don't get it met?«

Hollydeva knew from her observations in the dungeons of Georgeburg: »Sleep! When people don't have sleep, they go crazy!«

»Right! And it appears to be especially important in sleep that we dream. Dreaming helps cleanse our brains!«

Libra interjected, »My mother is a midwife, and during childbirth it's important to avoid infections!«

Sycamor nodded again, »Hygiene! Protection from infections! What else can you die from?«

Virgo knew, but he wasn't happy about it, »You can burn to death or freeze to death!«

»Exactly. We need our body temperature to be about 37 degrees! And to survive as a species, it takes sexuality, reproduction!«

»That's a basic need?«

»Well, you guys are still a little young.«

Hollydeva looked at Gemina, who was smiling superiorly, obviously knowing what was being talked about. The other novices, however, seemed rather innocent and irritated.

Gemina asked in a somewhat insinuating tone, »Zss. Do you teach us about sexuality and procreation as well, Master Sycamor?«

»No, I am celibate and have no expertise in that area!« informed Master Sycamor in a firm voice.

Hollydeva felt that Gemina would have liked to tease provocatively with, »Oh, too bad, actually!« The snake then bit it, however, for it was rather unwise to spoil it so early with the master of the art of self-control.

But the topic was now floating around the room, and Hollydeva felt that some were furtively looking around to see with whom they could explore this topic in self-instruction. Hollydeva was glad that she seemed of little interest in that regard. However, Gemina then glanced at her and winked, and Hollydeva felt herself blush, and got annoyed.

She quickly decided to deflect, »But if the right to live isn't fulfilled, it's not like we're going to die! What is that anyway, the right to life?«

»The right to life is our most fundamental social need. If our parents deny us this and even try not to let us live until birth, or even if we are denied the right to life because we are the wrong sex, this affects our soul. It doesn't lead to instant death, but it also doesn't support our lives in a way that allows us to fulfill our full potential.«

Hollydeva wondered if her mother had denied her this right to life before she was born, or if her rejection had come later.

Sycamor continued, »In childhood, these Basic Social Needs should be met, and they actualize in order: right to life, attention, belonging, respect for boundaries, space for expression, support, appreciation. This knowledge is part of a detailed psychological view that we will learn more about in the course of your training here.«

He looked insistent, »And please never forget that this is also only a model that we can work well with. When we come across other points of view or teachings, we look at them with open minds and adopt what we can use. I like the division into sevens. If someone provides me with an eighth basic need that doesn't fit into the other seven, I change my preference and immediately become a devotee of the eight!«

Dance of Dragons

Afterwards, they went back to the Novice's House to finish their work or study day with a lesson given by Maestra Fraxina.

In the morning, Ariëa and Hollydeva had been with Maestra Corvanya again. They had made their tour to King Krama and the ravens and to the ancestors of the Yana of Ravens.

Corvanya had led them to a small meadow.

»Here, do you see these mushrooms? They have strong mystical power! You will eat from them in three weeks and go on an inner journey to find your power animal!«

Shouldn't her power animal be the raven? What else could a power animal be? A lion? A cockroach? »I'd rather be a lion«, Hollydeva thought.

At their evening meeting, she almost fell asleep. But almost all novices of the first year felt that way. So they said the Green Prayer at eight o'clock and went to bed early.

But she woke up in the middle of the night. Overslept, she went to the small room where the novices could or should drop urine or excrement through holes. Hollydeva knew that good fertilizer was obtained from her excrement, and imagined that her mother was standing just below to collect the particularly valuable fertilizer that her daughter had produced. She smiled nastily as she heard a strange noise. She finished her emptying and followed the sound. So outside the novice house, she reached the weed meadow behind the building. There, Leo and Virgo were throwing a ball, generating the sound that had attracted Hollydeva.

»Can't you sleep?«

»No, it's all so exciting,« Virgo exclaimed a bit exaggerated.

Leo noticed that Hollydeva wasn't in the mood to be made fun of, and explained, »Virgo is probably worried about Piscio, who's just on night watch with the big Tauro! He doesn't believe that the two of them can stop the demons and wants to be ready!«

But Leo himself noticed that he had also exaggerated too much, and Hollydeva looked at him disapprovingly.

»And afterwards Shrimp and Gemina replace your two heroes, and they can be swallowed by the demons with pleasure?«

»Well, we can't stand the whole night extra guard! You can take care of them then!«

»No, I'd rather go back to sleep! Throw me the ball!«

So for a while, Hollydeva took part in throwing and catching the little ball of the two novices.

Then she asked Virgo: »Did you meet the druyds on your family's travels?«

Virgo didn't throw the ball any further and approached. »Vertigo! Yes, I know the druyds. I also went to the Yana of Bees because the druyds impressed me with their bees. I think Master Alyapis is connected to the druyds in the woods. The druyds and also the fire-maiden often protected our troop. In return, we entertained them and provided them with information about the lands and cities through which we had come! Hopplahopp!«

»So now your people are telling them about Linden Island!«

»That could be! Do you have secrets from the druyds?«

»No, not at all. The druyds and fire-maiden helped me too! I would have liked to have gone to the Bees too, but Alyapis didn't seem as dangerous as Maestra Corvanya to me!«

»Yes, he seems a little old and good-natured! Agora! But he can talk to the bees! You have never seen anything like it! I think he knows more about what is going on in the world through them than any other person!«

Hollydeva nodded and was a little impressed. Then she spoke to Leo, »And how is it with the Dragons, Prince Leo?«

Leo didn't like to be poked with his noble origins and answered a little reluctantly.

»Shyena also knows what's going on in the world! And she is also very impressive!«

But then he remembered and seemed almost romantic or adoring.

»When Maestra Shyena looks you in the eye, you feel her tremendous power and clarity. That goes through and through!«

Hollydeva agreed. She could well imagine that Shyena could impress a young prince from the North.

»What are the Dragons about?«

»Well, similar to what Master Sycamor explained today: self-mastery. "Find your true self and overcome it!"«

Leo pondered something, »Overcome who you think you are and become who you are when you discover or develop your greater self or something like that!«

»Sounds huge!«

»Yes, sounds a little megalomaniac,« Virgo agreed with Hollydeva.

Leo nodded, »Yes, the Dragons want to become gods themselves. We believe in nothing at all and doubt everything and find the truth within ourselves. But it is a long way, as everything that has been told us, who we are, is wrong and must be operated out of our mind and our soul!«

»Then you are no longer a prince!«

Leo shook his head and looked a bit helpless, »No, then we are no longer a prince! We don't know if we should like that either! But we chose it that way! So we have to do it! And if we attain the strength that Shyena has, then we can probably be a good king for my people in the North!«

»But that is what you have to forget about, especially!«

Virgo added with a played important tone, »You may only remember your future job when you have forgotten yourself!«

Leo sighed, »Yes, that's it. It sounds paradoxical. But we think it won't be that much different with you. What is a king different than an actor on stage or a jailer at the Nacharya?«

Hollydeva realized how well Leo had paid attention and how well he knew who his fellow novices were.

»Come, we show you something! But you can't make a sound, and you can't rat us out!«

Hollydeva and Virgo nodded. They followed Leo. He led them to the small hill in the east of the island, the highest point of the island.

»Look there. There is the dark grove of dragons, where the dragons of our Yana rest during the day. At night, Maestra Shyena lets them fly over the sea! They are black and hard to spot at night. But sometimes they emit fire from their mouths, and you can see the glow of fire! Then you can see the rest of the body of the dragon. There is no more sublime sight!«

Hollydeva and Virgo pierced in the direction pointed out by Leo. But there was only dark forest and black night.

Some miles behind the forest, there was a cliff, the edge of the island in the east.

»There is a figure!« Virgo exclaimed, who was the first to see it.

»Yes, that's Shyena! She commands the dragons! She gives them a little freedom, and then she catches the dragons with her strong spirit and will!«

And then the three novices saw the glow of fire from the mouth of a dragon flying over the sea. And when their eyes had become accustomed to the night, they saw five great bodies circling over the sea, sometimes roaring and playing fire with each other, and sometimes rising to the stars, sometimes flying up and sometimes whipping over the waves of the sea. They heard the cry of a dragon, and they felt the power of the great beasts and the spirit that was in contact with them.

»Come! We must go back! The first watch is about to pass!«

Impressed, they ran back, greeted Piscio and Tauro, whose guard had been quiet, and went into their bedrooms. Meanwhile, Hollydeva still found it difficult to fall asleep, and she felt that Gemina had noticed her disappearing and coming back and was quietly watching her.

Chapter 22:
Celebration Day.
Game of the Five Levels and Elements

Flowerday (Sunday)

The novicesses of the first year, Libra, Ariëa, Shrimp, Aquaria, Gemina, and Hollydeva, woke up as agreed upon at the sound of the bell at 5:00. It was still dark. Dawn would wake up the rest of the world in an hour.

They placed themselves in a circle in the middle of the room, grabbed their hands, and intoned the text of the Yellow Prayer, the Sunday Flowerday Prayer, which they had memorized the day before.

»I breathe yellow light into my third chakra, power chakra,
I let the yellow from the flowers flow into me!
It flows in my bones and joints,
I am ready for power and leadership,
I give belonging to myself,
I belong to the great whole, to humanity and to all living creatures!
I breathe forgiveness, sending it into the world!
May all living creatures be forgiven!«

They looked at each other and felt that they belonged together, that they were connected.

Then they stormed out to run with the other novices to meditate at the sea. They felt the yellow of the fruits and sunflowers continue to flow into them.

At breakfast, Bagatto told the novices of the first year, who were still in their first week, that the Flowerday would always be a special day. They would not go into their yanas now, but all would meet in the cathedral. This would be a hall at the back of the main building, where all the inhabitants of the monastery would fit in. There would be a sort of meta-mystical worship service. Then there would be a dispute at the square in front of the bell tower. If bad rain would come down, the dispute would take place in the cathedral.

There would be a common lunch for all. In the afternoon the games would take place.

»Games?«

»Yes, we know three kinds of games on the island!«

In the games, the eight yanas would compete. It would depend on intuition and prediction and mystical power. Today there would be a round of "Game of Five Levels and Elements" going on. They would start their attendance to the games as spectators, as they would not know the game rules yet.

Separated From the Great Whole of Totality?

So they sat down in the last row of the cathedral. There were all masters, adepts, and novices present. And Hollydeva saw a few of the cooks and helpers as well.

Tilia, the Grand Maestra of the monastery, stood up and announced that the meta-mystical worship service had been opened.

»Let us sing the song of the Great Whole Totality!«

Bagatto had quickly distributed booklets with the lyrics of some songs to the twelve youngsters.

»Let us all dance, all dance!
We are turning with the Great Whole,
singing a song with which we thank,
and we plead and pray for all the sick.
The compassion of the Great Whole Totality
makes us dance, lets us all dance!«

There was a joyous, solemn mood. Hollydeva liked the atmosphere, felt inspired.

Next to Grand Maestra Tilia now there were five adepts with musical instruments. She saw Jackdaw, who had a drum again. The musicians began to beat a rhythm with three beats, a waltz beat. The adepts with violin and guitar tuned in, a flute chirped over it, and a second violin tuned in.

To Hollydeva's astonishment, all the masters and adepts began to turn around in circles, to hunch their hips, and to have their arms up to heaven and to dance. The novices joined. It was a slow beat and all the mystics danced consciously and slowly for themselves.

When the music ended, Tilia exclaimed, »Let us meditate together for a quarter of an hour, let silence be a common silence in us that binds us together.«

Hollydeva was impressed by the silence that immediately spread throughout the cathedral. Everyone sat on their chairs or even on the floor and closed their eyes, went inside enjoying the inner silence.

Then a bell sounded. The music was soft and gentle. Everyone sat upright.

Grand Maestra Tilia rose her voice, »Masters, adepts and novices of Linden Island! We are in a special place! We all have come a long way to this place to find that all paths lead to the same goal, the reunion with the Great Whole Totality!

»The Whole contains the whole cosmos, the universe. Nothing in this world should not be part of the Whole. How could it be?

»Why do we feel separated from the Great Whole Totality? We are not! We just think that we are! The thinking of men is what separates them. They think that they are better or worse! They think they are higher or lower! These are all errors!

»Our biggest mistake is to think that we are separate units, that we are personalities. People develop and polish their ego and their selves and become increasingly unhappy. For happiness is not to be found in superiority, but in connection with the Great Whole Totality.

»We are parts of the Great Whole like waves in an ocean. Let us be a sea, an ocean!

»We are going on eight different paths that have been developed in the history of mankind, which have often struggled and fought in the history of mankind. We know that every path has its strengths!

»We respect one another and find out what is common to our paths. The common thing is that we want to enable ourselves to go the way of overcoming our personality separated from the Great Whole Totality! The common is our love for the Great Whole Totality and therefore for all other beings in this world!

»I thank you!«

The music started again, and now it was a bit wilder. The congregation had once again stood up from the seats and had begun to dance. Now some of them jumped up and higher up, and screams were also ejected, and some clapped into their hands.

In front of the cathedral, tables were set up with sandwiches and tea. Gemina and Aquaria had hooked up with Hollydeva and bounced together, as they saw some of the adepts and older novices doing.

Then the eight yanas took their places in the square at the bell tower.

Worldviews?

Again; High Maestra Tilia spoke up, »Our present issue of the dispute is life after death! Who starts? We begin with a single sentence!«

Maestra Urana, the Prioress of the Yana of Agnus, came forward, »After death, we return to the OneGod, who graciously welcomes us, with whom we are at peace.«

Maestra Shyena, Prioress of the Dragons, took a step and shouted, »This is just a faith! The body decays after death, and so does everything else that made us! There is nothing after death!«

Maestra Corvanya also proceeded, »Death sets our soul free and releases the soul back into the trees, flowers, and animals, and stones!«

Maestra Sura, the Prioress of the Angels, replied, »Depending on good or bad deeds, we are reborn in good or bad conditions, turning in the wheel of karma.«

High Maestra Tilia exclaimed, »Good, good! We have heard four views on life after death! Our four wonderful Lady Maestras have spoken!«

Then she asked, »Who can give us further illuminating commentaries on the problem of life after death?«

Master Sycamore, the teacher of the Inner Way, stepped forward, »We have heard of four views which are quite justified each. The question can only be answered when we know for sure whether we have a soul. Soul is meant here as something that is independent of body and mind within us.

»The human being who takes only that as true, which he or she sees with her or his own eyes or because he or she can measure it, will say that there is no soul and thus: No life after the death of the body!

»The human, however, who believes that there is only the soul, a non-physical universal consciousness, which in our perception generates the body and thus the mind, will say that we return from the illusionary world of perceptions back to the reality of a Universal Consciousness which is sublime to the realm of perceptions!

»We who are here in this plane of existence can not decide which perception is true. We can only perceive which worldview enables us to certain deeds and actions.

»The view that there is no life after death compels us to fill every moment in this life! For we only have this one life and, if we do not despair due to our finitude, we will make every moment significant! At best, this attitude leads to an intense awareness of the present!

»The point of view of returning to Universal Consciousness relaxes us a little, lets us hope that suffering and pain in this world are transient phenomena! This can lead to less intensity of experiencing this world, but it can also lead to undertakings that would otherwise be too risky for us!

»All views can be taken up and put down and taken up and put down at a time in a place according to how fitting they are then!«

Master Sycamore bowed and stepped back.

Grand Maestra Tilia exclaimed, »Thanks to Master Sycamore, that was very enlightening! We perceive that there are several perspectives! Each has its justification. May the questions be circling in you during this day and next week! May you respect the views of the others! Let us do contemplative walks!«

Hollydeva walked with the words of the dispute in her head. These were important questions. She was convinced of being more than just a body. But she understood what Master Sycamore had said. »We should have a multitude of points of view at hand,« she said to herself.

»We should live any moment as if it would be the only one that would ever be, knowing that we will finally return to a superior plane of existence!«

After lunch, everyone went in a direction that Hollydeva had not yet explored.

»We're going to the stadium,« Amantes explained.

The Fighting Game of Five Levels and Elements

The stadium was a large round grass area surrounded by benches. The outer seat rows were higher than the inner, so everyone could see well. Behind the last row of seats rose a wall, two meters high, protecting the stadium from the outside.

There was a stand from where Master Abiës called for the opening of today's match day.

»Today we play the game of inner levels, the "Game of Five Elements and Levels". With the arrival of the new novices begins a new game series. All results are therefore at zero. The title defender of the last series of the game of the seven inner levels is the Yana of Dragons. Maestra Shyena, please send the five players! The opponent today shall be the Yana of Agnus!«

As the five Dragons entered the center of the stadium, they laughed and were obviously very confident that they had to compete with an easy opponent. And the five Lambs looked a bit unsure.

»That is one of your brothers,« Libra whispered to Hollydeva. Einar was one of the five players from Yana Agnus, "Brother Avela". Hollydeva looked questioningly at Libra, who probably had an eye on Einar, especially as she was in the same yana.

Maestra Urana led her team of five, which consisted of her, Avela and three other adepts.

In the Dragons' team, Hollydeva saw Maestra Shyena and Master Fagus, the geomancer.

She felt a bit sorry for her brother. The team of Dragons clearly radiated more strength and conviction.

Master Abiës shouted, »Teams, decide who of you is "beast", "child", "actor", "master", and "god"!«

This deciding obviously took place in secret. The combatants should not know who of the opposing team would impersonate which function.

Abiës explained that there would be five rounds. Whoever wins three rounds or more would be the winner and would get an extra point. The elements in each round would be decided by a lot, picked on this day by the cook of the novice's house, the admired and popular Miss Emily.

Hollydeva was pleased to see the woman who prepared their daily supper filling a role she enjoyed here on Flower Day.

The teams lined up so that the master of the yana was in the center and the other four combatants were in a square around him or her.

In the center of the playing field there was a circle.

»Send a player for combat!«

Maestra Shyena went herself and met one of the adepts from Yana Agnus.

»This is Sister Bamba!« Libra whispered to the other novices.

»Show your level,« Abiës requested.

Shyena held up a white placard. »I am the "goddess"!« she shouted.

Bamba held up a blue disk. »I am "master"!«

In the middle of the stadium, a trapdoor opened, and a play area was pushed up from below.

The playing surface consisted of two large bowls set into the ground, both about two meters in diameter. Between these two bowls was a sphere whose wall was made of a transparent material. The sphere seemed to float in the air, but it was held there by the two tube-like pipes that formed a connection to the two bowls.

Shyena and Bamba stood opposite each other behind a bowl.

Cook Emily drew a lot and shouted, »"Fire"!«

Immediately, as if out of nowhere, small fires were kindled in the two bowls. The two fires had different colors. Shyena's fire looked rather white. The fire in the bowl, where Bamba stood, was almost blue. Only at the tips were the yellow and red colors, characteristic of fire, to be seen.

The two combat mystics were in positions with which they could best focus their forces on the respective fires.

Astrello had suddenly appeared in front of the lower rows of seats, had looked searchingly and then sat down next to Hollydeva, pushing the other novicesses a little to the side. Was he an enthusiastic observer of these games? Hollydeva was glad to be close to him again and to feel his touch.

»Shyena as a "goddess" is actually invincible in the element of "fire". Shyena is the strongest player in this game anyway! However, last year, an opponent defeated her once as "beast". "Beast" can win against "goddess" through savagery!« Astrello explained to the novicesses.

»What is the meaning of these levels?«

»Now, on the level of the "goddess", you are in the state of transcendence and can hold the connection to the whole! Your will as "god" is greater than the individual will! Thus, Shyena can fuse her fire with energy from the Yrth and the Heaven. Bamba as a "master" has a forceful will and can with this will ignite a strong fire! But her resources are limited by her personality! She is, however, brave! The one whose fire fills the sphere, forcing the other fire out, wins!«

Hollydeva saw the fires streaming through the tubes and into the ball sphere. There they tried to displace each other. A white fire and a blue fire struggled for dominance. It was late in the day and getting dark now, and so the blazing fires in the sphere looked impressive.

Ultimately, as expected, the white fire won and Shyena had made a point for the Dragons.

The audience applauded, the two fighters bowed and returned to their teams.

Abiës asked the next fighters to move forward. Master Fagus, the teacher of geomancy, stepped forward. On the side of the Lambs, Maestra Urana herself became active.

Fagus held up a red placard and shouted, »"Beast"!« Urana seemed surprised, but she shouted, »"Actor"!«, while she held a green placard.

The ball and bowls were again empty and pure. Emily picked another lot and exclaimed, »"Metal"!«

Astrello commented, »"Metal" should be difficult for both at the chosen levels!«

Hollydeva asked, »Why "metal"? I thought the five elements are: "earth", "water", "fire", "air", and "ether" or "akasha"?«

»Yes, it originally was probably like that. The masters, however, changed this game two generations ago when they learned about an eastern doctrine with the five elements "earth", "water", "fire", "metal", and "wood". There are no such spectacular battles in this game with "air" and "ether". "Metal" and "wood" are better suited for this purpose!«

»And what do you expect for this fight, Astrello?«

»I find these fights very fascinating, and I've also started to try astrological calculations to predict who's going to win. We prophets on the island predict the fights and keep statistics to determine who makes the best predictions!«

Hollydeva saw that a few rows of seats up, the Chynese master of the Book of Changes and Achillea, the cartomancer, were also surveying the fighters and taking notes. An adept was walking around collecting slips from them, as well as from some other adepts and, of course, Master Betula, on which they had probably written down their short-term predictions.

As this adept collected Astrello's slips, he teased, »Well, star boy, are you going to lose to the Chynese again?«

»No, today I'll beat him. He believes too much in the Lambs and Angels!«

Into the bowls, metal had flowed, liquid silvery shining metal. Maestra Urana made movements as if she wanted to direct the metal like a tamer. Master Fagus stepped forward and kicked in the air.

Both metals now flowed into the tube. The Dragon's metal was becoming red. Urana's metal was greenish-green.

Maestra Urana worked hard. She wanted to get this point. And she did. Master Fagus was obviously not a great lover of "metal". As the geomancer he probably would have preferred the element "earth".

Brother Avela, Hollydeva's brother Einar, came next. He held up a yellow placard. The enemy was a brother Harpio of the Dragons, who also held up the yellow plaque.

»It's going to be exciting,« Astrello explained. »Both are about equally strong and experienced adepts. Both have chosen the same level! Now it depends on the element! Your brother should be good with "earth" and "wood"!«

However, it was the element "water" that was selected.

Avela strained himself very much to let his yellow-colored water flow into the ball. Harpio's water was rather orange, so somewhat darker, dyed. He had created a lot of small trickles that attacked the water of Avela like a swarm. At the end they dismantled the yellow waves and Harpio won. Hollydeva's brother looked a little kinky, and Hollydeva saw that Urana was looking at him sternly while his companions tried to cheer him up.

Milvina and Danthonius started the fourth fight. Milvina had picked the level of "master", while Brother Danthonius had the level of "child".

Astrello explained, »The Lambs are rather bad in choosing the levels. They are almost always a level below that one which the Dragons have taken. An essential part of the game is to predict which level the opponent may pick. Higher levels usually have an advantage, although it is not a hierarchical model because "beast" is stronger than "god". But Shyena as a game leader is almost unbeatable in choosing the levels!«

It was about the element "wood" and both let branches and twigs grow into the sphere. As expected, Sister Milvina's wood fingers were more aggressive and were able to displace the branches of Danthonius.

The Dragons had already won, but the last game was also played, as for the overall score all the points would be counted together.

»But the Lambs are, of course, a bit down and depressed now, and the last game should be won by the Dragons,« Astrello said.

A Brother Accipiter of the Dragons was nominated to fight against a Brother Simso. Accipiter was level "child" and Simso was of level "god". The element "earth" was like dust blown into the ball. It was an exciting fight, but ultimately Simso could win. His dust had settled against the outer wall of the sphere and then stifled everything inside. Although this was not so easy to see from the outside, the result was obvious. So the Dragons had three victories and the Yana Agnus players had scored two points. The Dragons got the extra point for the overall victory.

»That could have turned out worse for Yana Agnus!« Astrello stated.

Hollydeva had understood that this game had three components: the choice of the inner plane, dealing with the level, the element, and a personal ingenuity and power in dealing with the element on the inner plane.

There were three more of these battles between two Yanas, which looked similarly exciting and beautiful as this first one.

Hollydeva saw that some spectators were very feverish. Most of them, of course, were supporters of their own yanas. And she also saw that like Astrello there were several gamblers among the spectators, who were also eager to watch the battles.

She tried to figure out how crucial advantages were gained. And then, at the last fight, she was curious as to how the Yana of Raven would fight against the Yana of the Tigers.

Before, the Bees had beaten the Snakes, three to two. And the Angels, with four to one, had been victorious against the Dolphins, who were somehow not quite at it at all.

Maestra Corvanya came as the first Raven fighter, ready to attack Master Baghora.

»This is the greatest personal rivalry here in the monastery, I think!« Astrello informed them. »It'll be a tough fight!«

And so it was. Both had chosen the level of "god". The element was "water", which was not favored by any of both. Baghora would have won with "fire" or "earth" and Corvanya with "wood" or "metal".

The water streamed into the sphere and was barely distinguishable. At one moment, it seemed as if it was raining around Corvanya as if she were pulling the water out of the air to fight additional power in the water that was pushing for her in the ball against the Tiger's water. Baghora always made jumps like a tiger, and his water attacked jump-like.

»Are there undecided fights?« Hollydeva asked.

Astrello nodded. »But that is very rare and unlikely. The umpire, Master Abiës, would not break off, as we all know that Corvanya and Baghora are going to fight for it, and only they can agree on a tie!«

Then Corvanya won. Her water had assumed the nature of rain, and the rain had covered and assimilated the water of Baghora, and he had to give up. He looked angry. He was probably not a good loser. Hollydeva saw that Corvanya had taken on her sharp gaze. She admired her Raven Maestra and felt again that she had made a good choice.

The other Ravens, however, were not quite so happy. The Vigilio, Brother Laburnum, the adepts Brother Crow, Sister Kolk, and Brother Jay all left the field as losers. At the end of the day, the Ravens stood at the bottom of the table together with the Dolphins. But Hollydeva guessed that Maestra Corvanya had made the point that was important to her.

Chapter 23:
In the Garden.
The Stories of the Twelve
Novices

Cloudday (Monday)

It was almost routine. With the 5 o'clock bell, the six novices jumped up, clasped hands, and declaimed the morning prayer. On Cloudday, day of the moon, it was the prayer of the Silver Light.

Then they ran with the other novices and sat with them at the edge of the sea, in silence and immersion.

After breakfast, Hollydeva returned with Ariëa and Appeso to the Yana of Ravens.

»She will not be in a good mood!«

»Because of the lost game against the Tigers?«

»Yes. She defeated Master Baghora, but the others were weak. But we cannot help it. We must tell her that we are the hope of Ravens!«

»And? Could you do better, Appeso?«

»I do not think so. But I have not got a chance to find out yet.«

»Is playing not being trained?«

»Yes, but rather little. We were practicing the harmony and influence of the five elements and the elements of "air" and "akasha". I do not really know the special ways of the five elements.«

»Hmm, I have not really understood that either.«

»If you're lucky, Maestra Corvanya will tell you! Ask her! Mention that I would like to learn it too!«

»Why did not you ask her during last year?«

»I was very intimidated and shy when I entered the Yana!«

»That was your way of immersing yourself into the swarm of Ravens!«

»Or that. Maybe Maestra Corvanya has to decide whether she wants a good swarm or good individual fighters!«

»We must show her that we can do both!«

»Ah, yes. "As well as". You seem to understand the principles of Linden Island well already!«

»I picked it up somewhere. Mystics live the as-well-as!«

Then they went to drumming and dancing with the Raven family. Afterwards, Ariëa and Hollydeva found themselves with the Maestra of the Ravens, who actually looked a little grumpy.

»And how did you like Flowerday, my dear novicesses?«

»Very good, Maestra! You've shown it to the Tiger Master!«

»Thank you. And did you see how the rest of the team was doing?«

»There were all sorts of narrow results!«

»Losing by a narrow margin is almost worse than losing fat! My adepts are all spoiled. They lack bite!«

»Can I say something, Maestra?«

»Yes, of course! Stop these phrases!«

»Appeso, Ariëa and I would like to train for the game! We would like to learn from you!«

»Appeso? I am afraid that he lives the state of being hanged too much and will have lost any fight before he has started to move!«

»But I know that he is unhappy in love, and would like to show his lady that he is a hero!«

Maestra Corvanya looked to see if Hollydeva had meant that seriously. Then she understood that both irony and genuine advocacy for a friend had been included in the sentence, and laughed approvingly.

»You cheered me up, Scorpio! That is already an improvement! Unfortunately, you can only compete in the team when you have completed the first half year with some visits to the other Yanas! Then we do it with the training! And I look at Appeso more accurately! Who is he in love with?«

»I'd rather not say that. It is probably hopeless!«

»As long as it is not me!«

»Appeso is not so daring now!«

They grinned at each other.

Corvanya gave them each a booklet with empty pages. »This is your dream diary! Dreaming is important for Ravens! Become aware of your dreams! It starts with writing them down! Begin tomorrow morning after waking!«

Hollydeva considered briefly how she could arrange that with the reciting of the prayer and the running. She would just have to wake up a little before the bells would toll!

The Art of Gardening

After the lunch break, Hollydeva met the other novices of the first year in the Moon Garden, which was far back left behind the abbess's building.

It was almost like at Grandmother Algard's garden. Inside octagonal areas a mixture of plants was growing. Bushes, shrubs, and trees were planted between the beds.

Maestra Castanea came to them, »I greet you on your first day in the Moon Garden! I am Maestra Castanea. I am the garden mystic. Mystics want to become one with nature, and a garden like this one is pure nature! So where could we better meditate than here?«

Hollydeva tried to see her mother as if she were just some woman, a teacher in the monastery school. She thought that her mother did her job quite well. Her address had reached the other eleven.

»You will sow and plant and weed and water here! You will do what you do with plants in a garden! But this is not a school for gardeners, but for mystics! It's about something different! It is about learning to communicate with the plants as living creatures! It's about learning to be plants! And you can also discover the worlds of insects and worms!

»Ultimately, it is about discovering and experiencing that this world is permeated by a very fine, very deep harmony! Whoever comes into alignment with this harmony can draw from an inner power, from an inner music!«

Maestra Castanea, Hollydeva's mother, made an arm movement that seemed to encompass the whole garden and seemed to invite them into it. »Please, look for a plant, a flower, a shrub, or a grass, and sit down in front of it. Try to connect with the spirit of the plant! It may not work at the beginning! But you signal to the plants that

229

you are interested in them! Go, look for a plant! You'll be there in front of it for half an hour until I let these cymbals sound again!«

Hollydeva heard the high tone of the cymbal and sat in front of an elderberry tree. »Hello, Elder! How are you?«

But everything was quiet. Hollydeva tried to free her mind and simply be in harmony with the elder.

She remembered Guuz and became sad. She had liked the plant deva. He had been very brave and had given his life for the survival of the plant world.

Yet, the elder deva did not show up.

They returned to Maestra Castanea who held a hand in the air. After a short time a tit, a little bird, sat down on her hand.

»It's not about being a good gardener! You could learn this in any nursery! It is about a mystical union, an "Unio Mystica", to experience a revelation! As you deal with plants, animals, nature and open up, you will experience that you are a single universal consciousness! This allows communication with all creatures! This allows love and connection! When the beings of the hidden world realize that you are well-minded, they will show themselves to you!«

Gradually animals had gathered around Maestra Castanea: rabbits, mice, hedgehogs, a cat, a chicken. Butterflies flew around her nose. And then the twelve novices saw the many little plant devas that were around the Maestra. They saw gnomes and trolls and elves and fairies. Was that real? Or had the Maestra hypnotized them and dreamed a dream world for them?

Hollydeva was not impressed. She wondered why the elder deva had not shown himself to her. »Does my mother control the devas here so well, that they dare not to show themselves to the daughter, who is rejected by the Maestra of the Garden?«

Hollydeva became even more defiant. »Here, she can mother these beings, but her own daughter she left to starve!«

She had muttered angrily to herself, but the others had noticed. And her mother saw her face expression. Quickly, Hollydeva looked indifferent again, looking expectant. But she did not really succeed.

»So, dear novices,« exclaimed Maestra Castanea. »We'll be enjoying times in the garden here together. We will not only plant and water and reap and rejoice in flowers. We will open ourselves to the revelation of a grandiose creation! Let us sing a song!«

As if out of nowhere, three adepts had appeared, musical instruments with them and now tuning a simple song with the Maestra, into which the novices quickly joined. All but one who had lost her voice.

After the lesson, Castanea asked her daughter. »Hollydeva, you promised not to disturb the lessons!«

»My name is Sister Scorpio!«

»Oh, excuse me. Sister Scorpio, what was wrong with today's lesson?«

»I was disappointed as I thought you are a liar, Maestra!«

»Good, Scorpio! As I heard, you can already speak with devas and all beings. You can not learn anything here! I would like to ask you not to appear in my classes anymore! From now on, you are free at early Monday afternoon!«

They looked at each other and the wave of mutual disapproval was flowing high.

»Thank you, Maestra!« Hollydeva pushed out contemptuously and walked away. Rarely had she rejoiced in the teaching of Maestra Fraxina, who was dry and secular. »Dry and secular, but honest and useful!« Hollydeva confirmed her anticipation for the hour after this conversation with her mother.

Hollydeva's Story

»What is it about you and your mother, Scorpio?« the others were asking at their meeting after dinner.

»My mother, when I was just six years old, had disappeared with my two brothers from one day to the other, leaving me alone! She had received a call to Linden Island and reckoned that I was not good enough for this place! I lived, so to speak, alone in our house! It took two years for my father to take me to Castle Georgeburg!«

»And that is why you hate your mother?«

»I do not hate her! I would rather not have anything to do with her! I think she rejects me! We had a talk with the Abbess who set her straight and my mother had to apologize to me! I should not disturb the lessons! But I have not done well today with that assignment! So now I'm not supposed to attend Maestra Castanea's classes, and you will probably be able to enjoy her without me!«

Aquaria pleaded, »We're sorry, Scorpio! I think we found your mother fascinating! Please do not blame us!«

Hollydeva swallowed and understood. »No, it's my thing! You can certainly learn a lot from her! She has learned to garden from my grandmother and my Granna has the most beautiful garden in the world!«

»You came with her!« Piscio knew.

»We both have come with her!« Hollydeva corrected. »Yes, before I came to the island, I was with my grandmother, who also had been a maestra here at the monastery. In her Refuge I have recovered for a few days! My grandmother cares for my father and tries to heal him.«

»Heal? What disease is he suffering from?« Libra asked.

»We repelled the attack of the wizardeurs at Castle Georgeburg, and my father had caught a curse, which three wizardeurs had hurled at the Nacharya.«

»Uh, that sounds dangerous!« The novices were eager for more adventure stories.

Hollydeva looked up. »I'm worried about my father. He was good to me and trained me! Currently, the nacharyas Nononn, Achmar, and Saphed are on their way to the alchymists. The alchymists have stolen the remedy for my father, a blue strawberry. We have sent bees to tell the Nononn that he must take the blue strawberry back from the alchymists. Then my grandmother can heal my father! Or, more precise, the wizardeur Ostreaux can heal him, after he made sure that I do not become the successor of my father!«

When Hollydeva saw that the others were looking at her, disbelieving or frowning, she tried to distract that attention.

»I think your stories are at least as exciting as mine. Perhaps each and every one of us should tell his or her story in the evening!«

But Leo was not so easily distracted. »The wizardeur was supposed to prevent you from succeeding your father as what?«

»I'd rather not reveal that!«

»And could the wizardo prevent it?« Tauro was curious.

»Yes, in a way, he has prevented it. My grandmother has forbidden me and my father to take over this function again, ever again. That's why she brought me here! To learn something different! So I take another path! That's probably the better way!«

Aquaria had been watching her and had most likely taken the impression that she was now to be taken out of the focus of attention. »Your suggestion of telling our stories is good! We should do that! Tomorrow evening Ariëa begins!«

»Why me?«

»Because the zodiac signs begin with the sign of Aries!«

»Alright then!«

Hollydeva listened intently on subsequent evenings as the other novices, her friends, presented their stories. She tried to feel where the deeper pain shone through. But all of them, of course, tried to look good without coming across as model boys or girls.

Hollydeva made notes in her dream diary. She tried to feel into the others to express what her friends had shared, although in her own words.

The Stories of the Other Novices of the First Year

Ariëa:

»I grew up in Afryca in an old caravan town on the edge of the desert. The desert grows, and the ways in which goods and water reach us are becoming longer and longer. My father is a scholar and a dervish. He secretly meets the other dervishes, and they spin around their own axis for hours. My mother is a good, industrious woman. I liked to be out in the desert, I had met the desert warriors in their blue robes. I have learned from them to survive and fight in the desert. I am the middle one of three daughters, and my parents have worried. Then we ought to leave the oasis, as it was too much for the government to provide for us or because they feared revolts of the nomads. I had actually participated in nomads' attacks, and my father feared I might be arrested. That is why he sent me here, far from the desert. I should be as wise as he has become, and he hoped that after puberty I was no longer a hothead!«

"Puberty"? Holly had written down the word. She did not know exactly what that meant.

Tauro:

»I've already reported that I was a son of a merchant family. But I'm too slow to be a good trader. It interests me too little. I was always interested in stories from distant lands, fairy tales and stories. I am the youngest son of three and have a sister. My father thought that I was not capable of becoming a merchant. But he said that I was probably a good eater. I am going to travel somewhere, to invite other merchants to eat, to go to whore houses with them, to make contacts which might become important to our trading house. Here I am supposed to learn some secret abilities and, above all, the ability to adapt to different religions in order to be able to elicit secrets from my conversation partners during eating dinners and enjoying the whores!«

"Whores"? Holly wrote in her book, noting that there were things she did not know enough about.

Gemina:

»I've lived on the street in a very big city. My father was a violent drunkard and thug. I've learned to survive as a thief. The thief's guild officer took me under his wing and taught me to be a perfect thief and fighter. He became my lover. But he was too old for me. I wanted to choose my own lovers. Or actually, I do not want any lover. I have one day tried to steal from a man who was more skilled than me. He kind of invited me to steal from him and so caught me in the act. He said that I had to go with him. This was Master Anguinaga, who saw the Snake in me, who has never made an inappropriate impression on me, whose successor and his secret weapon I will be!«

"She had lovers". Hollydeva wondered. She got the impression that most pain had to do with an uncanny world, the world of pleasure and passion. And she was aware that she had lived a life without lust and passion and could not speak with the others about her experiences. "I'm a damn virgin!" she wrote. She would have to talk to Maestra Corvanya about it.

Cancra, "Shrimp":

»As you know, I come from Chyna, far east. My mother is a cook and I learned everything from her. We operated a cooking kitchen on the street. My father is weak and sick. My siblings also help with the kitchen. But we could hardly survive. Then the city quarter was demolished and replaced by new modern high-rise buildings. We stayed in a cottage on the outskirts and continued to run the kitchen, but the people there had no money. I went to our old quarter and could work as a girl in a restaurant that sold modern fast food as the people on the western continent take it. One evening I came home and my parents had sold or rented me out. I should cook for a rich Westerner. The Westerner wanted eastern food, but it was supposed to be more like the Westerner's food because he did not want to be disgusted. But he was pleased with me and took me to his country. His wife, however, accused him of being a pedophile and told me that I could not stay in their house. She sent me to Chynatown to East-Asians, but they did not belong to my family and did not want me.

The Westerner, whom I had cooked for really well, had, however, searched for me and procured the job on the island here. He probably is a brother of Master Ulmus. Master Ulmus introduced me to the Abbess, who thought that I was to develop the meta-mysticism of cooking.«

"Pedophiles". Another word Holly could not fully grab.

Leo:

»I am the crown prince of a kingdom in the north. I should at the same time appear powerful and sovereign, yet not proud or arrogant, and so on. The requirements are really very high. When my tutors noticed that I was coming to the critical age, they thought I had to be sent abroad so that I could discover myself without the prejudices of the people who surrounded me. Above all, I would probably somehow have to "break the horns", as it is called with us. At home, I can only get to know princesses who are completely inexperienced. So I need somehow more experience. But I really do not think that I will get that here. But I should also learn humility. Or begin with renunciation.«

"Let Leo break any horns". Hollydeva shook her head internally. »Novices are here for seven years to become adepts later. This is not for crown princes. What is he really here for?«

Virgo:

»I belong to the traveling people. We move around and perform theater and acrobatics. I am rather small and light, so I could always climb to the top, on the shoulders of my brothers and uncles. My father, unfortunately, was lynched by a pack in a small town in the east where we had appeared because he had beaten one of the city's superiors, who had harassed my sister. Those were bad days. We had to flee, and it has always happened that we were hunted or humiliated. But mostly we were on the road and with friendly people. I do not know how we came here on the island. We performed our tricks and a small play. The Abbess asked my mother for me to stay here. I was a bee who could use a home.«

»He is the first of them to show me and the others his pain, and knows that he belongs to Linden Island forever.«

Libra:

»My mother is a midwife in a small town in the east from here, on the mainland. I help with births. I have seen births, after which I never wanted to have a child. But it is probably due to the anatomy of the pelvis of a woman and mine is well suited, and I will have relaxed births. I would like to have many children one day. Midwives are bearers of old knowledge. In the Middle Ages they were burned as witches, as they also have knowledge about contraception and at that time they needed soldiers and did not want people to prevent getting kids. My mother told me everything she knew. I shall supplement and preserve that knowledge here, and one day I will pass it on to the guild of midwives, and perhaps all the guilds of all midwives.«

»Are midwives a group like mystics, wizardeurs, alchymists? Birth. Okay, I know how the child got into the womb. Sex. But I have not experienced it or seen it.«

Sagittario:

»My parents are professors at a major university. I always wanted to know and explore a lot. My father thinks that the greatest enemy of science is faith. But then, one evening, I heard a conversation between him and a friendly professor who said that science was also a belief, based on faith as well. Since then, I wanted to understand faith. I am aware that I am too little interested in other people and that there is too much thinking going on in my head. Running in the morning is good to me, and these talks with the other novices are too.«

Hollydeva wondered how he could be so lonely, without seeming to be bothered by it.

Capricornus:

»I'm from Afryca like Ariëa. But there is no desert where I lived. I come from the jungle and from the savanna. I have run around a lot and have seen many animals. I love animals. But there are poachers who kill animals to sell ivory and horns or anything. That made me very angry. I understand that poachers are acting out of necessity and hunger. I wanted the world to be different.

»You have to meet the powerful in the world and make them change the world, then!« my grandfather said. I went to the capital and met the president of our country. But he said that his power was limited. The truly powerful ones would be in Eyropa and Ameryca. So I hiked north. I have seen the desert and wandered through it. I've been brought across a sea on a boat. I have also seen presidents in Eyropa. I asked and asked. And somebody told me that the center of all power on Yrth was on Linden Island. But I'm still looking for a way to save the animals.«

Hollydeva noted many questions about Capri.

Aquaria:

»I come from The Brytish Island. My ancestors were Celtic wizards and mystics, and many of my ancestors were masters here on the island. I am, so to speak, following what my parents and grandparents had already decided for me. But it is my destiny and I like to fulfill it. I want to help people. Nonetheless, in me there is also a pain. I loved a boy from our village, Celt like me, Branton. He went away to bring a dragon egg for my mother and did not return. That was two years ago, and he's probably dead. I hated my mother for it. So she sent me here. "So that I may have other topics to brood about!"«

Dragon egg? Is there such a thing? How does she know she loves Branton?

Piscio:

»I was the ship's boy of the ferryman who is bringing people from the mainland to Linden Island. I am an orphan whom he has taken in. He used to hit me, and he gave me food and shelter. I watched all the people who traveled from and to the island. I could look into their hearts. They are all liars. Except for one person: Scorpio's grandmother, Maestra Malus, Grandmother Algard. She looked me in the eye, and she knew that I was looking through people. And I knew I had found the one true person. When she said that I was to go to the monastery to help Scorpio, I was very pleased to be able to serve Scorpio's grandmother.«

»Am I also a fake now? He said Granna was the only honest one. I'm afraid, he's right. He protects me rather than I am protecting him!? He's with the Bees, that's good.«

Fourth Part:
A Festival Year at the
Linden Island Mystic
School

Chapter 24:
An Evening Fire at Samhayn.
Power Animal

Samhayn (November 1st)

Their first novice year had begun on the day of the equinox between day and night, which marked the beginning of autumn. The days of the solstices and equinoxes were special and distinctive dates and were observed and honored with small festivals on the island. The same was true for the four classical festivals at the beginning of the months of February, May, August, and November: Ymbolc, Beltayne, Lammays and Samhayn, as the Celtic peoples, who probably originally dominated the island and the lands lying on the mainland shore, had once named them.

On Samhayn, the first day of the month of November, the month of fog, which indicated the entrance into the dark half of the year consecrated to death, there had been a fire and delicacies roasted over open fires that varied according to yana and tastes and food taboos.

In the evening, the novices sat around fires in their year groups and told how they had fared in the weeks before.

Aquaria, as always, was adept at leading the conversation.

»Well, how have you been during the first month? How is it with the Snakes, Gemmi?«

»Zss. Lots of snakes. I mean the poisonous critters. I'm supposed to watch them first, and then next month I guess I get to sit in a room with one for an hour every day!«

A few quiet exclamations were heard. That sounded dangerous!

Gemina then said, »Zss, but I would rather sit in a room with a snake between male legs. I haven't had sex here since my arrival, and I'm not used to it. There's a master with us, Apophis, and he's very attractive. But the female adepts — they are named after snakes, so Boa, Mamba, Cobra, and so on — have already made it clear to me to stay away from him. Then there is a maestra Manasa, who would probably also do it with a woman. I'll take her as a consolation prize, then.«

Gemina sounded audacious and amoral as usual, and some admired it and others shook their heads.

Ariëa and Capricornus, the two Afrycans, sat close to each other and the others had most likely noticed that the two had sometimes taken evening walks entwined.

But when the eyes of the round were on them, Ariëa waved off with both hands and Capricornus blushed a little and everyone laughed. The topic of sex had been brought in by Gemina, and the uncertainty that came with it actually pleased most of them.

»And you, are you still missing your Branton, the dragon egg seeker, or have you already found a replacement, Aquarium?« asked Leo.

»Ah, would you be interested?« snapped Aquaria back.

But then she became more serious, »No, I'm a little unhappy about my choice of yana. The Dolphins are not my home. I guess Professor Griseo has little to offer me. I should have gone to the Tigers. Master Sycamore's classes are the ones I like best so far!«

»Hoppla! Sycamor, has the hots for you!« Virgo had observed.

»I think I've met him before, too! I think he's friends with my parents, and he used to be in our village in Walysia!«

Then Aquaria preferred to deflect. »But you, Sagittario, get along well with the Dolphins?«

Sagittario was uncomfortable being the center of attention, but he replied, »Yes, there's a well-stocked library, and I'm left alone!«

»Zss. He has sidelined himself in the sex games as well!« stated Gemina dryly.

Everyone laughed except Sagittario.

»Libra, who do you have your eye on?«

»Hmm, yeah, there's Scorpio's yummy brothers in particular with us. I would love to pluck them. But the older one is gone away right now, visiting your grandmother.«

Hollydeva, the addressed Scorpio, nodded. Einar had gone to visit the grandmother and she missed him. It had felt good to be reunited with part of the family. But really, he should be back on the island soon.

»So what did you like about the first month, Scorpi?«

»I don't like the way they from the second year pick on us! Especially Piscio they should leave alone in the future!«

General agreement.

»Those Luna and Torre from the Tigers are bad!« confirmed Leo.

There had probably been some arguments, and especially Piscio as the smallest had been teased by the second year novices. At one point there had even been physical altercations over supper, but they had been interrupted by Maestra Fraxina, the head of the novice house.

»What are they like in the Tiger House, Shrimp?«

»Oh, I not know. I kitchen at cook, Raelyn. Cooking hot for master!«

»Raelyn!« came from Tauro.

»Oh Amor, someone's got their eye on one of the cooks!« again, Virgo remarked.

»Si, I like Raelyn. After all, I'm often at the Cellerar to trade goodies, and I noticed that Cellerar Platanus was harassing the cooks. I confronted him and Raelyn noticed, and I think I would have a chance with her. I think she's bella. And I think the cooks are some kind of gang working together underground in the monastery, maybe with the Cellerar. I'm going to find out what's going on, and that's how my path to world domination will begin!«

»World domination? Why don't you run a lap around the island first!«

»Do you really think that running around the island will get you even one step closer to any position of power?« asked Tauro back sharply, and Leo winced in surprise.

»How about Shyena?« asked Aquaria to bring Leo back into the circle a bit.

»Oh, Shyena is wonderful. But until that one considers sex with us, we think we'll have to work on ourselves for a few years and probably shovel a lot of dragon crap like we are doing now. Because that's our spiritual exercise in the yana right now. And the three dragon ladies probably don't like us either, at least they don't talk to us!«

»But aren't there also some adepts who emulate Shyena in the Yana of Dragons?« teased Virgo.

»No, they're not our cup of tea, more ascetic and stuck-up. After all, they always win in the games of the five elements. We would love to be on that team!«

»You just like being with the winners!«

»Yeah, we guess we are! What about you, friend Virgo?«

»Acharach! Piscio and I have some fun together with Matto. But we also do mostly clean. Bees are like very small dragons, but millions. The adepts are all female and led by an Opalia. They, I guess, are not quite friends with Prior Alyapis. But yes, everything is actually quite good, isn't it Piscio?«

Piscio nodded. It could have been worse. Worse he had known, too.

»Maybe you should have given him the Raven feather instead!«

»Or you give him the lion's tooth!«

»What do you mean, Scorpio, Capri?«

Scorpio sat up. »Ariëa and I had a task with Maestra Corvanya: find our power animal! For that, she gave us mushrooms to eat, and we had to lie down in a certain meadow. We've been keeping dream diaries since the beginning of the novitiate, to be able to remember dreamlike visions precisely.«

»Come on, tell more already!«

»All right. It was a Cloudday last week. We girls had said the Moon Chakra prayer in the morning.«

»Do you boys remember that one?« asked Aquaria.

The boys fussed a little.

»Go on, do it now!«

»It's Cloudday today. Do you really want to do this twice a day?«

»Yes, double is better!«

»Alright!«

They joined hands and intoned the prayer of the chakra above the head, that of the moon.

»I breathe silver-gray light into my moon center, the lunar plexus chakra!
I let the gray, white, and black flow into me from the clouds!
It flows in my skins, hair, and nails!
I am ready to be lifted up by the higher power!
I give myself recognition and appreciation!
I have value, I am doing well!
I breathe out humility and send it into the world!
May all living beings be part of the whole and give birth to the whole within themselves!«

Lionheart and Liontooth

So Hollydeva told, »I don't go to my mother's garden on Cloudday anyway, and I guess Ari was exempted from gardening that day. After we took the mushrooms and lay down, I soon felt quite unusual.

»I was dreaming away like this, so I was waiting for some animal to appear to me.«

Ariëa intervened, »Before that, Maestra Corvanya had whispered something hypnotic to us. May I play that?«

Everyone nodded.

In a deep, slightly hoarse voice, Ariëa croaked, »You will now dream a dream! And in the dream, you will travel to another world! It is a wonderful world! And yet, it is also quite similar to this one! In that dream world, you will meet an animal! Your animal will speak with you! It will tell you something important! And it will promise you that it will be your power animal! And it will also demand a promise from you! Now fly away!«

The other ten novices felt that even without the mushroom, they were about to fly off and see an animal.

»I think a bear appears to me!« quipped Virgo. But no one laughed.

Hollydeva continued her tale, »I could actually dream while being awake inside. So I flew along, swam through rivers, glided through forests and meadows. Then I paused and waited.

»I knew that my spirit guide, my power animal, would show itself shortly. I felt insects around me, but no insect would be my power animal. I sensed birds in the air. But I am connected to ravens, and it was going to be a different animal. And other birds would be careful not to get in the way of the ravens!

»But then it happened. A large, stately, male lion with a flowing lion's mane came toward me. He stood before me and eyed me. I'm going to act this out.

»"What's your name, girl?" he asked.«

Hollydeva had tried to imitate the booming, deep voice of the lion. She had succeeded quite well, for none of the other eleven had laughed.

»I said that my name was Hollydeva and that I was called Sister Scorpio in the monastery on Linden Island!

»He boomed, "I am the lion, the king of the beasts!"

»"My respects, Lord King!"

»But he was a bit haughty, acting King of the Beasts: "I don't need your reverence! People have little honor nowadays! So they have little honor to offer! Or are you different?"

»I explained that I want to help animals and plants. He said that yes, that would be quite honorable!

»I wanted to impress him and exclaimed that I would fight the alchymists who adjust the clockworks in plants! He asked if I would be successful at that!

»I had to admit that I had been busy surviving and hiding. And now I would learn in the monastery on Linden Island in the Yana of Ravens! I wanted to become stronger and learn some things to be able to defeat the alchymists. And they were under the protection of the wizardeurs!

»The lion said that I hadn't gotten very far in my fight yet!

»I said that I also needed a power animal and asked him to be my power animal!

»He laughed and boomed, "Yes, you will need the heart of a lion, Hollydeva, poisonous scorpion!"

»Then he nodded. "I agree! I will be your power animal! If you can get a lion's tooth as you continue your journey, it would help you a lot. Then you would always have access to my power! Maybe there is a tooth of a lion on Linden Island?"

»He confirmed: "You need real hard tooth! Ask your maestra! What do I get from you?"

»"What do you want? A strand of hair?"

»"No, hair I have enough! I require a gesture from you! Lions are gracious and generous! But they also punish the devious! I want you to pardon one living creature every day! Do you understand what I mean?"

»"So I, if a mosquito bites me and I slap it with the flat of my hand, shall I instead make it fly away with my sucked blood?!"

»He liked that. Yes, I should be so generous and gracious!

»So I promised!

»He promised to always be near and to give me strength and courage when needed, lion courage!

»Then I felt myself drawn back to the real world! To Corvanya, Ariëa and the ravens that flew overhead. Corvanya liked that a lion would be my power animal. What was yours again, Ariëa?«

»I met a wolf!«

»Oh yeah, that's right. Also strong, a wolf!

»I still needed the lion's tooth, though, and Ari told me to ask Capri, who was actually carrying a very valuable lion's tooth that had given him power to get here!

»He wouldn't give it up so easily, of course. Corvanya gave me a sacred feather from King Krama to offer him in exchange. If he pricks his finger with it when in danger, the ravens will come to his aid in seconds. Capri accepted the exchange, for which I am truly grateful to him!«

»Did you have to do or get something like that too, Ariëa?« asked Aquaria.

»Yes, for the wolf I have to lay out a sacrifice, a piece of meat or bone on any given day. I've been doing it for a week now and the pieces are always gone in the evening. I don't know whether there are dogs or animals here on the island that take it. I think it's actually my wolf!«

Aquaria ended the first-year novice meeting with, »We're impressed! Strong practice you Ravens did there, I think! I hope something similar happens for me with the Dolphins!«

»Let's hope we experience exciting things where we can or have to use our powers!« exclaimed Virgo, somewhat theatrically.

»Are you sure?« asked the more cautious Piscio.

»As sure as the poison of the bees will drive away our enemies, my dear brother Bee!«

»The poison of the beelets! Will that be enough?«

Everyone laughed, and they danced around the Samhayn fire some more.

Chapter 25:
A Festive Dinner at Yule. Within the Yana of Tigers

Yule (Winter Solstice on December 21st)

On the evening of the Winter Solstice, the Yule Festival on December 21st, the novices found a table laden with food and drink in the dining room of the Novice's House. All, including the second and third year novices, were surprised to find seats with their name cards, next to which small wrapped gifts awaited them.

When everyone had arrived and was seated, novice Tauro stood up.

»Allora, you will wonder from whom this food and gifts for the celebration of Yule com. You will think that Maestra Fraxina or the Abbess are behind it, or that it is so common on Linden Island. But no. The food was prepared by my friends, the cooks of the yanas and the abbey. Please give the cooking maestras a round of applause!«

Suddenly, the nine cooks of the monastery stood in the room, bowed, curtsied, and received the applause gratefully and smiling joyfully.

»My friend the Cellerar, Master Platanus, has contributed a great deal by getting things that are not otherwise available here,« Tauro added.

»Mio dio, I am neither athletically nor mystically the fittest among us novices. But I am the descendant of a wealthy family, perhaps a little penalized here. Nevertheless, after all, I aspire to world domination...«

Everyone laughed in amusement. Only Hollydeva probably suspected that Tauro was not being funny.

»And, amici, for world domination I will certainly need you. So eat with me, rejoice in small gifts, and above all, let all discord between the year novices be forgotten for tonight!«

After dinner and good cheer, the first-year novices met in the boys' dormitory.

»Tauro, how did you do it?« asked Aquaria.

»Bene, the cooks helped me a lot. I helped them a little when I got Platanus to refrain from demanding sexual favors for better goods. He didn't need it at all, anyway. The cooks are a guild of their own here, and you shouldn't underestimate them! And their families on the mainland or on the Brytish Island provide for them and are provided for by them. Anyway, through them, I was able to make contact with my family's consigliere, who supports me and through whom this celebration was financed.«

Everyone was impressed.

Aquaria, meanwhile, cautioned, »You might also want to abide by the rules of the island, Tauro. I fear that the Abbess may not approve of these enterprises and today's feasting. But I'm sure you yourself know the best way to get by here. We are all visiting other yanas right now, and we have already been to others for two weeks in November. How have you guys been? What is there to report?«

Hollydeva immediately took the floor, »Bagatto wanted to show us the Tower of Tigers. But we were forewarned by Shrimp that she wants to make herself important above all. I was actually there with her on the second day and found out that I have problems with getting affection and have to work on it. Bagatto, however, then became a bit pushy and I also stayed away from her. I hope Baghora doesn't give me, us, a negative spin on that!«

Shrimp shook her head, »Baghora not like Bagatto. I only still kitchen. Also do not go Ravens!«

»You do not visit the Ravens, no other yana?«

»No, I free from Baghora. Only kitchen!«

»But maybe you're missing something!«

Ariëa said, »Well, from what I've heard, she's cooking a goose or several here for the Christmas feast for the masters and adepts of the Tigers! And for the visitors, too. She'd be in the wrong place with the Ravens, as we don't eat poultry!«

Virgo asked incredulously, »Holla, but as visitors with the Tigers, you don't mind poultry?«

Hollydeva and Ariëa laughed, »No, we do not mind, as we have to adapt!«

Capricornus still sat conspicuously close beside Ariëa. The two were probably still lovers.

»What did you think of the Angels when you visited them in November?«

»Yes, beautiful morning rituals, with invocation and offerings. And we were in the temple and Scorpio had contact with an ancient god!«

»Ancient god?«

»Yes, I spoke to Nynurta! Ancient and dark. I'm supposed to be wary of Nacharya Saphed. But I already knew that!«

Hollydeva concealed that Nynurta wanted her to murder Saphed within a year. But she was on Linden Island and would not have known how to do it.

And she remained rather quiet during the rest of the Yule feast, especially since Tauro naturally savored being able to be the center of attention for once, to appear as a generous patron of poor mystic novices. Hollydeva liked Tauro and begrudged him.

The memory of the dialogue with Nynurta in the Temple of Angels had brought her back to the beginning of November when Astrello took his leave. He had said that he was going to join the wizardeurs in their castle of Vowharts to study astro-magic.

»I can work out pretty good predictions with astrology! But I want to know how to meet expected dangers and adversities according to the stars! I intend to be able to appease the star gods! Or I wish to be able to strengthen and use the energies I recognize! I need to learn about magic, so I'm going to the Wizards' Castle for a time!«

»I'm going to miss you, Astrello! It was good to know you were around!«

»Oh well, I'm from the far reaches of space! From there, the distances here on Yrth are still quite short! I'll always be close to you as long as I'm on Yrth, dearest Holly!«

He hugged her and pressed a light kiss to her cheek.

It was a little too much for her to feel. But she liked that Astrello obviously liked her and didn't resent his time in the dungeon of Georgeburg.

Capricorno's Dilemma

After the banquet, Ariëa pulled Hollydeva aside. »Capricorno wants to talk to you! Or rather, with us! I need to hear what he wants to expose!«

Hollydeva did feel a bit that the wine, Tauro had dished up, made her a bit subdued in the head, but she agreed.

It was cold outside, and Ariëa led her to a hut at the edge of the Angel Grove. There were garden tools put inside and it wasn't that cold in there.

Capricornus was sitting on a stool. He was speaking in that kind of pronunciation of names and substantives again where the vowel of "a" was prolonged.

»Hello, Scorpio, I need your advice and possibly your help!«

»What is it about?«

»Well, I'm with Tauro at the Yaanaa of Angels, and I've been keeping an eye on him a bit. I think he was a little irritated or incensed right at the beginning that he found himself at the bottom of the hierarchy of the island, so to speak. He was or is untrained, overweight and rather not at all knowledgeable or even interested in the mysticism or spirituality taught here. He must have been sent here by his faather for some kind of punishment or reflection. I guess I also heard that his faather somehow made sure, probably with financial support for Tiliaa, that Tauro passed the exam. This, of course, also angers Tauro.

»Tonight's Yule dinner is to serve his status among us novices, understandably. However, we should not be deceived! But it is only a vague imprint of his activities in recent weeks. He started early to trade things with the Celleraar. He probably came here with gems that he had sewn into his clothes. The gems are used to get candy, dried meat, or whatever he needs from Maaster Plaataanus.

»At Plaataanus he met the cooks who go to the celleraar to get or buy things for their kitchens. He has become friends with the cooks, who I guess form their own grouping on the island! They are a kind of gang, in connection with their families on the mainland or on Brytish Island, from whom the Celleraar buys so that everyone earns and is happy. And the cooks are probably sexually pleasing to him. So the whole thing is a kind of underground of the Linden Island, which is important for the supply and is hardly noticed by the somewhat detached maasters and priors.

»Add to that the fact that Plaataanus was a maaster of the Angels and was booted out by Suraa and Betulaa and probably has a score to settle with them, which Tauro is supposed to help him with.

»Tauro, however, is up to much more, I believe!«

Ariëa had grown increasingly agitated during his communication to Scorpio and her.

»You're betraying your novice brother, your Angel brother! This is not right! I don't want anything to do with a denunciator and a traitor!«

Had Ariëa been looking for an excuse to end the love affair with Capricornus? Or were breaches of trust actually in fact taboo for her?

»I don't want to betray him after all! I want us to help him, to keep him out of trouble!«

»Without trouble, we'd be weaklings!«

Hollydeva was about to mediate when Capricornus, startled, shook his head and stormed off.

Ariëa did not want to be spoken to by her either and disappeared in the direction of the Yanas' groves and gardens.

But Hollydeva decided to follow her. What was really going on with Ariëa?

They had been visiting the Tigers together for a week. Was Ariëa running to the Tiger tower?

Visiting the Yana of Tigers

When they had knocked on the Tigers' door a week ago, accompanied and provoked by Sister Luna and Brother Torre, Prior Baghora had greeted them kindly.

»So you are with us for two weeks, Sisters Ariëa and Scorpio!«

Hollydeva had a great deal of respect for Master Baghora, who seemed more powerful than the Nacharya or her father or anyone on the island in terms of personal charisma.

»I understand, Scorpio, that you have been in the service of the OneGod!«

»Yes, I was a student of my father, the Grand Inquisitor of the Nacharya!«

»Your mother: you will have already heard that she wants to join the Yana of the Tigers! But that is rather still secret.«

Hollydeva made a face that showed him that the yana would gain nothing in prestige with her by this defection.

Baghora bristled and continued, »Very well, we are the yana of the OneGod on our way to the left hand! We do not seek the mercy of the One Almighty! We practice and improve ourselves to receive His power to perform deeds in His service! Reaching our full potential!

»It is all One! One great universal consciousness! We can unite with it and let its power and force flow through us! We can manage and direct this power!

»How do you feel about monotheism, novicess Ariëa?«

Ariëa shrugged her shoulders and remained silent. To her these days these philosophical questions seemed rather trivial.

Baghora looked at the two of them. »I must tell you that we are the yana on Linden Island, that is connected with the wizardeurs, sorcerers and magicians! And you,

Scorpio, have after all already encountered some of the most powerful wizardeurs, and have even driven them out of Georgeburg Castle!«

»I've only impaired them!«

»After all! You must know that there are factions in all power groups! There are wizardeurs allied with the alchymists. There are independent contract wizardeurs like Master Ostreaux. And there are wizardeurs who reject the pact with the alchymists and support the Nacharya, but again are divided within themselves.

»We, masters of the island, are also divided! Those of the right ways and those of the left ways do not like each other very much. We monotheists quarrel with the polytheists and atheists. I think I actually get along best with your Maestra of Ravens!

»You should know that the Nacharya Onthronn Achmar is my foster brother. We grew up together and were educated together. We have survived many battles together and are loyal brothers to each other. I am worried about Achmar, who rode to the alchymists to assist the Nononn!

»Very well, I burden you with too many of my thoughts! You may address and question me at any time, Ariëa, Scorpio! You may speak with Master Sycamor, and he will gladly give you further instruction in the mental, spiritual exercises!

»Most importantly, I want you to take yourselves under the wing of Sister Bagatto for the two weeks! You know her! I want her to show you a few things and, above all, I want her to discuss with you the philosophy of the OneGod!

»Beware of the novices Torre and Luna! They are deceitful and vile! I must tell you that they have energies that I intend to use, that I promote and cherish! So rather don't get in their way or even try to make them better people! They shall not be good! That concerns you just the same! I don't want good people here! That is rather the aim of the Yana Agnus! We here want to be above the law and conscience. We aim to do the right thing, in the sense that we grow to our full stature so that we can rise above.

»Come, I'll show you the tiger!«

But then Master Baghora remembered an appointment and promised that he would show them the tiger another day. They should now look for Bagatto, who already knew about it.

Bagatto, the third-year novicess and spokeswoman for the novices on the island, began with disparaging statements about these two Ravens, who obviously thought they were special.

Then she led Hollydeva and Ariëa to the Tower of the Tigers. They had already heard about this tower from Shrimp, who, however, had stopped interacting with Bagatto early.

The tower consisted of five floors, with seven rooms on each floor. In each room, a specific theme would be updated, so the seeker would receive feedback that would tell him or her what to work on.

Ariëa, annoyed by Bagatto's lectures, broke off even after an hour. Hollydeva at least walked with her through the rooms on the bottom and top floors.

But when she was supposed to get to know the orange room of affection on the second floor of the tower with Bagatto the next day and Bagatto wanted to press her weak point too much, she also ended the cooperation.

In the days that followed, Bagatto tried to get in touch with her again, but Hollydeva blocked. She would rather not talk to this ambitious novicess about her weaknesses.

They preferred to help Shrimp in the kitchen and see that they spent their time with the Tigers inconspicuously. Torre and Luna had also lost interest in them or had been admonished by the master.

But on the penultimate day, Master Baghora himself fetched them from the kitchen. »Come, Ariëa, Scorpio, you have earned something! You get to pet the tiger!«

»How did we earn anything?«

»You've shown the over-achiever her boundaries! If she can't handle you, she thinks, she must try harder or change. I'm getting tired of her ambitiousness! And I don't think she'll ever get with herself that way! You have done her a favor! Unfortunately, she doesn't recognize it yet! But I don't want you to feel bad about your time with the Tigers! Come along!«

Then Master Baghora had actually shown them one of the tigers in the enclosures, and he had it so under mental control that it actually let Ariëa and Hollydeva scratch its neck, purring.

They felt the powerful presence of the noble big cat. »Thank you, Master Baghora!«

»Remember that you never know the whole story and rarely the very broad framework in which this story happens, Scorpio, Ariëa! Cut yourselves some slack! And allow yourselves to be forgiven! And forgive the ones that have harmed you, too!«

Hollydeva knew that he meant especially her mother, who, after all, would become a maestra of the Tigers. And she felt that she had a long way to go if the goal was to be "forgiveness".

Chapter 26:
A Festival of Lights at Ymbolc.
Back at the Refuge

Ymbolc (February 1st)

At the beginning of February the Celtic festival of light, "Ymbolc", was celebrated on the island. Everywhere lights were lit on the evening of the first day of February, probably to drive away winter, to declare the dark season over.

But the round of novices was quickly dispersed. Ariëa had most likely finally broken up with Capricornus and seemed a bit lost. She had complained in the days before that her father wanted her to give him insights into what was happening in the world. But she didn't learn anything on the island, even though she had the impression that the masters of the island were constantly meeting with nacharyas and other important people and concocting activities concerning the world. She would not have known how to convey messages to her father in the Afrycan desert anyway.

She was probably especially angry with her Raven sister Scorpio, who was favored by Prioress Corvanya and now had also been taken with masters of the island to fight outer-world beings. Ariëa would have very much appreciated conveying some critical information to her father back home in Afryka. But this Scorpio had come back distraught and silent, and Piscio, who had also been on this expedition, had told her that Scorpio would tell it herself when she was ready.

Capricornus, since his betrayal of Tauro had brought him the painful termination of Ariëa's love, was apparently no longer interested in the developments of the other novices or of Linden Island. He seems to have distracted himself with love affairs in the community of Angels. He had been seen with the mandala maestra Coryla, the older novicess Sister Sol, and with the palm reader Achillea. And from the gathering at the Ymbolc festival, Maestra Betula herself called him!

Aquaria had been invited by Master Sycamor to look with him at the lights at the Tigers. The other novices looked at each other questioningly. Love relations with masters were surely not allowed.

Aquaria noticed the irritation of the other novices and signaled to Master Sycamor to leave, but this caused even more curiosity or a kind of gloating.

Sycamor understood and left, and Aquaria was in a terrible hurry to ask novicess Scorpio to come with her.

»Come, Scorpi, let's sit somewhere together, and you tell me exactly what happened at your grandmother's. It's heavy on your mind, and it will help you to tell me!«

Back at Granna's Refuge

»Scorpio, we have all heard about the creatures in the Refuge and that something happened to your grandmother, who used to be an important maestra here. But what exactly happened in the Refuge, Scorpio? Tell me! Please!«

»Why do you want to know?«

»Because you are my friend! And because I've already heard about your grandmother, about Maestra Malus, the Apple Tree Maestra, from my parents, who were also novices, adepts, and even masters here. My mother must have hoped at that time that your grandmother would become abbess here and not the Vritra of Dragons, Tilia. Please tell me how Maestra Malus fared!«

Hollydeva looked at Aquaria and faltered. But then she nodded.

»All right, Aquaria, I'll tell you exactly what happened on that expedition to my grandmother's Refuge.

»A force had been assembled: the masters Baghora, Sycamor and Maestra Corvanya, Nacharya Rokudan Aoi, my mother. Corvanya had with her the adepts Kolk and Kitta, who kept the connection with the ravens above them. From the bees had come an adept Opalia, who mentally connected with a swarm of bees. Oh yes, and Piscio was with us, since he knows well the ferry and the area between the ferry dock and the Refuge. And there are probably other reasons why Piscio is so promoted and pushed forward by my grandmother and some masters!

»Tilia said goodbye to us, we got to the Refuge unmolested and entered my grandmother's croft. She must have been amazed at how all at once this troupe filled her good parlor. Ravens had perched on the roof. Bees populated the flowers in the front garden.«

Aquaria interrupted, »Wait, you said Rokudan Aoi! Hadn't he attacked you on your escape from Georgeburg?«

»Yes, he had, along with the Nacharya Quavert! But now it turns out that Rokudan Aoi is the nacharya assigned to the Ravens! Quavert is with the Snakes! My grand-mother was already kinder to him than I would have expected! He appeared in our Yana house just after New Year and Maestra Corvanya mediated between us. And then he actually apologized to me in such a way that I had to see him with different eyes. Anyway, he reported a dramatic increase in creatures in my grandmother's Ref-uge, so a squad from Linden Island had to go and see. That was the right thing to do, and unfortunately, it didn't end well.

»Anyway, we reached the Refuge. The nacharyas Daman, my uncle, and Quavert were there, too. I checked on my father, who was still weak but watching everything from his bed. You do remember that my father had been badly caught by a curse from the wizardeurs?«

Aquaria nodded, showing that she was eager to hear the rest of the tale.

»The wizardeur Charles Ostreaux had stayed in the background, as wizardeurs are just not so well regarded among us at present. But the grandmother explained that because of that wizardeur's actions, the father would be much better off.

»"Please show us the creatures!" Master Baghora had then asked in a tone that indicated his readiness to fight.

»So we all went out into the gardens of the Refuge to the spot on the outer hedge that Daman showed us.

»There squatted these creatures. They appeared to be eating carrots.

»They had gray skin or were dressed in something close-fitting gray. Their shape looked like that of small humans with arms, legs, torso, and head. But instead of a face, we saw only a blank surface.

»The creatures probably perceived that a threatening force was approaching them. They jumped up and stood in our direction.

»I had sat down a little apart. I wanted to feel if I could get access to the beings. Master Sycamor had sat down next to me. He most likely had heard of my talents and possessed similar ones himself.

»Opalia had sent the bees to the beings. They quickly returned, however, and Opalia reported that the bees thought these beings were completely alien and could not establish any communication with them.

»A raven tried to peck at the creatures. But the creature held up a hand, from which, as I had seen before, a spike shot out in a flash, killing the raven.

»Quavert shot an arrow. The targeted creature raised a hand, from which a kind of shield shot out that easily intercepted the arrow.

»I sent them a question, "What do you want? Who are you?". But I got no answer.

»Then we saw more of these beings coming over the hedge so that their troop had now grown to about twenty beings.

»Wizardeur Ostreaux sent a magic pulse with one of his Latyn spells. This was the first thing that seemed to impress the beings. They backed away a bit and made their strange movements that looked like random twitches.

»"It is imperative that we first close the crack, the door through which they enter!" decided Baghora, who had become something like the leader.

»Maestra Corvanya nodded and asked, "Who has experience with such doors to other worlds?"

»"There has been such a thing in history!" recalled Rokudan Aoi, "We must sew it up!"

»Adept Opalia said that the bees could sew it shut. But she didn't know which thread would have the power to keep the door closed.

»"My mother has silk!" suggested my mother, Maestra Castanea.

»"Let's try it!", Corvanya confirmed.

»So Opalia, Corvanya and Castanea went to the crack to close it.

»The creatures did not seem to have noticed this plan or did not want to stop it.

»I reported that I could not get access to them! I could talk to plants and animals, put myself in their place! But I can't do that with humans! Therefore, I suspected that the beings were probably humans or human-like beings! They were wearing some kind of highly technical suit! They seem to have eyes and ears like we have, but they were shielded by the suit!

»Master Sycamor nodded and agreed with me!

»He called out to Baghora and the nacharyas that those creatures could be human-like beings wearing a high-tech suit.

»"We need to find out how they communicate with each other!"

»"Probably via high-frequency thought transmission!"

»The creatures, however, seemed to eat the vegetables from the grandmother's garden. When they ate, they bent to the side and their mouths were not visible.

»"They're hungry!" commented Daman.

»My grandmother put some vegetables in a basket and made an effort to go to the creatures.

»"Stop! Mother, what are you doing!" Daman tried to stop her. But she just went.

»Corvanya, Castanea and Opalia came back and reported that the crack could be closed by the bees with the silk.

»My grandmother now actually approached the creatures and showed them her basket of vegetables. She wanted to show them with a gesture that they were welcome, that the residents and visitors of the Refuge were peaceful.

»I had the impression that the beings had perceived and understood the grandmother. They came closer.

»My grandmother put down the basket and took a step back.

»But at that moment Corvanya must have given a sign to the two raven adepts so that they ordered the ravens to attack the creatures!

»The ravens swooped down on the creatures and tore into their gray protective suits with their beaks! A glow of light or something red shone through the cracks. Desperately, the creatures sought to help each other and close the cracks! Opalia had now also set the bees on the beings, which were stinging the protective suits or even the open areas.

»But most of the creatures had gone over to fight. Sharp extensions shot out of their fingers again. They were killing the ravens they could reach. Some had also turned their fingers into fly swatters, which they tried to kill or drive away the bees. Two of the creatures had turned toward the humans and were trying to hit them or keep them at a distance with the beams protruding from their fingers. They could not hit anyone, however, as the distance was probably too great. The only person within their reach was the grandmother, who had stopped at her good-natured offering, the basket full of vegetables and fruits. Everyone cried out when a long beam from the finger of one of the creatures hit the grandmother, who immediately fell to the ground.

"Stop the attack!" yelled my mother, Maestra Castanea.

»Ostreaux was again able to force the creatures back a bit with some incantations. Castanea, Daman and I rushed to the grandmother, who was breathing weakly. They carried her out of the beings' area and laid her on a grassy bed.

»"Mother, can you hear me!" My mother bent over her.

»Grandmother Algard opened her eyes once again, saw her daughter and son. Blood was shooting from the wound in her chest. I put a hand on her upper arm.

»"Let the creatures stay here in the Refuge!" whispered my grandmother. "They are starving!"

»Then my beloved Granna had sunk back and died.

»I felt as if the worst thing I could imagine had happened.

»My mother was furious. "Why did you let the ravens attack?"

»Maestra Corvanya was very distressed, but preferred to remain silent. Baghora looked at Castanea and said seriously, "We had to do this! I am sorry for mother Algard! She should have gone back!"

»My mother wanted to say something back, but Baghora must have been a master she had to respect, and she bowed her head. "It is only grief that speaks from me!!! Forgive me, Maestra Corvanya!"

»They carried my grandmother back to the house.

»The next day, we buried the grandmother in the Refuge she had cherished and loved so much.

»Nacharya Daman, my uncle, gave a speech at the grave. He then decided to stay in the Refuge. He would know the protective magic that his mother had set up, even though it probably couldn't do anything against the beings.

»Daman said that he would try to make contact with the beings peacefully. They were free now to go into the garden and feed themselves. Baghora suggested that everybody else should return to Linden Island.

»Ostreaux reported that he would stay near the Refuge.

»The creatures were injured and in distress. They huddled in a corner of the Refuge. Some probably ran to the crack, but it was now closed. They would be glad to be left alone for now.

»I then supported my father, who was also to come with us to Linden Island. "Your grandmother loved you very much, Hollydeva!" he said to me.

»I replied, "Yes, she did! But she also kept me away from her just as my mother did!"

»"Hmm," my father grumbled in agreement. "She still loved you!"

»"Yes, I would have liked to know that here was a place and a person where the world was all right, where I could always go! I guess that's destroyed now!"

»My father then said, "We must find the peace, the home, within us! Pardon this platitudinous wisdom!"

»And I, "I wish for a real home!"

»Then Corvanya had stepped in and grasped my hand. "Your home is forever the Yana of Ravens, Scorpio!"

»That was meant sweetly, but I felt that this home would not be enough for me, that the wound was already greater than the well-meaning Maestra and her Ravens would be able to close.«

Aquaria grabbed Hollydeva's hand and held it.

»I have always had a home in our village in Walysia. My mother was a maestra in the Yana of Dragons, and now she guards our village like a Dragon princess! I have felt safe and can go back there anytime! If that was lost, and I had to rely on the Yana of Dolphins, I would despair! But you will always have me as a friend, Scorpio! And I have you, haven't I?«

»Yes, Aquaria, Ellianne. From now on, when we're among ourselves, let's call each other by the names we'll have outside the island when we get to your village in Walysia! I am Hollydeva!«

Aquaria nodded and squeezed Hollydeva's hand.

Chapter 27:
Eggs and Garlands at Oystara.
A Spyess

Oystara (Spring Equinox at March 21st)

At the spring equinox in March, the beginning of spring, the Oystara festival was celebrated on the island. There were countless eggs, painted and unpainted. The individual yanas organized dance and music. Everyone was happy to have survived the cold, stormy winter.

For the first-year novices, this first winter on Linden Island had been an exhausting time. They had had to learn a lot in the academies and with Master Fraxina. The respective yanas had also kept them fully occupied. Cold and wet had contributed to colds and coughs.

The first year novices met again in the evening for a round around the fire behind the novice's house.

Leo was the first to speak: »We have something to tell you! The dragon ladies have finally spoken to us! We've been shoveling their crap and bringing them food for half a year, and now they've accepted us!«

Virgo asked what they had said.

»Oh, they teased us a little, and they knew who we were, even more than that. They know our mother, Queen Sigfreya of the Ice Kingdom. They said they owed us something. But they always sound a little threatening, and we don't really know now if they are well-disposed towards us or if they want revenge for something.

»But then we helped Tilia to meet and talk to the dragons! She knows what the dragons would have to do with us. We think she wants to tell us later this week.«

»Tilia? The Abbess?«

»Yeah, that's the one. We think she used to have a position in the Yana of Dragons. It's called 'the Vritra'. And the dragon ladies are mad because she would have given up or neglected that position for the post of abbess.«

»Well, that sounds exciting. And did you tell Shyena everything?«

»No, we are careful about that. If we try to make ourselves interesting or seem like a good student, she will ignore us! We have to be as arrogant as she is.«

»Zss. Well, arrogant you will be able to do, little prince!« teased Gemina.

Virgo: »Agora! Piscio is also increasingly successful at communicating with animals here! I'm afraid I can't even talk to the bees! I'm supposed to learn how to do that, but I have no idea how!«

»You'll be able to do it! Take your timelet!« Piscio tried to cheer up his friend.

»What animals have you been talking to now, Piscio? Any flowers as well?« asked Libra.

»Oh, all kinds of small animalsies: Hedgehogs, martens, mice! Songbirdsies! And I think I can talk to little fishlets, too. I am not sure, though. Scorpio, you'll have to come with me sometime and tell me if what I'm hearing is actually their language!«

»I don't know the language of the fish! I've never talked to fish before! But, Piscio, I'll be happy to come along!«

Capricornus asked, »Scorpio, you did speak to a deity in the Temple of Angels, didn't you?«

»Yes, I did. His name was Nynurta. It seemed real, but I was in some kind of trance. I don't quite know what to make of it!«

»Yes, I've experienced something like that, too. Suraa also had me meditate in the little temple and something opened up on me and an Afrycan goddess appeared to me, Iëmaanjá. Iëmaanjá was my favorite goddess already! She explained some things to me. And it must have been a real contact because what she said made sense, and it was a realization which I didn't have yet and couldn't have had!«

Everyone indicated that they found this interesting.

Aquaria now was all in too, »What did she say, Capri?«

»She asked if I had a wish. I said that I am faar from Aafryka on this trip because I want the dying and suffering of the animals to end. And I said that I wished at all for the world to be harmonious and peaceful!

»The Goddess answered that I would misunderstand the character of this world in which I would be. This world would be created because the builders in her world would have succeeded in eliminating death and disease and murder and the like. But that would be a completely boring world in which there would be no more chance for awakening and traanscendence, as the development of the soul would require pain.«

»Oh!« exclaimed Scorpio »I've heard something like that as well!«

»Go on, Capri!«

»She said that only those threatened with death could become awake and stay awake. I would have to accept that there would be death and suffering in this world. My activism would cause a separation between me and this world, which would prevent me from developing to the next level!

»Then she said that I should support you, Scorpio, in your fight against the alchymists, your fight for the survival of plaants and insects and animals!«

Scorpio nodded and mumbled agreement.

»But I thought that was unfair. I should support you, while I should let go of my own fight for the survival of animals! But Iëmanjá said that we were at different stages and that I first had to accept and embrace this world as it was. You would already be ready to admit the pain of this world, and it would be important, however, that you save it and take care of its further existence.«

Hollydeva was just embarrassed by this excessive appreciation, and she tried to play it down a bit, »And now I'm sitting here on the island, far away from the battlefield, immobilized! But thank you, Capri, that was beautiful and deep, the way you said that. Will you keep talking to Iëmanjá?«

»Yes, I will. She wants to tell me more!«

»Zss. I have a goddess like that, too!« volunteered Gemina.

»Really? Tell us, Gemina!«

»Zss. Yes, really! It surprised me, too. Prior Anguinaga wanted Maestra Manasa to show me the gods in the Temple of Serpents. It's a mostly underground complex full of rooms with statues and paintings. All gods of some sort, and in the case of the Snakes, of course, the more dark and voracious gods. Are gods memories of aliens, or are they projections of subconscious human abysses? Did I just say that? Something is happening to me!

»Zss. Anyway, Manasa showed me around, and then she showed me an even deeper tomb, a room with ten large paintings on the wall, the ten so-called Mahavidyas. They are the goddesses of a religion from Yndia called Tantra.

»These ten look dangerous, I tell you!

»One had a necklace with skulls around her neck and danced on the corpse of a man. Another had her own head cut off. Manasa wanted me to choose one or let one choose me.

» But I had already been chosen by one of these, who had somehow begun to come alive in the painting and speak to me!

»Manasa explained to me that was Dhumavati, the Mahavidya of the outcasts. Well, that suited me!

»Dhumavati lives in graveyards is old and unsightly, full of ashes of the dead. But she is so very powerful, a mighty protector. But there's a catch!«

»What kind of catch, Gemmi?«

»Zss. Manasa said that Dhumavati lives without sex and celibate. If I want her power, then I have to go her way and live equally without sex and pleasures!«

»Is it worth it?«

»Zss. Yes, I'm afraid it is! I guess Dhumavati is my way!«

Tauro had started handing out delicious looking cookies.

»Cibo! Are these your drug cookies, Tauro?« asked the well-informed Virgo.

»He's not that brazen!« reassured Capricornus.

They nibbled cookies, and Hollydeva wondered what drug that could have been on the cookies. True, Capricornus had become a traitor to a friend in Ariëa's eyes. But it was good to know what was going on.

Aquaria asked the group, »Who are these gods? Where do they live? Are they imaginary or do they have an existence of their own?«

»Who could know?«

»Is the OneGod also just one of many?«

»If I understood it correctly, Iëmaanjá said that the world we live in here is created! Who are the builders? Are they our gods? Or are the gods still somewhere else?«

»We cannot know, we are not supposed to know! We are to have an experience that is real, that we do not separate ourselves from.

»Or are we supposed to have an experience and watch ourselves, and learn, and wake up?«

»Master Shishumara would know!«

»The black mystic? Are you sure about that, Sagittario?«

»Yes, I think he has done a lot of research and understood. I'm studying his notes in the library of the Dolphins right now! I think he is being misrepresented by the Abbess!«

»The Abbess? The Grand Maestra! Surely, she wouldn't do such a thing? She banished him to protect the island!«

»Or to give Griseo and the alchymists a yana of the island for a lot of money!«

»Sagittario! You are a heretic!«

Everyone laughed at this idea, or at the fact that the novice, silent in himself, was possibly the one who nurtured the most audacious thoughts within himself.

Even on the nights before the great festivals, a guard had to watch that the island would have early warning of an attack from the sea. The night of the beginning of spring was one of those nights when Hollydeva would be awakened in the middle of the night to make the rounds of the island with Libra. However, they had both decided to keep the feast alive until the start of their watch shift to stay awake and pull an all-nighter.

In the weeks before, they had sat for long periods of time on the bench at the Grove of Lambs that Libra loved so much. Hollydeva had probably noticed that Libra was questioning her. Why did she want to know everything about the Nacharya? Why was she asking so specific questions about the wizardeurs and alchymists?

But Hollydeva liked to be asked, and she liked that this friend believed her granting her to be experienced in the world, knowing the mighty of the Yrth.

And Hollydeva was aware that Libra was in a yana with her mother and brother and that she could probably ask her father, the former Grand Inquisitor, who was being cared for in the infirmary there.

»Do you miss your grandmother, Scorpio?«

»Oh yes, I do. She was the wisest and most loving person I knew!«

»Do you want to take revenge on the creatures?«

»No! They couldn't help it! They were just defending themselves! It was more the impetuosity of the ravens and bees that triggered it! But Corvanya and Opalia had also only meant it right. Master Baghora made that at once clear to the whole party! But of course, the creatures are strange and dangerous, and they most likely are our enemies from that encounter on! Nonetheless, I think the nacharyas have already thought about how to deal with them!«

Libra nodded, and then she must have dozed off after all.

Hollydeva was also feeling heavy eyelids then, after all it was just before sunrise early in the morning when she thought she was addressed.

»Hollydeva, listen to me!«

»I am hearing you! Who is speaking?«

Vimala, a Spy and a Saboteur

»Am tree on whose trunk you sit! Am an old copper beech tree and have seen many things. Am in contact with all the other trees and plants here on the island, exchange ideas about everything continually.

»Listen to me carefully! You may have wondered why you haven't had any contact with the plant devas here before. We know that you were friends with Guuz. But your mother controls the plants here and forbade us to help you or talk to you!

»Am old and was a good friend of your grandmother, Maestra Malus! Am not in your mother's garden and don't have to obey her and have to tell you something!«

»I hear you, friend Copperbeech!« Hollydeva let herself be heard softly, so as not to wake Libra.

»It's about your friend here next to you, who often sits here and whose thoughts I can hear!

»She is not who she says she is. And in the meantime, she's on a dangerous path that you should know about in order to save her!«

Libra seemed rather a bit staid to Hollydeva. What was the copper beech trying to tell her?

»Libra, Vimala, daughter of a midwife. Midwives, guild that in the history of past centuries suffered a lot from the orthodox churches of the OneGod! Knowing about births! Knowing about avoiding fertilization or killing unwanted pregnancies early. Midwives want to harm the right-handed OneGod worshipers, to take revenge on them. Yana Agnus here on the island is a central place of the worshipers of the One-God. Vimala, spy and saboteur.

»She making move on your mother, knows also averse to the Yana, at odds with Prioress Urana.

»You also watch Tauro! Asked Vimala who in Yana Agnus interest drug cookies. He insight and control over finances! He knows Libra wants harm Yana Agnus!«

Hollydeva thanked the copper beech tree for talking to her, providing her with access to the extensive network of plants on Linden Island. She had already thought that no deva had shown itself to her because her mother had stopped it. She promised the copper beech to ensure that the peace of the island would be preserved. For the trees wanted peace and quiet in their surroundings and in general.

So Hollydeva decided to quiz the just-waking Libra over the coming days and night watches about Maestra Castanea, the garden maestra, and her own daughter-rejecting mother, to find out if Libra was indeed seeking the garden maestra's proximity to find ways of sabotaging the yana.

And perhaps, she maybe would want to support this agent of the midwives.

Chapter 28:
A Witch Dance to Beltayne.
Messages by the Bees

Beltayne (May 1st)

The night before the beginning of May was known as the Night of the Witches, night of Valpurgys. On Linden Island, the trees were decorated for the beginning of May, the festival of Beltayne. This was the festival of the sun, which would usher in the bright summer in May. The night before, however, the worshipers of the night would have their say.

»Come along!« urged Maestra Corvanya to the novices of the Ravens, Hollydeva, Ariëa, and Appeso. On the northern shore of the island, the other adepts and masters of the Ravens were already gathered. Hollydeva also saw some adepts of the Bees and Snakes.

They were rowed over to the shore. Boats and rowers had probably been hired from the port city, which was thirty kilometers north of the island.

Then they headed inland about a kilometer to a clearing where some of Hollydeva's old friends, druyds and fire maiden, were already gathered.

Adept Jackdaw, as usual, quickly provided rhythmic music, there were slightly intoxicating drinks and a boisterous mood.

The seeress Medea had soon approached Hollydeva. Hollydeva embraced the sturdy woman who had stood by her eight months ago.

»How are you doing on the island, Hollydeva?«

»Oh, thank you, Maestra Medea! Quite well. I am with the Ravens and very happy with Prioress Corvanya. But I'm also still worried about the world, and I still feel that I need to intervene, that I need to stop the alchymists from tampering with the clockworks of the plants.«

»Yes, I understand that. And yes, the situation has become rather more threatening. More land has been contaminated by their altered plants, many insects have died. The birds are getting fewer.«

»And the wizardeurs still protect the alchymists?«

»Yes, I suppose they do. The wizardeurs need money and the alchymists have it. It's a new time when money is important. Everything has to be financed and paid for. The alchymists allow the wizardeurs to continue living in their magical dream world!«

»Then we need money too!«

»No, we should leave it alone, retreat to the woods and wait! They'll dig their own grave, and one day they'll be out in the woods looking for food!«

Hollydeva didn't look convinced. But she was aware that her talk was cheap! She was just a novicess in the sheltered, remote monastery world!

»How is your father?«

»He's still impaired and mostly in bed!«

»Didn't your grandmother have a cure procured?«

»Yes, the wizardeur Ostreaux felt that only a blue strawberry could ultimately remove the curse, and we had sent bees to tell the Nononn to reclaim the last blue strawberry from the alchymists! I don't actually know what happened to that!«

»Well, ask Master Alyapis. He'll know what the bees in the distance know!«

»Can I also ask Opalia?«

Opalia was the adept of the Bees, who had also been with them at the Refuge. She was accompanied by a gaggle of Bee adepts. They were dancing exuberantly around the fire.

»No, you'd better ask Alyapis! Opalia may not want your father to get better!«

The feast went on all night and Hollydeva was warmly greeted, hugged and later seen off by all the fire maidens and druyds.

Messages Delivered by the Bees

On Beltayne Day, May Day, Hollydeva asked Piscio if he could ask Master Alyapis to ask the bees about the whereabouts of the bees they had sent to the alchymists.

In the evening, Piscio reported that she should come with him to Master Alyapis the next morning.

Master Alyapis asked her to come with him to the bee garden. There were beehives everywhere and the air was buzzing with thousands of bees.

»Bees are constantly talking among themselves and a message reaches them very quickly over very long distances. But they are seldom interested in what is happening far away!«

He pulled on a pipe and sat down on a bench. He motioned for Hollydeva to sit next to him. Piscio took place down on the grass some distance away.

»Did I understand that correctly? You sent bees out to deliver an order to the Nacharya Nononn?«

»Yes, that is so. These bees had once protected me and led me to a group of druyds. Then they had led me to the Refuge of my grandmother, who has now just sadly passed away. My father needs a blue strawberry for his recovery, which the flies of the alchymists had just stolen. I asked the bees to tell Master Nononn to reclaim the blue strawberry from the alchymists so that my father could be cured!«

»Good, good. That's a lot of information! I am really sorry about your grandmother! After all, she was Maestra Malus here for several years, Yana Agnus like her daughter. I always got along well with her!

»I'm going to ask some of my bees here if they've heard about those bees you sent out there!«

Hollydeva tried to listen in on the master's conversation with the bees. But he seemed to be able to have a lot of conversations at the same time. It was as if he were talking to the whole field of bees around him at the same time. Thousands of whispering voices came back to him.

Master Alyapis was very concentrated and she forgot time and space beside him. Then he straightened up and turned to her.

»I have heard very much, Scorpio! And little you will like it!«

Hollydeva nodded. What worse could happen! It seemed to her that she was unjustly in a haven of peace on the island, and all around the earth was crumbling.

»The bees have met and spoken with the nacharyas at the alchymists. The flies also arrived there with the blue strawberry that they had stolen from the grandmother's garden. But when Nononn heard that he had to bring them back to the Refuge to save the Grand Inquisitor, he was killed by the alchymists! The Nacharya Saphed betrayed and deceived him! The Nacharya Achmar defended him and fought back, but is now in a dungeon of those alchymists on Lead Mountain.«

This was more shattering news!

»Come, Scorpio! Let us go to the High Maestra and convene the Council of Masters, to whom we must report this! The death of Nacharya Nononn is a weighty matter! It changes the power system on the Yrth a lot! And a new Nononn must be found and trained! Come! Piscio, you please join the other adepts and fulfill your duties!«

Master Alyapis went with her to the Abbess and reported what he had learned. She immediately instructed the masters working in the abbey and had the priors of the eight yanas summoned. Then she also sent for Maestra Fraxina and Master Sycamor.

»Is your father up and about yet?« she asked Hollydeva.

»Yes, he can walk around! But he's still kind of reduced by the wizardeurs' curse!«

»Tell him to come here, too! Go get him, please! Your mother too!«

Hollydeva ran to the Yana Agnus and had herself brought to her father, who was sitting in a chair in his room, musing to himself. »Father, you would please come with me to see High Maestra Tilia!«

The father rose and shuffled after her. »What is the matter?«

»The Nononn has been murdered by the alchymists!«

Seren stopped. »That is what I feared! And I could not stand by him! What about Onthronn Achmar?«

»They have put Achmar in a dungeon!«

»And Saphed?«

»Saphed is a traitor!«

»I feared that, too!«

The father made a worried face and asked some more, »Have you heard from the Executive?«

»No, I guess the bees didn't mention him!«

»That's good! He's very skilled in these situations! I'll follow you!«

»I have to go get the mother too! She's probably in the Moon-garden! Actually, I'm not allowed to go there!«

»She'll make an exception! Run! I'll go to the abbey myself!«

Hollydeva found her mother in the garden of the monastery.

»Forgive me for coming into the garden here and disturbing you, Maestra Castanea! You would like to come with me to the Abbess, please! It is a meeting of all the masters of the monastery!«

»And you are already one of them?«

»No, of course not! But I have triggered the events it's about!«

»You overestimate yourself!«

»But I feel guilty!«

Her mother looked at her.

»Once you start repenting, you won't be able to stop, Hollydeva!«

»Don't you have anything to regret?!«

Her mother looked dismissive.

»I meant besides the fact of giving birth to me?«

»Don't do that now! What is the meeting of the masters about?«

»The Nacharya Nononn has been murdered by the alchymists!«

»Oh no! Things are getting worse and worse!«

»Yes, so it is!«

A Strategic Headquarters!

So that's how everyone met in the abbey. Master Alyapis reported everything he had learned from the bees in the meeting of the leading masters of Linden Island.

The Grand Mistress ordered, »We must send news to the Nacharya who are not on Lead Mountain! They should come here! Then we must find out if the Nononn has reincarnated somewhere or if we should find and train a new Nononn or designate anyone else!«

Seren explained, »The alchymists only dare do such a thing because the wizardeurs are on their side and attacked us!«

Baghora added, »It takes not only a Nononn but also a fit Grand Inquisitor who can organize the Nacharya forces and troops!«

»Yes, that's right!« Seren replied. »My daughter and I had to make a promise that we would not fill the position of Grand Inquisitor again, or ever!«

»Do you have another representative?«

»None with the necessary competence for such exceptional situations!«

»Then we must think carefully about how to build a strategic center that can fulfill this task!«

»Yes, that could be the solution! I am reduced and tired, but I have all the information and know where agents and troops and allies are! You, Master Baghora, and Maestra Corvanya surely have the strategic assets to take the lead in this war!«

»No!« objected Corvanya. »The most strategically gifted among us is Maestra Shyena!«

Everyone turned to the rather young prioress of the Yana of Dragons, who looked proud and sharp as an eagle. At that moment, Hollydeva knew that here was indeed a maestra who could replace and even surpass her father.

»Thank you, Maestra Corvanya!« agreed Shyena. »I think building a strategic command center is a good idea. I am willing to be a prima inter pares with Baghora, Corvanya, the Abbess, the retired Grand Inquisitor, and the eventual arriving nacharya!«

Master Griseo spoke up. »I also want to be involved in strategic leadership!«

High Maestra Tilia replied to him, »Master Griseo, you are very much in league with the alchymists! That is right and good! But it appears that we need to put the alchymists in their place! We would rather not bring you into internal conflict! Nor do we want to risk you betraying plans or strategies!«

»I would never do that! My loyalty is here on the island and in this circle of Linden Island masters!«

Shyena relented, »Perhaps it is indeed good to involve Master Griseo, as he knows the alchymists best of all of us! However, I must say, Master Griseo, that I will be watching you very closely, as I am also not sure that you will not run into conflicts!«

»I promise that I will reveal my inner conflicts and withdraw if necessary!«

Everyone agreed.

Grand Maestra Tilia turned to Hollydeva, »Dear masters, you will find it unusual that a novicess, Sister Scorpio, is present at this meeting! I could say that she is here as the right hand of her father, the Grand Inquisitor Emeritus. But it appears that Scorpio is involved in all the happenings of our day and is in part a victim of those happenings. On the other hand, some of us already know that she has abilities on a level that some of our adepts will never reach! There should be no objection to her presence here! Novicess Scorpio, don't let it go to your head that you are allowed to be here in the circle of masters!«

Hollydeva suddenly felt ashamed. She nodded to indicate that she understood the Abbess. And she was aware that she actually felt superior.

»I am not a good and humble person!« she affirmed to herself.

»And I don't want to be!«

Then, in the first two weeks of May, Hollydeva and Ariëa visited the Yana of the Snakes, but it seemed a little scary to them.

»Can we also get a mahavidya like Gemina?« they asked Maestra Manasa, who responded with a contemptuous shrug of her mouth.

Gemina's encounter with the Mahavidya Dhumavati had clearly changed her. She had become quieter, more reserved, less threatening, no longer making lewd remarks.

They were both able to talk to the snakes, so they were able to get through the exercise of staying in the room with a snake well, as after some coaxing the snake fell asleep peacefully in a corner. The adepts of the Snakes, as well as especially the novices Giudicia and Mondo, were disappointed. They most likely had chosen an especially aggressive snake for the exercise to then be able to demonstrate the burning out of the bite wound to the two impudent Raven novicesses in a dramatic and painful action.

Chapter 29:
A Summer Roundelay at Lytha.
Nereïde Lykoria

Lytha (Summer Solstice at June 21st)

On the shortest night of the summer solstice, there was again a boisterous novice feast with music and dancing and a round around the fire with roasting of potatoes on sticks.

Leo related that the Abbess had actually invited him to the abbey to read to him from records that said something about whether the dragonesses, who had said they had an open account with him, were settling a debt or a credit.

The Abbess had read aloud that the dragons had once lived very depleted in the Ice Country, his homeland, almost frozen to death. His mother, Queen Sigfreya, an ice and fire mage, had saved the young dragons. She had helped them to get to Linden Island. The last two male dragons probably had been brought to a hidden valley by Nacharya Peredur.

The dragonesses would be sympathetic to Leo because of his mother! For her helpful information he was feeling grateful towards the Abbess, who, as Vritra, should have some power over the dragons, but who would have to deal with Shyena.

Virgo had heard, »Agora! There are rumors that the sea demons may attack again!«

Others confirmed, »Yes, the Black Mystic, the Dark Master, is inciting them against us!«

Hollydeva had been watching Sagittario, who shook his head but preferred to remain silent.

»Say it, Sagittario!« Hollydeva urged him. »We know you see it differently. And it could be that you are right!«

Sagittario overcame his timidity, »All right! I think that this master is misrepresented. He was, after all, the prior of the Dolphins, which were called Sharks at that time. I found some of his records and found them very intriguing. Maybe your good opinion about the Abbess is unjustified! Shyena is not the only one who has kept her distance. The Abbess is strong and wants to keep this Master Finster out. But some things have happened in the history of the island that I would like to know more about before I pass judgment!«

Aquaria nodded, »Yes, Sagittario, that is important! You may be right. My parents and my uncle Mannech were also once masters here on the island, and they probably went back to Walysia because of Tilia too! We should be careful in our judgments!«

Later, Hollydeva and Aquaria went to Sagittario and asked him what he had found out about the Dark Master.

»Oh, a few things. And I found mysterious diary entries. I'll read them to you.

»26.6.33

Arlecyna has been reborn. I must find her. Tilia continues to interfere with the Nereïdes. They will have to attack the island.

»27.6.33

The Nereïdes do not know where Arlecyna was born. It must be far from the sea and not by a river. Kalima might know. I must go and see her.

»14.7.33

I went to see Kalima. I could have her crater. Arlecyna was born in the Nacharya environment. Saphed knows where, but wants to get power over her himself. He wants me to support the alchymists more. I am afraid they are doing more harm than good.

»15.7.33

Tilia has spoken against me in the Council of Priors. She wants me gone so she can take undisturbed action against the Nereïdes. Only Corvanya is on my side. Sura and Urana accuse me of nihilism. Nihilism? What would my prior say to this accusation? Unfortunately, I cannot ask. He has left. But I hear his words inside me. "When you truly surrender to nothingness, the nothingness of being, and stop seeking meaning and significance with your mind, then, only then, will you become one with the world, a great energy and bliss will flood you, and you will know that this primordial ground of all phenomena, is a great potential. But you will have to go further and reach the silence and emptiness that lies beneath, where there is eternal peace. Act from the absolute non-being and nothing can kill you!"

»20.7.33

Saphed arrived. With him came the professors, leaders of the alchymists. A certain Professor Griseo is with them, offering a lot of money to the monastery. Does the monastery need money? Is Tilia greedy? Yes, it can be, the donations by the Nacharya have decreased. The churches have lost importance and don't send so many donations anymore. I am tired of fighting. I will retire. But what will become of my people here? What will become of the inhabitants of the sea?

»21.7.33

The Council of Priors has decided, Tilia has prevailed. I have released the adepts. Most of them are coming with me to the crater. Master Cuda wants to go to his homeland, to the river of his childhood, somewhere in Siberia. Carcharias stays on the island. Alarias wants to go to his native village. They would rather have fought and are disappointed in me.«

Aquaria exclaimed, »There are unanswered questions with me. Who is Arlecyna? Who is Kalima? Alarias is probably my uncle Mannech. Who is Carcharias? What is that crater?«

»Oh, Kalima I met. My father had imprisoned her, but the Bhogi was furious, angry and apologized to her and released her. She is very beautiful and fiery and seems to be a special person!«

Hollydeva had noticed another name: »Arlecyna? Somewhere I've heard that name before too!«

Aquaria asked, »Sagittario, how are you anyway? What are you doing? I feel a little guilty that I'm in the same yana with you but have barely spoken to you. It's not because of you, but because of my discomfort here in the yana. What do you do?«

»Oh, I'm researching and studying. And I've made friends with Baston, who is a good engineer and inventor, but a bad player on exchanges. Every master, adept, and novice in the Yana of the Dolphins has a share in Professor Griseo's stock market account and can speculate with it. I haven't touched my subaccount yet. Baston has already gambled away his share. After Griseo shamed him for it in front of all the adepts of the house, he was given the chance to make up for the loss through his energy project. In fact, he has already succeeded in making small mechanical flying bodies that look like flies, powered by an energy that drives them directly from the environment, from what Baston says is an omnipresent energy field!

»Meanwhile, these flies are delivering stock quotes that are more current than the numbers on the business pages of the newspapers that the airshiplet brings in the morning!«

At this, Hollydeva had to interject, »I've already seen these flies in action and it wasn't good! I don't know if your Baston is for the good of the Yrth!«

Somewhat meekly, Sagittario defended the older novice, »Yes, but Baston is fine.«

Aquaria and Hollydeva didn't quite know what to make of Sagittario. But they thanked him for his information about the Dark Master.

»I guess we shouldn't be quite so uncritical of the Abbess!«

»No, she's in the same boat with that Professor Griseo and the alchymists!«

»Let's hope Leo can protect himself from her!«

Nereïde Lykoria

In the further weeks of midsummer, this critical attitude toward Abbess Tilia was to intensify dramatically when Piscio delivered to Hollydeva a summons for a meeting with the Nereïdes.

Piscio had sought Hollydeva's proximity. He wanted to act as her somewhat diminutive protector. Hollydeva gave him to understand that she could very well take care of herself. Since they would now be in competing yanas, there would be a natural distance. Piscio had nodded, and she often saw him with Virgo and Matto, the other novices at the Bees. When they weren't cleaning and tending beehives, they were concocting pranks and jokes.

But then at the second week after the Lytha festival at the summer solstice, Piscio had pulled her aside.

»Scorpio, I need your help with something!«

»Yes, what is it, Piscio?«

»Scorpio, this morning I met a woman in a yellow dress at the place by the bay. She said she was a nereïde, called Lykoria, and she asked me to have you come there with me tomorrow morning, since the nereïdes need to talk to us!«

This sounded a bit strange, but Hollydeva went together with Piscio to the place the next morning. A woman in a yellow robe and long reddish-blond hair was indeed waiting there.

»I greet you! May I address you by your birth names? I greet you, Hollydeva! And I greet you, Pierre!!«

Hollydeva and Piscio greeted back together. »We greet you, Lykoria!«

»I, of course, know that these names are just passing denominations, labels, like your novice names are! We, the nereïdes, know both of you since long with different names. But there are more urgent things right now than to reveal our whole story!

You just should know that there is an old bond between you two and the inhabitants of the sea!

»You owe us not. It is rather the other way around, that we are indebted to you two! But I was sent to ask for your help! As your help would be essential for our survival! Or, it more likely could be that we and the seas are stronger and you and your commitment would be needed to prevent us from destroying Linden Island and the monastery for good!«

Hollydeva and Piscio involuntary grabbed each other's hand. Lykoria's words sounded really dramatic! They were just kids, youths! What was this heavy burden placed upon them?

But Hollydeva felt a rage at the sea-dwellers who had killed novicess Papessa, whose grave she visited every morning. Before accepting any assignment, she first wanted to know why the nereïdes and the sea-demons had attacked the island almost two years ago and why they would do it again.

»Tell me first, Lykoria! Why have you killed Sister Papessa? Why had you killed masters, adepts, and novices of Linden Island?«

»The answer to your questions is known to the Abbess!« was the reply of the yellow clad nereïde.

»But I ask you, Lykoria! Why did you kill Sister Papessa?«

»We are sorry for the death of novices, adepts, or masters! But the survival of so many living beings more than these was at stake and still is! Please, we can discuss this in detail at some point and possibly count it up! But right now, we and also your friends here on the island need your help badly, Hollydeva!«

»Good! So, how can I help you?«

»As you know, your grandmother has made sure and sworn that you cannot be used against us!«

»Yes, I know that, and I will never fight you!«

»That's good. The Abbess is harming us! Make her stop her behavior, or we will have to attack again, as she is endangering the survival of the creatures of the sea!«

»The Abbess? I can't believe that!«

»You would realize it if you watched her better! In the place where you sit now, she always stands in the middle of the night on the day of the week before this day! Watch it!«

Hollydeva nodded, and Lykoria disappeared back into the sea.

»The Abbess? I really can't believe that!«

But Piscio was not so sure. »I have heard from Virgo that she sneaks around the island during their night watch trying to stay secret. We were already asking ourselves what she is doing then!«

Hollydeva couldn't very well swap the night watch shift with a boy. She did want to get up at night the next week, but the day had been exhausting, and she was oversleeping. She asked Leo, who had been on guard duty that night, if he had seen the Abbess that night. He was surprised by her question. He looked at Virgo, with whom he had the shift.

Virgo nodded. »Yes, hopplahopp! She walks around more often in the middle of the night! But we don't know where or what she's been doing!«

Hollydeva now suspected that the nereïde had spoken the truth. What was the Abbess doing? She would have to find out.

The following week, she had Virgo wake her and waited for the Abbess. Sure enough, the Abbess appeared at the beach area, stood up to her knees in the water and performed some kind of incantations.

The Abbess affected the nereïdes or the ocean in such a way that they felt compelled to attack!

But Hollydeva was aware that a confrontation with the Abbess would go badly for her. Or Tilia would simply refuse to answer her.

She decided to gather more information. There had to be a way to stop the Abbess.

She told Aquaria what she had learned and seen.

»We should send a message to this Master Finster. Maybe Sagittario knows how to reach him by now!«

Sagittario had indeed already contacted the Master Finster and promised to deliver the fresh warning from the nereïdes.

Hollydeva then confided in Maestra Corvanya as well.

»Yes, we priors know about the problem and about Tilia's unfortunate activities. There is nothing we can do about it! We can only be prepared for the attack by the sea dwellers!«

Maestra Corvanya pondered for a while and explained, »In her childhood in an ocean port town, her family was wiped out in a tsunami, a strong storm surge. It haunts her to this day, she can't get rid of it! Each of these masters has a pain point like that somewhere! Tilia used to be called Tyuria, and she had sworn that there should never be such a storm surge again. That motivated her to learn so much and come so far!

»This is how she calms the sea. And prevents big floods. But this is unnatural, and it is against the rhythms of the sea. The animals and consciousnesses living in the sea suffer from the forced rigidity that Tilia causes. It is a form of wizardry that she uses! Actually, it should be forbidden here on the Island of Mystics!«

»Very well!« thought Hollydeva. »Life is combat and probably these attacks have been around forever and Tilia is making sure that the novices, adepts, and masters of Linden Island don't fall asleep and get challenged and tested in combat!«

A Warning For Libra

Then she had night watch with Libra again, and they sat under the copper beech. Hollydeva decided to enlighten Libra about the copper beech's knowledge of her.

»Libra, this is where you often sit and come to, isn't it?«

Libra nodded in affirmation.

»You know, I can actually talk to the plants. Or rather, there are devas living in the plants that I can talk to. The plant devas of the island tend not to talk to me because of a spell my mother put over them. But the copper beech we're sitting under here, your favorite tree, doesn't abide by it and has been talking to me. About you!«

»About me?«

Libra turned to the tree, startled, and put a hand on the trunk.

»What is the beech tree saying about me?«

»She is worried because you are an agent of the midwives and want to harm your yana. To achieve this, you have approached my mother, the garden mistress, and act as if you were her student or assistant.«

Libra had gone a little rigid, caught.

»Libra, I know you are someone else. You're not a somewhat womanly young girl, plodding around a bit awkwardly in the Yana of Lambs, making 'meh' like a sheep grazing!«

»What do you want from me?«

»The copper beech is worried about you! Maybe she'll talk to you too! Open up, listen carefully!«

»All I hear are leaves rustling in the wind!«

»Wait. It will take a moment. Turn off your thoughts and just be open to the beech!«

After a few minutes, Hollydeva heard the copper beech speak again.

»Thank you, Hollydeva! You are trying well. Libra, Vimala do you hear me?«

Libra nodded, »Yes, I hear a deep voice and feel a vibration!«

»Libra, beware of the fat angel!«

The tree seemed to back away again.

»What does the tree mean? You should beware of Tauro?«

»Yes, Tauro wants to get all the yanas under his control by supplying important adepts with his cookies. The cookies are coated with a drug that makes the adepts temporarily better at the games and more charismatic. But they become addicted and want more, and Tauro then makes demands. In our yana Danthonia is the bookkeeper and right hand of the prioress, and she would like to join the team where her brother Danthon is already playing rather badly. They are probably interested in improving their performances. And I'm brokering Tauro's cookies...«

»Because that way you support Tauro's effort and your interest in harming the Yana Agnus is fulfilled?«

»Yes. Please don't judge me. There is a long history of suffering that wise women have experienced at the hands of the OneGod churches. Your mother is a worshiper of the Great Mother, who is also a version of the OneGod. But a goddess who would never harm women and especially wise women!«

»You know that my mother and I are estranged!?«

»Yes, I know that. Will you report me to Prioress Urana?«

»No, but I advise you to comply with the copper beech's wish and not give Tauro any help! There are more important battles at the moment that we all need to prepare for!«

Libra seemed to agree, and Hollydeva decided to give Tauro a run for his money. But she also realized that she was already taking on a bit much again. What happened with acting like a regular novicess?

This summer was a good time on the island. But she kind of indulged in her bad conscience as she was aware that there were adverse powers in the world outside like alchymists and wizardeurs who were attempting to distort and pervert nature and the beauty of the world.

Chapter 30:
Heat at Lammays. Slua.
Conspiracies

Lammays (August 1st)

It was high summer, the end of July, the feast of Lammays on the first of August, celebrated at the warmest time, the weeks filled with the joy of the sun's rays. Or was the feast supposed to summon some rain in order to water the dry earth, to save the harvest from drought, to make sure that life could grow and blossom?

Hollydeva had visited the ravens in their grove and was now making her way to the novice's house, where there was to be a gathering and drinks.

It was strangely peaceful, the heat of high summer seemed to make time stand still.

»But time doesn't stand still!« Hollydeva was concerned. »The enemies surely continue to work to destroy nature or upset the natural order. They want power and wealth, and in their greed don't realize that they are also destroying the foundation of their own lives, harming their own mental health!«

But the alchymists and wizardeurs were far away. They had representatives on the island, but Hollydeva was not threatened or affected by them here and now.

There were concrete threats or irritations on the island. What was Tauro up to? How far was he with his plans? Who had he gained as allies?

How was Libra's connection with Maestra Castanea, the garden mistress who wanted to join the Tigers, developing?

What was the deal with the Black Mystic, Master Finster, a former Prior of the Dolphins?

When would the sea demons attack again?

How could she stop Abbess Tilia from doing things that would force the sea demons to attack and possibly destroy Linden Island and the monastery?

A few days ago, Ariëa had approached her with a strange story, and she wondered if another front was developing here, or if surprising allies were presenting themselves.

The Slua

»Can I speak with you, please?«

Ariëa's request came as a surprise. Actually, they were rather avoiding each other by now. Ariëa pouted a bit, defiant because she felt unequally treated in the Yana of Ravens.

»Yes, of course, Ari. What is it?«

»I was watching the ravens and practicing understanding their language. Then a little raven woman approached me. She was called Slua, or she was a slua. The slua had a strange request for me. She wants me to become the mother of a child, at whose birth I am to strangle the slua so that her soul can take the body of that child.«

»Uch, that sounds gruesome!«

»Yes, and the slua wants your brother, the younger one, to be the father of the child! Could you please ask your brother if he is willing to become the father of my child, the newborn Slua?«

»I hardly know Baldar, among the Lambs his name is Eragrostis. I suppose he will hear me out, and I can introduce you to him. But are you sure this is all a good idea? Have you talked to Maestra Corvanya?«

»Yes, I spoke with Maestra Corvanya about it! She told me that connecting with the slua and with their tribe could be powerful! The slua are special beings who are not allowed into heaven or hell when they die because of their misdeeds!«

»They won't be let back into heaven or hell? We should find out what that means! And we should talk to Baldar. I don't know if he's already taken or how he feels about fatherhood!«

Then a little raven, the slua herself, hopped in front of them.

»You want to know why I can't go to heaven or hell!?«

Ariëa and Hollydeva nodded.

»We slua are the embodiment of souls who have harmed others in such a way that they cannot return to Heaven. Because the souls of the harmed do not want to or cannot go to Heaven, we, the perpetrators, should not be allowed either!«

The slua saw incomprehension from the two Raven novicesses and explained the somewhat broader framework.

»You must think of this life here as this: In Heaven we set ourselves tasks, developmental steps to take, down on Yrth. This may well include misdeeds because only through repentance and understanding we reach to higher levels. The soul, that has nothing to repent from his or her life within a body, stagnates!

»But there are misdeeds where repentance is not enough, where other souls are so damaged that they do not want to wake up, do not want to leave the body to return to their true embodiment in Heaven! The causers of these conditions are expelled and must remain here as sluas. There is only one possibility for me: I must help these damaged souls, souls damaged by me, there are five in number, in such a way that they can let go of the pain and the madness and return to Heaven! I cannot do that as a slua, as a kind of bird! I can do that only as a human being, possibly already as a child. As a child of Ariëa, Cita Yaboah!«

»This all sounds very dark and confused! How does Ariëa know that you are not harming her as well, that you are not rotten and incurably bad?«

The slua nodded, looking distressed. »Yes, you ask legitimate questions! I will first make sure for three months that Ariëa gets the information to send to her father that she asks for. She may have questions for you, and I ask you to answer them for her! Her father is a dervish and an important man in the order of dervishes, at least in the North-Afrycan desert. He can contribute to peace and health of the people and countries there! You will want that the people there do not plant the grain whose seeds they got from the alchymists!«

»How do you know about these plans of the alchymists?«

»Oh, the ravens and their relatives, like the gulls and magpies, know a lot, and we slua get around too!«

»But you will probably be able to pretend for three months and appear helpful and friendly!«

»Well, I'll tell your maestra my whole story and what I learned from it, and then she'll tell you if you can trust me to mean what I say!«

»You don't want to tell us right away because we might be or become put off and prejudiced?«

»Yes. And your maestra has the life experience with which to judge whether my insight, remorse, and will to make amends are real or fake!«

Ariëa spoke up, »Yes, that's a good start. And Scorpio goes ahead and introduces me to her baby brother!«

A few days later, Maestra Corvanya told Hollydeva that she believed Slua's story, and that Ariëa could cautiously yet bravely take the venture with her, provided she could find a suitable father for Slua's rebirth.

But by then Ariëa had already spoken with Baldar alias Eragrostis. Hollydeva had thought that the only way would be to tell him everything openly and honestly.

Eragrostis, Hollydeva still called him "Baldar", had looked Ariëa in the eyes for a long time. She had withstood his gaze.

»We should take it slow. Maybe we can take walks and hold hands first and talk and see how it goes!« he suggested.

Ariëa had to laugh, since she probably had some more experience in love than he did and actually preferred a more direct approach.

»True, this is about making a baby and not about romance and love. But well, let's start with walks and holding hands. How about tonight?«

»Tonight's fine. And please, Scorpio, don't gossip and tittle-tattle about this with your girlfriends. It would be good if it could remain our secret, at least for a time!«

Hollydeva nodded in agreement and Ariëa asked: »May I call you Baldar, too? Eragrostis sounds so stilted!«

»Yes, call me Baldar!«

Tauro's Conspiracy

Hollydeva had been watching Tauro for the past month and then approached him.

»Tauro, what are you up to?«

»I'm making the best of my predicament!«

»What predicament?«

»I am here on an island where there is not a single restaurant, establishment or any culture or enjoyment! I am not interested in mysticism, magic, or religion! No deity appears to me in the temple of angels!«

»You want to leave from here?«

»Yes and no. I can't leave from here so easily! My father is powerful and sent me here. Maybe this was a prova, a test. But I don't know if he wants to see if I'll fit in here or if I'll rebel here and find ways to control the monastery or use it as a stepping stone to return to civilization!«

Hollydeva nodded and fell silent. Tauro appeared honest.

»Very well, I have met with my father and the consigliere of our family, Cefalú, on the mainland. I have presented a plan, and they support me, although cautiously and with reservations. I already have the cooks and the cellerar on my side and power over the one in the Yana of Angels who manages the money, Adept Jehadiel, soon to be Master Jehadiel.

»Those who have the highest title to show do not have the power. Those without whom things would not work and those who control the money and the flow of money do have the real power. Sura and Betula act big and act bossy. But without one like Jehadiel they would be nothing, for they know nothing about the management of their house. Without the cooks and the cellerar, there would be nothing to eat here. That is what counts in the end: Food, drink, roof over their heads, clean water for washing, procreazione!«

»Procreation?«

»Yes, without procreation, we humans become extinct. Apart from that, procreation gives pleasure. But you won't know or want to know about that yet, Scorpio!«

»Yeah, I guess you're right! And now you attack the Yana of the Lambs?«

»Yes, the Lambs come next. These Danthon fratelli are easy prey. All those who are capable of little but want to appear significant and successful are easy prey!«

»Then make sure you are not one of them, Tauro!«

»Uh, that was wicked! I love you like that, Scorpi!«

»Libra's helping you with the Lambs?«

»Yes, she does. But now she wants me to get poison and give it to her. I was going to refuse, but I owe her. I referred her to Gemina!«

»And how far are you with the other yanas?«

»Oh, far with the ones on the right. The ones on the left are more difficult. I haven't gotten anywhere at all with the Ravens, though!«

»You just don't want to tell me because I would tell Corvanya!«

»No, I have no access with the Ravens so far, and you or Ariëa won't give it to me either!«

»You think Ariëa could be your ally? Because she left Capri when he tried to tattle on you to us? Make no mistake about Ariëa!«

Hollydeva had become angry and wanted to provoke him more.

»And then, when you have power and money, your father will welcome you with open arms, will give you a rank in the family?«

»No, the family would then be too small, too insignificant for me!«

»So, the world?!«

»Yes, the world!«

»And then what are you doing with your position? All the effort just for good food and procreation?«

»No, then I'll save it with you, the world!«

»Save it from what?«

»From those who are as greedy as I am, the alchymists! Or from the Master Finster, the black mystic!«

Hollydeva was surprised that Tauro had talked to her in a way that motivated her to sympathize with his endeavor. She gave him one more tip.

»Remember the name of the Nacharya Zronn Saphed, Tauro! Saphed is the enemy! He is the nacharya who is directing the wicked!«

More Conspiracies

At the summer feast of the novices of the first year, there was a lot of the traditional red berry compote with cream to indulge in.

Hollydeva addressed Gemina, »Did Libra ask you about poison?«

»Zss, no, Tauro asked if I could get Libra some poison!«

»So, have you given her poison yet?«

»No, I have to ask Anguinaga first!«

»Don't give her anything, Gemina! Libra is under my mother's spell, and she's up to no good! We shouldn't be splitting our forces on the island in internal battles!«

»Zss, oh come on, Scorpi, you don't really believe that! We've visited almost all the yanas now. There is competition and fragmentation between the yanas and within the yanas. Competition forces us to do better. When the Lambs fight among themselves, they become stronger!«

»Or they die out because they kill each other!«

»Zss, that would be acceptable to me too! I didn't like it with the Lambs!«

Hollydeva realized she couldn't argue with Gemina, especially since she probably shared her attitudes. She went to Libra.

»Libra, what does my mother want with poison?«

She had asked it aloud, so the other ten would overhear. She wanted Libra's agenda to be revealed. All eyes were now on Libra.

»Your mother wants to be either Maestra of the Tigers or Prioress of the Lambs! I just water this flower!«

»By eliminating the Prioress of the Lambs?«

»Blame your mother! After all, I'm just a helper, a midwife!«

»But you are the ones on the right path!«

Leo interjected, »But your mother, Scorpio, doesn't seem to want to be on the right path anymore!«

Virgo added, »She felt coerced by your grandmother into joining the Lambs and being garden maestra, when she'd rather be wild and wicked! Agora!«

»What do you know about my mother? Leave my grandmother out of it!«

But Libra felt challenged and supported by the general sentiment of the other novices, »Your grandmother was a maestra of the Lambs and her son is the Nacharya Daman, the nacharya assigned to the Lambs. Together, they have provided for the unification of the monotheistic churches into the Church of the OneGod, to have even more power to make the good old patriarchal OneGod the dominant religion on Yrth! And don't you had doubters of the OneGod, like animists, polytheists and atheists, in the dungeons of Georgeburg and tortured them?«

Hollydeva was shocked at the accusation! And she realized she couldn't answer, since she didn't really know what religious or philosophical beliefs the inmates had had.

»No, we had mostly politicians and rich people! The nine nacharya represent different concepts. Just like the eight yanas here. Each of the nacharyas is assigned one of them! I also don't know why the OneGod is propagated by them together. Probably that's the best way for them to keep order in the world!«

She realized she was on the defensive and her performance had become embarrassing.

»Oh, do what you want. Let my mother poison whoever she wants. At least I know I'll stay away from her!«

Virgo saved the mood: »Hustle bustle! What themes for a summer night! Come on, let's drink. Piscio and I organized some honey wine from the Bee's cellar. Shrimp brought some strong rice liquor! Let's party!«

And Aquaria also shouted, »Yes, let's dance and bawl until Fraxina tells us to be quiet!«

»Fraxina is making amore with the Cellerar right now!« knew Tauro.

»What, since he stopped bothering the cooks, he's grabbed our dry teacher?«

»Si, but I think, there's more going on and has been for a long time!«

Chapter 31:
Thanksgiving at Mabyon.
Prior Alyapis

Mabyon (Autumn Equinox at September 21st)

At the autumn equinox on September 21st, the Celtic festival of Mabyon, the first-year novices on the island were to gather wild fruits and sweet-grass stalks. It would be a harvest and Thanksgiving festival.

It was late summer, over half a year after the confrontation with the creatures in the Refuge and almost five months after the news of the murder of Nononn by Saphed and the alchymists.

The masters of the island and the visiting nacharyas had established a Strategic Headquarters where intelligence was gathered and plans for counterattack were formulated.

But on the island, the threats posed by the alchymists were rather distant. And Professor Griseo took pains to portray the alchymists' work and deeds as harmless. As far as he could find out, the Nononn's death would have been a tragic accident. He possibly had been stung by too many excited bees.

Hollydeva felt that considerably more should be done to curb the activities of Nacharya Saphed, the wizardeurs, and especially the alchymists. But she would not have known how to do it, either. She was in a monastic school on Linden Island and had enough to do with learning and gaining experience and getting along with her novice friends as well as novice enemies from the advanced grades.

Some priors of the yanas eyed Professor Griseo suspiciously, but he seemed mostly interested in playing at some world exchanges that no one else on the island could ascribe any significance to.

Maestra Shyena had made Hollydeva understand early on that she did not think a novicess' presence at the Strategic Headquarters was appropriate and that she should rather confine herself to her training.

Abbess Tilia had issued a warning regarding the Dark Master, Master Finster, Black Mystic, and some priors had warned that the threat from this heretic might become acute. Hollydeva suspected that Tilia was trying to distract from both the alchymists and her own nocturnal activities on the island beach.

She asked Maestra Corvanya what to make of the Abbess's warning regarding this Dark Master.

»Tilia and the Dark Master do not like each other! Don't let her influence you too much! Master Finster is not an enemy of our house!«

A week before the Thanksgiving at Mabyon, Piscio had come to Hollydeva and whispered, »Please come with me, Scorpio! Masterlet Alyapis must speak to you!«

There had been great excitement in the house of the Yana of the Bees. Hollydeva saw novices and adepts, buzzing around like insects. And even the small insects, instead of producing honey, seemed to be busy exchanging information.

»Novicess Scorpio, there are two critical issues I need to discuss with you! Please sit down! Piscio, go get Virgo, please. I also need to speak with the three of you together!«

As Piscio hurried away, Master Alyapis turned to Hollydeva with a serious face, »As you know, Scorpio, I get a great deal of information through the bees, provided I can motivate them to take an interest. And you also know that every yana here on the island has one of the Nacharya as a worldly protector and also as a spiritual companion. The nacharya of the Bees is the Master Bhogi, whom you know well.«

Oh yes, Hollydeva remembered the Bhogi. She had last seen him amid smoke and flames at Georgeburg Castle. He had been preparing not to live much longer and then to depart forever. Involuntarily, she groped for the metal medallion hanging on a chain around her neck, well hidden under her novice robe. She was sure, or believed, that no one on the island knew that the Bhogi had given her this proof of her claims of succession.

»I am sorry to tell you that the Bhogi passed away yesterday. The last thing he did was have the bees send you and me a greeting!«

Hollydeva felt relief and joy on the one hand, knowing that the Bhogi wanted to be redeemed. But in her heart, she grieved, as another hole had now been created next to the one her grandmother had torn. She would never see the Bhogi again, hear his wise or crazy explanations, or have adventures in big cities with him. This was bitter.

»Show me the medallion, please, Scorpio!«

Hollydeva was surprised that Master Alyapis knew. And she was also surprised at his tone. Who did he think he was, to be able to order her to do something?

»What medallion?«

»The medallion with which you think you can declare your claim to succession to the Bhogi!«

»Me? Succession to the Bhogi?«

»I know you have it! I will prevent you from becoming the new Bhogi! A woman cannot be a nacharya!«

»Oh, why not? The Bhogi didn't think so!«

»Yes, I know, unfortunately. But we know this from the bees: A woman who is chosen, who is given an exalted position, changes drastically, becomes a queen! I don't want a human queen in my beehive!«

»Well, Master Alyapis, if I had such a medallion, I would declare the candidacy for the function of Bhogi, the Septonn of the Nacharya, before the Council of the Nacharya and not here before you! I do not know what you want from me or what you have against me! But be aware that you are also already at an age when you should think of your own succession! Who is able to talk to the bees the way you can? I saw Opalia during our fight with the creatures in my grandmother's Refuge. She would probably be suitable for your succession! But Opalia would also be a woman! You will hardly think of Matto, Piscio or Virgo for your succession! These three novices are probably a bit too immature for that!«

And as if on cue, the two Bee novices came running. True, they saw that a discord had arisen between the prior and Scorpio. But they told themselves that their own good humor would soon drown out that sound.

»Listen!« growled Master Alyapis. »Something has come to my ears. The bees have heard a rumor. The sea demons will attack again, soon! The nereïdes are still angry with the island and want to destroy us! And I've learned that you, and especially Scorpio, of course, already know more about this. So, what do you know?«

Hollydeva looked firmly at Prior Alyapis, »Piscio and I had been approached by the nereïde Lykoria! We have heard their side! It is about Abbess Tilia affecting the inhabitants of the sea! She is affecting them so much that it is a matter of life and death for the sea dwellers! If we don't put a stop to Tilia, they will have to attack us!«

Alyapis looked serious. »Yes, I know the story about Tilia's youth and the storm surge that destroyed her family. But she is the most developed maestra on the island! That's why she is the abbess! She will not do anything against the nature of any creatures or animals! I don't want to believe it! After all, I gave her access to the power of the element Earth!

»I want you to warn your fellow novices of a possible attack! I will talk to the Abbess herself! Or we will bring it up in the Council of Masters of the Island! I hope I don't make a fool of myself!«

Then the Master of the Yana of Bees prompted Hollydeva, »Good, Scorpio, you may now leave the house of the Bees! We will now hold a funeral service for our protector, the Nacharya Bhogi!«

»And I may not be attending?«

»No, you are a Raven! You can have your own celebration somewhere! You're not a Bee!«

Hollydeva realized that part of Alyapis' rejection stemmed from the fact that she had not chosen the Yana of Bees at the first day of the novitiate, although the bees had assisted her on several occasions. The druyds and fire maiden were clearly associated with the Bees. She had become a Raven novicess and the Bees were in particular competition with the left-hand path version of nature belief, animism, a worldview in which divinity was found in nature. For the right-hand path nature devotee the divine was found in blossoming; for those on the left-hand path it rather manifested itself by withering.

What should she do now? Should she declare her right to the position of Septonn of the Nacharya? With whom could she speak about it? She wished that at least the Nononn was there. But she was sure that the council of the Nacharya would wish her to continue and finish her education on Linden Island. And to finish it would take more than four years. Possibly, it would be good if at least the Nononn knew that there was a new Bhogi, a Bhogeva. But the Nononn was dead. Should she talk to Rokudan Aoi, the nacharya of the Ravens? She was still uncomfortable with him. The same was true of her uncle, Nacharya Daman. She trusted Tatu Njena and Peredur the most. Peredur, however, was absent. And perhaps the whole story with the Nacharya was also unreal or history. Maybe the incarnation of the Bhogi she had met had been the last in a long line, and it was just as well to be finished for good.

Would the father be able to give her good advice? He was still lying in the Yana Agnus. But he was weak and mostly dozed off as if absent. Hollydeva did not want to disturb him. She had also moved away from him, did not trust him.

»If the Bhogi is the nacharya who knows about ecstasy, I haven't gotten very far into the experience!« she said to herself. Or was the Raven dance in the morning an exercise in ecstasy? The druyds and fire maiden in the soma rush had no doubt been more ecstatic. But Corvanya had certainly prepared experiences along those lines for them.

Can Not Tilia's Mind Be Changed?

In the evening, Aquaria and Hollydeva called a meeting of the first year novices. They reported their observations and the information they had about the danger that threatened everyone.

»Who else observed something?«

Sagittario knew that Professor Griseo had met with Abbess Tilia several times. He would have given her a chymical substance. He also knew that the professor would be involved in a stock market project related to the energy harvesting inventions Baston was developing.

»And there is something else strange!«

»What is it, Sagittario?«

»I think one of the leading alchymists, Doctor Albedo, is with us! He has a woman with him, his wife. He calls her Lotus. She's rather small and strange. I think she's one of the beings that you met at your grandmother's garden, Scorpio!«

»What? I can't believe that!«

»They want to drill for oil and metals in the ocean floor! This woman built them a boat, a kind of balloon made of a special material!« reported Sagittario.

»So Griseo is influencing Tilia, who wants something from him, and together they are harming the inhabitants of the sea so that they fight back and want to destroy us all with them!«

»We have to somehow tell the nereïdes that we have nothing to do with this, that we are innocent!«

Cancra spoke up, »With us, a secret couple arrived. They came in the night, hiding. Master Baghora in search of Achmar. Master Sycamor substitute, not pleased with visit, these young wizards. Gave me notes with requests for food.«

Aquaria knew what this meant, »The Nacharya Achmar is the nacharya, the protector, of the Tigers. He had traveled with the Nononn to the alchymists and is missing! Do you know anything more about this couple?«

»I think are young wizardeurs! The woman black-skinned. She like Ariëa!«

Hollydeva snapped, »Ah, I know her! That's Miona Yaboah! I've had her in the dungeons!«

And that's when she bit her lips.

»Miona Yaboah?«

Ariëa was suddenly wide awake. »That's my sister! What do you mean, you would have had her in the dungeons!«

»I'll tell you when we have time, Ari, I promise! Your sister is a wizardeur, and she's the girlfriend of Cevaine Mire, the Prince, the boy wonder of the wizardeurs!«

»Are there any more strange happenings in the yanas?« asked Aquaria.

Leo asked Piscio and Hollydeva, »Are you still in contact with the nereïdes?«

They had to answer in the negative. Lykoria had not been seen or called in recent weeks.

»We should find a way to talk to the nereïdes directly, to meet them to ask for leniency!« suggested Leo.

Aquaria asked Gemina, »Aren't there sea serpents?«

»Zss. Yes, we have contacts in the sea! I can talk to the master and see if he can get us a meeting with the queen of the nereïdes!«

Everyone was optimistic. »Gemina, that would be excellent! You can do it! Anguinaga won't refuse you!«

Aquaria explained, »Sagittario and I will take a closer look at what the powder is that Griseo is giving Tilia, and what else we can find out about these projects and Albedo and his wife!«

Sagittario had the idea: »We'll send him stock messages that will irritate him or even turn him away from the project!«

»Can you do that? That's good, Sagittario!«

»What's the situation with the Lambs?«

Libra shook her head, »I don't know. After all, I work a lot with Scorpio's mother, the gardener. She's not on Tilia's side either. But she's also at odds with Prioress Urana and the prior is probably influenced by the Abbess. Nacharya Daman, Scorpio's uncle, is coming soon. Then there will be a family council of Scorpio's family. But I don't know if you'll be invited, Scorpi. You're most likely still worried about your older brother, Adept Avela, too!«

»I'll ask my brother Baldar, Eragrostis, what this is all about and what they're up to!«

»And Sura?«

Capricornus reckoned that Sura didn't particularly like Tilia, but neither did the other masters. She would mostly confer with Maestra Betula, and they would work out predictions together. They would probably miss Astrello, though.

Tauro asked, »Can't Tilia be changed? Who is her maestro, and who is her nacharya? Who does she listen to?«

Aquaria knew, »Tilia is Yana Dragon! We would have to speak to Shyena! Leo, do you know how Shyena and Tilia relate to each other?«

»There's some old strife. We had to help Tilia to be able to visit the dragons! Nacharya Peredur has been with us a lot lately. We think she and Shyena are lovers!«

But Leo probably realized that at least Scorpio and Aquaria were irritated by his statements and didn't believe him, and he decided to rather tell the truth.

»Very well, we adore Maestra Shyena, and we don't want Peredur to be with us so often, as we have a good chance with her in the long run!«

Leo saw the ironic looks of the other novices and now had to bring in something really exciting to distract from his weakness.

»All right, then. We helped the Abbess talk to the three dragons with us in the grove. In return, she helped us find out what history connects us and these dragons. Because our mother saved the last dragons from freezing to death, they owe us and our family!«

»Zss, and now you're thick as thieves with the Abbess?« asked Gemina, somewhat snappishly.

»A little, I suppose, yes. But we also don't want her to harass the people of the sea to the point where they have to attack here!«

Aquaria would rather not stir up any tension. »Leo, ask Shyena gently if she would listen to Scorpio and me!«

»Fine, we can try that and ask her!«

Later that evening, of course, Hollydeva had some explaining to do to her Raven sister.

Ariëa was upset, »Why didn't you tell me this a long time ago? Did you think I would go rogue? Or that it would make me like you even less? I have to go to the house of the Tigers! I want to see her! It's not like she knows I'm here!«

»Ariëa, I'm sorry. But be careful! Your sister is involved with that wizardeur boy! I've seen him! He is not harmless! And I don't know what Master Baghora thinks of him! Please ask Maestra Corvanya first!«

The slua had accompanied Ariëa and explained that she wanted to observe the Tiger house and these wizardeurs. She flew off.

»So you told Maestra Corvanya about Miona!«

»Yes, she wanted you to focus on the Yana of Ravens here! We're supposed to forget our old family after all, and have a new one here, with the Ravens!«

»That's easy for you to say! Your whole family is here on the island!«

»But I rather avoid them!«

Ariëa shook her head, muttered an Afrycan curse, and stomped away.

Fifth Part:
The Battle of Linden Island

Chapter 32:
Master Finster.
Dragons and Sea Demons

The Arrival of Master Finster

At the evening of the day after Mabyon, the feast at September 21st, at dinner shouts rang out. »The Black Mystic is coming on the ferry!«

Everyone ran to the jetty. There the ferry, piloted by Piscio's foster father, was about to dock. It was carrying a single man, dressed in black. On the other bank of the ford over which the ferry crossed, the gathering masters, adepts, and novices saw a carriage with two horses that were being fed by a groom.

Grand Maestra Tilia and Master Ulmus had rushed to the very front, in front of the crowd, and were opposing the ferry that was about to dock.

»You can't go to the island here, Finster!« shouted Tilia, upset. »What do you want?«

»You can't stop me, Tilia! I have things to do here!«

»What do you have to do? Why don't you stay in your volcano?«

»You'll soon find out!«

The black mystic threw a bundle over his shoulder and got out of the ferry. He was very determined and stern looking, and he just did what he wanted. The crowd and even the Grand Maestra avoided him, so there was always an alley for him wherever he was directing his steps.

He walked up to the bell tower, looking around. »Is Maisy still your cook, Tilia?« he called out. The Abbess gave no answer.

The Black picked up his bundle again and simply went into the abbey, where a supper, prepared by the good-natured Maisy, would probably be offered to him.

The novices went back to their dinner and excitedly discussed the incident.

They heard and saw nothing further of the man. The night was quiet. But at the next morning, when Hollydeva was about to go to the Grove of Ravens after the Raven Dance, she overheard Master Finster in conversation with Maestra Corvanya.

»Blacks among themselves!« thought Hollydeva.

Then Maestra Corvanya called her over already.

»Scorpio, I want to introduce you to a friend of our yana! Please say hello to Master Finster! I myself rather call him by his real name, Master Nikor! And in fact he still is Prior Shishumara of the Yana of Sharks who want to be Dolphins nowadays!«

Hollydeva took a bow. She avoided touching the Black Master. But he didn't put out a hand either.

»Sister Scorpio is the daughter of the Grand Inquisitor of the Nacharya, who is unfortunately injured and being cared for at the Yana Agnus. Maestra Castanea, the garden maestra, is her mother!«

»Scorpio, then.« The master laughed lightly. »If your parents are followers of the OneGod, what are you doing here with the Ravens?«

»I'm nothing like my parents!«

»Oh, sorry! That's good! So you're already alone and to yourself!«

»I'm not alone! I'm in the Yana of Ravens, and I'm friends with the other first year novices!«

Now the Black Master looked rather sad.

»I know how alone you are, Hollydeva!« he threw at her.

He knew her name, the name by which she still addressed herself! And he knew how she felt deep inside. She looked Master Finster firmly in the eye.

He must have been 60 years old, gray and weathered, scarred by life. His eyes looked implacable and kind at the same time. She felt a strange connection.

»Thank you, Corvanya, for taking care of her.«

»It's an honor!«

Hollydeva was now confused about the conversation between the two masters.

»Thank you, Scorpio!« Maestra Corvanya relieved her, »Please help in the kitchen!«

Peeling the potatoes, she still had to think about the Black Mystic. What was he doing on Linden Island?

Maestra Corvanya's Worry

At lunch, the Dark Master was not with them, and while clearing the dishes, she asked Corvanya to talk to her. Corvanya nodded, signaled her to just put the dishes back on the table and follow her.

»What is it?«

»There are two important things I need to tell you, Maestra! The Master of Bees has information that the sea demons led by the nereïdes will soon attack to destroy the island, as they feel they are under massive threat. This threat comes from Abbess Tilia and probably from the leadership and connection of the Yana of the Dolphins!«

»Good, yes. I have already been informed of these things! What is the second?«

»Further, the Prior of the Bees has informed me that the Nacharya Septonn, Master Bhogi, has passed away. I had contact with Master Bhogi several times at Georgeburg Castle, and I know that he will not be reborn. He gave me this.«

With that, Hollydeva pulled out the medallion that would affirm her claim to Bhogi's succession.

»I am the successor of the Bhogi!«

Corvanya shook her head in disbelief.

»You're taking on too much, child!« reckoned Maestra Corvanya, and she sounded a little worried.

»I plan to finish my training here and only then inform the Nacharya Council and present my claim. The Bhogi wanted me to become the first female Nacharya!«

»You should already announce your claim to our friends among the nacharyas. But Rokudan Aoi is not on the island right now! I don't know if he would be thrilled with you, either. How do you feel about the Bees?«

»Alyapis doesn't like me and doesn't want me to take over the Bhogi's function!«

»Yes, I thought so!«

Corvanya pondered for a while.

»Come along, we need to talk to Shyena. Tilia, as you know, is from the Yana of Dragons and Shyena and Peredur could possibly forbid her behavior towards the sea! How do you stand with Peredur?«

»Oh, very well.«

»How do you stand with your uncle, Nacharya Daman?«

»I'm not sure. He's at the Yana Agnus with the rest of my family. They're kind of playing their own game!«

»Your mother is a problem. She doesn't really want to be a garden maestra. She wants to aim high, to be a prioress or the abbess herself! Or maybe she wants something else entirely. I've known your mother for a long time. We were novicesses together! She was always dissatisfied with herself and everyone, and probably still is!«

»Yes, that may be!«

»Is there anything else?«

»In the Yana of the Tigers they are visited by the new prince and princess of the wizardeurs, with whom I had already had contact, or rather confrontation. Cevaine Mire seems to be a young wizardeur with some power. His escort is named Miona Yaboah. She is Ariëa's sister! And Ariëa only knows from today that I have already met Miona at Georgeburg under what she considers as adverse circumstances!«

»Yes, I already thought so. We have to be careful with Ariëa. I don't want to lose her! The connection with the slua could be powerful!«

»My friend Gemina wants to ask Master Anguinaga if he can arrange a meeting with the queen of the nereïdes. Perhaps there will be another way for her if we promise to dissuade Tilia from her actions.«

»Who do you want to attend from the island side?«

»Well, I was thinking Master Anguinaga, Sister Aquaria and me. Do you want to be there too?«

»You and Aquaria. That would be the first time first year novices have the initiative on the island.«

»Yes, but Aquaria is the result of a long line of masters and maestras of the island! And I'm...«

»Yes, I know, forgive me! You are indeed of a different quality than the novices who usually show up here like this. There should be a nacharya at the meeting. Maybe Shyena has an idea! Come, let's go to her!«

Dragons Versus Sea Demons

Maestra Corvanya and Hollydeva met the Prioress of Dragons, Maestra Shyena, behind the house of the Yana of Dragons. She was practicing stick fencing with a long stick made of hardwood.

When she became aware of the two Ravens, she paused. »What do you want?«

»Shyena, we have learned that the nereïdes and the sea demons are planning to attack again. Moreover, there seem to be wizardeurs and alchymists on the island. They are in the houses of the Tigers and the Dolphins!«

Shyena nodded. »Yes, so I heard already. My dragons will defend the island against the sea demons! As for the wizardeurs and alchymists, we should wait for them to show themselves. Maybe it's just a visit!«

»Yes, well. It's good that your dragons are fighting the sea demons. But we should rather ask the nereïdes to refrain from attacking as soon as Tilia stops her behavior!«

»Tilia? What is she doing?«

»She's trying to paralyze the waters of the sea with magic and alchymy to avenge the storm surge that once killed her family or something! She is a yana sister of yours, and you should have the power to stop her from her behavior!«

»I will question her. I can hardly imagine Abbess Tilia doing such a thing. That would be foolish. But I must also say that the dragons have a long feud with the sea demons. We will fight them and win! Actually, we are waiting for the sea demons to attack again! You lost an important novicess last time! You should be less lenient with the sea monsters!«

»From what Scorpio says, the nereïdes and the sea demons can't help it, since their very existence is threatened. Some ventures of the alchymists, probably supported by Griseo, add to the threat posed by Tilia!«

»But what do you care? Ravens are not fish, after all. The sea is the sea.«

Hollydeva interjected, »What do the dragons have against the sea demons?«

Shyena seemed reluctant to answer the impertinent novicess at first, but then did. »It's a long story, started a long time ago. Dragons, after all, can live on land and in the air. And they can also swim and glide on water. Once a sea demoness fell in love with a dragon man and showed herself to him. This dragon was not even reluctant to get to know this sea demoness. They met secretly several times. But it probably finally led to the fact that a great dragon drowned in the depths of the sea as he tried to follow her.

Shyena took a break and made a sad face. Hollydeva thought that she was practicing her stage actor's skills.

»His dragon family did not take the incident, the loss, well and avenged him with the death of the sea demoness, who in fact was even more despairing over his death than those angry dragons. So it escalated at that time. Dragons and sea demons understood that there could be no love between them. But they both claimed the surface of the waves, the spray, the surf, the surface of the sea. The demons could stay in the depths, where the nereïdes also have their palaces. The dragons could stay in the skies, and if they want water, visit any inland lakes. But both sides are strong and powerful and stubborn and fight each other. I once tried to bring the dragons to some understanding and to give in. They, however, made me understand that they have made an ancient oath not to yield one step to the sea demons. And I, as Prioress of the Dragons, must be well-placed with them. I am yet very confident. My dragons here have grown stronger and deadlier in the last year! Just let the sea demons come!«

Corvanya sighed, »I fear we underestimate the concern or even despair of the sea dwellers! Still, I would appreciate it when you or Peredur could have a word with Tilia!«

»Peredur? What does he have to do with this?«

»He's your nacharya, and as such may have influence with the Abbess, and I think he's more likely to understand what's at stake! He just doesn't have an ancient history with the sea demons to overcome!«

»I'll talk to Tilia! Leave Peredur out of it! It'll all work out!«

»You're taking it all a little lightly, Shyena!«

Shyena made a dismissive hand gesture and said, »Pah!« Then she continued her exercises.

What Is It Really All about?

In the evening, Master Finster intercepted Hollydeva and wanted to ask her a few questions. He approached her politely and really had nothing threatening to her.

»What have you learned here, Hollydeva?«

»I can change what I believe! I can choose in the way that will get me the farthest in the situation. There are no more true or more false beliefs or worldviews, they all have their justification. And truth is something else.«

»Good, good. Is that all there is? What is mysticism? Isn't it a monastery of mystics here, even meta-mystics?«

»Yes, I suppose that's true. I guess mysticism is an attitude that says the world is perfect as it is, divine, animate. When I become one with the Yrth, I am fulfilled. I'm not supposed to reject anything. I am to experience it. I don't want to change the world.«

»Is there good and evil?«

»Yes, that's what I asked myself once. Back at Georgeburg.«

»What is it all really about?«

»I don't understand!«

»Who are you? Who are you really?«

»I'm Hollydeva!«

»It's a name, that's all!«

»I am a Raven.«

»That's a temporary connection to a yana of the island. Are you really identified with it? Who would you be if you didn't identify with anything?«

»I don't know.«

»That's right, stop trying to know. There is no good or right answer! It's a consciousness! You are the one who wonders who she really is. It's a state within you, an observer wondering, wondering who or what or where she actually is! Do you know that?«

»Yes, I know that!«

»They teach something like meditation here on the island, don't they?«

»Hmm, I don't know. I'm only in my first year, after all.«

»Yes, with meditation, I guess it has decreased here. But that's also specifically the technique of the trans-theistic, so the Dolphins and the Dragons. With the Dolphins, after all, there's nothing going on in the direction of mysticism. And the Dragons I can't judge. Is there one of you novices in that yana?«

»Yes, Brother Leo.«

»Ask him what meditation they do there. I'd be interested to know. But some day, and perhaps it is not so far off, I will teach you meditation, Hollydeva, and you will let go of all thoughts, and all identifications with them also, and you will realize who you are in truth and always have been.«

»I don't think I want to learn from you!«

»Yes, I don't have the best reputation here. Don't let that affect you. And please be aware that this, this world, is a kind of theater or training platform. Don't take it too seriously. There are challenges! Threat sharpens our perception and develops our powers! Be grateful to the enemies and opponents for challenging you! Be grateful to the sacrifices you must make, the dead and the traitors, for giving you the opportunity to understand and forgive!«

She nodded understandingly, and he lightly touched her forearm and went into the night as if he had a secret sleeping place in one of the groves.

Chapter 33:
Sea Goddess Nammu.
Sea Scorpion

Audience with the Goddess of the Seas

Hollydeva had consulted Aquaria, and they had decided to find out if they could expect support from the priors of the other yanas. A battle with the sea demons and nereïdes had to be averted!

»Let's go see where Tauro and Capri are! Let them take us to Sura!« suggested Aquaria.

So they strolled to the house of the Angels. They did not want to enter uninvited. Most of the houses were secured, either by adepts keeping watch or by some protective spells.

But there they saw Capri holding hands with a woman in the small garden on the right side of the house. It was the colorfully dressed fortune-teller, Achillea.

»Capri, can you please take us to Maestra Sura?«

Since Ariëa had broken up with him, Capri had become dismissive of her friends as well. He had had a series of love affairs: with novicess Sol, adeptess Coryla, and this cartomancing visitor to the Yana of Angels.

»What do you want from her?«

»That's what we had discussed! We have to motivate the priors to make the Abbess restrain herself!«

»And you want that right now?«

Then Tauro also arrived, together with the cook of the house, Laënna. The two were in animated conversation and seemed to have come together from the cellerar's storehouse. They had no wagon or bags with them, and Aquaria and Hollydeva wondered what Tauro and the cook had been up to.

They both startled when Aquaria approached them. Did they feel caught doing something?

Tauro immediately pulled out his now famous jerky.

»Hello Aquaria and Scorpio, do you want some dried meat?«

»No, we're more in the mood for fruit now that it's autumn!«

»Fruit? Laënna must have some cherries in her cucina!«

»Yes, with pleasure. Because we would need you to escort us into the House of the Angels. We want to talk to the Prioress and find out if she can influence the Abbess!«

»Si, naturalmente. Wasn't Capri going to help you?«

»He's probably romantically busy right now!«

»Mah, Capri is consoling himself over Ariëa in his own way. Is she really with your brother now, Scorpy?«

»Yes, but this is a mystical trial, not love!«

»Oh well, that explains a lot. Come along, first we'll go to the cucina. We'll have cherries there. Then I'll show you how to get to Sura!«

Hollydeva and Aquaria looked at each other. It seemed that Tauro was closer to the cook than to the other novices, adepts or masters of the island.

The Yana of the Angels had developed a lot anyway. In the Games of the Five Elements and Levels, they had won some victories, which had been largely due to the appearance of the Adept Jehadiel. It was almost as if he had been boosted by some substances. Because otherwise, he still seemed more pompous than empowered or even charismatic.

»What can I do for you?« asked the Prioress of the Yana of Angels, Maestra Sura. Nacharya Tatu Njena and Maestra Betula happened to be present as well for a meeting of the leadership of the Yana of Angels.

Aquaria and Hollydeva reported what they knew about the situation and the threat to the monastery.

Sura had a plan right away. »Come, we must speak with a sea god!«

They went to the small round temple in the holy park of the Yana of Angels.

Maestra Sura, along with Tatu Njena, Betula, Aquaria and Hollydeva, sat down in the center of the little temple. Each of the five took the hands of their neighbors, and so they sat in a tight pentagon.

»Close your eyes and follow me!« murmured Maestra Sura, who began intoning a kind of mantra over and over.

Hollydeva became woozy, and she felt herself slipping over into another dimension, as she had when she had met the Babylonian god Nynurta. She felt the hand of Aquaria in her right hand and was glad that her friend was with her on this journey in a different kind of world. It was also good that the strong Tatu Njena was with her. And Betula? Hollydeva felt a sharp, clear alertness in her travel group and no doubt it was an asset, as was Sura's friendly warmth.

»I call to the goddess of the sea! Nammu, appear to us! Nammu, we call to you!«

Hollydeva felt like she was drowning. She was sinking into an endless, wet, cold ocean. She saw fish and jellyfish and creatures all around her. But she felt that she didn't need to breathe, so she didn't get any water into her lungs.

»It's a journey within my inner imagination!« she told herself, and this self-reminder was reassuring.

Then she also saw Sura, Betula, Tatu Njena and Aquaria floating down in the imaginary water as she did.

Then they fell through the bottom of the sea and arrived at a kind of large cave. There, sitting on a throne, was a being that seemed to be made of water. This was probably Nammu, the goddess of the sea.

Sura was the first to regain her composure. She knew such journeys well and had most likely been down here before.

»Nammu, we salute you!«

»Maestra Sura of the Angels! Are you here again! It's been a long time! You rather prefer the flying gods in the skies!«

»Yes, that may be, honored Nammu. But it is an important matter that brings me here to you with these companions!«

»Who are your companions?«

»This one is the Nacharya Tatu Njena, one of the guardians of the Yrth! The lady is my prediction maestra Betula! And these two girls are novicesses in our monastery, named after astrological signs, Scorpio and Aquaria. These two have received information that an attack of your subjects, the nereïdes and the sea demons, on Linden Island is imminent. They know that a conflict with Abbess Tilia is the trigger for these attacks. And we want to promise that we will dissuade the Abbess from her doings so that an attack will be unnecessary.«

»Oh, the Shishumara once promised that too! It is not easy to dissuade the Abbess from paralyzing the sea! Do you have anything on her? Will she listen to you?«

Aquaria now raised her voice, »She accomplishes the paralyzing with a substance and a magical spell that she gets from the alchymists and wizardeurs. Professor Griseo, who is the successor of Master Shishumara in the Yana of the Dolphins, provides her with this substance! We have made sure that it is weakened. And soon it will be completely replaced by a harmless substance. Abbess Tilia won't notice the difference, though!«

»Dolphins?«

»Yes, the Yana of Dolphins!«

»Under Shishumara it was still the Yana of Sharks! We don't like dolphins and whales very much! They're not fishes! They're not really sea creatures! They won't accept any advice from me!«

»Yes, the yana is now named like that! We will see to it that Griseo is degraded. Then it will be named again as before!«

»You promise so much! People keep few of their promises to the sea in the last centuries! The sea is getting dirtier, more polluted, more abused! I know you, Sura, and think you are one of the better people and want to keep promises!«

»Yes, I definitely do and so do my companions here!«

»I will speak with the Queen of the Nereïdes! We will watch the developments!«

»Thank you, honored Nammu! We cannot ask for more!«

Nammu pondered a bit.

»You may leave us. The novicess Scorpio may yet remain!«

The Sacred Dagger of the Sea Scorpions

When the other four had left the cave, Nammu advised Hollydeva, »Swim out of my throne room through that opening there. When you are outside, you will see a kind of coral reef some distance away. Swim there. There you will meet the Sea Scorpion, one of my familiars. He will give you something that you must keep well and always have with you in the coming days. You will need it to avert the misfortune from your island! Do you understand?!«

Hollydeva nodded and did as she was told.

Sure enough, the sea scorpion was waiting for her at the coral reef.

»I greet you, Scorpio! Here, I give you the sacred spiked dagger of the sea scorpions!«

He had a long, pointed, black dagger in his pincers. Hollydeva received the dagger and thanked the sea scorpion.

»When you have deployed it, throw it back into the sea! We like to keep such sacred objects here!«

»Deployed? How do I deploy it?«

»You will know when the situation for which it was created arises! We know you are the Scorpion that was prophesied! You will do the right thing!«

»Good, yes. Thank you, Sea Scorpion!«

And Hollydeva also rose again, up to the surface of the ocean, and when she came up for air, she woke up in the little temple in the holiest of the Yana of the Angels.

But, how wonderful, the spiked dagger of the sea scorpions, received during a kind of inner journey, was actually in her hands, hard and cold!

»What did you get there?« asked Tatu Njena.

»It's the sacred spiked dagger of the sea scorpions!«

The other four seemed impressed.

»Come, let's go back to the house and talk about what else we can do to avert a war with the sea demons!«

»Was that helpful?« asked Maestra Sura Aquaria and Hollydeva.

»Oh yes, Maestra! Nammu will surely have an effect on the nereïdes! And we now have a spiked dagger!«

»Good! I have a request for you!«

Aquaria and Hollydeva nodded, ready to fulfill any request of the angelic maestra.

»In a way, the most problematic yana for me is that of the Tigers. We have a long history of controversies and disputes. As I'm sure you know, they are connected to the wizardeurs, and since the Tigers are treading the path of the left hand, their access to black magic is not far away. Black means here: Using magic for power, for imposing one's will. I understand you are well acquainted with Master Sycamor?!«

Sura had addressed Aquaria, who blushed slightly. Hollydeva was a bit surprised. But yes, Aquaria spoke remarkably often of the Tigers and also of the spiritual exercises they had learned from Master Sycamor. But Sycamor was celibate!

As Aquaria nodded, Sura continued, »With Master Baghora, I have a sort of non-aggression pact. But I understand he's not on the island because he's worried about Nacharya Achmar, who was with the Nononn at Lead Mountain and is probably still there. And now other wizardeurs have arrived at the Tigers! Is that right?«

»Yes, Maestra! The wizardeurs have a new star in the sky, a boy wonder called Cevaine Mire. He appears to stay in the house of the Tigers right now along with his lover Miona. Miona is also the sister of one of our fellow novicesses, Ariëa. But Scorpio knows them better!«

»Yes, Ariëa is also in the Yana of Ravens! And I made the acquaintance of her sister and Cevaine Mire at Georgeburg Castle!«

»You can tell me more about that at another time! I want to know what these two young wizardeurs want in the Yana of Tigers!«

»Yes, we've been wondering the same thing!«

»Perhaps you'd like to do a little spying! You have another novicess of your year in the Tigers, don't you?«

»Yes, Sister Cancra. She works there almost exclusively in the kitchen, though!«

»Kitchen is always a good place to learn things!«

»Yeah, we'll ask Cancra!«

Tellers of Fairy Tales

Tatu Njena asked Hollydeva if she could accompany him to the House of Ravens and take him inside. It was late, but Hollydeva didn't mind another word with Maestra Corvanya.

»Have you met the master called Finster? He's supposed to be in and out of the Ravens?«

»Yes, he seems to be on good terms with Corvanya! Once upon a time, I think he was the prior of the Dolphins, who were just called "Sharks" then!«

»What impression do you have of him?«

»He was eager to talk to me and asked me some questions about my understanding of what is taught here. He seems serious about mysticism and the search for enlightenment. But it may be that he is actually trying to stir up the sea demons!«

»Yes, he has a long relationship with the denizens of the sea!«

»Why did you ask me, Master Njena?«

»It may be that Finster is going to thwart efforts to appease the nereïdes and the sea demons. He may well be interested in an attack by the sea demons! Watch out for him!«

»Yes, thank you for the warning!«

»And one more thing!«

»?«

»Sura makes a very nice and friendly impression, and she is the prioress of the Yana, of which I am the Nacharya protector! But she is indebted to Tilia, has given her access to the element of Air. If Tilia has all five essential elements at her disposal, she will be very powerful! And Sura is one of her most important allies! You will be able to harness her for a pacification of the nereïdes and sea people. But she won't do anything about Tilia's activities!«

»Thank you for telling me that, Master Njena! I guess we will have to convince Tilia! Or stop her from going to the shore of the island!«

»Yes, that would probably be the easiest solution!«

They reached the Ravens' house and went together to Corvanya's study, where Master Finster was already waiting.

»Oh, Nacharya Tatu Njena! It's my pleasure!« Finster had immediately risen to shake the nacharya's hand.

Corvanya also greeted him in an almost friendly manner. »Tatu Njena, be welcome to the Ravens!«

»I thank you, Maestra Corvanya! I somehow learned that you wanted to share something with me!«

»Yes, I think you are the right nacharya to know! Scorpio, show him!«

And she looked at Master Finster and warned him, »This will even surprise you, Nikor!«

Hollydeva understood that Corvanya was referring back to their earlier meeting. They needed a reliable nacharya as an ally and as a mentor for her application to the Council of Nine.

She took out the medallion and was somewhat surprised at the apparent surprise of the nacharya and the Dark Master.

»You are the successor of the Bhogi!?«

»Yes, he wanted me to be his successor. He would rather not be reborn, and he wanted a woman to join the council! Possibly, in the long run, he wanted the Council of Nine to be made up of women!«

»Yes, it is not without sense! We men are tired and about to fail!«

»May I comment?« Master Finster began very cautiously.

Hollydeva looked at him. He looked very distressed.

»Hollydeva, you must not become Nacharya! You must let go of this world! You can't guard it or rule it or save it or whatever the task is!«

»No? Why not?«

»You are here to attain final liberation, not to bind yourself! Life as a nacharya and in repetition is a sacrifice, a tremendous sacrifice! Master Tatu Njena knows what I am talking about!«

Tatu Njena nodded and remained silent.

»Final liberation, it sounds like a fairy tale! This world is threatened. Now the seas are threatened! Intervention must be taken! If I have the power as Nacharya, I want to do it!«

»But there will always be something to save! This world is continually changing, and all things pass away and new ones arise! Do not bind yourself!«

Master Finster had spoken with vehemence, almost desperation.

Hollydeva looked at Corvanya. She did not quite know what to make of this performance,

»I'm afraid it's too early for that insight, Nikor!« Corvanya tried to reassure him.

He nodded and sat down. »Do you have another raven whiskey?«

»Yes, I suppose we could use a drink!«

Corvanya retrieved four glasses and a bottle from a cabinet.

Hollydeva wanted to wave them off. »Well, I'm too young for anything, so more like no whiskey!«

»Oh come on, you're the oldest one here!«

»Tilia had said something like that to my mother, too. It's all spin!«

Tatu Njena took the floor, »But, Hollydeva, if it were true, and you've already tried in countless lifetimes to save or change or influence this world, and it's now where it is, and you realize that all that influencing didn't really accomplish anything, and now you're just going to let things take their course...«

»No, I can't! I have to stop this battle with the sea demons!«

Master Finster was at it again, »Alright, I understand you! I'm asking you to do one thing. You will be in the battle, in the middle of it. Watch everything and yourself in the process. Keep a distance from yourself and from everything that happens! Do not judge, just perceive! And the moment comes when you have to act! And you act! You do it with full awareness, very awake! But you also perceive that you are like an actress in a play, who fills a role! Have I made myself understood?«

»Yes, I understand! Is that also the way of the Ravens?«

Corvanya: »Yes, Scorpio, this can also be an exercise in the Way of the Ravens! Come, drink your first whiskey in this life!«

And so she drank with her maestra, the dark one and the dark-skinned nacharya. It burned her throat and warmed her stomach, and the smoky taste was intense on her tongue and palate. She wondered if she had drunk with these three many times before, and it seemed likely. For these masters were laughing at her and acting as if they had waited a long time for this evening.

Chapter 34:
Master Anguinaga. Sea Snake. Kymothoë

Master Anguinaga Calls a Sea Serpent

Gemina reported at the next meeting of the novices that Master Anguinaga would expect them on the north shore in the evening. Three of them were to come. Hollydeva looked around and decided that Piscio should go with her and Aquaria, since he was already known to the people of the sea as a ferry boy, and it would be good to have a male speaker. Piscio was a bit surprised, but he also felt honored and quickly got ready.

Gemina led them to where Master Anguinaga was waiting and withdrew at a sign from him.

Master Anguinaga immediately addressed the issue. »You want to dissuade the nereïdes from attacking the island?«

»Yes, that is so!« confirmed Aquaria.

»What can you offer?«

»We will do everything we can to dissuade Tilia from influencing the sea!«

»You mean the nereïdes and the sea demons will attack because of something Tilia does?«

»Yes, Tilia pours something into the sea and makes incantations and such to calm or paralyze the sea.«

»So there's no flooding! That's good!«

»If high tide and low tide are the natural rhythm of the sea, then there must be stronger tides that cause floods every so often. Nobody is forced to build a house in an area that is in danger of being flooded regularly!«

»I'll ask the sea snakes! Come along!«

Master Anguinaga seemed to Hollydeva like the most dangerous person she had met so far. It was certainly good to win him as an ally. But there was nothing friendly

319

about him. He didn't seem like anything would impress him or make him friendly. She could only hope that his interests coincided with hers.

Anguinaga stopped right at the edge of the sea. Loudly and commanded with his strong voice, »Samudri!«

He stood there with his arms outstretched. Hollydeva, Aquaria and Piscio stood about two meters behind him, eager to see if "Samudri" would show.

Then a water snake came slithering up and straightened up in front of the headmaster of the Yana of Snakes.

»What do you want, master of Snakes with blunt teeth!«

»Samudri, if you can address me so blasphemously, you seem to be doing wonderfully! These here claim that the inhabitants of the sea are impaired, and that the mistresses of the waters are contemplating an attack on this island!«

»My blasphemy is but gallows humor! We here in the waters of the sea are indeed not well! The sea is not as alive as it once was. The queen says that the Abbess of the island is the main culprit. She wants it to be stopped. The Abbess allows machines to drill in our depths, cables to stir up our ground, dirt, sewage and unnatural substances to spread in our sea. You who are the allies of this Abbess will have to go down with her!«

Hollydeva could not stop herself, »But we want to stop her! We are allies of the dwellers of the sea, as we are allies of the dwellers of the forest and the heavens!«

Anguinaga made a reassuring gesture with his hand.

But Samudri laughed, »That about going down together scared you, girl? Yes, there you are in a boat with the Abbess, being shaken by the nereïdes until it sinks.«

Then Samudri changed the tone, »But I understand you. After all, we are also in a boat with the sea demons, and actually, we don't like them. We actually don't like all these fish. After all, we are air-breathers like you, like dolphins and whales!«

And then Samudri seemed to come to his senses. »Yes, actually, we who live in the sea, although we are not fish, are quite fine with the activities of the Abbess. That way the fish and especially the demons and those imaginary fairies leave us alone!«

Anguinaga shouted, »Samudri! I command you not to speak so blasphemously! Fetch one of the nereïdes now!«

Samudri laughed, »You think you can command me like you command the snakes in your terrariums, Toothless?«

Then the sea serpent slithered closer.

»But there is one with you with which I can press the nereïdes very nicely. For that one, they'll be quiet for now. That should be fine with you, too!«

With these words, the sea serpent had wriggled incredibly fast onto land and around Piscio's legs!

The sea serpent pulled Piscio, who was kicking and flailing trying to fight back, into the sea! Hollydeva and Aquaria rushed to him to free him from the snake. But they came too late.

»Samudri, he is going to drown!« screamed Anguinaga as she pulled Piscio further into the sea.

»No, he won't!« interjected a woman's voice.

Lykoria, the yellow-robed nereïde, had emerged from the waters behind the sea serpent and grabbed Samudri by the scruff of the neck.

»Luck! That's Lykoria, Piscio's friend!« cried Hollydeva, who had, after all, already met the nereïde.

Samudri made a bitter face and had to let go of Piscio. Lykoria threw the sea serpent with a high arc far out into the sea. She held the still startled Piscio under the armpits.

»Serpent Master, why do you call this malefactor? What do you want?«

Hollydeva replied, »Lykoria, we need to talk to you! You have been out of sight, even though Piscio and I called for you! We thought that Anguinaga would call the sea serpent, and it would bring you here!«

»Which is kind of what happened!« sighed the Prior of the Serpents, who must have been a little embarrassed by his lack of power over Samudri.

»Good then, here comes the ambassador lady of the nereïdes, my beloved Kymothoë!«

Ambassador Kymothoë

From the waves rose a boat pulled by large fish, made of a large shell, in which a woman sat whose long hair seemed to be made of seaweed. She had blue robes flowing down her like flowing water. Her large blue eyes seemed to be directed into a far distance.

»Master Anguinaga! Raven novicess, I thank you for fulfilling the request Lykoria made at your previous meeting! Piscio, my friend! And you must be Aquaria, another friend of the waters! I thank you for coming and for your concern!«

Master Anguinaga made a deep bow and the three novices followed suit.

»Ambassador Kymothoë, greetings!«

»I greet you, too, Master of Serpents! I must speak with the Raven girl, whom I have known longer than she has known herself! How may I address you, girl, who I know as Arlecyna?«

»I have never heard that name before! My name is Hollydeva! And now as a novicess with the Ravens, my name is Scorpio!«

»Hollydeva, then! Listen, Hollydeva, you are in possession of a sacred weapon, a sting dagger of the Sea Scorpion, which Nammu herself had given you! Against whom will you use this weapon?«

»I don't know! I will defend myself and my friends with it!«

»You don't remember! Are you familiar with the concept of rebirths, of multiple lives?«

»Yes, somehow I am!«

»I addressed you as Arlecyna, as that is what you were called in a previous incarnation. Or rather, that is your name in the world from where our souls come!«

»World from which our souls come?«

»Yes, a part of you was born and grew here in this world. But don't you feel there is something inside you, an unchanging consciousness, that is watching, taking in new consciousness, something that feels like the real you?«

»Yes, I think I know what you mean!«

»Good, you are Arlecyna, a special person, a special consciousness. We were allies once before, during the fall of a great civilization, Atlantys. We finished off that Atlantys together!«

»Atlantys? I don't believe it! You're telling fairy tales!«

»Snake master, you tell her!«

»Kymothoë, let it be! That was a very long time ago! She wants to help you. And her friends too! The distribution of sympathies among the masters and adepts of the island, on the other hand, is not so clear.«

»Where do you stand, serpent master?«

»I'm staying out of everything at the moment! I will defend my house against attacks, from whomever! I'm not giving Tilia access to the element of stones. But she doesn't want that right now. She needs the power of Water to master the five essential elements!«

»I wish you not to be shipwrecked with your attitude, Anguinaga!«

Then Kymothoë turned to Hollydeva, Aquaria, and Piscio,

»Your grandmother has vouched that you cannot be used against us! The boy next to you was a witness!«

»That's right, and that's not what I intend!«

»But we will destroy the island and the monastery!«

»Then, like Master Anguinaga, I may have to protect what I see as belonging to me!«

»Good, so we are to leave the houses of the Ravens and the Snakes in peace! But the girl next to you is from the Yana of the Dolphins, if I am correctly informed!«

Aquaria replied, »Yes, I chose the Yana of Dolphins on the first day of my novitiate here based on false information. But I was mistaken. The Yana of Dolphins is not my home. You should destroy it! I would be happy to help with that!«

»You said that you have rendered harmless the things that the Abbess pours into the sea?«

»Yes, we already have diminished the power and next time she will only pour salt and sugar into the sea! However, we know that she activates the whole thing with incantations, and we probably don't know how to render them harmless! We'd have to be wizardeurs to do that!«

»Yes, that's true. Can you harness wizardeurs for yourselves?«

»The Yana of Tigers is connected to the wizardeurs, and young wizardeurs have arrived there as guests. But they're most likely more on Tilia's side! We'll question them!«

Hollydeva intervened, »Doesn't Master Sycamor perhaps know something more about wizardry?«

Aquaria blushed slightly and nodded, »I will question him!«

»Let the ferryman's boy come to me!« Kymothoë, the ambassador of the nereïdes, ordered Lykoria who had carried Piscio to the shore.

Piscio walked back towards Kymothoë until he was up to his waist in water.

Hollydeva and Aquaria looked at each other in wonder. Anguinaga hissed softly.

»Get in the boat, boy!« urged Kymothoë.

»What are you doing, ambassador? What do you want with him?« cried Hollydeva.

»He is a hostage. He will be fine with us. But we'll make sure you remember your promises this way!«

»But how will he breathe and survive underwater?«

»Oh, he's a fish! His name is Piscio, after all! He'll be fine!«

Piscio actually got into the clam boat, which quickly veered off and disappeared into the waters.

»Well, that was a success!« stated Master Anguinaga somewhat sarcastically.

»Yes, you are right, Master. Actually, we accomplished nothing and lost a novice whose disappearance we also have to explain!«

»Maybe he is in the safest place of all of us!«

Chapter 35:
Tondeuse Family. Prioress Urana

Family Counsel

There they were sitting together in the house of Yana Agnus, Hollydeva's family.

»Anyway, what is our family name?« wondered Hollydeva. Her mother's last name was "von Valmere", she knew that. But her father's last name wasn't "Stone", after all. She had never met paternal grandparents, had never even heard of them, oddly enough. Daman was a von Valmere, too.

But, oh yes, in school she had been called by her last name. "Tondeuse".

»Dear Tondeuse and von Valmere family and relatives!« she began, then. »I have called you here because I need your support! There is an important matter at hand, and we should stick together, as a family!«

As she said this, she already knew that this family did not exist. Besides, Einar wasn't there, who would have been the most likely to stand by her.

»What is it about, Hollydeva?« asked her father, who still looked stricken, but was probably on the mend.

»Yes, what is it about? What do you want from us?« her mother also asked a little impatiently.

»I have sure information that the next attack of the nereïdes and the sea demons is imminent! They attack to protect themselves from an interference of the sea coming from Abbess Tilia and the alchymists, who have their local chapter with the Yana of the Dolphins! I have spoken with the nereïdes. They are waiting to attack and see if I can make good on my promise to dissuade the Abbess from her behavior!«

»You sure do run your mouth!«

Daman intervened, »Listen to her, Rosa! I'm afraid it's true what she says! We should consider whether we can get Tilia to give in!«

»Why do you support her delusions of grandeur? All she wants is war and fighting! It makes her feel good!«

Baldar spoke up, »Let's think about what we can do! After all, we are all in the Yana of the Lambs. We should talk to Urana first!«

Hollydeva had noticed that this attempt to swear her in to the yana had caused a twitch in the corner of her mother's mouth. After all, the garden maestra wasn't really a maestra within the Yana Agnus anymore. She had become a Tigress. She was only staying at the Lambs because she felt obligated to Seren, who was in the best place to heal.

»I can talk to Griseo and the Dolphins! I'll try to find out what they're up to and if they can reduce or reverse it!« suggested Seren.

Hollydeva nodded. »That would be a start!«

»I can talk to Prioress Urana. But I don't think she has much influence over Tilia!« agreed her mother, Maestra Castanea.

Daman commanded, »Let us all talk to Urana!«

Prioress Urana's Sermon

So they went to Urana, prioress of Yana Agnus, the House of Lambs.

»Maestra Urana, can you dissuade Tilia from interfering with the sea dwellers so that they are not forced to attack the island?«

»No, I don't think I can! As prioress of the Yana Agnus, I have power over the element called the Akasha or Quintessence. It is, in a sense, the highest of the five essential elements.

»In the tradition of the island, the priors of the yanas of Bees, Angels, Dolphin, and Dragons grant the abbot or abbess access to the power of the elements of Earth, Air, Water and Fire. The prior or prioress of the Lambs gives access to the Quintessence, which contains the power of connection of the four basic elements. So then the abbot or abbess of the island has a lot of power, which he or she uses to protect and seize the island and to let this power radiate for the good of the Yrth.

»But then the predecessor of Griseo, the unfortunate Master Finster, at that time he was called Shishumara, took away the power over the Water from the Abbess! He gave very flimsy reasons for it. As if Abbess Tilia were conspiring against the sea because she had once experienced a storm surge as a child!

»This master was then deposed by all of us and had to leave the island! Tilia then invited Griseo! The alchemists associated with the Yana of the Dolphins had introduced him to her. But he had no experience with the elements and did not know how to master the element of Water or how to give access to the Abbess. But he's working on it, I'm told.

»In addition, the nereïdes must have stated that they had stopped cooperating with the island after the Dark Master was thrown out. They would actively prevent the island from gaining mystical access to the water. We live in the midst of a hostile element, so to speak.

»Tilia is doing something so that we are not continually beset by storm surges and floods!

»Then the sea demons attacked and killed masters, adepts, and novices! There had never been anything like that before!

»If Tilia gets the power over the Water through the help of the alchemists, and thus peace returns to the island and our worship, I am fully on her side! And so should you be!

»But Castanea, you've been struggling with everything for some time! And then the Abbess has also reprimanded you for your behavior towards your daughter!

»And you, daughter of Castanea, are just as much a rebel as your mother. The good thing about you rebels is that you can't get along with each other!

»May the OneGod lead you back to the right path! I am most likely unable to do so!«

Hollydeva had to swallow. Prioress Urana had piled up some anger. She looked questioningly at Daman and her mother.

Her mother shook her head and explained, »I have little sympathy for Abbess Tilia, not least since the conversation in which I had to make amends with you, dear daughter. I am also completely indifferent to the sea dwellers. It has long been clear that I have little in common with you, Urana. I ended up in this yana and the monastery garden because of my mother. She is now dead, and I am free from her power!

»So now I declare that I have belonged to the Yana of Tigers for some time! Prior Baghora has given me the new name of Maestra Manducate! And I think I have sympathies for the new star in the wizardeur sky, Cevaine Mire. So, I am out of here. I'm not interested in your war! The Tigers have little to do with it. I will protect the house of the Tigers in case of a battle! Otherwise, frack you all!«

With these words, she gathered her robe and wanted to leave the room.

Daman, her brother still wanted to stop her: »Rosa, your daughter is probably right. We must also protect the sea dwellers! The water worlds are gardens too!«

But Castanea, now Manducate, formerly Rosa de Valmere, had only an »Oh no!« for him too and had left.

Daman pushed Hollydeva and Baldar out of the prioress's room, who was staring dead ahead rather gloomily.

»I guess we can't do anything here!« he commented. »Baldar and I can try to influence the adepts and novices not to blindly follow Tilia or Urana, but to prepare to defend the house!«

»That's good!« confirmed Hollydeva. »Novices? Where is my friend Libra, any-way?«

Libra's Love

Hollydeva had a suspicion. She said goodbye to Daman, her uncle, and Baldar, her brother. Of late, the novices were to be found in the kitchens of the houses. It was the same here. Libra sat with the cook of the Lambs. The midwives' and cooks' guilds were probably a good match. Or weren't they even in a common guild with doctors and healers!?

»Libra, Urana is very firmly on Tilia's side!«

»I'm not surprised! Urana is only prioress because she fits well into the hierar-chical system! Obedient to authority! That's what makes right-handed monotheists so dangerous! They always form an army quickly!«

»But you're one of them!«

»No, I'm here as a saboteur! Midwives have always suffered under the minions of the OneGod everywhere! The OneGod wants the suffering of mothers! And he wants children! Multitudes of children will grow into strong armies! Midwives are not only helpers of birth! They are also helpers of women who do not want a child!«

»And how far have you gotten in your sabotage here?«

»Not far. I'm too much of a woman and have too much to do with my love affairs, all of which go unhappily! After all, your brother ran away!«

»He didn't run away! He went to our grandmother's place and never got there! Where the hell did he go!? I have a feeling: he disappeared in the crack through which the creatures came!«

328

»Creatures?«

»Yes, they are such small beings with horns on their foreheads. One of them is probably with the Dolphins as the wife of the alchymist Doctor Albedo. She builds a device that Tilia can use to draw energy from the sea!«

»Uh, that doesn't sound very believable!«

»It is!«

»I'm going to go over there and try to find out something. Maybe I can question this creature and find out where Avela is! I mean your brother, Einar!«

»Alright, Libra, you do that!«

But then Hollydeva still stopped her novice sister. »Libra, you've been hanging out with my mother a lot lately, haven't you?«

»Yes, I'm helping her in the garden!«

»Just now we were with Urana and that's when my mother explained that she was now Maestra Manducate with the Tigers. Are you now with the Tigers too?«

»No, my assignment is here with the Lambs, the priests of the OneGod. As garden maestra, your mother will have to stay on here as well. She just likes to make a big fuss and provoke Urana.«

»But you must be at home somewhere. You must belong to a yana! I'm happy with the Ravens!«

»I am at home with the midwives! And maybe I'll find a husband here and be at home in a marriage!«

Hollydeva shook her head. The concept was foreign to her.

»Who is it going to be, Libra? Who will be your husband? Have you picked out a husband yet?«

Libra didn't answer that, of course. Hollydeva told Aquaria about the conversation later, and the elected spokesgirl of the first year novices had her eye on Libra anyway.

»I can tell you who she has picked. You won't guess!«

»She was after my older brother. But he disappeared. My younger brother is now claimed by Ariëa. I guess she wanted something from Leo, to be queen in the north someday. But he only has eyes for Maestra Shyena. Who is it? One of the masters? Sycamor?«

Aquaria blushed, and Hollydeva realized that she had found a sore spot in her friend here, where she had better just keep asking carefully.

»No, not a master, adept, or novice of Linden Isle!«

»Yes, but who else is here? After all, she can only cast eyes here. At the moment!«

»Exactly. Nice puzzle, isn't it?«

Hollydeva thought. It couldn't be her recovering father, after all. Then she knew.

»Uh, my uncle, the nacharya.«

»Yes, your uncle, the nacharya. And, if I am not mistaken, that nacharya enforced the unification of the churches into the OneGod and the elevation of the OneGod to the main faith in the world. And your uncle is the nacharya of the OneGod yana here. So he has prevailed in the council of the Nacharya! He has much more power and political skill than we think. And he is what Libra is supposed to fight as an agent of the midwives above all!«

»You're right, Aqui! And she doesn't realize that in her urge to be someone significant through a marriage, she will as well not have the home that she can't find in her yana!«

»Should we warn her?«

»No, perhaps she will indeed find happiness with Daman. We must not deny her that!«

And they giggled at the tragedy that was unfolding, like the young girls they actually were.

Chapter 36:
A Meeting at Tiger's Kitchen

Ariëa and Miona

»Come with me!« urged Hollydeva Ariëa after dinner.

»What do you want from me? You're just lying to me anyway!«

»I want to set you up with your sister! Surely, you've already tried to get in with the Tigers! But they've closed everything down because they have enough to do with themselves!«

Cancra, novicess with the Tigers, however, was there with her novice friends, »I sneaked out. I you bring to sister! Come, Ari!«

So Ariëa went with her Raven sister Scorpio and the little Chynese called "Shrimp" to the house of Yana Tiger.

The house looked locked and inaccessible, but Shrimp, of course, knew a vendor entrance for the kitchen, through which they entered the Tiger house.

Crouching down, they followed Shrimp through several hallways and up a flight of stairs. Then she pointed to a door.

They heard voices behind the door.

»What are you really up to?« It sounded like head-novicess Bagatto.

»Who cares! The main thing is to have something going on!«

Hollydeva shook herself, Brother Torre, the impertinent second year novice!

»I'll explain!«

That was Cevaine Mire, whose voice she had heard only briefly some time ago in the basement of Georgeburg!

»We must take the Yana of the Tigers! It is the yana that is in contact with the sorcerers and wizardeurs. But unfortunately, Prior Baghora and Nacharya Achmar, both rather mediocre wizardeurs, are unwilling to relinquish leadership, for one thing. And for another, they are in disagreement with the wizardeur's leadership, and so we are tasked by that leadership to take over here in the house!«

»You want to depose Baghora?« That was Luna.

Shrimp signaled Hollydeva and Ariëa to stay where they were and keep quiet. Then she knocked on the door behind which Cevaine Mire had gathered the novices of the Tigers and stepped into the room.

Hollydeva heard through the door as Shrimp greeted that gathering surprisingly blatant. »Hello, friends!« she greeted, »I bring you some more drink! Is ready. You come and help me, Miona? You strong!«

Indeed, Miona followed Shrimp out of the room and came into the hallway, in the corner of which Hollydeva and Ariëa were waiting.

When Shrimp and Miona were close, the two Raven novicess girls stepped out.

»Miona! It's me, Cita!«

Miona stumbled and stopped. Her arms and hands she had spread, ready for a magical spell. Defense or attack?

»Cita? Really? What are you doing here?«

»I'm novicess Ariëa in the Yana of Ravens! This here is my Raven sister Scorpio!«

Miona looked sharply. The light was dim, but she had to laugh.

»The Nacharya Bhogi's disgusting little bitch who hypnotized me into the dungeon! What do you want? What are you doing with my sister?«

»I'm a friend of your sister! We are here in the same house! I could be your sister too!«

»Ha ha, what would I get out of it? But Cita, let me give you a hug!«

The two Afrycan girls hugged each other.

»How is father? How is Yamina?«

»When I left our village, they were fine. Father sent me here. This is where all the threads on the Yrth come together, he said. So far, though, I haven't discovered many threads. Scorpio is a little better at that.«

»Scorpio? Yes, that sounds fitting. A poisonous stinger! Cevaine Mire will be happy to give you back your burps!«

»Oh, thanks, no need! So you guys are here to take over this house?«

»Yes, that's the order! But Cevaine sort of forced it on our head wizardeurs. Actually, nobody wants trouble with Baghora and Achmar!«

»Then what's the point?«

»Shh!« whispered Shrimp between them. »Go into kitchen, no one can hear!«

They went into the kitchen of the house. Shrimp put on tea and got pastries from a cupboard. Here in the Tiger kitchen was her domain by now.

»Listen, Miona! Please! The island is about to be attacked by sea demons and nereïdes, as it was about two years ago! The survival of the island is at stake! It's not a good time to bring discord to one of the eight yanas! You must get Cevaine to leave again!«

»Oh, nonsense! You're just making that up!«

»No, Miona! It's actually true!« confirmed Ariëa.

»But your Tigers are probably at odds anyway! The three novices we're talking to right now are eager to depose Baghora!«

»And these are supposed to be your allies? Novices so quick to betray their prior? What kind of Tigers are they? You're welcome to take them with you!«

»Yes, there's something to that. I didn't have the best impression, either. But one of them is a beautiful girl. She even is the spokeswoman of all novices in the monastery! What's she got against Baghora?«

»Probably he doesn't pay enough attention to her!«

Aquaria and Master Sycamor

Then they heard soft voices and noises at the door leading outside. Someone was trying to insert a key into the keyhole.

Hollydeva signaled to Shrimp, and she quickly turned out the light.

The door opened, and two figures entered the kitchen. And these two jumped in surprise, as Shrimp turned the light back on so that the two stood somewhat dazzled in the middle of the kitchen, gazing in disbelief at the four young women.

»Aquaria!? Master Sycamor!?«

The two did not want to be known as lovers. They had thought themselves unobserved and holding hands, and were now visibly in a state of being caught.

»So what? Sycamor and I are lovers!«

»Is that allowed? Master with novicess and even from different yanas?«

»No, not really!« confirmed Sycamor, somewhat contritely. »But Ellianne is not a normal novicess, and actually, she belongs in the Yana of Tigers. And I'm a master who-«

»Is living celibate!« added Ariëa with a laugh. Hollydeva and Shrimp joined in the laughter. And then Aquaria and Sycamor laughed, too.

»Master, you said "Ellianne". You call each other by your worldly names?«

»Yes,« Sycamor confirmed, »I knew Ellianne through her mother before she came here as a novicess. And my name for her is Altaïr, which is my real name. Sycamor is a tree, after all, and many of the masters here at the monastery just have tree names!«

»Like my grandmother, "Maestra Malus", who was called like the apple tree!«

»Exactly. And your mother is named after the chestnut!«

»Why are you mentioning my mother now?«

»You will know that she defected to the Tigers! I supported her in that! I think very highly of your mother, Scorpio!«

»Yes, you'll have to forgive me, Master Sycamor. I'm not a great admirer of my mother!«

Miona interrupted, »I'm going back to Cevaine and the others!«

»No wait, Miona! Please, Master Sycamor, confirm to her that a sea demon attack may be imminent!«

»I don't know anything about it!«

Hollydeva became indignant. »You are the acting prior of the Yana of Tigers these days, one of the preeminent yanas here on the island! And you don't even know what is happening in your house and around you because you are in love with a novicess right now? You are the master of self-mastery! I'm not very impressed right now!«

But Hollydeva saw Aquaria's pleading look. And she realized that she regretted her harsh words. Aquaria was an important friend!

»I'm sorry, Aquaria! I don't begrudge you your happiness!«

»But it's not the time for love! We must be ready for battle now!« announced Ariëa. She grabbed her sister's hand, »Miona, Scorpio is right. You have to help us!«

»I don't know how I could help you!«

Sycamor and Aquaria had not relocked the outer door to the kitchen, and it was now opened again from the outside. In stepped the Abbess herself, Grand Maestra Tilia.

Overcrowded Tiger Kitchen

»What is going on here?«

Master Sycamor stepped in front of the girls. »We're having a little meeting here, where I'm explaining the basic exercises of self-mastery in detail!«

»Nonsense, Sycamor! What's going on here?«

»Abbess! Here at the Yana of Tigers, Ariëa's sister, the wizardeur Miona, is visiting, and we wanted to give the two of them a chance to meet! We're having a reunion!«

Hollydeva had pointed to Miona, who made a short bow toward the abbess.

»A visit from wizardeurs? That should have been reported to me!«

Cevaine and the three Tiger novices must have heard voices, and now they too came into the kitchen of the Tiger house, which fortunately was sufficiently spacious.

Bagatto approached the Abbess, »Abbess Tilia, this is Cevaine Mire! The wizardeurs have sent him to spruce up the Yana of the Tigers!«

Tilia shook her head. »I'm still wondering what's actually going on here. What a mess! And these lies and stories!«

Meanwhile, Shrimp had slipped out of the kitchen and returned with the remaining Tiger Masters, Maestra Simhana and Master Abiës.

»Perhaps you have already heard, Abbess!« now Bagatto began. »Scorpio here is spreading the word that the sea demons will soon attack again because you, Abbess, are interfering with the inhabitants of the sea and are planning the exploitation of the sea together with the alchymists and Professor Griseo!«

»So, that's what she's spreading! Is that right, novicess Scorpio?«

»Yes, that is so true! I beg you, Maestra, to stop this and not carry out what you are planning to do to suck the essential element of Water from the sea! The nereïdes and sea demons must then attack and destroy the monastery!«

»As if I hadn't considered that! Then we'll just have to beat them back like we did before!«

»But consider the losses we suffered two years ago!« exclaimed Master Abiës.

»Well, now we still have the active support of alchymists and wizardeurs and will know how to fight back better! As soon as I use the device the alchymists built me in time, they will already be too weak to attack!«

Hollydeva became really indignant. »You can't be serious! You can't want to harm the sea's inhabitants like that!«

Tilia was probably about to say that these sea dwellers had already caused her greater harm when two more people entered the house through the kitchen door: Hollydeva's mother and novicess Libra.

Maestra Castanea, Maestra Manducate now, immediately took the floor: »I have overheard everything or already knew. I currently have the priory of Yana the Tiger!« With these surprising words, she showed up a mummified tiger claw, which must have been the sign of the Prior of the Tigers.

Maestra Simhana frowned and shook her head somewhat in disbelief.

»Prior Baghora has asked me to look after things here while he is searching for Nacharya Achmar. So right now, I'm the housemaster here. Masters Sycamor and Abiës know about it! Abbess, I must ask you to leave the house and not to cause any more trouble here! Cevaine Mire and Miona, you please prepare your departure and stop dreaming about taking power here in the House of Tigers. My name is now Maestra Manducate, and I am the acting prioress of the house!«

Abbess Tilia nodded and walked out the door. Cevaine Mire pulled Miona with her, who still hugged her sister tightly for a moment, and they probably went to follow the instructions of the Tiger maestra, who now wanted to be called Manducate.

»Now to you, daughter. Novicess Scorpio, you are causing a lot of wind everywhere here! We should keep you here in the house for now! Bagatto, Luna, Torre! Seize her and constrain her into the basement room!«

Just as the three Tiger novices were about to carry out the order, Cancra boldly threw herself between them, assuming the stance of a martial artist.

»Stop! I'm protecting Scorpio!«

Then Ariëa, Aquaria, and Libra stood beside her, and the forces were probably even, especially since the two male masters also seemed undecided about whether to go along with the order of the prior's second-in-command, which was still unclear to them. That Maestra Simhana would not stand by her anyway was probably clear to Hollydeva's mother.

»But Libra, I thought I had your support!«

»Yes, Maestra Manducate, you do! But I don't want to be partly responsible if Scorpio is right and the sea demons attack, and she has the power to resolve the situation or dissuade the sea people from their plans!«

Hollydeva's mother sighed and nodded. »Then go! All of you who do not belong in this house, please leave now!«

And soon the Tigers' kitchen was emptied again, and Cancra made herself some tea.

In the next room, she heard the masters of the Tigers arguing with the garden mistress about who would be in charge of the house during Baghora's absence. And she suspected Raelyn, the young cook of the Tigers, of having stolen the tiger's claw from Baghora's room in order to give it to the new maestra Manducate via the cook of the lambs. What had been her price, her reward?

Chapter 37:
Griseo, Albedo.
Mrs. Lotus aka Fapha

The Aquumulator!

After leaving the house of the Tigers, Hollydeva, Aquaria, and Ariëa ran to the house of the Yana of the Dolphins. Libra went back to the house of the Lambs, probably because Daman had announced that he had to leave, as he had an important appointment somewhere in the world.

»How far along is Sagittario in sabotaging Griseo's chymical substance for Tilia?«

»Very far. He's been working on it for some time, it seems. What Tilia pours into the ocean and what she does her incantations with should be attenuated!«

»That's why the nereïdes may be daring to attack again now!«

»Yeah, they'll probably have to, as eventually Tilia and Griseo will realize what's going on!«

»And what about the stock market and fake stock news?«

»Let's ask him!«

But Sagittario was not to be found in his office in the house of the Yana of the Dolphins. The three novicesses, however, saw him sitting with Master Finster at the bell tower. What were those two talking about!

»Why is he talking to Master Finster?«

»I have a confession to make, Scorpio!«

»What?«

»Sagittario and I called this Master Finster and invited him to come here. Well, he was probably planning on it anyway! We found out that he is the former and the actual Prior of the Yana of Dolphins, Master Shishumara. Tilia disempowered him and kicked him out for two reasons!«

»And those would be?«

»He has become a heretic. He doesn't believe in a mysticism where everything is ultimately good or even reasonable. Rather, he teaches that everything is ultimately emptiness and nothingness.«

»A nihilist!«

»Yes, but a nihilist who nevertheless seeks ecstasy and love, or something like that. A non-cynical nihilist, so to speak.«

»What was the second?«

»Tilia needed money, and the alchymists offered her that! Plus, of course, their access to agents that enable the paralysis of sea creatures! She gave them licenses so they could drill and lay cables in the ocean floor and use the sea as a dumping ground, since Linden Island probably owns the ocean floor quite a few miles off the island!«

»I find all this hard to believe. Tilia actually makes a sovereign and morally exemplary impression!«

»She must have gotten herself into something she thinks she can only get out of by getting in totally!«

They had reached Sagittario and Master Finster.

»Hello, Hollydeva, Cita, and Ellianne! This young man is capable! You have a good plan! The nereïdes will refrain from attacking, I think!«

Something about his voice irritated Hollydeva. »You don't really mean that! You wouldn't really be happy about it!«

»No, I'm sure that Tilia should be taken out! But I don't have many allies here to take her out! Actually, probably only Corvanya!«

»And us!«

»Well, yes, that's something! But it takes a majority in the Council of Priors! And the Nacharyas have a vote in the council too!«

»What is it even about that? It has to be about more than just Tilia's unhappy childhood!« Aquaria wondered.

Sagittario knew something: »I'm afraid I know something about that! After all, a leading alchymist has been in the House of Dolphins for several days now. With him has come a little woman, whom I believe to be one of the creatures from your grandmother's garden. She has such horns! This being comes from a completely different world and has superior technological skills and knowledge and builds the alchymists and Griseo a device with which Tilia can absorb the power and energy of the water, of the sea. It works on the principle of energy accumulator with layers of organic and inorganic material. They call it Aquumulator!«

Master Finster seemed shocked. »Is that possible? That would be tragic! The abbot or abbess of Linden Island have the power of the four, five, or even the eight elements. But they have them only if the priors of the eight yanas give them to him or her! I have made sure before my expulsion that Tilia does not get the power of the Water. The nereïdes supported me in this. But then they wanted more than I could give them! I had to settle far away from them, in a dry volcanic crater! Griseo doesn't have the knowledge and skills to lift my lock! So Tilia doesn't have the power of the five elements, let alone the eight, especially since Corvanya probably denies her the power of Wood as well. Although if she finds such a technological way, it would be critical, then she could kill the nereïdes and the sea demons and enslave all the sea dwellers. We must prevent that at all costs!«

Hollydeva, Aquaria, Ariëa, and Sagittario nodded in agreement.

»Please, go to the House of Yana Dolphin and find out exactly what this otherworldly woman is building and if you can sabotage it too!«

Ariëa said that she would inform Corvanya about everything and took her leave.

Griseo's Stock Market Investments

Aquaria and Sagittario knew an entrance to the House of Dolphins through the basement. They led Hollydeva to a room from which they could eavesdrop on Professor Griseo, who was having a very interesting conversation with Doctor Albedo.

»Griseo, tell me, how are your stock market transactions going?«

»They're going great soon!«

»So right now they're not doing so well?«

»What do you want, Albedo? I get the paper here in the morning, with the stock market prices from the day before! I'm here, far away from the places where the crucial things are happening right now! And why am I sitting here making losses? Because the triumvirate of the alchymists has decided so. Because I hold the position here for you! But now something will change soon!«

»Something change? You're leaving here, leaving the post?«

»No, don't worry! I've set up a corporation, and I'll be making the information and the stock prices myself soon! We will be able to pull energy from the sea and sell it! "Aquanergy" will be one of the most successful stock market openings ever! The investors and speculators will be clamoring for the shares and make me more than wealthy! I will gladly give to the guild of alchymists! But I also have to pay off my friends here, like this Abbess. And, as you know, things can change at any time, and there are forces here in the monastery that would love to see us lose access to the energy of water again!«

»So we'll strike while the iron's hot!«

»Right. But I have gained a weighty ally! And he'll be here soon enough to support us, and maybe he can also make sure that access lasts a very long time!«

»Who is it?«

»It is the Nacharya protector of this Yana, the Nacharya Saphed, also called the Boss of the Nacharya!«

»Saphed?!«

»That's the one. After all, you reported that he took out the Nononn, making him the highest Nacharya himself!«

»But that happened at Lead Mountain! And there he still is!«

»Saphed has informed me that he knows a way by which he can and will be here rapidly!«

»Uh, there's possibly another exchange company in it then, a transport company! From here to there in no time!«

»Sounds good! Another drink?«

»Give it a rest! I've got to see what my wife is doing!«

»Crazy story, about your wife! How did you manage that?«

»Oh, Griseo. We had learned that these beings had come into this world through a crack and had sought refuge in Mrs. Algard's garden. You can imagine that we, as scientists, were fascinated by this. What is this crack? What does it say about our world? What is behind the crack? Where did these beings come from? Who are they anyway? So the first thing was that we had to be able to communicate with them.«

»Yes, language is the key! How did you manage to do that?«

»Well, after the Mrs. Algard was probably killed in an unfortunate action by the priors and the accompanying nacharyas, there was something like a controlling hand missing in the Refuge. The Nacharya Daman was on travel and a freelance wizardeur were still there, to be sure. But he was rather half-hearted! We occupied the refuge with a rather small force. Then we were able to use a program that deciphers languages. Languages have a certain basic pattern. Just syntax and semantics. We were able to train the device that we had so that it could decipher the vocabulary and syntax of these creatures! We eavesdropped on them with very sensitive microphones. They were very surprised when we were capable of talking to them. It is true that they are technologically advanced. But in their world there are probably no language problems, and they encountered the problem of communication only here. But they lacked the resources to build a device like we now had.«

»Exciting!«

»So I was able to establish communication and especially with Lotus, my current wife. She's truly interested in this world. She's also a scientist, an alchymist!«

»Wonderful! Yes, feel free to see what your wife is doing and if she finishes the aquumulator soon!«

Sagittario nudged Hollydeva and Aquaria and led them into his study. He reported to them that he had established contact with this woman Lotus. She would have needed him and Baston as intelligent interlocutors. He would know that she was committed to Albedo, but was also basically more in favor of nature and beauty. It might be that her device would not work the way Tilia wanted it to.

But she was very strange, he said, and he could not say with certainty what she would undertake. But the chymical Griseo would give Tilia would probably be almost ineffective.

Mrs. Lotus aka Fapha

There was a knock at the door, Sagittario opened and a small, strange-looking woman with two small horns on her forehead entered.

»May I present Mrs. Lotus!« exclaimed Sagittario delightedly.

Hollydeva, however, was not so pleased, »She killed my grandmother, the dearest person I had!«

The little outerworldly woman, Mrs. Lotus, had a flat box in her hand, on which texts miraculously appeared and disappeared. A mechanical voice could also be heard, uttering sentences in the strange singsong and chatter of the otherworldly.

The device had probably translated Hollydeva's accusation.

Mrs. Lotus looked at her with surprise and wide eyes.

»Grandmother dead? We didn't mean to! Please forgive us!«

She cackled something into the box, and it then spoke in English, »We ask for your understanding and forgiveness. We were attacked and one of us reacted wrongly!«

»Did you kill my grandmother, Mrs. Lotus?!« asked Hollydeva directly and with an angry undertone.

Mrs. Lotus shook her head. »No, I didn't! Please, me not Lotus. Name get from Whity. Me Fapha.«

»Fapha!« exclaimed Sagittario.

»Hello, Fapha!« added Aquaria.

»Who is Whity?« asked Hollydeva.

»The alchymist you know as Doctor Albedo now also likes to call himself Doctor White in modern English!« Sagittario knew.

Fapha talked again into the box that translated their language, »White and troop came to garden of grandmother. Had translation apparatus. Could talk with us. Took me with him. Want to learn. We must find way back.«

Hollydeva nodded. She understood the situation of the outerworldly woman. But she was not relaxed with her yet.

»You build aquumulator for abbess?!«

Fapha nodded. »Yes, Whity please. I can. I scientist!«

»The device is used to extract energy from the sea!?«

Fapha nodded.

»The inhabitants of the sea don't want that. They will attack Linden Island! You must not help the Abbess and Griseo! You mustn't build that!«

»Already done!« admitted Fapha.

Aquaria intervened, »Does Griseo have the device already?«

Fapha nodded again, looking a bit saddened and confused.

And she saw the desperation that showed on Hollydeva's and Aquaria's faces.

»Must go.«

And already the little woman from a strange world had disappeared out the door.

»We won't be able to stop this!« concluded Aquaria.

But Sagittario replied that he had seen her dismay. She would think of something else. They should trust. He would be sure that this Fapha would only cooperate with the alchymists because she had had no other choice. He had talked to her a few times, learned from her, and got the impression that she would think similarly mystically as they did.

»She has very advanced scientific knowledge and thinking, with knowledge of technologies we've never heard of. But she wants to use that in harmony with nature and not destroy anything. That's how I heard it out, anyway.«

»Or interpreted into it!« Aquaria lectured him.

Sagittario shrugged his shoulders.

»We can only hope and trust and be prepared!« stated Hollydeva.

Chapter 38:
In the Dragon's Grove

Kalima and Peredur

It almost seemed as if a confrontation with the sea demons and the nereïdes could be averted. It almost seemed as if Tilia and Griseo could be put in their place.

But then Kalima appeared. And she came together with Nacharya Peredur. Horses were probably not allowed on the island, and the small ferry boat of Piscio's foster father could hardly transport them.

Somehow Kalima and Peredur had managed to ride into the central courtyard of the monastery on two proud, fiery horses. They laughed and winked at each other and looked like lovers who were completely indifferent to the judgments and sympathy or antipathy of the surrounding society.

But what did they want?

The first to approach them was Master Finster: »Kalima, Peredur! What are you doing here? This is an inopportune time!«

Then Maestra Shyena, who supposedly was also involved with Peredur, came running as well.

»Peredur, dearest, you're just in time! We must keep the dragons at bay!«

But Peredur responded rather coolly. »I can barely keep this fire horse in check! And certainly not Kalima!«

This was probably a kind of verbal boastfulness in front of the wrong audience.

»Kalima, come down, tie your horse, I need to talk to you!« ordered the Dark Master.

»But father, aren't you even going to greet me?« teased Peredur.

Hollydeva and Aquaria had been watching the scene and were close enough to overhear the speeches. Peredur was the son of the Master Finster? And the nihilista Kalima seemed to be connected to him, too!

»Peredur, son, go with Shyena and take care of those dragons real quick now!«

Peredur actually seemed to obey his father. He swung off the horse, tied it to the bell tower, and walked toward Shyena, who eyed him angrily and turned abruptly to go back to the house of the Yana of Dragons. Peredur followed her.

Hollydeva nevertheless thought that Shyena and Peredur made a handsome couple. Both were rather slender and elegant, and sharply cut in the face.

But no man could well resist Kalima's charms. Meanwhile, Master Finster did not seem to be her lover, rather her father. But Kalima and Peredur were probably not siblings.

Aquaria said she wanted to keep watching Griseo and possibly Tilia. She would also have assigned the other novices to observer posts.

»You see what this Kalima wants, Scorpio!« she advised Hollydeva.

So Hollydeva walked up to Kalima, »Hello! Do you remember me?«

Kalima narrowed her eyes, eyed the small, rather nondescript novicess in front of her, and made a somewhat disparaging face, »Yes, you remind me of a rather unpleasant incident!«

»But I saw to it that you were released!«

»No, the Bhogi saw to that! May he rest in peace!«

»Yes, as I say!«

»You are not the Bhogi!« But Kalima bristled, as if she was getting information to the contrary on the side from some unseen information service.

»All right, you were involved in the release. What do you want from me? I need to confer with the Dark Master!«

»What do you need to confer about? I want to come and attend the meeting!«

»You do?!« Then Kalima exchanged a look with Master Finster and surprisingly changed her mind, »Yes, good. Come along. We'd best go to Corvanya's anyway!«

So the four of them sat in Corvanya's study. Then King Krama came flying in through the window and sat down on a perch that Corvanya had already placed for him next to the desk.

»All right. What exactly is the situation?« began Master Finster.

Corvanya knew the answers, »Tilia has power. She controls four of the five elements. Wizardeurs and alchymists support her. In exchange, the alchymists get her permission to tap the energy of the sea! But for that, she first needs the power over the element Water. The nereïdes withhold this power from her. For the known reasons or probably the reservation of the nereïdes is far older, and they already tried to wipe her out with a storm tide when she was still a child, but only hit her family.

»And Tilia is from the Yana of Dragons and Shyena is on her side or is using the dragons for her or wants the power of the five elements herself, which she already excels at in the game.«

»Yes, Shyena will possibly wipe out Tilia the moment she unites all the power in herself. Shyena may be more power-hungry than we think.«

»What are the wizardeurs in for with this?«

»Didn't you talk to the wizardeurs, Hollydeva?«

»Yes, I talked to Miona Yaboah. She is the sister of our Raven sister Ariëa. We could question her. I think they're recounting their experiences somewhere here in the house right now.«

»Yes, you can go get them both right now. But first we need to initiate you in some way!«

»Initiate?«

»Yes, perhaps you have heard that in the ancient mystery schools there was such a thing as initiation? We must open your eyes to the whole truth!«

»The whole truth? Yes, gladly.«

»Listen carefully. We can only tell you right now. It would be better if we could show you! But that will have to wait right now.«

»The entrance is in the Dragon's grove, and it's well guarded.«

»Exactly. Maybe Peredur can distract Shyena enough for us to get to the gate. But still, we have to let Hollydeva in on it.«

Master Finster spoke to her with intensity in his voice, »This world here is not real. You're taking it all too seriously!«

Hollydeva objected, »It all seems very real to me. It hurts!«

»Yes, the pain in this world is real. This world is an installation that allows for soul growth. Soul growth requires pain. Pain motivates us to take a new perspective, to reevaluate an unpleasant occurrence in a larger perspective.«

»Well, what are you trying to tell me? It's unreal, and I'm not supposed to care so much about Tilia and the beings of the sea? I'm supposed to be indifferent to whether Linden Island exists or not?«

»Yes, in a way, dramatic things happen. Drama helps to wake up.«

Kalima wanted to support Master Finster, »The master doesn't want you to act and care for peace. The battle must come!«

Hollydeva was now confused and had a startling realization, »I've weakened the sea people by promising them that I'll make sure the masters of the island put a stop to Tilia and her activities?«

»Yes, you could say that!«

»But I have to protect the island, and the sea people too!«

»We have to show her! Let's go back to the Dragon's grove!«

Finster nodded in agreement. Corvanya and Krama stayed behind to consult and keep an eye on what was happening in the monastery.

Prioress Shyena

Outside the Dragon house, Kalima called loudly for Maestra Shyena. Just then Brother Leo, the novice in the Yana of the Dragons, ran by.

»Leo, will you please get Shyena out?!«

»The Prioress won't listen to me!«

»Please inform her that we are standing out here waiting for her! We need to get to the door in the grove and if she doesn't open it for us, we'll paralyze her dragons and open the door ourselves! Can you keep that and tell her?«

Leo looked slightly irritated, but he nodded and went into the Dragons' house.

After a while, Shyena and Peredur stepped out.

»You are threatening me and the dragons? And this is supposed to make me let you guys to the door?«

Master Finster tried politeness,»Shyena, please let us to the door! It's important! You want there to be no attack from the sea demons, too!«

Hollydeva had to pause, think and laugh inside at this attempt to persuade Shyena. Finster wanted the attack after all! So he was pretending to have a false motivation! But maybe Shyena wanted the attack and the war as well. In any case, her dragons were eager to take on the sea demons.

Kalima now intervened, »Peredur, can you please have an effect on your beloved?«

Shyena now mimicked Kalima: »Peredur, your beloved. Don't try to fool me, Kalima. You would rather have me out of the way and out of the bed of your beloved Peredur sooner than later!«

Peredur stood beside Shyena and tried to reassure her. »There will be a solution after all!«

Hollydeva now wanted to make her presence felt as well. »You want to show me that this world is just a game, a pretense of the senses! To make me not take this threat to the island so seriously!«

Shyena became even angrier. »This world is very, very real! And wonderful! Breathtaking dragons! My dragons! Pratikora! Dvesha! Nrishansya!«

Master Finster let out a short curse, one of the smelly kind.

»She summons her dragons!« clarified Kalima for Hollydeva.

Mighty wings rustled in the treetops of the grove. Nostrils blew fire into the night air. The rumbling of three throats made the grove tremble.

Peredur shouted, »Shyena, there's no need for that! Calm the dragons again!«

But Shyena was angry.

»The dragons are needed to protect Abbess Tilia anyway, when she absorbs the power of Water!«

Hollydeva, Master Finster and Kalima's mouths dropped open in astonishment. Shyena was throwing herself fully into the scales of Tilia!

Kalima protested, »The power of Water can only be given to her by the rightful Prior of the Dolphins, and he stands here! Or the nereïdes give it to her. But that's out of the question!«

Shyena knew better, »You are mistaken! She has found a way! She has powerful alchymists and wizardeurs on her side!«

Saphed Appears

Rather slowly and deliberately, Master Finster and Kalima had led the conversation group into the Grove of Dragons and to a hidden, half-overgrown door.

Then, suddenly, a glow of light came from the door to the supposedly other, encompassing world. The door, the entrance, was opened from the outside!

When the door was fully opened and the dull glow of light shone into the grove, a figure strode out.

As soon as he left the glow of the door, those gathered could see who it was.

»Saphed!« exclaimed the astonished Peredur.

»He took the door at Lead Mountain and traveled through the Otherworld to arrive here!« Kalima seemed to know how he had arrived so quickly from Lead Mountain.

»Nacharya Saphed, you know that I forbade you to use the doors without my permission to fast travel in the Jaghat!« Kalima hissed at him sharply.

»Oh, the cheruba of Jaghat 4! You can't order or forbid me at all! I had to come here because something big is happening today. The Abbess unites the five essential elements in herself and makes my great work possible!«

»Your great work? What is it?«

»I am building a simulation within the simulation and so this world can no longer be shut down, formatted or ended! The first step was to turn the Nononn cold! But I know that Arlecyna also wants this world preserved!«

Hollydeva didn't actually understand a word of the argument between Finster, Kalima, and Saphed. She looked at Peredur, the only one in the group whom she had already met, who had been at her side, who had shown her his Sacred Valley, who seemed to be a good friend to her. What was it with him and his women?

Peredur also looked at her at Saphed's words and made a barely noticeable head movement toward Master Finster. He told her that she should trust the Dark Master. That was fine with her, as Saphed was obviously a bit of a megalomaniac,

»Arlecyna wants to preserve nature. Like us, she wants no high technology, no tampering with the internal systems of plants and animals! She wants no exploitation of the sea today! Do you?«

Master Finster had spoken loudly and powerfully and Hollydeva nodded and actuated, »That's right! What's happening?«

»What's happening?« outraged Kalima. »He's stopping us right now!«

Then King Krama flew up and sat on Hollydeva's shoulder.

»Quickly, you must go to the east coast! Tilia is going to the coast with a device to drain the energy from the sea! Nearly all the other masters and adepts are under her spell and accompanying her!«

Hollydeva loudly repeated Krama's words.

»Exactly!« exclaimed Shyena. »That's where Nacharya Saphed and I are rushing to! Come, Saphed, I'll lead the way!«

Then she paused and called her dragons again, »Pratikora! Dvesha! Nrishansya! Keep the sea demons at bay!«

»The sea demons are already attacking! I can feel it!« shouted Kalima.

»Hurry to the bell tower!«

»I once had to swear that I would not interfere in the war against the sea demons!«

»You will not interfere against the sea demons, Hollydeva!« confirmed Finster to her. »Come!«

Kalima looked at Peredur, »Which side will you be on, Peredur, my love?«

Shyena held Saphed by the sleeve, stopped and looked at Peredur too.

Nacharya Fionn Peredur looked firmly at Saphed. »I know that Saphed has gone down a wrong path! And I don't know what path you are on, Shyena! But I also think that you, my father, have a dark motivation in mind and still detest this island and want to punish its masters!«

Peredur took a deep breath and stated loud and firm, »So my concern is Hollydeva, who I will protect with my power!«

Hollydeva grabbed him by the hand. »Then come with us, Master Peredur!«

They had to find Tilia and stop her from affecting the sea, the ocean.

Kalima, however, turned abruptly, shouted to Master Finster, »I must find the Nononn!«, and disappeared through the mysterious door in the Dragon's grove.

Hollydeva wanted to ask what this door was and where it would lead. Behind the door was a world where Kalima would be able to find the murdered Nononn? But they had to quickly follow Saphed and Shyena!

Chapter 39:
Abbess Tilia's Assault

The Activation

Finster, Kalima, Peredur and Hollydeva were just about to leave to look for Tilia. Saphed and Shyena apparently already knew where she could be found. The bell tower in the center of the monastery began to rumble. Suddenly above the tops of the grove the head of a sea demon appeared. Everyone paused.

The sea demon continued to rise! He or she had dragon wings! The creature that looked over the grove was a mixture, a half-breed of sea demon and dragon! It was the child of the couple who once loved each other, drowned in love and murdered because of love, the dragon man and the sea demon woman!

This dragon demon child was obviously looking for the three siblings, cousins. He thought that the three dragon ladies of the Yana of Dragons were related to him. These three had raised their heads and were hissing fiery at the half-breed. They rather did not want to have anything to do with the offspring of their unfortunate relative.

The dragon demon child stumbled and made a sound that sounded like sobbing and howling.

Prioress Shyena called out to him, »Get out of here, you don't belong here! Stay in the sea!«

Master Finster now raised his voice as well, »Obey the Dragon Mistress! And go to the Queen of the nereïdes, go to Oaëia, and tell her that Tilia is doing something today that must be stopped at all costs! Tell them to attack the island now and destroy it if necessary!«

Shyena turned to face Master Finster. »Shishumara, have you became insane?«

Hollydeva was shocked! What was the Dark Master saying? Why was he endangering them all like that? Who had she gotten involved with!

»Understand how dramatic the situation is! He has to advise the sea-dwellers to do so!« Peredur told Hollydeva with intensity, looking very directly into her eyes.

The dragon-demon child looked towards Master Finster. Hollydeva felt him sending a silent message with his spirit. The young demondragon seemed to have understood, and sank behind the treetops and into the floodwaters.

Shyena called to Saphed, »Quick to the bell tower!«

Finster, Peredur and Hollydeva followed them.

At the bell tower stood Abbess Tilia, holding a large round device in her hands.

In front of her and around the bell tower now all the other inhabitants of the monastery on Linden Island were standing and watching anxiously.

And Hollydeva also saw the visitors: Alchymist Albedo with his strange wife, Cevaine Mire and Miona, the wizardeurs.

From the nacharyas there were only Tatu Njena and now Peredur, who stood by her side.

The masters, adepts, and novices seemed to be under a spell. Only Maestra Corvanya and her Ravens stood a little apart, not seeming to know exactly how to act.

Even Tigers and Snakes seemed to be attending the meeting as if in a trance.

»I got this wonderful device from the alchymists! It contains a technology we didn't know before, and we got it, thanks to Mrs. Lotus, Doctor Albedo's wife! It is a so-called reverse energy accumulator. We shall call it "Aquumulator", as it absorbs the essential energy of Water, of "aqua", sucking it up to transfer it to me!

»Energy accumulators are made of layers of organic and metallic material! This one is especially powerful because the layers are made of gold and diamond. I don't know how Mrs. Lotus was able to liquefy diamond and cast it as layers around the gold metal, but she can, and she gave it to us. For that, we thank her and the alchymists. I will be able to draw the energy, the true energy of the water from the sea with this device! This will enable me to absorb the power of the four essential elements plus the Akasha. I will be an abbess as powerful as the abbots and abbesses of former times! Together, we will lead the monastery on Linden Island to the highest, to flourishing and blooming!

»But we have enemies! There stands one, the Dark Master, Master Finster! In former times he was called "Shishumara" here and denied me the power of the Water as Prior of the Dolphins, which were called "Sharks" at that time! Surely, he wants to prevent me from getting the power of Water now, too! Too late!

»For I already have the power of Earth from Master Alyapis!«

Alyapis bowed and his Bee adepts clapped their hands. All the other yanas except the Ravens began to applaud as well.

»And I have the power of Air from the Angels! Thank you, Maestra Sura!«

Applause again! Sura was on Tilia's side? Hollydeva was horrified!

»And I got the power of Fire from the Dragons! Thank you, Shyena, Prioress of the Yana, to which I myself belong!«

»I thank you, Prioress Urana of the Lambs! And take the power of Akasha from you!

»And thanks also to the holders of the elements of Metal and Stone! Thank you, Tigers and Snakes!«

»Thanks also to the Ravens who deny me the element of Wood! I don't need it!«

»We now go to the shore in the east, and activate this device, and you witness the energy of Water flowing into me! I will share it with all of you, and we will feel the five essential elements, making our monastery flourish! Follow me!«

The entire assembly began to move. The Ravens also followed, though at a distance. Ariëa, meanwhile, had apparently been instructed by Maestra Corvanya to stand beside Hollydeva and be ready to assist her. The raven-like Slua flew about a meter above them.

The "Averterer"

When Hollydeva and Ariëa were just attempting to follow, Master Finster held them back.

»Wait here! All hell is about to break loose, and we'll be safe here! Besides, you're not allowed to intervene against the sea demons like your grandmother promised them!«

Then Miona stood in front of them.

In the meantime, a storm had moved in. It had begun to storm and rain. Thunder could be heard. Lightning flashed through the dark sky some distance above the sea.

Miona called out, addressing her sister in particular, »Cevaine and I have received an analysis of the situation based on astrological data from astro-magician Astrello. He advises us to leave! Something will happen here that we could not and should not prevent. Farewell, sister! Farewell! Maybe we will meet again! I wish you luck. Please don't have a bad opinion of me, Hollydeva!«

She ran away, and Hollydeva saw her take Cevaine Mire by the hand, and they both got on a kind of broom that rose into the air and on which they flew away quickly.

Then the alchymist's wife stood before them. Mrs. Lotus, wife of Doctor Albedo, who had built the device for Abbess Tilia, the Aquumulator, with which the Abbess would be able to extract the basic energy from the sea, so that the alchymists would be able to drill, lay cables, dispose of garbage, discharge sewage, unmolested by sea demons and nereïdes on the ocean floor.

»You not happy?« asked this little she-devil with two horns.

»No, we are not happy, Fapha! You have built an evil device!«

»Not evil! Energy!«

»The energy of the sea! The sea is wonderful! It should live, it is the cradle of life! You are destroying it!«

»Destroy?«

Albedo had approached. »Come, Lotus, dearest, we must go! We must go to the Lead Mountain! The zeppelin is waiting at the back of the Dolphins' house!«

The she-devil looked at Hollydeva. »I'm sorry! Grandmother! Not wanted! For-giveness! I, Fapha! Aquumulator breaking with this! "Averterer"!«

She handed Hollydeva a small box with a field that could probably be pressed to trigger something in the distance.

Albedo was horrified, »What are you doing, Lotus?«

»Toys!« she placated the alchymist, her "husband". He must have been pacified, or preferred to be pacified, as Master Finster and Nacharya Peredur had taken on a threatening body posture. Albedo quickly pulled his outerworldly wife toward the house of the Dolphins.

Hollydeva gave Ariëa the "averterer".

»Quick, run to where Tilia wants to use this aquumulator and press on this field. Maybe it's not a toy after all! I have to stay out of it!«

Ariëa nodded and ran! Slua hovering over Ariëa reminded Hollydeva of her brother, Baldar, who was supposed to be Ariëa's husband. But he must have been well-placed in the troupe of Yana Agnus, under the direction of Prioress Urana.

Hollydeva was still wondering about this strange creature, Albedo's wife. "Fapha" was her name. She had to secure her place in this world by marrying the alchymist who had taken the trouble to learn her language. And she was sorry for Granna's death. She had given her name and given them a device, probably to be able to render harmless what was her contribution in the marriage with the alchymist. Hollydeva hoped that this averterer that Fapha had given her would work.

The Dare

Abbess Tilia, Grand Mistress of Linden Island, maestra from the Yana of Dragons, placed the device, the size of a book case, on the shore of the eastern edge of Linden Island. The island ends here with a steep shore about ten meters high and the view goes far over the sea.

It was late evening. Only sparsely, the twilight illuminated the sea. In a wide semicircle around the Abbess, the masters, adepts, and novices of the island had spread out.

Torches were set up and lit.

»Now and here we use this device, the Aquumulator, which a kind genius from another world built for us with the help of the alchymists, to supply us with the strength and power of the element Water. With the element of Water, I unite the five essential elements within me, and so with the power thus gained, we can ward off further attacks from the sea demons, the nereïdes, and all sea dwellers.

»Priors of the yanas of Bees, Angels, Lambs, and Dragons! Step forward and repeat your blessing with which you give me the element granted to you at my disposal!«

Alyapis, Prior of the Bees, stepped forward first. He held a sturdy wooden staff. As he stretched it aloft, it seemed to glow and shine. Loudly Master Alyapis announced, »I hereby confer upon you, Abbess Tilia, the Element of Earth!«

Sura, Prioress of the Angels, stepped forward. She held up a metal disc in which a pentagram was engraved or inlaid with another metal. This disc also began to glow. »Herewith, venerated Abbess, I give you the element of Air!«

Urana took a step in front of the Lambs accompanying her and called out, »I give you the quintessence, the Akasha, with which you can bind all the other four elements and bring them to their full strength!« She held an ancient lamp that emitted a similar light to the staff and the pentagram disk.

And finally, Shyena, Prioress of Dragons, holding up an equally luminous sword, spoke, »I give you the power of Fire, dear Maestra of Dragons, Abbess Tilia!«

Abbess Tilia held a chalice in her hand, which, meanwhile, did not glow or shine. But the Abbess was about to change that. She had placed the ominous device, built in the Yana of the Dolphins, on the floor and attached the chalice to one side, where the foot of the chalice could be slid into a rail.

So she spoke, »This device is made of layers of metal, diamond, precious fabrics and precious woods! And possibly other layers of secret materials! Now, if I point this chalice like a funnel to the sea and place my hand on the device, the element of Water will flow into me!«

The entire congregation held its breath. In a moment, Tilia would accomplish her great work. Soon she would overcome the sabotage of the Dark Master. And it seemed that the beings of the sea would not be able or willing to interrupt this ritual.

But then a novicess with dark skin stepped in front of the semicircle. She had emerged from the ranks of the Yana of Ravens, the yana which viewed Tilia's project with suspicion, which had boycotted her claim in previous years. The dark-skinned first-year novicess, whom Tilia knew as Ariëa, the Ram, held up a device.

Ariëa shouted loudly, »Listen to me! The alchymist's wife, who comes from another world, has given me this device with which I can immediately destroy the Aquumulator! For she was not sure if she had done the right thing! Step back, Abbess Tilia, for the first year novices believe you are making a mistake!«

»How dare you! You have not even been in this place a year! You still have much to learn!«

Dragon Mistress Shyena shouted, »Arrest her!«

Some adepts from among the Dragons and Lambs tried to get to Ariëa. But other adepts, Ravens and Serpents, put themselves in front of them.

But then Ariëa was attacked by a swarm of bees, had to drop the device and already Capricornus, novice of the Angels, had taken it.

»Capri, give it back to me!«

»No, I can't! I have to do what Maestra Sura wants!«

Sura stepped close to them. »Hand me this device, Capricornus!«

Capricornus wanted to give Sura the device, but his friend Novice Tauro, tall and a little overweight, stood in his way.

Nacharya Tatu Njena had also interrupted the handing over of the device when he placed a strong hand on Prioress Sura's shoulder and held her back.

»What does your goddess want, novice? What does Iëmanjá want?«

Capricornus stood there rooted to the spot, at a loss. But the averterer was out of action for now.

Maestra Sura angrily shook off Tatu Njena's hand and shouted, »Tilia, just continue!«

Maestra Fraxina and Master Ulmus, Tilia's deputies, had stepped next to Tilia. They held up the funnel and pointed it toward the sea. A few feet away, Nacharya Saphed, the Zronn, supervised the ritual. Or was it not a ritual, but a scientifically based energy generation?

The Beginning of the Battle

But from the sea now giant figures rose, the sea demons, eight in number, rapidly approaching the shore.

Maestra Shyena called her dragons: »Pratikora! Dvesha! Nrishansya!«

Three dragons tried to confront the sea demons. But they faced superior numbers. The demons extinguished the fire breaths from the dragons with great quantities of water spewed from their huge puffy mouths.

Maestra Shyena had her dragons mentally under control and wanted to force them to attack further. But out of nowhere novice Leo appeared in front of her.

»Maestra, give up! Let the dragons save themselves!«

Giving up was not in Shyena's mind. This prince from the north, however, was right. Where was Peredur? He probably was helping this daughter of the Grand Inquisitor, who was also on the side of the Sea Demons. Shyena nodded, ordered the three dragons to retreat and told her masters, adepts, and novices to do everything to protect their house and the dragon grove.

Ravens, Tigers and Snakes were already retreating to their houses for the same purpose.

Master Alyapis had called back the bees that had attacked Ariëa. He wondered where the novice Piscio was. He was about to question his friend Virgo when the first large chunks of mud were thrown onto Linden Island by the sea demons.

»Save the bees! Protect the beehives!«

Tauro yelled at Capri, »Give Ariëa back the averterer! You are not a traditore, not a traitor!«

Capricornus looked over his shoulder at the powerful sea demons. If turning off the aquumulator could still avert the battle, that would probably be considerably better.

But he hesitated, and Abbess Tilia activated the aquumulator. It, however, would take some time for it to run up to full power. Eventually, it would be tapping the sea's energy and weaken the sea demons.

Ariëa could yet still turn it off! No, because Sura and Betula, the masters of the Angels, had used the attack of the sea demons to tear the averterer from Capricornus' hands. They threw it on the ground and trampled it with their feet, destroyed it.

Two of the sea demons were striving towards the place where Tilia was standing. Those gathered could see that they were being directed by angry nereïdes standing on their shoulders.

Tilia, Fraxina and Ulmus began to shout incantations. They spread their arms and erected a kind of rampart of spirit power in front of the shore, slowing down the sea demons. The Angels and Lambs joined them. Shyena saw what was happening, and the Dragons also paused to support Tilia.

The Dolphins? A battle was obviously not Professor Griseo's world. Those missing him on the shore of the island could not have known that a novicess he had ignored had trapped him in the house of the Dolphins. But it would not be long before he would figure out how to break open the locked door of his room from the inside.

Where were the Tigers? They were without clear leadership. Maestra Manducate, Scorpio's mother, was arguing with Master Sycamor, who saw himself as the representative of Prior Baghora. Maestra Simhana shook her head and told the other Tigers to retreat as well to protect their house.

Then a sea demon came from the eastern shore and seemed to want to stop the other eight. To their surprise, the masters, adepts, and novices of the island saw that the rather small novice of the Bees, Piscio, was standing with a nereïde on the demon's shoulders. He seemed to be calling with her to the other sea demons, causing them to pause.

Nacharya Saphed called out to Abbess Tilia to take the chance and set the Aquumulator to full power.

Chapter 40: The Redemption of Tilia

All the Five Elements

Aquaria came running from the Dolphins' house, shouting, »I've locked Griseo in! But he'll probably be able to free himself soon!«

Master Finster now decided, »Come! We have to get to Tilia! She must not absorb the water energy!«

So Hollydeva, Aquaria, Nacharya Peredur, and Master Finster ran to the spot on the shore of Linden Island where Abbess Tilia was about to raise the aquumulator to full power.

The Abbess probably thought that the delay in the sea demon attack caused by the appearance of a sea demon with Bee novice Piscio on her shoulder could be used to her advantage.

But Hollydeva would now intervene, as she had promised the nereïdes, and put an end to the Abbess's undertakings. But a semicircle, composed mainly of the adepts of the Lambs and Angels, had been formed to prevent them. When Hollydeva tried to force her way through them, they closed their ranks and formed an impenetrable wall of backs.

Hollydeva saw that the Ravens were standing apart. »Master, send a raven to tell Ariëa to use the averterer!«

Corvanya had to answer, »She has already done that! But Sura and Betula took it from her and destroyed it after she was attacked by bees!«

»Are the bees still with her?«

»No, it appears that the novice Virgo is influencing Master Alyapis to send the bees to their baskets! They are retreating right now!«

»Where are the dragons?«

»Your friend Leo got Shyena to make the dragons refrain from further attacks against the sea demons! Because they would have been harmed in the process! The

358

prince from the ice country seems to like the dragons! And Shyena must have realized that she should stay out of this!«

»We have to get through here! We have to get to Tilia!« shouted Hollydeva to her companions in the roar of wind and lightning and the whipped up surf of the sea. Peredur and Finster tried to push adepts aside, but those had hooked on and remained stubbornly steadfast.

Then a troop approached, led by Hollydeva's mother, Master Manducate formerly Castanea, and her friend midwife-agent Libra, who were supposed to know how to handle the Lambs.

»Lambs, make way!« shouted Hollydeva's mother.

But Master Urana had stood in front of her troop of Lambs and countered: »In the name of the OneGod, let no one, absolutely no one, pass! And the Kingdom of Heaven of the OneGod will be open to you!«

But Master Manducate changed back into Master Castanea, for as such she still had power and influence in the Yana Agnus, »Eragrostis, my dear son, get out of there! Tilia must be stopped!«

»You only want to sabotage Tilia because she rebuked you for your daughter!« Urana tried to irritate.

»But now my daughter is on my side!« Maestra Castanea triumphed.

Hollydeva shook her head. Now, that was not how she wanted it to be! Her mother had her own agenda! But if she could get a clear path through the backs of the flock of Lambs, it would be fine with her.

»Your Raven friend is talking down to the Angel novices!« reported Peredur.

Aquaria saw it now, too. Hollydeva was smaller and actually still only saw the backs of those trying to shield Tilia.

Aquaria shouted, »Ariëa is storming Capricornus to do something! Tauro is standing by her! Now they go towards Sura and Betula, who are still cheering the other Angel adepts to stand firm. Now Capri and Tauro are holding back the two angelic masters with their large bodies!«

The actions of their fellow novices had led to uncertainty among Lambs and Angels, and Hollydeva was able to squeeze through the front row of backs.

Meanwhile, however, Abbess Tilia, protected by Masters Ulmus and Fraxina, instructed by Nacharya Saphed, had powered up the Aquumulator. She was in the process of drawing energy from the sea. The sea demons sensed this and roared. The nereïdes on their shoulders and backs roared and screamed, and Hollydeva understood that they were now urging her intervention.

Then she, Peredur and Finster had fought through the semicircle of adepts. But when they went to Tilia, Nacharya Zronn Saphed confronted them.

»No further! The work must be completed! In a moment, the Abbess will have united the power of the five essential elements, and then you will not be able to do anything against her! We need the power of the sea to save the world!«

Saphed had his arms outstretched and was building some kind of energy wall. Peredur began to build a counter-wall, while Finster threw something towards Saphed, but that action failed to effect anything.

Hollydeva saw Cancra coming from the right side with the Tiger Masters Sycamor and Abiës.

The sea demons howled again, and now in turn began to pelt the island with mud and silt and water. They did not have such great aim, and even those who wanted to assist the sea dwellers had to be careful of their projectiles.

Above them, they heard a strange noise, a continuous rattling and humming. Then they saw a small flying machine with wings and something spinning very fast in front, a propeller. In the flying machine was obviously Professor Griseo. He probably wanted to defend Tilia from above and throw something down. And that's what he did. It looked like a stone at first. Then on the ground it burst with a loud bang and firelight, a bomb. Fortunately, it had not seriously hurt anyone. Griseo couldn't aim exactly, as all the opponents were standing close together, and he was in danger of hitting the ones he wanted to help.

Hollydeva saw Aquaria running to Corvanya, who sent out a raven. Possibly Sagittario was sitting somewhere from where he could disable or interfere with the flying machine.

Hollydeva was watching all this, and now Master Finster was standing next to her. »Crazy, isn't it, a battle like this? There you are in the middle of all this fighting and strife and yet somehow you are completely uninvolved, an observer. You understand that any action is basically pointless. Fighting is good, is energy, forces you to stay awake! But this fight must now come to an end. You must stop Tilia!«

Hollydeva's Act

Hollydeva looked to him. »How am I supposed to do that?«

»You do have the dagger, the sea scorpion's spiked dagger! You must use that now!«

»But I can't kill Tilia!«

»You have to do that. Only you can! Only you have the power and the distance to her!«

Hollydeva nodded, pulled the dagger from her belt, advancing.

But there was still Saphed.

Griseo with his flying machine had to turn away. Apparently, Sagittario had been successful.

But as Hollydeva went ahead, a raven flew up. She wanted to greet him, thinking that this one would come to her support. But he pecked at her eyes. As she was startled, she realized that another, it was King Krama himself, had snatched the sea-scorpion's dagger from her hand, into which a third attacker had pecked, so she loosened her grip in fright.

Corvanya shouted in her direction, »You must not do this, Scorpio! You're supposed to not accumulate any karma!«

King Krama flew to Corvanya with the spiked dagger and placed it on the ground in front of her.

»I have to do it!« yelled Hollydeva, Raven novicess Scorpio.

Out of the corner of her eye, she saw a misty cloud billowing out. Gemina stood by the cloud, from which emerged an old woman who looked very gray and almost translucent.

The old woman walked up to Corvanya and Gemina stood by Hollydeva. »This is Dhumavati, a powerful goddess who has become my friend. She will get you the dagger!«

The old woman seemed to walk on another plane, like a transparent figure. Corvanya wanted to pick up the dagger, but she must have caught a glimpse of Dhumavati and hesitated.

»A beautiful greeting from my sister, the Great Kali, dear Raven Mistress. Do not interfere here! Your novicess wants to make a great sacrifice and it is right!«

Dhumavati grabbed the dagger, turned and threw it in a high arc right at Gemina's feet, who picked it up and handed it to Hollydeva, her friend Scorpio.

»Come on, Scorpio, we can do it!«

At that moment, a bundle flew through the air and hit Saphed in the head, knocking him to the ground. But it wasn't a bundle. It was Shrimp! She must have known a fighting technique that allowed her to make these leaps. Or had Sycamor and Abiës thrown her? Probably Peredur and Finster had also managed to weaken the energy wall.

But by then, Abbess Tilia had also achieved what she had been striving for: she had absorbed enough Water energy to combine the power of the five essential elements within her. She seemed to have grown taller and more radiant.

»Earth to the North, Air to the East, Water to the West, Fire to the South! Above me, the Akasha! Power of the Five Elements, secure my space!«

A kind of cone of light arose around Tilia. The sea demons threw silt in Tilia's direction, but it bounced off that cone.

»It's too late! She's done it!« shouted Peredur.

Tilia now hurled some kind of energy ball in the direction of the sea demons. One of them was hit and fell into the sea.

The others retreated. They looked weakened and desperate. Piscio looked back and shouted as loud as he could, »Hollydeva! Scorpio! Only you can save the sea now!«

Tilia seemed to have averted the threat from the sea. Amid the lightning and thunder of the still-raging storm, the Abbess turned and faced the congregation.

»Where are my opponents? Who wants to doubt me now? Who would like to mess with me?«

She turned to face Master Corvanya and the Raven adepts crowding around her.

»Ravens? You are traitors! I guess I'll have to punish you now!«

She hurled a force toward Corvanya, who doubled over as if she had been punched in the pit of the stomach. The other Ravens cried out. King Krama and his raven brigade rushed boldly toward Tilia, but also bounced off her invisible protective wall.

Tatu Njena had drawn a whip and was trying to affect Tilia with it. Sura and Betula had freed themselves from the novices' grasp and fell into Tatu Njena's arms.

Tilia shouted, »All I want is peace! I want Linden Island to bring peace and protection to the world!«

Master Castanea was now all Tiger, Master Manducate. She contradicted Tilia as loud as she could, »Your peace is death, Tilia! A paralyzed sea and the houses of the island that dare not contradict you: This is the peace that the grave offers! Let's talk about it, let's talk it out!«

»Talk? Discuss? I am Dragon and we Dragons are seeking to become the superhuman! We just rule and use our power! It was good that the Nacharya enforced the

OneGod and monotheism! But now we go one step further and let the human be God and make the world according to human's will!«

»This is madness!« exclaimed Peredur.

And it seemed as if the priors and masters and adepts of the yanas hitherto supporting Tilia were bristling and frightened and undecided whether they might not be participating in a sacrilege.

Master Finster stood beside Hollydeva, who held in her hand the sea scorpion dagger that Gemina had handed her.

»Only you can get to her, Hollydeva! You must free her from herself now!«

»How can I get to her?«

»The spell of the Five Elements does not affect you! I'll explain why later. Trust me and go to her!«

So Hollydeva let go and actually got to Master Tilia, in front of whom she now stood, the drawn spiked dagger in her hand.

»Forgive me, Lady Grand Master!« she cried, plunging the dagger into Tilia's heart. Fraxina and Ulmus cried out. The Abbess collapsed.

In an instant, the roar of the sea demons ceased. The storm also seemed to stop. The whole world seemed to pause. The cone of the Five Elements with which Tilia had protected her field collapsed.

»Thank you, Arlecyna!« the nereïdes shouted.

Hollydeva supported the head of the Lady Grand Master. She felt no guilt or sympathy. She had had to redeem the Abbess from a curse. She had had to save the island.

The Black Mystic had put a hand on her shoulder.

The Grand Mistress looked into her eyes once more. »Now I understand! Now I know who you are! I thank you! I am now free!« With these words, the Abbess died.

»What have you done!!!« cried Fraxina.

»Come, come quickly!« The Black Mystic shook her out of her deep connection with the Lady Grand Master.

He dragged her toward the abbey. »You're coming with me!«

»No, I won't! You are too dark for me! I don't know you!«

»Nonsense! You can't stay here now! We don't have time for murder charges and trials! I command you!«

»You can't order me to do anything! I have to go to Corvanya! Only she can give me orders that I'll obey!«

Several people had rushed up and saw the dead Abbess lying there. Fraxina screeched, »Scorpio stabbed her!«

Angry cries rang out to her. Nacharya Saphed, who had been standing next to the Abbess, suddenly held a weapon, a pistol, in his hand. He looked at Hollydeva with anger and hatred. But when he fired, his shot missed because a small figure had pushed him aside. It had been Piscio, whom his sea demon had set down right where Tilia and Saphed had been standing. Shrimp, too, had probably pushed at his legs with his feet.

As the masters approached, the Black Mystic made a wide hand gesture and shouted, »Stay where you are! Don't come one step closer!« He had a strong, commanding voice and a shout that made them pause.

But Corvanya came forward. »I must speak with my novicess!«

»Come, Corvanya! You must tell her to come with me!«

Corvanya looked astonished. She shook her head slightly.

»Corvanya! Order her to go with me now! It must be done! It is the only way of saving her soul! You love her as I do, and you must do this now!«

Master Corvanya looked dumbfounded. Then King Krama sat down on her shoulder. »Do as he says, Maestra!« he croaked. »Only he can protect and save her!«

»I don't need to be saved after all!« Hollydeva wanted to shout.

But Corvanya nodded. »Scorpio, my scorpioness! Listen to me. I love you with all my might, and I pray that one day you will remember who you are! Once again, you sacrificed yourself and your soul to save the island! One day, you will understand! Go with Finster! He will save you! I order you now: Go with Master Finster and do whatever he tells you to do!«

Hollydeva was astonished. What was the fuss about! But yes, she had the blood of the Abbess on her hands!

Sagittario had rushed to the aquumulator and pressed almost invisible switches, causing the device to stop its humming.

»We need the energy of the water back that she absorbed!« one of the nereïdes shouted.

Master Finster called back to her, »Queen Oaëia, how can we return that energy? It looks like Tilia has used it up!«

»Bring me the dagger that Arlecyna used to free her!«

Master Finster went to Hollydeva, who was still crouching next to the Abbess as if frozen, wrung the dagger from her hands and went to the edge of the water where the queen of the nereïdes was waiting. Once she had the sea scorpion dagger, she held the tip into the sea, where it immediately billowed and swirled.

»Thank you, Shishumara!« exclaimed the Queen of the Sea. »You are forgiven! We consider you a friend of the sea again!«

As Hollydeva was still pondering the words of the Raven Lady Master and the other masters were again approaching menacingly, Master Finster murmured mysterious words, picked her up off the ground and carried her across the square on both hands. She felt as if she was about to fall asleep. She vaguely noticed that he was carrying her to the ferry landing, where the ferryman was waiting to ferry her across. At the other landing, there was a carriage with two horses. Finster put her on the carriage seat, sat next to it, clicked a word and the horses started to move.

The night was still stormy, rainy, and restless. But the nereïdes had retreated with their sea-demons into the wild sea, and the hope of the world, Linden Island, center of the union and further development of all mystical world perceptions, had remained alive.

Hollydeva Reviews One Week Later

A week after the events on Linden Island that led to the death of Abbess Tilia, Hollydeva tried to remember what had happened, what she had left behind.

She was in a cabin on a ship that was to take her and Master Finster across the ocean to a distant land.

No. It didn't take her much effort to remember that she had stabbed Abbess Tilia. That was very present in her mind, and she knew that she had had no other choice. And she also still heard in her ear that Tilia had seemed and spoken as if freed from an evil curse.

But she wondered where her father had actually been during the events. He had been lying in the house of the Yana of Angels all this time, continuing to recover from the triple curse of the wizardeurs. But had he felt no impulse to intervene at all? He who had once held the fate of the Yrth in his hands as Grand Inquisitor? Within a year, he had become very small to her, and she felt sorry for him, too.

»Or do I feel sorry for myself, who had once been a supposedly powerful person as his assistant and disciple and had become insignificant with him?«

She, however, felt no less significant than she had a year ago. She had learned that significance was not what this world was about.

But what was it about?

Did Master Corvanya know what it was about? They had never talked about it. Hollydeva thought she heard Corvanya's voice calling her to the Raven dance, telling her to arrive in this world in the first place before worrying about meaning.

Hollydeva thought of her mother, the garden mistress who had come to her aid in the battle with the nereïdes, who had enabled her to make her way through the ranks of the angelic adepts to reach the Abbess. Why did the mother reject her? She had hinted at knowing something about misdeeds and a bad eternal character. But it seemed to Hollydeva that this knowledge about past lives was made up and used to have justifications for negligent behavior in this life.

She remembered the good masters in the past months: the Bhogi and her grandmother, the former Master Malus, Lady Algard. These had seen in her a girl who could contribute to the welfare of the Yrth and the people. She would gladly conform to the ideas of the Bhogi and her grandmother.

Then she thought back to the Sacred Valley and the nacharyas Tatu Njena and Peredur. Both seemed sympathetic to her and had shown her how beautiful the Yrth could be.

The Druyds and Fire Maiden, the seer Medea and Odiën were in tune with nature. They had taught her that pain was inevitable, that everything in nature was also fleeting. But pain, they said, was real and a gateway to growth, to expansion of consciousness.

Hollydeva remembered that while still in Georgeburg Castle, she had thought about whether she was a good person or a bad person. Odiën had then so inflated her self-doubt by saying that it was good that she was evil that the subject had somehow ceased to matter, especially since the grandmother had joined in the judgment of the bees.

But weren't the alchymists and the wizardeurs evil who had attacked Georgeburg?

»Of course, we call the enemies evil. They probably also think they're the good guys, acting for the good of their own, or even the good of the Yrth!«

On Linden Island, Hollydeva had learned the attitudes of both-as-well-as and neither-nor. There was no such thing as good or evil. There was no choice between black or white. It was all gray. Everyone had both sides in them!

She was on the side of the nature and the naturalness. The alchymists and the followers of magic wanted to change the world, to shape it. Perhaps they were partly successful with it. But the success was bought dearly. Those who changed the world and made it easier for themselves in it had a harder time becoming one with it, with its true essence. That much she had understood in the lessons and in the discussions at the Flower Days on Linden Island.

Then she had to think of the eleven friends she had just had to leave. She was sure that she would see those novices, her friends, again.

End of the First Volume of Hollydeva

Register of Persons

Main Character

Hollydeva, novice Scorpio, Arlecyna

Hollydeva's Family

Her mother: Rosa of Valmere, Master Castanea or Manducate
Her father: Seren Tondeuse, the Stone, Grand Inquisitor of the Nine Nacharya
Her eldest brother: Einar, Adept Avela
Her second brother: Balder, Adept Eragrostis
Her grandmother, called Granna: Mrs. Algard, Master Malus
Mrs. Bromholle, neighbor

Hollydeva's Companions

Astrello, the star boy
Guuz, a daisy-deva

Nine Nacharya, Georgeburg

Nononn, primus inter pares of the Nacharya
Onthronn Achmar, associated: yana the Tiger
Tworonn Daman, an uncle of Hollydeva, associated: yana Agnus
Dresonn Tatu Njena, associated: yana the Angel
Verionn Quavert, associated: yana of the Serpents
Fionn Peredur, son of Master Finster, associated: yana of Dragons
Sessionn Rokudan Aoi, associated: yana of Ravens
Septonn Bhogi, associated: yana of Bees
Zronn Saphed, associated: yana of the Dolphins
The Informant
The Executive
Castellan Allman
Cook

Druyds and Fire maidens

Medea
Odiën
other druyds and fire maidens

Alchymists

Magnificentia Negara, Lady Black
Doctor Albedo, "White"
Professor Rubedo, Ben Redding
other alchymists

Wizardeurs

Cevaine Mire
Miona Yaboah
Madame Owleya
Andalf, the Theurg
Charles Ostreaux, Freelancer
other

Linden Monastery: Masters, Adepts, Cooks

Lady High Maestra Tilia, Abbess of the monastery, origin yana of Dragons
Master Ulmus, deputy abbot, the bursar of the monastery, yana Angels
Cellerar: Master Platanus
Cameraria: Maestra Arla
Guard: Master Quercus
Maestra Fraxina, Prioress of the Novice House
Master Alyapis, Prior of the yana of the Bees
Maestra Corvanya, Prioress of the yana of Ravens
Master Anguinaga, Prior of the yana of Snakes
Maestra Sura, prior of the yana of Angels
Maestra Urana, prioress of the yana of the Lamb
Master Baghora, prioress of the yana of Tigers
Maestra Shyena, Prioress of the yana of Eagles
Master Griseo, Prior of the yana of Dolphins, calls himself Professor
Master Abiës, Master of the Faculty of Martial Arts, yana Tiger
Master Fagus, master of geomancy and construction, yana Dragon
Master Salix, teacher of healing arts, yana Snake
Maestra Betula, teacher of the art of prediction, yana the Angel

Master Sycamor, teacher of the Inner Path, yana Tiger
Master Cedrus, teacher of mental martial arts in the faculty of martial arts
further Master of the Ravens: Crataegus, Labernum
other masters of Snakes: Wadjet, Vasuki, Apophis, Manasa
Cooks: Emily, Maisy, Marjorie, Raelyn, Babette, Laënna, others

Adepts and Animals in the Yanas and Houses

Yana of the Bees: Opalia
Yana of the Ravens: Jackdaw, Kakula, Jay, Kolk, Kitta, Rosehip
Ravens: King Krama, Rakra, others
Yana of the Angels: Coryla, Teacher Mandalas,
Achillea, cartographer, guest yana angels
Ai Min, Yi jing master, guest yana angels
Yana Angels: Jehadiel, Barachiel
Yana Snake: Boa, Mamba, Cobra
Yana Agnus. Bamba, Simso, Danthonius, Danthonia
Yana Tiger:
Yana Dolphin:
Yana Dragon: Harpio, Accipiter, Milvina.

Novices of the First Year

Sister Ariëa, Cita Yaboah, yana Agnus
Brother Tauro, Leonardo, yana the Angel
Sister Gemina, Dirt, yana of the Snakes
Sister Cancra, "Shrimp", Lin Tao, yana of the Tigers
Brother Leo, Prince Bjarkerik, yana of Dragons
Brother Virgo, Gaudio, yana of the Bees
Sister Libra, Vimala, yana Agnus
Brother Sagittario, Jack Goedel, yana of the Dolphins
Brother Capricorno, Ndenju, yana of the Angels
Sister Aquaria, Ellianne, yana of the Dolphins, spokeswoman for the novices of the
first year
Brother Piscio, Pierre, Eoïao, yana of the Bees

Novices of the Second Year

Brother Matto, yana of the Bees
Brother Appeso, the Hanged, yana of the Ravens
Sister Sole, the Sun yana Angel
Sister Giudicia, the court. yana of the Snakes

Brother Mondo, yana of the Snakes
Brother Temperan, yana of the Lamb, spokesman for the novices of the second year
Brother Torre, the Tower, yana of the Tiger
Sister Luna, the moon woman in the yana of the Tiger
Brother Bastoni, also Ass di Bastoni, yana of the Dolphins
Brother/Sister Diavolo, yana of the Dragons

Novices of the Third Year

Bagatto, later Adept Felisa, spokeswoman of all the novices, yana the Tiger
Brother Amantes, yana Angels
Sister Giustizia, yana Agnus

Nereïdes

Oaëia
Lykoria
Ianira
Kymothoë
other

The Black Mystics

Master Finster (Nikor Norhard, Master Shishumara)
Kalima

Beings from Other Worlds

Fapha, Lady Lotus
others

Subsequent Hollydeva Volumes, Continuing the Legend of Hollydeva

You can find more stories, background descriptions, explanations and hopefully much more about Hollydeva on the website hollydeva.com.

There you will also find information about the writing progress of books that tell how the story of Hollydeva, the legend, continues. These may come as follows:

Volume 2: Hollydeva, Hermitess

In which Hollydeva lives with Master Finster and is initiated into meditation and mysticism. They take part in the fight of the anti-island Avalonya.

Volume 3: Hollydeva, Seekeress

Hollydeva travels with Nacharya Peredur to oppose the activities of alchymists and wizardeurs. Later she arrives at Vowharts, the castle of the wizardeurs, where she is imprisoned and takes the time to meditate for attaining a very profound state of consciousness.

Volume 4: Hollydeva, Guerillera

Hollydeva and her companions set out to put an end to the alchymists. They find the labs in Lead Mountain and a powerful machine brain in Gold City.

Volume 5: Hollydeva, the Cursed

Hollydeva returns to Linden Island to stop Saphed and Griseo. Kalima leads her to Heaven where she realizes her true nature.

Volume 6: Hollydeva, World Wanderer

In which Hollydeva travels to Fapha's world to fight the Space Huns with her and Astrello and Miona and some other novices. Hollydeva learns of compassion.

Volume 7: Hollydeva, Saviouress

In which Hollydeva reaches the plane above Heaven and explores the realm of the Child Empress to save the Heavens and Yrth.

Other Fantasy Book Series Written by Abella Blunk:

The Contest of the Seven Princes

published so far: Volume 1, Fatal Masteries

The Secret of the Seven Days

published so far: Volume 1, Cursing Mothers

For more explanations, instructions, information about Hollydeva and her path, please visit:

hollydeva.com